I0639751

A World of Dinosaurs

MINTARI
A World of Dinosaurs

DANIEL ARENSON

Copyright © 2023 by Daniel Arenson
Illustration © Sergey Krasovskiy

All rights reserved.

This novel is a work of fiction. Names, characters, places and incidents are either the product of the author's imagination, or, if real, used fictitiously.

No part of this book may be reproduced or transmitted in any form or by an electronic or mechanical means, including photocopying, recording or by any information storage and retrieval system, without the express written permission of the author.

CHAPTER ONE
The King

The Tyrannosaurus rex was stalking them. He had their scent now. He would not stop until he fed.

Joe ran through the dark forest. Roots snagged his feet. Thorny branches whipped his face. Sweat soaked him, and his heart pounded against his ribs.

He's hungry. He's after us. Oh God, we're going to die.

A rumble sounded behind him. Deep. Echoing. Ravenous. A deep bass that rolled through the forest like thunder.

There was no mistaking that sound. It was the rumble of a T-rex. And not just any T-rex but King Ivan himself. The tyrant of Mintari. The most dreaded predator evolution had ever produced.

Joe ran faster.

Mina was struggling to keep up. Her face was pale, her eyes sunken. Thorns had slashed her cheek, and her blood beaded. As she ran, she cradled her pregnant belly. A mossy root grabbed her boot. She cried out, stumbled, and nearly fell. Joe caught her.

For a moment, they stood panting.

"Joe," she whispered. "Joe, we can't run forever. We have guns. We can fight him."

A tear rolled down her cheek, mingling with the blood.

He hungers for us, Joe thought. *For my flesh. For her flesh. For the flesh of our unborn child.*

"Mina, bullets won't stop him," Joe said. "Ivan would shrug them off like spitballs. Tonight we're prey. Tonight we must run. We're almost at Crater Lake. We can lose him in the water. I'll carry you."

She shook her head. "No. That'll slow us down. I can keep going."

She took a deep breath, then resumed running through the brush. Joe ran at her side.

The daylight was almost gone now. Shadows cloaked the ferns, ginkgo trees, and towering conifers. The sun's dying rays pierced the canopy like bloodied claws. Most predators would be settling down for the night. But not Ivan. The beast could see in the faintest starlight. Even in pitch-darkness, his uncanny sense of smell and sound would guide him. Over millions of years, evolution had crafted tyrannosaurs for one purpose. To kill. And Ivan was the greatest killer of them all.

"We must reach the water," Joe said. "We can lose him in the water."

Mina did not reply. She could barely breathe. Her arms trembled as they cradled her belly. Eight months pregnant. A baby girl. A dream of a beautiful family. Now the beast's teeth threatened to rip this dream to shreds.

Footsteps thudded behind them.

The beast was closer.

The two humans had gotten a head start. But even the fastest sprinter could not outrun a T-rex for long. Soon the dinosaur would catch them.

Mina cried out. Sweat drenched her hair.

"We can make it!" Joe said. "Come on, cheesecake, just a little farther. You got this."

It should not have come to this. This all seemed like a bad dream.

Joe was a rookie Ranger. He had just taken his vows last year. And he took those vows seriously. The Mintari Rangers had a simple mission statement. They swore to protect the dinosaurs of Mintari. On this world, humans were only caretakers, not masters. This planet belonged to the dinosaurs. This was their home. Their sanctuary. Their only chance to survive. Scientists had brought these majestic animals back from extinction. The Rangers made sure they never went extinct again.

Like all Rangers, Joe wore a khaki uniform and sturdy boots. The traditional Mintari hat, colloquially known as a ceratop, topped his head. It resembled park ranger hats from ancient Earth. A good Mintari Ranger wore his ceratop day and night, only removing the hat to honor a fallen comrade. Joe's badge gleamed on his chest, shaped like a stegosaurus's dorsal plate. The words MINTARI RANGER were engraved into the brass. To wear this badge was the honor of Joe's life.

He wore a second symbol. Smaller. Hard to see unless you stood close. It adorned his lapel, forged of silver but left to tarnish with age. The brooch was shaped like the head of a triceratops. The crest of Clan Triplehorn.

Clans were important on Mintari. A unique dinosaur represented each prominent lineage. Most people displayed their crests with pride. For Joe, displaying his family crest was an act of defiance. He noticed the stares. He heard the mutters. Sometimes men spat at him. Several times they had tried to rip his crest off, to stomp on it. But he still displayed the silver triceratops on his lapel. Someday he would restore his clan to honor. He vowed that the name *Triplehorn* would be uttered in admiration, not scorn. Only that day would he polish the silver until it gleamed again.

But first he must survive tonight.

He looked at Mina. She was struggling beside him but still so strong. Unlike Joe, she didn't wear a Mintari Rangers uniform. Instead, she wore blue scrubs and a white lab coat. Dr. Mina

Clubber-Triplehorn was a paleonarian. A veterinarian who treated dinosaurs. A dino-doc, as folks sometimes called her. She too had sworn to protect the wildlife on Mintari. Wherever a dinosaur was sick or injured, Mina would be there. Joe's job was to shoot poachers. Hers was to heal any dinosaur who survived a poacher's cruelty.

Earlier today, both had answered the call of duty. A Ranger satellite reported an urgent situation. Poachers from another planet, armed with heavy guns, were stalking a tyrannosaur family. Joe and Mina responded at once, entering the wilderness to save the dinosaurs. For even the fearsome T-rexes were worthy of life.

When they arrived at the scene, it was too late. The poachers were dead. Ripped apart. Pieces of them here and there. Before dying, they had managed to kill several T-rexes. A big female lay on the grass, riddled with bullets. Her hatchlings lay dead around her. Above the carnage stood the sole survivor. A gargantuan T-rex with black scales, blood on his teeth. King Ivan himself. The mightiest dinosaur on Mintari.

The poachers had killed his family. And now the beast was after Joe and Mina. He had shattered their tricopter, so they fled on foot. Just prey animals. Tonight one of the dinosaurs they had sworn to protect would kill them.

They ran onward through the forest. A thorn ripped Joe's cheek. He stumbled over a rock, twisting his ankle, but managed to keep running. The ground sloped into a shadowy valley.

Another rumble rolled through the forest. It sounded closer now. Waves of bass pounded Joe, aching in his bones.

"Joe, I can't ..." Mina panted. "I can't."

"You can, Mina. You can! We're almost there. Look."

He pointed. There in the valley. Salvation. Crater Lake gleamed in the light of Hypnos and Thanatos, Mintari's twin moons. They were running through hell, but there ahead shone heaven.

Mina nodded and wiped her eyes. Her fingers twined around Joe's. Holding hands, they ran downhill together.

Footsteps pounded the forest.

The ground vibrated with every footfall.

A bellow shook the trees. It was so deep human ears could barely hear it. But Joe could feel those punishing ripples of bass in his chest. It was the sound a Tyrannosaurus rex made before feasting.

Joe looked over his shoulder, and his heart seemed to stop in his chest.

The foliage was rustling. A ginkgo tree crashed down. A boulder rolled. A dark shadow moved between the conifers. Ivan was coming.

"We're not going to make it!" Mina cried.

"We will! Come on, Mina! Come on!"

They ran downhill through the ferns. The footfalls grew louder behind them. The forest trembled. The trees swayed. The sky itself seemed to tremble. Joe knew the facts. In peak condition, a human could run about ten kilometers per hour. In this dark forest, exhausted, bleeding, Mina pregnant—at best they could hope for half that speed.

A T-rex could run at thirty kilometers per hour without breaking a sweat.

To hell with the facts! Joe thought. *We're going to make it.*

He gripped Mina's hand tighter. There ahead—Crater Lake.

They were almost there.

So close.

Rumbles sounded—this time from ahead! The ferns parted. An ankylosaurus family burst out from the brush.

Joe's heart seemed to stop in his chest.

Ankylosaurs were essentially living tanks. They weighed more than elephants and wore suits of thick, bony armor. Spikes rose across their backs, lined their sides like scythes, and framed their lumpy heads. Their tails ended with bony clubs the size of pumpkins. Those tails could shatter bones, crack boulders, even plow through brick walls. Joe had once seen an ankylosaurus bull charge through a pack of allosaurs, kill two of the fearsome predators, and send the rest fleeing. These armored brawlers were among the toughest dinosaurs on Mintari.

And even they feared King Ivan.

The ankylosaurs howled, nostrils flaring, eyes wide with panic. Joe counted five of them—a male, a female, and three juveniles. The heavy herbivores rumbled down the hillside, fleeing for their lives. Their feet tore up roots and shrubs. Boulders rolled and little mammals fled into their burrows. Dust and moss filled the air. Like tanks charging across a battlefield, the armored brutes ran.

Joe and Mina skidded to a halt, then leaped back. They just barely dodged the stomping feet of the male ankylosaurus. The bull didn't notice them. He was too busy herding his family to safety. As he ran, the dinosaur swung his armored tail from side to side. He wasn't aiming at anything in particular. It was an instinct, similar to a cat bristling, meant to deter any predators. Even the mightiest carnivore would fear approaching a swinging club that could shatter boulders. Joe and Mina ducked. The tail whooshed overhead, nearly cracking their heads like eggs.

The tail's club *thunked* into a conifer like a wrecking ball, cracking the trunk. The tree swayed like a drunkard. The armored dinosaur kept thundering downhill, braying and rousing more ankylosaurs. More and more of the spiky giants burst from the forest. Soon an entire herd was stampeding downhill, fleeing the oncoming predator, leaving a trail of devastation.

The cracked conifer tilted farther. Wooden splinters burst from the trunk with a series of *cracks*.

Joe winced and grabbed Mina's hand.

With a sound like shattering bones, the trunk *snapped*.

The mighty conifer came pitching down.

For a moment—just a moment—Joe forgot about the pursuing T-rex. He pulled Mina back. The tree slammed down before them, shaking the hill. Both humans fell into the mud.

The conifer lay across the hillside. The trunk was enormous—as wide as a train. Hundreds of branches thrust out the top like spines, reaching taller than a house, so dense a cat would have trouble squeezing between them. The fallen tree formed a wall of wood and moss, blocking their way to the river.

The ankylosaurus herd vanished into the distance, leaving the humans trapped. Joe and Mina turned around, placing their backs to the fallen conifer. The last beams of sunset faded, leaving only the eerie moonlight.

The trees uphill parted.

And there he came, stepping into the moonlight. King Ivan. The tyrant of Mintari.

All tyrannosaurs were terrifying. They were born to kill. Even the juveniles could take down a stegosaurus. And as adults, the T-rexes dominated every other dinosaur on Mintari, from the bulkiest sauropod to the fastest raptor. Only the mighty triceratops stood a chance against a T-rex, and even he gave the king a wide berth. T-rex teeth could crunch through solid bone.

Their claws could rip the toughest scales. Their nostrils sniffed prey across vast landscapes, and their eyes pierced the darkest shadows. Even their arms, mocked for being disproportionally small, were no joke when they slashed at you. They were larger than human arms, and they could disembowel a man with a single swipe.

And Ivan made other T-rexes seem puny.

Nobody knew how Ivan had grown so big. No scientists dared study him. A few had tried. Nobody ever found the bodies. Most likely, Ivan was a mutant, the next step forward in the evolution of tyrannosaurs. He was as long as a sperm whale, as tall as an oak tree. His teeth were like swords gleaming in the moonlight. Spikes crested his back, sharp enough to impale anyone foolish enough to attack from behind. Most tyrannosaurs were green or gray, but not Ivan. His scales were black as coal, and his eyes blazed red like two torches. Those eyes perhaps seemed small in the gargantuan lumpy head of the beast, but they were larger than a man's heart, and when they stared at you, it was like they could see inside you.

There he was. The king himself. The most dreaded dinosaur on the planet.

He was still a good distance away, far on the hilltop. From where he stood, Joe and Mina must appear as mere specks. But he could see them. He could smell them. And he was thundering right toward them.

Death.

It was death personified coming for them. Death was not a pale man in a black cloak, holding a scythe. Death was a dinosaur.

Joe lit his flashlight and scanned the darkness for a way out. The conifer blocked their path to the lake. They could try to climb over the gargantuan log. Maybe, just maybe, if they were fast enough, they could cross the fallen tree before Ivan reached them.

But they would not get much farther. To Ivan, a fallen conifer was a speed bump. He'd leap over the tree, catch the humans, and feast.

Joe looked at the rampaging T-rex. The beast was stomping downhill, knocking down trees. He was only a moment away now. The gargantuan jaws opened with a deafening rumble. The land shook. The earth cracked. That nightmarish maw could swallow a man whole.

Trembling, Mina drew her gun. She let out a howl of her own. Compared to Ivan's cry, it sounded like a whimper. But the pregnant woman would not be easy prey. Fire burned in her eyes now, drying her tears.

"Go to hell, you son of a bitch!" she shouted and pulled the trigger.

She was a good shot. Bullets pounded Ivan's black scales. Amazingly, the T-rex stopped and shook his head. It was hard to see from here, but he didn't seem hurt, just surprised. Maybe one or two bullets had actually embedded themselves into the scales. Most had probably just fallen to the ground. The monstrous T-rex bellowed. The gunfire only made him angrier. He burst into a run again, feet shaking the hillside.

Joe had a gun too. He doubted it would do any good.

"Mina, climb with me!" he said.

"We won't make it over that log. Even if we do, it won't hold Ivan back, and—"

"Not over the conifer log. Up that ginkgo tree! Come on!"

He pointed. A ginkgo tree soared nearby. Ginkgos were among the tallest trees on Mintari. Even the great titanosaurs, sauropods with necks as long as buses, had to rear on their hind legs to reach the top branches. Ivan was tall, but even he couldn't reach that high.

As the T-rex stormed closer, Joe and Mina began climbing.

Thankfully, the ginkgo sprouted many branches for easy purchase. But they had a long way to climb. And not much time.

They scurried upward in a frenzy. Sap covered their hands. Bark scraped their skin. Twigs scratched their faces. Ivan thundered closer. Closer. Every footfall shook the tree. God, the stench of him. It wafted on the wind—a smell like bad breath and rotting meat. Between the branches, Joe saw the great shadow fall. The eyes of the beast burned in the night, two red flames, seeing him, lusting for his flesh.

Joe climbed faster. Mina slipped, screamed, and he caught her wrist. They kept climbing. Bark ripped Joe's palms. Blood dripped down to his elbow. He kept climbing through the pain.

Ivan crashed through the brush, heading toward the ginkgo tree.

Joe and Mina climbed another branch. Another. Hot, foul breath washed over them.

They were only a few meters up when the T-rex reached the tree.

Ivan rumbled. The sound was deafening. Mina screamed and Joe winced. His ears rang. The terrible maw widened, lined with teeth, a portal to hell.

Hanging from the branches, Joe unslung his rifle from across his back. He had avoided firing until now. It seemed pointless. When it came to King Ivan, you chose flight over fight. But flight was off the table now.

He was a Mintari Ranger, and he carried the traditional weapon of his order. They called it the sleep-or-die. The rifle had two barrels. One barrel fired tranquilizer darts. Sometimes even Rangers ran afoul of dinosaurs, and they must sedate an angry beast. The second barrel fired bullets. That barrel was for poachers only, never for dinosaurs, for the Mintari Rangers swore to protect all wildlife.

Tonight Joe broke his Ranger vows.

Tranquilizer darts would do little against a behemoth like Ivan. So tonight Joe flipped the switch from "sleep" to "die."

He pulled the trigger. A bullet flew toward Ivan's open mouth. Joe dared to hope he could pierce the soft gullet.

But as the shot rang out, Ivan snapped his mouth shut. The bullet slammed into the dinosaur's scaly snout ... and crumpled.

Joe stared in shock. The bullet actually crumpled like a tiny tin can ... and fell to the forest floor. It left little more than a dent in one scale.

Dear God, what the hell is this beast? Joe thought.

He fired a tranquilizer dart next. What the hell. Might as well try it. As Joe suspected—no good. The dart bent against Ivan's scales, then clattered to the ground, joining the crumpled bullet. It was like shooting at a hurricane. Pointless. Even if the darts *could* pierce Ivan's scales, so what? The dinosaur was so heavy, so furious, he would probably just shrug off the sedative. Might as well sing him a lullaby.

The infernal jaws opened again, hungry for humans.

Joe curled his legs inward. Ivan's bear trap of a mouth snapped shut only inches away, nearly severing both legs. God, that mouth was huge. It was like a sinkhole lined with teeth. The dinosaur glared up at him. His eyes were like cauldrons. Red eyes. Eyes full of furious fire. And Joe saw more than hunger in those reptilian orbs. He saw intelligence. Awareness.

Joe's upper lip rose in a snarl. He fired his sleep-or-die again.

He aimed for one of those blood-red eyes.

The bullet slammed into the scaly ridge above the eyeball. So close!

At this range, the bullet did some actual damage. Scales cracked. Blood splattered the branches. Ivan let out a furious howl.

He can bleed! Joe's heart sang. *We can hurt him!*

He fired again and again. But Ivan closed his eyes and mouth, protecting the softer parts of his head. The bullets hit only scales, chipping them. Nothing more than flesh wounds. If Joe kept firing at one spot, maybe he could—

His gun clicked. Out of bullets.

Tar it. He reached for more ammo, ready to finish the job. But blood slicked his fingers. His fresh magazine slipped from his grip. The bullets tumbled down to the forest floor. Joe could only watch in horror.

Ivan opened his eyes. They gleamed. Maybe Joe was imagining it, but the bastard actually seemed to be gloating. The dinosaur leaped up, jaws opening to feast.

Joe scurried higher among the branches. Mina, who was already several branches up, caught him and pulled him. The jaws snapped shut below Joe's boots, shattering the branch where he had just stood.

He scampered up the tree, Mina pulling him along. Ivan reared. T-rexes normally walked with their spines horizontal, their tails thrust out straight, balancing on their muscular legs. But now Ivan rose upright like a rearing bear. His teeth shred branches in a demonic imitation of a herbivore as he tried to reach the humans.

Mina fired her own gun. A bullet hit Ivan in the head, cracking a scale that Joe had already chipped. The dinosaur fell to the ground, grumbling more in anger than pain. The tree shook. Within only a moment, Ivan recovered and leaped up again.

By then, both Joe and Mina were high enough.

Ginkgos grew two hundred feet tall. The couple hadn't climbed the entire height of the tree. But they had climbed enough to escape the terrible teeth. Breathing heavily, his limbs slung over the branches, Joe stared down at the dinosaur.

Ivan glared up at him, a low growl in his throat. His eyes narrowed. He knew his prey was out of reach. It began to rain. The plump drops steamed as they hit the dinosaur's cracked scales.

Joe allowed himself to relax. Just a little. The rain ran down his face, clearing the blood. He looked at his wife.

"Mina, are you all right?"

"I'm all right." She clung to the branches, pale and panting, and scratches bled across her arms and face. But they were both still breathing. Right now that was a miracle.

"The baby?" Joe whispered.

Mina gave him a wan smile. "Kicking. Scared but strong."

They both looked down at Ivan. Joe pointed his flashlight at the great Tyrannosaurus rex. Ivan's pupils narrowed to pinpricks in the light, but he did not blink. He just stood there, staring up at them. His eyes were calculating. His breath steamed. His nostrils flared, and his scaly lips rippled with every growl.

"Why does he hunt us?" Mina whispered. "Humans are so small. He can hunt far larger prey by the watering holes and on the grassy plains."

Joe stared at the dinosaur. Ivan stared back. The two maintained eye contact.

"I thought he was hungry," Joe said softly. "I was wrong. He's *angry*. Remember what we found on the plains. Poachers killed his family. This is about revenge."

"But we're not poachers!" Mina said.

"To Ivan, it's enough that we're human. In his madness, all humans are now his enemy. He doesn't know we're here to help dinosaurs. To him we're no different from poachers. And he wants his vengeance."

"Joe, he's only an animal!"

"He's intelligent, Mina. Maybe not as intelligent as us. But at least as smart as chimps or dolphins. I see it in his eyes."

As if he understood, Ivan broke eye contact. He took a few steps away, vanishing into the shadows.

Mina breathed out in relief. Tears flooded her eyes. "He's leaving. Thank God, he's leaving." She let out a sob. "We made it."

But Joe did not smile, did not sigh in relief. He tensed and clutched his gun, wishing he still had ammo.

"Mina? Hold on tight."

She blinked at him. "What?"

His heart burst into a gallop. "Grab a branch and hold on tight!"

A bellow pealed through the night. Footfalls thundered. Ivan came racing out of the shadows and barreled into the tree trunk.

The ginkgo shook.

Mina screamed and clung to the branches. Joe winced, hugging the trunk.

Ivan retreated again, then ran and slammed into the tree.

Wood snapped. The tree shook and tilted. Roots burst from the underground. Branches trembled and leaves rained.

A third time Ivan bulldozed into the tree … and the trunk shattered.

The tree, with Joe and Mina in it, came crashing down.

They screamed as the tree tumbled down.

With splintering wood, shattering branches, and clouds of dirt, the ginkgo slammed onto the hillside.

Joe and Mina clung to the branches. Thankfully, the opposite side of the trunk hit the ground. Otherwise the tree would have crushed them. But the crash still jostled them around between the branches. Joe bloodied his nose and banged his shoulder. He didn't care. He held on to Mina with one hand. Only she and the baby mattered now.

The fallen trunk began sliding downhill. The two humans clung on, riding the trunk like a giant toboggan. If Joe weren't so terrified, he might have laughed. The rain kept falling. Mud sluiced down the hillside. The fallen tree gained speed.

And the T-rex followed.

Roaring, Ivan raced alongside the sliding trunk. His foot-long teeth tore through branches, seeking his prey in the foliage. Joe cried out, leaping back from the terrible fangs. He felt like a field mouse fleeing a lawn mower. He nearly fell off the log. Mina pulled him back to safety.

The tree slid faster through the mud.

Ivan lowered his head and rammed the trunk. The tree spun through the mud. Joe and Mina scurried from branch to branch. The trunk began to roll. They raced along the bole, arms windmilling. Joe flashed back to a game he would play as a child, trying to run atop a rolling log in a lake. He had never lasted long, always falling into the water. Now, if he fell, the gullet of a tyrannosaur awaited.

The jaws came at them again, snapping madly. A tooth scraped across Joe's leg, ripping skin and flesh. He screamed.

Seized with bloodlust, Ivan lunged at him again. But just then, the log rammed into a boulder and leaped into the air.

Both humans flew from the tree.

For a moment, the world spun. Joe saw only branches and ripping leaves and then the ground rushing up toward him.

He splashed into the mud.

Mina landed beside him, crying out in pain.

The baby. Oh God, the baby.

He scampered toward Mina through the mud. She had landed on her side, not her belly. He grabbed her and pulled her to her feet.

He stared into her eyes.

"Run!" he shouted.

They ran.

There just ahead—Crater Lake. Safety.

Ivan crashed through the fallen ginkgo tree, shattering it into a million pieces. The tyrannosaur thundered after the two humans. Strings of saliva dangled between his teeth like harp strings. Lightning flashed, reflecting across his black scales. Thunder boomed.

Another lightning bolt cleaved the night, slammed into a tree, and fire blazed. Ivan burst through the flames, teeth red in the firelight.

Joe and Mina kept running. They were almost there.

The enormous head of the tyrannosaur swooped toward them. The tongue quivered as the beast rumbled.

Mina fired her gun.

Her bullet punctured the lumpy tongue.

Ivan reared, a cry of pain replacing his cry of hunger.

"That was my last bullet!" Mina said.

But it was enough. It bought them time. Before Ivan could regain his bearings, the couple reached the lake.

Holding hands, they jumped into the water.

The icy water flowed over them. Their legs kicked in the depths. The lake had formed about a million years ago, seawater rushing in to fill an asteroid impact crater. Years later, landslides separated the flooded crater from the sea, isolating the saltwater lake. The crater's lip still formed the shoreline. The water was deep right from the first step.

Both Joe and Mina were strong swimmers. They had met in the water. It was during the great floods of 3021. Joe had been just a Ranger trainee; he hadn't even earned his badge yet. But he swam through rushing water to save a drowning sauropod, a hatchling not much larger than a pony. He brought the poor, shivering dinosaur to a clinic in Dinovia City. The floodwaters had rushed into the city too, and many people had fled onto the rooftops. But Mina, the paleonarian on duty, stood with the water up to her waist, treating the hatchling. She saved the animal's life. A year later, that sauropod was the size of an elephant, and Joe and Mina were married.

It seemed like a lifetime ago.

In the dark forest tonight, they had almost lost this marriage, this life together. But the water washed away their blood and fear. Now they would live. Now they could grow old together.

They swam under the twin moons, and Joe's tears fell. Tears of relief. They had fled the beast.

Mina let out a strangled cry.

She pointed behind them.

Joe stared. His heart seemed to shatter in his chest.

He was a Mintari Ranger, and he knew a lot about dinosaurs. At least he had told himself that. Tonight he learned something new. T-rexes could swim.

Joe still remembered the first time he had seen a dinosaur.

Mintarian children grew up with dinosaurs. To them, the beasts were ordinary. Large and dangerous, yes, but ordinary. Joe, however, had been born on Cloventia, a planet where the largest reptile could hide in your pocket.

Originally Clan Triplehorn came from Mintari. Their last name was a dead giveaway. So were their strong jaws and dark, hard eyes. But they had left long ago. After all, Mintari was a backwater. A wild world overrun with monsters. You had to be crazy to live on Mintari. Tobias Triplehorn, the family patriarch, prided himself on immigrating to a more civilized world. Among the glittering skyscrapers of Cloventia, Clan Triplehorn had grown wealthy, comfortable, and domesticated. With every year, they smoothed out more of those rough Mintarian edges. They lost their crude outer world accents. They ate fine vegetables and delicate fruits, not just meat and potatoes. They wore modern silks, not khakis and boots. Instead of battling dinosaurs, they fought corporate rivals at court. Like many emigrants from frontier planets, they considered themselves more sophisticated than those remaining in their so-called "old worlds." And they always had something to prove.

Until Joe was nine, he had never seen a dinosaur. Not until his mother left Tobias Triplehorn. She fled the icy stares. The cruel jibes. And sometimes, yes, the fists. When his temper flared, Tobias lost his veneer of elegance, and he was a wild man again. Battered and homesick, his wife ran, taking young Joe with her. She returned to Mintari, a planet with barely any humans and billions of dinosaurs.

Joe saw his first dinosaur before they even landed. They were flying inside an astrolite, a vehicle designed to descend from a starship, enter an atmosphere, and deliver passengers to the ground. Joe remembered gliding over a forest, heading toward

Dinovia, the only human settlement on the planet. He was in the back seat, hugging himself, so afraid. He was Mintarian by blood and birthright, but he had never seen this world. He missed Cloventia. Missed the skyscrapers, the neon lights, and mostly his friends. He had never even seen a plant—unless you counted the plastic ones some Cloventians kept on their shelves. The forests rolling by below seemed alien to him, dangerous, and as his father would say—primitive.

This was before he had fallen in love with the wilderness. Before he understood the majesty of this world. Back then, he had been afraid.

When he saw his first dinosaur, the young boy pressed his face against the window, and his eyes widened. It was a sauropod. Which species, Joe didn't know. A brontosaurus? A diplodocus? Something else? He never found out. But the dinosaur had a long neck, and it reared on its back legs and looked at the astrolite flying above. Joe imagined that across the distance he made eye contact with the gentle giant. The dinosaur looked bigger than the starship that had carried him here. But yes, it was gentle. Joe's fear eased. And he realized that Mintari was his home.

Today, swimming for his life through the icy lake, Joe remembered that boy, so full of fears and hopes.

How would I have felt, he wondered, *if the first dinosaur I saw was a T-rex?*

Most likely, that young boy would have sneaked into the first starship off this planet and fled back to his father's penthouse.

But now Joe was here. A young man. Swimming for his life as a terror from his deepest nightmares pursued him through the water.

As Joe swam, he looked behind him. Ivan was still following. His mighty legs paddled underwater, keeping him afloat. His tail whipped back and forth, propelling him forward.

His scaly head was mostly submerged like a crocodile's head. His nostrils rose from the lake, draped with algae, sniffing for his prey. His eyes stared, two red orbs blazing like floating water lanterns. It had to be a trick of the moonlight. But to Joe, it seemed like Ivan's eyes burned with their own malevolent light. He seemed like some mythological beast of fire, and more than ever before, Joe understood how the early discovery of T-rex bones had inspired the legend of dragons.

Thankfully, T-rexes were slower in water than on land. But Ivan moved with dogged persistence. Land, treetops, water— nothing would stop him from catching his prey.

And he was still faster than human swimmers.

Joe looked at Mina. She swam beside him, pale in the moonlight. Her eyes were sunken, her lips purple. She had almost no strength left.

Joe looked ahead. Crater Lake was not large. The moonlight limned the distant shore. But for two exhausted humans, it seemed a light-year away.

Between strokes, he glanced over his shoulder. Ivan was significantly closer.

"We're not going to make it," Mina whispered, echoing his thoughts. "Joe. Joe, I love you. We'll be together ... at the end."

She was swimming wearily, slowing down, losing her will and strength.

"We're not giving up, tar it!"

"We have no bullets. Our radios are dead. All we have are our flashlights."

Then it hit him. "So we'll use our flashlights."

"What, by blinding Ivan?" Mina said, panting as she struggled to keep swimming. "You know that won't work. T-rex can hunt by smell and sound alone. Remember the blind T-rex we observed last year at Naraka Gorge?"

"Not by blinding Ivan," Joe said. "But by summoning help."

There was only one animal in these parts that could challenge a T-rex. Only one animal as big, as powerful, as deadly.

The pliosaurus.

Joe had never seen one in real life. Heard of them? Of course. Suffered nightmares about them? Yes, he admitted it. They mostly remained underwater, prowling the depths for prey. The beasts were massive, as large as Earth's whales. Their flippers could shatter ships. Lined with rows of devastating teeth, their mouths could engulf a small boat. They made Great White sharks seem like minnows. If T-rex ruled the land, pliosaurus ruled the water.

Most of these leviathans lived in the vast oceans of Mintari. But according to legend, one pliosaurus lived in Crater Lake—a grand old female, grown too large to fit down the river and escape to sea. The Rangers nicknamed her Pearl. According to some stories, she had grown so large by devouring misbehaving children. Watch out, kids. If you swim too far from the shore, Pearl will grab you.

Ivan perhaps ruled the land. But he was now swimming in another predator's territory. Joe just had to wake that predator up.

At night, pliosaurs slept underwater. The sunlight woke them. Joe hoped his flashlight was bright enough.

He looked behind him. Ivan was gaining on them. He was almost close enough to bite. The tyrannosaur's nostrils flared with every breath. His scaly brows pushed low over his eyes. He was tired. He was not used to the water. But he was not turning back.

This will be your watery grave, Joe swore and reached for his flashlight.

For a terrible second, he worried that the flashlight was dead. That the water had killed it. But when he flipped the switch, the light came on, sharp and blinding. Ivan's pupils shrank to angry pinpoints.

Then Joe pointed the flashlight down into the murky waters.

He and Mina kept swimming.

Nothing happened.

Ivan growled and swung his tail, shoving himself forward with a burst of speed.

"Come on, Pearl, wake up," Joe muttered.

He waved his flashlight through the water, sweeping the beam across the murk. The light was clearly too dim.

He glanced behind him. Ivan was only meters away.

The predator opened his mouth wide, sucking up water and fish, and surged toward the two humans. Joe and Mina cried out and swam faster. The scaly mouth snapped shut behind them, just missing their feet. Water splashed.

They swam forward as Ivan loomed, mouth opening for the coup de grâce.

From the water ahead burst a monstrous, scaly head.

Another hellmouth opened before them, teeth gleaming in the moonlight.

The pliosaurus was awake.

Joe and Mina floundered in the water, trapped between two titans.

Behind them—King Ivan. The largest Tyrannosaurus rex on Mintari. His scales were black as night, his jaws powerful enough to break solid iron. But he was out of his element, swimming in the water where he was weaker.

Ahead loomed Pearl, a terror risen from the depths. The pliosaurus was old. Her teeth were a little shorter than Ivan's, and her bite was a little weaker than it used to be. But she was still a colossus. A living legend. Her lower jawbone was the size of a canoe, full of water, algae, and floundering fish. Most importantly, she was in her element, lady of the water. If Ivan was King of Mintari, she was the queen.

Clearly Ivan still nurtured a grudge for humanity. But despite the tall tales, Pearl had no taste for human flesh. What were humans to an animal this big? Just a snack. Barely worth the effort. At her advanced age, Pearl often let prey go, preferring to sleep than hunt. But a T-rex in the water? That was another predator. A challenger. The king of land had dared invade the watery domain of the queen. That could not stand.

With a gurgling cry, Pearl beat her flippers and charged at Ivan.

Joe and Mina swam aside, desperate to flee this clash of titans. Waves lifted them and hurled them away.

With a sickening *crack* that rippled across Crater Lake, the two predators slammed together.

Scales hit scales. Teeth clattered against teeth like dueling swords. The two legendary beasts, each an apex predator in its environment, howled and clawed and bit, locked in battle for supremacy. Blood darkened the water.

Joe only caught glimpses of this epic duel. With each swing of their tails, the two gargantuan carnivores raised higher waves. Joe tumbled through the water. His head went under, and the salt water stung his eyes and burned through his nostrils. He held Mina's hand with all his might. His legs kicked underwater, and his lungs ached for air. He burst over the surface, and Mina's head popped out a second later. Rain streamed down. The whole world seemed made of storming water. Lightning cracked the sky, painting the T-rex and pliosaurus brilliant white.

Pearl was used to swimming in the dark depths. Sensitive to light, the beast screeched and closed her eyes. Ivan seized his chance. The black T-rex whipped his tail, propelling himself closer in the water, and closed his legendary jaws around Pearl's flank. Just under the neck.

A typical T-rex had a biting force of 35,000 newtons. It was the strongest bite force of any animal in history. It made a lion's bite seem like a gentle nibble. It made a crocodile's bite seem like a puppy's playful nip. A Tyrannosaurus rex could crush a car in his jaws like a man biting an apple. And Ivan was far stronger than a typical T-rex. His swordlike teeth drove through Pearl's scales and deep into the flesh.

The leviathan mewled. Her blood filled the water.

Joe and Mina bobbed in the roiling lake. They tried to swim, but the whipping tails swirled the water. Currents pulled the couple under. For a second, they floundered underwater, kicked their feet, and burst over the surface again. It was impossible to swim in the churning chaos. Blood whirled around them. All they could do was struggle to stay afloat.

Thunder boomed and Pearl bellowed just as loudly. The behemoth was wounded but still in the fight. And while smaller than Ivan, she was no slouch. Like the humans, the T-rex was struggling in the water, kicking madly to stay afloat. The pliosaurus smacked the larger predator with her flippers, then leaned in, closed her mouth around Ivan's shoulder, and bit deep.

Ivan had thick scales and massive layers of hard skin beneath. His armor was so thick it could stop bullets. Pearl's teeth, terrifying as they were, would not reach anything critical. But the pliosaurus had other plans. She locked her jaws tightly ... and pulled Ivan under.

With a great maelstrom, the two mighty reptiles vanished underwater.

She's going to drown Ivan, Joe realized.

Then the waves hit him and Mina. They swept across the lake, hurtling toward the distant shore.

They swam the last stretch, then crawled onto the shore, exhausted, panting … and miraculously alive. They collapsed onto the sandy bank, gasping for air, coughing, but laughing too. They flipped onto their backs and just lay there, breathing, smiling. The rain pattered against them. Their hands were still clasped together.

"We made it," Joe said.

Mina laughed weakly. "Can we never leave the city walls again?"

"Never again," he swore.

But he already knew he was lying. He was a Mintari Ranger. His job was to go into the wilderness of a planet where dinosaurs lived again. To hunt poachers. To save dinosaurs in trouble. To keep this planet's ecosystem alive. That came with unspeakable danger. There weren't many old Rangers on Mintari. Tonight Joe had learned why.

But next time, he vowed, he was leaving Mina at home. Tar it, she was a doctor, not a Ranger. He would never more allow her to—

A great wave washed onto the shore, interrupting his thoughts.

Joe propped himself onto his elbows.

Lightning flashed, illuminating the scene.

His heart nearly stopped.

"No," he whispered. "It can't be."

In the darkness, a great shadow washed onto the shore like a beached whale. Another lightning flash confirmed it. It was her. Pearl, the legendary pliosaurus of Crater Lake, was dead.

On her neck, still bleeding profusely, appeared the unmistakable teeth pattern of a T-rex.

The water roiled.

Another shadow rose from the depths like a bubble of tar.

Red eyes blazed in the dark. The shadow rose higher. Higher still. Moving toward the shore. Lightning slashed the night, illuminating black scales. King Ivan trudged onto the shore. He placed one great foot onto the dead pliosaurus, tossed back his head, stuck out his little arms, and gurgled in triumph.

Dinosaurs couldn't roar like mammals. It was a common misconception offworlders had. Even the mightiest T-rex could not roar. They sounded more like crocodiles than lions. But the sounds were no less terrifying. Ivan's gurgles were deafening. They were so deep they scratched the lower edge of what human ears could hear. The waves of bass rippled the forest and pounded Joe's chest like invisible clubs. A T-rex's rumble was the most terrifying sound on Mintari, far worse than any roar could ever sound. And now Ivan was rumbling with relish.

Joe pulled Mina to her feet.

"Run!" he said.

He was alive.

The bastard was still alive.

He had survived bullets, the bite of a pliosaurus, and being drowned. But Ivan was still going. His talons tore through the sandy lakeshore. Blood dripped down his scaly hide. But he had lost none of his rage. His hatred for humanity still burned hot. Humans had killed his family. He now lived for nothing but revenge. He would not stop until he died, yet he seemed impossible to kill. At this point, Joe doubted that a blast from a tank could knock Ivan down.

What the hell are you? Joe thought. *What kind of animal can survive so much?*

Then Joe focused only on running.

He was tired. Bone tired. His body screamed to lie down, curl up, and nurse its wounds. With sheer force of will, Joe kept moving his legs. And if *he* felt this tired, he couldn't even imagine what Mina was going through. His wife's skin was gray in the moonlight. She kept her arms wrapped around her pregnant belly. She seemed half dead, moving on momentum alone.

Behind them, Ivan's growls rippled the air. The T-rex was wounded. He was still losing blood. He had slowed down. But step by step, he kept advancing toward them.

Mina stumbled and fell to her knees.

Joe helped her back up. She swayed, took another step, nearly fell again. The rain dripped down her face, mingling with blood.

"Joe, it's over," she whispered through purple lips. She was shivering with cold.

"We're going to—"

"We can't escape him."

He gripped her hand tighter. "Listen to me, Mina. Listen to me! He's wounded. He's losing blood. He's slowing down. We just need to run a little farther, and Ivan will have to stop. Home stretch, babe. Come on!"

She nodded, took a step, then froze.

Her eyes widened, then flooded with tears.

"Mina, what is it?"

She looked at him, her face like a wax statue. "Joe, my water broke. The baby is coming."

His head spun. All he could think of saying was, "You're not due for another—"

"The baby is coming, Joe!" She trembled, then clenched her jaw and moaned.

Joe looked back toward the lake.

Ivan was moving closer. The T-rex was too wounded to run now, but he kept trudging forward. Getting closer. Closer still.

Joe's head spun. His belly churned. This was a nightmare, had to be a nightmare. How could this be real? How could his life have become such a hell? Blackness was spreading across his vision. His knees shook. He felt close to fainting.

Then he tightened his lips.

You are a Mintari Ranger, he told himself. *You are a warrior. Your wife needs you. Deal with things!*

He lifted Mina in his arms and began carrying her uphill.

Each step was a battle.

Each breath was a war.

Mina grimaced in his arms, her jaw locked in pain, her hands on her belly. Joe kept carrying her uphill. He didn't have a plan. Maybe he didn't have a hope. He just knew that he must keep going, must keep taking step after step, winning battle after battle against oncoming death.

He seemed to walk for miles. For eternities. To cross continents. And Ivan kept following. The dinosaur was limping. Blood leaked from the pliosaurus bite. At one point, Ivan slipped, crashed through several trees, then pushed himself back up and kept climbing. The great carnivore was breathing heavily, but his eyes never looked away from Joe. So long as he drew breath, Ivan would hunt.

Finally Joe reached the hilltop. The land leveled out. He took a few stumbling steps forward, carrying Mina in his arms.

Cycads grew toward the moonlight, their fronds forming a canopy. Fluffy little cynodonts scurried below, feasting on fallen fruit. The cynodonts were the ancestors of mammals. Like the dinosaurs, they were brought back from extinction and let loose on Mintari. Superficially, they looked similar to shrews. They were prey animals. And they attracted predators. Several feathered dinosaurs stood among the trees, chasing the fuzzy critters.

Joe froze, body tensing.

"Dakotaraptors," he muttered.

The last creatures he wanted to meet now.

Dakotaraptors were fearsome carnivores, roughly the size of horses. Like the much-larger T-rex, they were theropods, and they had the same general body plan. Two powerful legs. Big toothy jaws. Long tail. Short arms. But unlike their scaly big brothers, the raptors sported a coat of brown and white feathers. At a glance, they looked almost like flightless hawks. If hawks had teeth like steak knives and claws that could disembowel a rhino, that was.

Dakotaraptors were ruthless predators, but tonight they were here among the trees, pathetically picking at the scurrying cynodonts. They weren't happy about it. They knew this was below them. It wasn't easy being a lesser predator in T-rex's kingdom. The raptors, deadly as they were, knew their place in the food chain. Tonight they made do with morsels.

At the sight of Joe and Mina stumbling into the grove, the raptors looked up hungrily. A few licked their chops. Perhaps, after all, they could feast tonight on larger game? Then Ivan growled in the distance, still cloaked in shadows. The raptors tilted their heads, sniffed the air, then turned to flee. They knew a T-rex when they smelled one. And they knew who was king. This meal, like so many others, would go to their master.

Seconds later, Ivan crashed between the cycads, ripping off fronds, shattering trunks. The king lowered his head, swept up a fleeing raptor, and crunched the horse-sized dinosaur in his mighty jaws. With a sickening *snap*, the raptor's spine shattered. Ivan tossed the corpse down, bit off a mouthful, and swallowed the hot meat. After his quick snack, Ivan kept advancing toward the humans, his true quarry.

Joe ran between the falling ferns, carrying his wife. Ivan seemed stronger after his meal. He grumbled in fury, knocking down more trees. His low-frequency rumbles seemed to shake the very sky.

"Watch out!" Mina cried.

Joe skidded to a halt, feeling dizzy.

A cliff plunged down into the darkness.

He had reached Big Bend Cliff. The end of the world. Realm of flying giants.

He stared down into the void, head spinning, too scared to move. Even in the light of Mintari's two moons, the ground was too far to see. Screeches rose from the void. Huge, winged shadows glided through the misty depths. White eyes lit the darkness.

Joe recognized those animals. These cliffs were the realm of *Quetzalcoatlus northropi*, lord of the skies. The largest flying animal to ever exist. Q-pis, as the Rangers called them, were a type of pterosaur. Flying reptiles. Many pterosaurs lived on Mintari, but Q-pis were the mightiest. Their wingspan was the length of a bus. Their skulls were longer than most cars. On the ground, with folded wings, they would stand as tall as giraffes. Tonight they swept through the misty depths, their shrieks echoing in the abyss. Anyone who fell off that cliff would be lucky to die by hitting the ground. More likely they would be swallowed alive, doomed to slow, agonizing digestion inside a flying creature from the land of nightmares.

Joe snapped out of his paralysis. He stumbled back from the abyss, turning away from the terrors below.

But he faced a terror no less formidable.

Ivan stomped closer, licking his chops.

Joe stood with his back to the cliff, holding his pregnant wife, trapped.

When he was younger, Joe never imagined he would someday become a Mintari Ranger. He had wanted to become a musician, of all things. He played the piano and guitar. He wasn't bad at it either, if you asked the locals at the Fossil and Firkin pub. Why leave the walled safety of Dinovia, the only human settlement on Mintari, when enormous, man-eating reptiles roamed the planet? Hell, why even leave the pub? There was beer, there was a piano, the shepherd's pie was heavenly, and the only dinosaur was the fossil that hung behind the bar. Seemed good enough for humble Joren "Joe" Triplehorn.

But as he grew older, he learned more about his family.

About Triplehorn Incorporated. Ticker symbol TRPL on the Cloventia Stock Exchange.

His mother had fled the clan long ago, taking young Joe with her. It was years before he learned the truth. The other kids at school would mutter, spit on him. Later on, drunkards at the pub would hear his last name, curse, and toss bottles.

He was a Triplehorn. And his name meant death.

His clan had abandoned Mintari. *Betrayed* Mintari. Today the family ran one of the largest hunting supplies companies on Cloventia, and they owned seventeen outlets on Earth. The poachers who came to Mintari all proudly brought traps, bait, camouflage, and weapons made by Triplehorn Incorporated.

Joe came from a family of dino killers.

And so, on the day he turned eighteen, Joe joined the Mintari Rangers. An organization sworn to fight the poachers who came from offworld to hunt the magnificent wildlife of Mintari. Legendary beasts lived here. Animals brought back to life through cutting-edge "time-casting" technology. Joe could have changed his last name. He could have disavowed his clan. Instead, he chose to reclaim his name. To own it. To redeem it. At least one Triplehorn would do good on Mintari. To him, the triceratops skull on his lapel was more than just a brooch. It was a promise. A vow to restore his clan's honor.

Mina knew all this when marrying him. She knew his struggle, knew the burden she was taking on. On her scrubs, she wore a golden ankylosaurus club—the crest of her father, Chief Ganzorig Clubber. On her right lapel, she displayed the silver triceratops of Triplehorn, the clan she had married into. She too got the stares. The curses. Sometimes people spat. She endured it. She loved Joe too much to remove the silver crest. The couple was united with love—not only for each other, but also for the dinosaurs of Mintari. They had sworn to protect these majestic animals—him with a gun, her with a stethoscope.

And tonight one of those majestic animals was going to kill them.

Gently, Joe placed Mina down by the cliff. She was convulsing with contractions. The baby was coming. Joe placed himself between her and the T-rex. He stood, facing his nemesis.

The rain stopped. The clouds parted. Full moonlight bathed Ivan, revealing the king in all his glory.

He was the largest predator on Mintari. Possibly the largest predator who ever walked on land. Ivan looked like a creature from a monster movie, a *kaiju* who stomped on cities. It was hard to imagine that evolution could have produced such a nightmare. Yet produce Ivan it did. He was not the product of some mad scientist weaving strands of DNA, crafting a Frankenstein terror from the imagination. Yes, scientists used time-casting to scoop up dinosaurs from the past, to preserve them on Mintari, but they were merely collectors. Not creators. Evolution had forged this beast. This unstoppable machine of ultimate carnage. Here was Mother Nature in her beastliest form. Ivan was not a mere animal. He was a force of nature, as unstoppable as a hurricane or erupting volcano.

There was a reason almost nobody left the walls of Dinovia City. You had to be crazy to roam the wilderness where carnivores like Ivan roamed. Joe was one of those crazy people. And now he would die.

Ivan took a step forward. Joe couldn't take a single step back, not without falling off the cliff. Trapped.

Maybe Joe was imagining it, humanizing the beast. But in his exhaustion, it seemed to Joe that Ivan's jaws parted with something like a smile. A cruel smile. A mockery of a smile. The smile a predator gives his prey before the feast. The king lowered his head toward Joe, nostrils flaring. His terrible mouth creaked wider like some medieval gateway, lined with teeth like a portcullis, large enough to swallow him with a single gulp.

Mina rose to her feet.

She stepped closer to the dinosaur.

Ivan hissed and turned his head toward her. His eyes narrowed. His foul breath fluttered her bloodstained scrubs.

Mina was in labor. She was exhausted, wounded, maybe dying. Blood dripped down her thighs. But she fixed Ivan with a glare.

"You will not touch us, you son of a bitch."

Grimacing with effort, Mina knelt, lifted a boulder the size of her head, and hurled the stone toward the king.

The boulder slammed into Ivan with the power of a cornered woman protecting her baby. It was the most powerful known force in the universe.

Ivan reared, howling in pain.

One of his teeth fell to the ground. It pierced the mud.

The king's bellow was so loud the sonic waves knocked Joe down.

But Mina stayed standing. Panting, she faced the dinosaur. Her hair clung to her face with sweat and blood. She bared her teeth, and at that moment, she was no longer prey. She was as fierce a predator as any tyrannosaur.

Then, as swift as a robin plucking up a worm, Ivan lowered his head down, closed his mighty jaws around Mina, and tossed his head back.

Mina barely had time to scream before the dinosaur gulped her down. Ivan's throat bobbed as he swallowed his meal.

Lying in the mud, Joe stared.

Ivan licked his chops.

Mina was gone.

Their unborn child was gone.

Something exploded inside Joe like an erupting tar pit.

"Tar you!" he cried hoarsely, tearing his throat. "Tar you black, you overgrown freak!"

Tears gushed from his eyes. His body shook. Mina. Oh God, Mina was gone. The love of his life was gone.

With a bloody hand, Joe grabbed Ivan's fallen tooth. It was as long as his forearm.

Ivan drove his head toward Joe, still hungry for human flesh.

With a wordless cry, Joe swung the tooth. It did what bullets could not. The tooth sliced through Ivan's thick black scales, cutting deep into the flesh. Joe carved a six-foot-long gash across Ivan's snout. From under his eye to his chin.

The T-rex reared. A curtain of blood sprayed from his muzzle. The scales parted to reveal the raw, red flesh within. Joe even saw a hint of the skull.

Joe's eyes stung. His legs trembled. Mina was gone. Oh God, Mina was gone.

He took a step closer to Ivan. He still gripped the tooth. He raised his weapon high.

"Do you want some more?" Joe shouted.

Ivan hesitated. Had the king met his match?

Then the tyrant's eyes hardened. A growl bubbled up his throat and emerged from his bloodstained gullet.

He took a step closer to Joe, already salivating. His tiny clawed hands flexed, revealing his eagerness for the next meal. It was an instinct T-rexes had before feeding. They used their small arms to clutch still-living prey as they tucked in. His cheek was carved open, but so long as the king still breathed, he would hunt.

Joe took a step back.

His heels reached the cliff. Stones cascaded into the depths. In the abyss, the winged reptiles screeched, their cries echoing like the song of demons in hell.

In the east, dawn was rising. Joe had been battling this beast all night. The wind died down, and the faint hints of morning gilded the mountains, gorges, and forests of Mintari, this fierce wilderness Joe called home.

He looked into the eyes of the dinosaur.

Ivan stared back, silent, almost contemplative. Who knew what thoughts were going through the mind of a killer?

Then the king let out a howl that shook the world and rippled the sky. He lunged toward Joe. Nothing would stop him this time. No blow from a boulder. No cut from a tooth. His hunger for humanity eclipsed his pain. All he cared about was the kill.

Gripping the dislodged tooth, Joe leaped off the cliff.

As he fell into the darkness, he gazed upward toward the top of the cliff. Ivan stood there, a shadow in the dawn, crying out in fury.

Mina, I love you. I love you so much.

He tumbled through the air, turning to face the shadowy depths, and a shriek washed over him. Leathern wings the size of a yacht's sails flapped. A quetzalcoatlus flew below, mouth opening wide to catch the falling morsel.

Joe pointed his T-rex tooth at the flying reptile.

The Q-pi turned its head aside, fearing the bony blade.

Joe tumbled past the pterosaur's head. The beak alone was larger than him. An instant later, he slammed onto one of the animal's wings.

He rolled across the leathern membrane and nearly fell off. But he drove his tooth down, piercing the wing, and clung on to the tooth like a handle. The Q-pi screamed and beat its wings and flew onward. Joe held on. He was weak. He was bleeding. A part of him cried out to let go, to fall, to join Mina in death.

But he clung on.

The Q-pi flew into the distance, shrieking. The beating of its wings rippled the grasslands below and sent a herd of hadrosaurs fleeing. As Joe held on to the wing, he stared at the retreating cliff. Ivan was growing smaller and smaller in the distance, but Joe could still hear the predator's cry on the wind, and all who heard it knew who was King of Mintari.

Joe closed his eyes and wept.

But there was something that Joe did not know.

Something he *could* not know.

In the darkness, he had not seen it. As the T-rex rumbled, he had not heard it.

It had happened while Joe stood before the T-rex, shielding his wife behind his body. While his back was turned, while the terror gripped his heart, while King Ivan glared with his burning red eyes, Mina Clubber-Triplehorn had given birth.

Mina was gone now. Ivan had devoured her, ending her short life—like the lives of so many creatures on Mintari. But her child still lived. The baby lay on a pile of bloody grass, crying for a mother's warmth.

Ivan did not bother feasting on this morsel. His wounds ached. The human had carved his snout down to the bone. His vengeance was quenched for tonight. He would leave the baby for some lesser predator. Let the raptors eat the scraps. Growling in pain, the T-rex stomped into the distance to nurse his wounds.

The baby cried for a long time. Long after Ivan was gone. Long after Joe had flown off on the pterosaur, mourning the loss of his wife. As the sun reached its zenith, bathing the land with heat, still the baby cried. A baby girl. Born prematurely. Small and red and angry.

As the sun dipped into afternoon, her cries began to weaken. Without milk or warmth, the baby was dying.

For hours, predators had stayed away from the place. The stench of a T-rex still lingered. But now a breeze from the sea dispersed the smell, and a handful of little dinosaurs crept forward, sniffing. The whimpers drew them. The smell of meat intoxicated them.

They were a group of eoraptors, among the smallest and oldest dinosaurs. Members of the sauropodomorph clade, they were among the first dinosaurs to evolve. Back on Earth, they had lived in the Triassic era. They roamed the world a hundred million years before their larger, more famous descendants like T-rex, stegosaurus, and triceratops. Eoraptors were no larger than chickens. Blue feathers covered their slender bodies, and their beady eyes blinked. They were omnivores and far from picky eaters. They devoured insects, frogs, carrion, fruits, nuts—whatever they could get. Sometimes they sneaked into Dinovia City and ate trash. A human baby though—that was a rare feast. Predators so low on the food chain rarely got access to such a banquet. Licking their chops, they bounded forward.

The baby opened her eyes. Her vision was still blurry. She saw only blue smudges, red eyes, and opening mouths lined with tiny white teeth.

Then—a larger smudge.

A stick that swung from side to side.

The eoraptors squealed and fled.

The large blurry figure stepped closer. Bells chimed, woven into checkered fabric. A necklace of raptor claws jangled. The figure knelt. The baby blinked, unable to focus her young eyes, but she could just make out a face. A human face. Red and yellow paint covered the cheeks, and a skull with sharp teeth topped the head. But this was a human. The baby had never seen a human, but she knew this by instinct.

Is this my mother?

"What is this?" the woman said, "A child! A blessing from Ivan, the God of Hunger."

The baby could not understand those words. But she understood the softness and awe in the woman's tone.

Hands with long fingernails reached forward. Bone bracelets clattered. The woman lifted her, held her to her breast, and the baby suckled. No milk came out. But she could not stop suckling. Another instinct. Perhaps in time the milk would flow.

"A blessing," the woman whispered, nursing the girl. "King Ivan has answered my prayers. You are a miracle, child. A miracle."

The baby fell asleep in her arms, feeling safe for the first time in her life.

The woman wandered into the forest, her dreadlocks jingling with amber beads, her lips moving with silent prayers. She was barefoot and savage, a shaman of the wilderness, a worshipper of reptiles. Many called her a witch, and some called her a holy woman. Today she was a mother.

FIFTEEN YEARS LATER

CHAPTER TWO
Welcome to Mintari

Simone was scared of animals.

Terrified of them, in fact.

Any animal. No matter how small. Even puppies. Once she had gotten trapped in an elevator with a Shih Tzu and suffered a panic attack.

She was the girl who found cat videos scarier than horror films. Birdsong sent shivers down her spine. Spiders? Forget spiders. If she found a spider in the house, goodbye house. She was burning it down.

The doctors called it zoophobia. Simone couldn't even imagine visiting an entire *zoo*.

And now she, Simone LaRue who once fainted when a kitten jumped on her, was flying to Mintari. A planet overrun with dinosaurs.

No big deal. She was simply going to die. Probably in the jaws of a dinosaur. Maybe just of fright. She accepted it. She was doomed.

She closed her eyes and focused on breathing. Oh, her kingdom for a paper bag! She was close to panic now. There were no animals on the starship. Simone had checked. Three times. No lap dogs, no support animals, no ants on the deck. But she was *thinking* about animals, and that made her hands tremble. Her heart raced. Her hair clung to her forehead with cold sweat.

Oh, Simone LaRue, get ahold of yourself! she thought. *You covered wars on Earth. You interviewed serial killers and cannibals. You are a fearless journalist. Surely you can survive a few dinosaurs.*

She brushed red curls back from her forehead. Her hair was her only vanity. She boasted long tresses the color of fire. They had become her trademark. Simone liked to think that her audience—God bless 'em—tuned in for her uncompromising investigative journalism. Deep down, she knew her hair was part of it. Maybe the biggest part. Hey, it's that pretty redhead again on *Gazette TV*! What was her name again?

Well, sooner or later her hair would turn gray, and her beauty would fade. But her stories were forever. And right now, there was a real cracker of a story waiting on Mintari. So here she flew. There was nothing to fear. Dinosaurs were harmless! After all, tourists visited Mintari all the time, right? It was just like whale watching. That was all.

And the whales could run on land. And had teeth the length of her arms. And like bulls, they probably went mad at the sight of red.

She was going to faint. Oh God, she was going to faint right here on the starship.

"Breathe, Simone, breathe," she whispered to herself.

A drone floated toward her. "Madame, would you care for some refreshments? A Valium? Perhaps a Prozac? Galaxia Spacelines offers a variety of pharmaceuticals for the nervous traveler."

Simone forced a sickly smile. "A cup of water please."

The drone was just a floating box, but somehow it managed to look disappointed. "Very well." A hatch opened on its body, and a cup of water emerged.

The water did help. So did the drone, in an odd way. It was comforting to see a being from back home, a thing made of metal and plastic. Most of planet Cloventia was like that.

Synthetic. Oh, they had *some* animals, of course. Once in a while, a bird sang a dreadful song of death. A few women in Simone's building had pet dogs—terrible little things that rode in purses, yapped ferociously, and no doubt nurtured a hunger for the flesh of redheads. But the big animals? The wild ones? No, those did not exist on good old Cloventia. No lions, no tigers, no bears, and thank God *no dinosaurs*. For a woman like Simone, it was the planet to be.

She looked around her, trying to distract herself. Each seat on the flight came with a personal hologram generator. The child beside Simone was playing with holographic dinosaurs on his lap. A tourist. He even wore a stegosaurus hat, complete with plastic spikes.

"Gimme a turn!" his little sister cried. She was holding a plastic pliosaurus. It was pink and had a ribbon on its head.

"You have your own holograms."

"But I want yours!"

Simone looked away from the siblings. At her other side, an old man was watching a holographic film. Seemed to be about dinosaurs devouring tourists. Just as Simone glanced over, a hungry T-rex gulped down a screaming actress. She was even a ginger. A glimpse into Simone's future? She gulped, looked away, and brushed back damp curls.

"Do not panic, do not panic," she whispered. Maybe she should have ordered that Valium after all. Where was that drone?

She looked around the starship, seeking the floating box of complimentary chemicals. But she saw only hundreds of tourists, traveling from the civilized world of Cloventia to the wilderness of Mintari.

They came of all stripes. Retirees looking for one more adventure. Families with excited little ones, bored teenagers, and worn-out parents. One young couple was here on their honeymoon. Another couple was heading to their destination wedding—along with an army of bridesmaids in uniform. A few rowdy lads seemed to be out on a stag weekend. Some tourists wore hats with triceratops horns. Many held plastic dinosaur toys. One teenager carried what looked like a real T-rex claw. They weren't even at Mintari yet, and they already had souvenirs. The spaceports were good at getting tourists to spend early.

But not everyone aboard was a tourist. There were the other types. The quiet ones. The ones who sat at the back. The ones with weapons.

Poachers.

Poaching was illegal on Mintari, Simone knew. But the planet had trouble enforcing the law. Not enough Rangers. Billions of dinosaurs roamed a planet the size of Earth, and only a few crazy cowboys were trying to defend them.

One cowboy was crazier than them all. If the stories were half-true, he was the craziest man on Mintari. Maybe in the entire galaxy.

They called him Jurassic Joe. And Simone was traveling on behalf of the *Cloventia Gazette* to interview him. She was the only one on this spaceship who wasn't a tourist or poacher. The only one who did not want to see dinosaurs.

She wanted to find a man. A wild man. A man who shunned society, who lived out in dino country. Maybe just a legend.

"Who are you, Jurassic Joe?" she whispered.

The boy beside her heard her. He lifted an action figure. A little plastic man with a ceratop hat and a badge on his chest. "Jurassic Joe is a hero!" the boy said. "I have fifteen of his action figures *and* a poster of him at home. They say he wrestled a T-rex once and beat him! And that he flies on pterodactyls and he beats bad guys with his fists."

The boy began demonstrating, unleashing the action figure's fists on an unsuspecting plastic sauropod.

His sister raised her chin. "Billy, your toy is ridiculous. I prefer Princess Pearl, thank you very much."

She held up her pink pliosaurus. The ribbon on its head wobbled.

Billy snorted. "Princess Pearl is lame. Just like you, Becky. I have King Ivan, the best dinosaur ever!"

He held up a plastic T-rex with black scales. The toy began chomping on Princess Pearl. The girl whined, and the kids almost came to blows. Simone ducked as a plastic stegosaurus flew overhead.

Just then, the pilot emerged from the cockpit. He was a tall man with a white handlebar mustache. His uniform was splendid, adorned with polished buckles, buttons, cuff links, aiguillettes, and other assorted bits of flair. The job of pilot was mostly ceremonial. These days, starships were fully automated. Once in a blue moon, a modern pilot might have to tweak a dial or two. Mostly they were showmen.

"Ladies and gentlemen!" boomed the pilot, his shiny bits of metal jangling. "Thank you again for flying with Galaxia Spacelines. If you look out the starboard windows, you'll see a view of Borealis, infamous planet of the Ice Age!"

The tourists blinked at him. A few looked around in confusion.

"The starboard means your right side," the pilot said.

The tourists nodded, mumbled, and looked out their right portholes. Simone had to lean over young Billy and Becky. Thankfully, the siblings had forgotten their tiff and were peering out the little round window.

Simone squinted. At first she saw only stars. Then she made out a little white sphere. From here it seemed no larger than a marble.

"Behold the realm of icy horror!" the pilot said.

"Boring!" said Becky, holding her pink pliosaurus.

The pilot seemed to overhear. He stiffened, his mustache bristled, and he cleared his throat. "Planet Borealis is full of terrors, danger, and adventure. It is on Borealis that the brave scientists of Earth placed the creatures of the Ice Age. On Borealis, these wonderful and terrible beasts live again! The thunderous mammoth trumpets his song! The lumbering Neanderthal wields his club! The saber-toothed tiger stalks his victims … who are mostly little girls."

The pilot glanced toward Becky. The girl blew him a raspberry.

"And remember, folks," the pilot continued. "Galaxia Spacelines offers flight and guided tours to Borealis as well. Remember to book your next vacation with Galaxia Spacelines! Five percent off if you book today."

Simone looked at the little snowy planet in the distance. There, on that white marble—all those animals? Mammoths and tigers and Neanderthals? It was hard to believe. Those creatures seemed like myths to her, no more real than dragons or unicorns.

But once, Simone knew, humans and animals had shared a planet. On Earth, they had evolved together. Lived together. At first the animals preyed on the humans. Then the tables turned, and the humans drove most animals into extinction. Lions and tigers and bears—bye bye. And good riddance, if you asked Simone. Don't let the door hit you on the way out.

"Okay, okay, I don't really want animals dead," Simone muttered under her breath. "I don't hate animals. Honestly. I fear them. I'm terrified of them. Sure, to others, animals look cute. To me they all look like predators. It's a mental illness. If anyone doesn't like it, too bad!"

Beside her, Becky began to cry.

Simone bit her lip. She realized she had spoken much louder than intended.

"Sorry, kid. Here, have a candy."

She handed Becky a cough drop. Closest thing to candy she had. But it calmed the girl.

Simone took a deep breath. She was getting worked up. The chip on her shoulder felt heavy today. Animals. They did that to her.

What had she been thinking about? Ah yes, the salad days when animals were extinct. A paradise for zoophobes! But two hundred years ago, everything changed for the worse. The animals rose from the dead. Those were dark days.

Some do-gooder scientists discovered time-casting. A way to reach into the past, grab samples of animal DNA, and recreate the monsters in the modern day. Now, you couldn't just unleash redhead-eating predators onto an unsuspecting Earth. Even the do-gooders knew that. But they came to a solution.

Around the same time, as chance would have it, scientists also discovered the Nyx star system. Nyx was an ordinary star, similar to a billion others. They named her after the Greek goddess of the night, but despite her name, she shone brightly. The star had five habitable planets, which was highly unusual. It was also within a thousand light-years from Earth. Pretty close. Piece of cake for the newfangled warp drives, which were also coming out around the same time. It was all a perfect storm.

The powers that be gave one planet to humans. Cloventia. The best planet in the galaxy, if you asked Simone. Along with billions of other humans, she lived on Cloventia, enjoying an animal-free life. Unless you counted the yapping little dogs. But no place was perfect. Earth today was a dying world, a spherical slum of urban decay, but Cloventia became a new bastion of science, art, and human flourishing. Not that Simone LaRue was biased, of course. Hey, she was a patriot. Nothing wrong with that.

A second planet, Dagon, they dedicated to farming. Dagon was three times the size of Cloventia. The gravity was too high for most humans. But a few hardy farmers lived there. As did billions of pigs, chickens, and cows, genetically engineered to survive the higher gravity and thicker atmosphere. Over five hundred years, the Dagonites had plowed over the forests and meadows of Dagon, creating a planet-sized farm. Dagon fed billions of people across Nyx. Nothing grew on Cloventia. Dagon was their breadbasket.

The scientists gave the three remaining planets to animals.

One to the animals humans had driven into extinction. Tigers, lions, and elephants happily devoured one another on that hellish world. Humans could assuage their guilt. Their victims were no longer extinct.

A second planet they gave to the Ice Age creatures. Simone was looking at it now through the window. A frozen ball of nope.

The fourth planet was the worst one. By far.

A world beyond time. Mintari. Planet of the dinosaurs.

It took thirty-seven hours to fly from Cloventia to Mintari, and Simone spent them in coach. The cheapskates at the *Cloventia Gazette* could have splurged on an upper deck. The travelers there enjoyed private cabins and a luxurious dining room. She bet that whenever they sent Blake Benway on a mission, he got to travel on an upper deck. Oh, of course the star of *Benway Tonight* would get the royal treatment. Smug anchor with his coveted prime-time spot. Simone LaRue was still a young journalist, only thirty-one years old. Her own show, *LaRue's News*, was way down the ratings list, often flirting with cancellation. She vowed that someday she would be the famous broadcaster, traveling in style.

Maybe, if she could grab the scoop on Mintari, that dream could come true.

She just had to land on a planet swarming with dinosaurs, find a crazy hermit who lived in a cave somewhere, and hope he agreed to give her an interview. As opposed to dismembering her with a machete, feeding her to his pet raptors, or whatever else crazy Mintarian hermits did to Cloventians.

"I'm going to find you, Jurassic Joe," she vowed. "I'm going to make you famous."

"Jurassic Joe is already fam—" began the boy with the action figure. Simone shushed him.

It wasn't an important story, all things considered. Simone knew that. This was not like her earlier assignments, interviewing warlords in the slums of Earth. Those were serious topics. Profound issues. And ... they got no ratings.

But Jurassic Joe was intriguing. Fascinating, even. The man was a myth. Granted, Simone had never heard of him until two days ago. But judging by the action figure, yes, she supposed he was already famous. At least among dino-obsessed boys. Which meant all boys across the galaxy.

If Simone could truly interview him ... millions of views. *Billions* of views! Simone LaRue with her famous red hair, interviewing the wild dino hunter of Mintari! A ratings bonanza. Next time, *she* would be the one traveling on the upper decks. Eat your heart out, Blake Benway.

The pilot emerged from the cockpit, rubbed sleep out of his eyes, and cleared his throat.

"Ladies and gentlemen, we are approaching Mintari! I've positioned our portside toward the planet. If you'll look through the port windows, you'll see Mintari approach." He paused. "Port means left."

Simone turned in her seat. Beside her, the old man had fallen asleep while watching his dinosaur movie. His mouth hung open, drooling. Simone leaned over the slumbering oldster, peering toward the portside windows.

"Hey, lean back!" said Billy. The boy was still holding his Jurassic Joe action figure.

Simone ignored him. She barely heard the child.

There it was. Right outside the window. Hell.

Surely this was hell, wasn't it? From a distance, Mintari seemed green. Not fiery red like the old depictions of Satan's underworld. But surely Mintari was just as awful. A planet overflowing with dinosaurs … and she was still traumatized by poodles.

"Behold—Mintari!" boomed the pilot, chest puffed out. "A world of dinosaurs! When scientists first invented time-casting, they could not imagine that someday their invention would lead to Mintari. A planet of terror. A planet where stegosaurus impales his victims with his mighty spiked tail! Where the colossal brachiosaurus crushes his enemies beneath his feet! Where the allosaurus, the Butcher of the Jurassic, slashes through—"

"You're not helping!" Simone muttered. A bit too loudly.

The pilot glowered at her, fixed his tie, and cleared his throat. "Ladies and gentlemen, thank you for flying with Galaxia Spacelines. Please remember to post your five-star review on the NyxNet. You may proceed through the gift shop to your landing craft."

The planet grew larger and larger out the window.

Simone took a shaky breath.

"Here we go. Simone LaRue against the Butcher of the Jurassic," she mumbled.

The tourists left their seats, gabbing excitedly about the dinosaurs they were going to see. And, in the case of the poachers, shoot. Simone forced herself through the starship's gift shop, trying to ignore all the dinosaur toys around her. Some of them were surely possessed. That plush triceratops was giving her a dirty look, she was sure of it.

She was almost relieved when she finally reached the astrolite bay. No more dinosaur toys. Then she remembered that an astrolite was about to ferry her down to Mintari, where she would see the real thing. And she finally did it. What she had been wanting to do the entire flight.

She passed out.

"Dude! Wake up, dude! We're here! At dino world."

Simone blinked and moaned. She lay on her back, her hair splayed out around her. Thankfully, she had fainted onto a pile of suitcases. Would be a shame to crack her head open and bleed all over her pretty hair. A tourist couple were reaching around her for their luggage. The husband spent a second too long looking at her aforementioned pretty hair. His wife glowered and nudged him with her elbow. The couple shuffled off toward a claw machine full of plush dinos.

"Dude, are you all right? You look spaced out. Hey. Spaced out. 'Cause we're in space. Pretty funny!"

Simone blinked and turned her head. Her cameraman, Cody, was looking at her. She didn't know his last name. Even payroll didn't know. He went by a mononym. Like a rock star, which he aspired to be someday. Sometimes, with a wink, he joked that his full name was California Cody. He wasn't even from Earth, let alone California, but Simone let that detail slide.

California Cody sported long, shaggy hair, earrings shaped like guitars, and a surfing tiger tattoo. He was only a cameraman until his band took off, he told anyone who'd listen. And those who wouldn't.

"Um, I think I fainted." Simone pushed herself off the pile of luggage. "Yeah, pretty funny."

"Whoa." The tall cameraman took a step back, eyes widening. "You fainted? Dude. My aunt Alice once fainted, and it turned out she had some parasite in her stomach, and one day, we all had potato salad, and—"

"Cody, I'm sure your family life is fascinating, but please help me up. I'm still dizzy."

"Oh. Right." He blushed. "Sorry, dude. Here. Grab my hand."

He hoisted her up. Simone stood for a moment, taking deep breaths, steadying herself. Cody hefted his camera equipment across his back. He wore Bermuda shorts, a Hawaiian shirt with little dinosaurs on it, and a headband.

"How was your flight, Cody?" she asked.

He cracked his neck. "It was a bummer, dude. Let me tell ya. Third class is straight up *not* a good time."

Simone sniffed and frowned. "Cody, is that you? You stink."

"Yeah, well, what do you expect, dude? They got us traveling with the sheep. Big crates of them. Man, I can't wait until my band takes off. Then I can fly coach like you. They got chairs and everything!"

"Sh-sheep?" Simone whispered.

"Yeah, I guess they gotta feed the dinos something, huh?" He hefted his camera across his back. "Now come on, dude! There's only one astrolite left. You wanna miss the dinos or what?"

"Yes, I kind of do," Simone said.

But Cody was already racing toward the last astrolite. With a sigh, Simone followed.

The Galaxia starship could cross the vast distances of space, but it could not fly in atmosphere. Most starships could not. To reach the planet surface, travelers took astrolites. They were slender shuttles with heavy engines and folding wings, designed for atmospheric entry and flight through air.

Simone and Cody entered the last astrolite. Several other travelers were already strapped into their seats. Simone recognized Billy and Becky, the bickering children with the dinosaur toys. A few tourists from Earth were here too. Most Earthlings were too poor to fly around the galaxy, but a few were wealthy—mostly arms dealers, slavers, and charity workers. You could always spot the Earthlings. There was no mistaking their quaint clothes and old-world ruggedness. Why was it that everyone from Earth looked so … worn out? They must have used Cloventia as a layover. If you asked Simone, they'd be better off staying there.

Another man shared the astrolite with them. This was no tourist.

He was a rawboned man, his skin like leather. It was hard to tell his age. His face was so weathered he seemed as ancient as a mountain, but there was strength to his jaw. He could have been forty or eighty. He sat with his head lowered, and his wide-brimmed black hat hid his eyes. The smell of soil and dry blood clung to his dark coat. A bandoleer crossed his chest, and a rifle hung at his side.

A poacher.

Simone studied him.

He looks dangerous, she thought. *He looks like a killer. This is the type of man Jurassic Joe fights.*

Her eye was drawn to the poacher's rifle. It was enormous. As long as the man was tall. The barrel was as wide as Simone's arm. A glint of silver caught her eye. A symbol gleamed on the gun—a triceratops head. Beneath the horned head, etched in silver, appeared the word: TRIPLEHORN.

That name! Triplehorn!

Memories shot through Simone. Old pain. Grief that still lingered. Memories she dared not dredge up now. The name *Triplehorn* was forever scarred across her heart, as surely as it was engraved onto that gun.

The poacher spoke with a low, grainy drawl. "You have a cameraman, my darling. Why not take a picture? It'll last longer."

Simone felt herself blush. And when you had skin as pale as hers, you blushed hard. She could feel every freckle on her face leap out. "I'm sorry, sir. I didn't mean to stare."

"Yes you did." His voice was like dry leather crinkling under a man's boot. "You know what I am. And I know what you are."

He raised his head slowly. The brim of his hat rose to reveal his eyes. He had completely black eyes. No white to them at all. The eyes of a shabu addict. A drug often used by soldiers and gangsters on Earth. A drug to keep you going. To keep you killing.

"And what am I, pray tell?" Simone said, raising her chin. She had met worse than him in the slums of Earth. She would not be intimidated.

The man gave her a predatory grin, revealing yellow teeth. "An opportunistic, greedy media vulture who gorges on the corpse of what journalism once was. I hope you choke on it."

"Dude, that's uncalled for!" Cody said. "At least, I think it is. I'm not sure what you said there. Something about a gorge?"

"Ignore him, Cody," Simone said. "The bitter old man clearly has a bone to pick."

"Tarry right I do," growled the weathered man. "You journalists call us poachers. Call us murderers. Well, I got news for ya, toots. I'm no different from you. We're both killers. I just have the decency to use a gun instead of a pen."

Simone frowned and tilted her head. The astrolite was flying now. She hadn't even noticed it launch. She almost forgot about the dinosaurs below. Almost.

"What's your name?" she said.

He spat onto the deck. "They call me Rattlesnake."

Another mononym. Must be a trend.

"Well, Mr. Rattlesnake, would you like to tell your story to the camera?" Simone said. "The world would love to hear your perspective."

"It would?" Cody asked, scratching his head.

"Shh!" she whispered. "We'll edit him together with Jurassic Joe. It'll make good drama."

But Rattlesnake only chuckled—a crackling sound like breaking twigs. "I got only three words for your interview, toots. Go to hell."

"Can we use four words and include the toots?" she asked.

But Rattlesnake had already lowered the brim of his hat over his eyes. He seemed to be asleep. Or ignoring her. Either one was fine with Simone. She feared dinosaurs. But, she decided, she would tolerate the sight of one stomping on Rattlesnake.

The astrolite dived into Mintari's atmosphere with a blaze of fire. The g-force pounded the passengers like an ankylosaurus tail. Flames washed over the windows. The astrolite jerked. Tourists yelped, clung to one another, and a few threw up into paper bags. Simone yawned. Atmospheric entry was no big deal for her. Been there, done that. Now, if there were a puppy in the astrolite, she'd be trembling.

Rattlesnake seemed as unaffected as she was. The lanky poacher still slouched in his seat, his wide-brimmed hat pulled low over his eyes. His boots were scaly, she noticed. The skin of a dinosaur? And he wore spurs on them. Now why would a man without a horse need spurs?

Probably to kick kids, Simone thought as little Billy threw up beside her. She had to wriggle aside to avoid being slimed. Maybe she needed some spurs of her own.

Finally their flight steadied, and the astrolite glided through blue sky. Drones showed up to clean the mess, carrying an array of sponges, mops, and air fresheners. Clearly the little robots were used to such cleanups. She hoped they weren't conscious.

Simone looked out the porthole. They were still high up, and Simone beheld a view of Mintari's sprawling wilderness.

"Darwin's beard!" she said and rubbed her eyes.

For a moment, she was dumbstruck.

"Whoa!" Cody whispered, leaning over her. "Dude."

Simone had spent most of her life on Cloventia, a planet of glittering skyscrapers, purple skies alight with a billion flying cars, and masses of apartment buildings that rolled into the horizons. She had never seen so much … what was it called? It didn't exist on Earth anymore either. Come on, what was the word … Nature! That was it. She had never seen so much nature.

On Mintari, she knew, there was only one city. A city? Barely more than a village. You couldn't even see it from up here. What you did see was endless greenery. The trees didn't grow from little pots along the roadsides. And they didn't seem like plastic either. They grew right from the ground, it seemed, clustered into great clumps of ... what did you call it? Simone frowned, thinking back to school. Forests! That was it.

"Mintari has forests," she whispered.

"Gnarly!" Cody whispered, eyes alight.

Mountains rose from the forests like islands from green seas, capped with snow. A few volcanoes were belching smoke. Lava trickled down one, gathering in a valley and hardening into basalt before their very eyes. Gorges carved up the land, and mist floated over flowering valleys. Beyond the smoky mountains, grasslands swept toward a golden sunset.

Simone sighed and placed her chin on her palm. Something stirred deep inside her, some ancestral memory. She had never seen nature before, but this seemed so, well, natural. It seemed *right*.

Humans evolved in such a place, she reminded herself. *Nature is where we belong.*

Tears filled her eyes, surprising her. She almost never cried.

"Beautiful," she whispered. "It's beautiful."

Then she cleared her throat, wiped her eyes, and raised her chin. Silly, romantic notions! She was a modern woman. Humans had evolved beyond life in nature. They were civilized now. More like drones than animals. Missing nature? Ha! She might as well miss life in the sea before those troublesome tiktaaliks decided to crawl onto land. People like Jurassic Joe, eccentrics who lived in the wilderness, were a relic of the past. Just as much as the dinosaurs who roamed this planet.

Speaking of dinosaurs, Simone peered at the planet, seeking the monsters. The other tourists were doing the same.

"Mommy, where are the dinosaurs?" Becky demanded, her little fists clenched. "I want to see dinosaurs!"

Everyone had their faces pressed to the windows, searching for the terrible reptiles. All but Rattlesnake. The poacher sat still, legs splayed out, face hidden beneath the brim of his head, presumably sleeping.

Gasps sounded across the astrolite.

Becky whimpered and hid behind her mother. Her brother gasped and dropped his Jurassic Joe action figure.

At first Simone didn't see it.

"Where is it?"

"Whoa!" Cody whispered, eyes nearly popping out. He pulled out one of his smaller cameras and began filming.

Simone squinted down at the forests, trying to see. Then she noticed that Cody wasn't filming the landscape below. He was pointing his camera straight out the window. Simone raised her eyes, and ...

Her head spun.

She couldn't breathe.

The astrolite fuselage seemed to be closing in on her. The tourists' exclamations of wonder faded to mere echoes. Blackness spread around her vision, letting her see only a small area before her.

And in that little circle of light ... there they flew.

"Dinosaurs," she whispered.

They flew right outside, an entire flock. They had no feathers like those few dreadful birds Simone had seen on Cloventia, only some peach fuzz. Their wings were more like bat wings—skin stretched over ridiculously long fingers. Claws sprouted from the tips. The creatures opened their beaks, revealing rows of teeth, and cawed.

Simone clutched Cody's arm so tightly she probably left imprints on the bone.

A deep, grainy voice rose behind her.

"Pterosaurs aren't dinosaurs, Ms. LaRue. They are reptiles. Flying reptiles who evolved to hunt from the air."

She turned to see Rattlesnake staring right at her. His black eyes blazed like coals.

"Well, look who's up from his beauty sleep," Simone said.

A sneer found the poacher's thin lips. "These particular pterosaurs belong to the pteranodon genus. Their wingspan is longer than this astrolite. Their claws could disembowel you with a single swipe. Their beaks could swallow children whole." He glanced toward the tourist children at his side.

"*Cool!*" said young Billy.

Simone gulped. Suddenly she wished she had grabbed a barf bag from the starship.

"These creatures are small compared to other pterosaurs, Ms. LaRue," said Rattlesnake. "There are flying reptiles on Mintari that would make pteranodons seem like sparrows. My suggestion to you, Ms. LaRue, is to return to your so-called civilized planet. Go hide in your plush apartment among your pretty little trinkets. The wilderness of Mintari is no place for you, Ms. LaRue. You will not find the object of your quest here. You will find only death."

Simone squared her shoulders and tossed back strands of her fiery hair. "You do not know me, Mr. Rattlesnake. Or whatever your name is. I'm not some pampered damsel who never left the comfort of her condo. I covered the Slum Wars on Earth. I crouched behind barricades as the bullets flew. I interviewed cannibal warlords. I saw horrors that would shrivel your little heart."

For the first time, Rattlesnake rose from his slouch. He slammed his boots onto the deck. The spurs jangled. He leaned forward, his pure-black eyes glinting.

"Do you think the slums of Earth are dangerous? They are a playground compared to Mintari. There are horrors here you've never seen, Ms. LaRue. You're not dealing with starving wretches reduced to cannibalism here. There are creatures on this planet who could crush one of your slums in an afternoon. Monsters are real, Ms. LaRue. And they live on Mintari."

"If Mintari is so terrible, why are you here?" Simone said. "Just to prove how tough you are? You must be very tough indeed. You're sharing an astrolite with tourist children, a snack bar, and a claw machine."

The poacher grinned, showing his sharp yellow teeth. "I will not be taking a tour inside a reinforced jippi, peering at dinosaurs from behind an electric fence. Of that much I can assure you, Ms. LaRue. I will enter the wild. The greatest predators that ever lived are dinosaurs and men. On Mintari, we will determine who is mightier."

She narrowed her eyes, studying the leathery man.

Jurassic Joe kills poachers like you, Simone thought. *I hope he kills you too.*

Before she could say more, Cody tapped her shoulder. "Dude, look!" The cameraman was hopping with excitement. "A brontosaurus!"

"Cool!" the children cried, pressing their faces against the glass.

"Oh wait … it's only a tree," said Cody. "Sorry, little dudes."

The children groaned.

Simone settled back in her seat, hugging herself. The two greatest predators indeed. Dinosaurs and men. Maybe dinosaurs weren't the worst creatures in the galaxy after all.

The astrolite flew lower, gliding over a wilderness of lakes, grasslands, and forests. Simone closed her eyes, trying to imagine herself back home on Cloventia. She was not flying over a land of man-eating reptiles, she told herself. She was leaning back on her recliner, a glass of wine in hand. The most exciting thing awaiting her this evening was her pad thai delivery. It should arrive any moment now.

A familiar, booming voice filled the astrolite, interrupting her reverie.

"Ladies and gentlemen! May I have your attention please!"

It was the starship pilot. Great. Simone had thought herself rid of him.

Physically, the pilot was still in the starship, orbiting Mintari. The astrolites were remote controlled. But a hologram of the tall, mustached man materialized inside the shuttle. He was probably projecting the same hologram to every astrolite now descending toward the planet. As always, the pilot wore his fine uniform with its many polished buttons and badges. The flair shone even brighter in hologram mode. Simone squinted.

"Ladies and gentlemen, you're in for a treat this morning," the pilot said. "We happen to have spotted a herd of dinosaurs. We're going to dive lower to give you a look."

Simone cringed. "Please don't."

Her belly flopped as the astrolite swooped. She gasped and clutched Cody's arm. Billy threw up again.

Their altitude dropped at a dizzying speed. The other astrolites, ferrying more tourists, dived at their sides. Soon they were flying alarmingly close to the surface. Everyone peered out the portholes.

"Where are they?" said Billy.

"I want to see dinosaurs!" insisted Becky.

The astrolites swarmed over a snowcapped mountain, then glided over a valley, and there they were.

Simone clutched Cody tighter. Her fingers would definitely leave bruises.

Dinosaurs.

Fifty or more, plodding across the plains.

Simone could not even look away. Her terror gripped her. She was like a deer in the headlights. The dinosaurs had fat bodies, thick tails, and long necks tipped with small heads.

"Ooh, brontosauruses!" said Becky. "Like my toy." She waved a plastic sauropod. Rainbows were painted onto its lavender haunches.

"Those are brachiosauruses," said her brother, nodding sagely.

"Ladies and gentlemen, behold the mighty patagotitan!" the holographic pilot boomed. "Patagotitan is a genus of titanosaurian sauropod dinosaurs."

"That's the same as a brachiosaurus," Billy whispered to his sister.

"Liar!" she whispered back.

The pilot kept speaking on-screen. "Patagotitans are longer than blue whales, and they weigh over seventy tons. If you stood next to one, you would not even reach his knees. You would need a ladder to tickle their underbellies. You could drive a car between their legs, and they wouldn't even notice. If a patagotitan reared on his back legs, he could stare the Statue of Liberty in the eyes. Yes, ladies and gentlemen, the patagotitan lives up to his name. These are the third-largest dinosaurs on Mintari. What a privilege it is to observe these gentle giants!"

Gentle? Simone wasn't so sure about that. She couldn't imagine any creature that could stomp on a mammoth being *gentle*. If these were the third-largest dinosaurs on Mintari, she hated to see whatever was bigger.

"They're herbivores, right?" she asked Billy. The boy seemed to know a lot about dinosaurs.

Okay, so Billy got the entire species wrong just a minute ago. But Simone needed some reassurance, and she'd take it where she could get it.

Billy nodded. "They're plant guzzlers. People think their necks are for eating from the tops of trees. But really, they sweep their necks from side to side like vacuum cleaners, inhaling grass and shrubs." He pointed. "They're probably heading toward those trees."

"I thought they didn't eat trees."

Billy blushed. "Well, maybe they ... like the shade."

Everyone watched. Even Simone. The titans lumbered toward the trees. They had thick, wrinkly legs like elephants—but much larger. They could probably flatten an elephant under one foot. Their tails flapped. Up close, their grunts and moans must be deafening. Simone could hear them even from inside the astrolite.

"I guess they're not that bad," Simone said. "So long as we stay far away."

The herd was almost at the trees when it happened.

The trees parted, and out burst another dinosaur.

Simone screamed.

This one was clearly *not* a herbivore. Even she knew that. It looked like a terror from Simone's worst nightmares. The monster thundered forth on two powerful legs, claws ripping the earth. Its jaws opened with a hungry rumble, revealing rows of sharp teeth. The skin was brown and scaly, and two crimson horns grew from its head. Devil horns. And this indeed seemed a demon from hell.

Simone wasn't sure what species this was. By the looks of it—some kind of theropod. She had heard of those. A type of carnivorous dinosaur with two legs and short arms. Tyrannosaurus rex was the most famous theropod, but the clade boasted many species. All with sharp teeth, terrible claws, and an appetite for redheads, no doubt. As if that wasn't bad enough, *this* species—whatever it was—added horns to the mix. Because why the hell not? Might as well go full-blown demonic. Simone shuddered and crossed herself.

The tourists *oohed* and *aahed*, crowding around the astrolite windows.

"Mommy, look, a T-rex!" said Becky.

"It's not a T-rex," said Billy. "T-rexes are bigger and don't have horns. This is clearly a giganotosaurus."

The pilot's hologram beamed. "Ladies and gentlemen, we are indeed in luck! Behold—the mighty carnotaurus cometh! The carnotaurus first lived in South America during the late Cretaceous period. Thanks to Mintarian scientists, this butcher feasts again upon his victims. Carnotaurus is a relatively small predator, only about the length of a city bus. But don't let his humble size fool you. He is a ruthless killer who can take down prey many times his size."

"Just the size of a bus," Simone muttered. "Tiny, really."

The patagotitans noticed the approaching predator. Massive as they were, the sauropods bugled in fear. The sauropodlets raced between the legs of their parents. Of course, even the babies were probably larger than Simone. The adult patagotitans—and they were truly colossal—whipped their tails through the air.

Thunderclaps shook the sky. The astrolite jolted. Simone covered her ears.

"What was that?" she cried.

"Sonic booms," Billy explained.

"Whoa, their tails broke the sound barrier!" Cody said. "That's *gnarly*, dude!"

The charging carnotaurus paused. The carnivore took a step back, shaking his head wildly. The tails whipped again. Sonic booms rippled the grass. The carnotaurus seemed to rethink his choice of dinner. The predator was perhaps the size of a bus, but next to the mighty patagotitans, he seemed minuscule.

Then, with rumbles that shook the wilderness, five more carnotaurs burst out from the trees and charged.

"Carnos—as we call our carnotaurus friends around here—are among the fastest predators on Mintari," said the pilot. "They can chase down virtually any prey. See how they run!"

The carnos raced toward the herd of sauropods, devil horns pointing forward. The patagotitans stood their ground. The largest bulls moved to the front of the herd, reared in the air, and bellowed.

The carnos fanned out, snapping their teeth, herding the patagotitans closer together. Smaller prey animals would likely have panicked by now. But these sauropods, while herbivorous, were no pushovers. They were big and powerful animals. They could hold their own. Trumpeting with fury, they cracked their tails and kicked the air, a display of dominance.

For the moment, the titans were successfully holding off the carnos. The horned carnivores hesitated, then took a few steps back. Was this too much even for a pack of predators? Surely there was easier prey elsewhere.

But their hunger must be great. After a moment to regroup, the pack of carnos attacked.

The patagotitans bellowed and lashed back. A tail like a tree trunk slammed into one carnotaurus, hurling the theropod into the air. Another carno managed to reach a sauropod. But the herculean herbivore reared, then brought his massive front feet down, crushing the predator. Bones snapped. The earth shook. The surviving carnos bustled around, desperate to dodge the swinging tails and stomping feet.

"Why do the carnos attack?" Simone cried out. "The patagotitans are too big for them."

"They're hungry, Ms. LaRue," said Rattlesnake. The poacher wasn't even watching the drama unfold below. He simply reclined in his seat, his hat pulled low. "Have you ever known hunger, Ms. LaRue? I don't mean that peckish feeling you get between your breakfast mochachino and afternoon salad. I mean real hunger. Hunger that twists up your insides. That howls in your muscles. That clamors through the bones. That is how hungry they are. Mintari is home to many predators, Ms. LaRue, and carnotaurus is only halfway up the food chain. He can only hunt when his larger brethren are away. Unlike you, he does not have the luxury of being a picky eater."

"Blah, blah, blah," Simone mumbled. She was barely listening to the poacher. She could not tear her eyes away from the battle below. The other Galaxia Spacelines astrolites were also flying above, giving the tourists their money's worth.

Two carnos lay dead. A whipping tail had shattered one. A stomping foot had crushed the other. But several of the ravenous reptiles were still alive. They snapped their toothy jaws, herding the sauropods closer and closer together. These were the stronger predators in the pack. Nature had culled the weak and stupid— those who rushed too eagerly to battle, who allowed their hunger to dull their senses. Their genes were flowing into the soil with their blood, lost forever.

The living predators were smarter. Faster. Stronger. Three of them leaped together onto one patagotitan—a big bull, old and scarred. The carnos' claws pierced the behemoth's thick legs. They scampered onto his back, slashing and biting all the while.

The sauropod reared on his hind legs. One carnotaurus lost its grip and fell off. Before the predator even landed, the titan swung his mighty tail. The carnotaurus flew through the air, bones shattered. The carnivore was dead before it hit the ground.

But two carnos were still clinging onto the prodigious herbivore. They climbed higher, reached the sauropod's long neck, and sank their teeth in. The titan bellowed, but the carnivores would not let go. They ripped out chunks of flesh, dug deeper, and kept chomping.

"They're eating him alive." Simone covered her mouth. She felt sick.

"Gnarly!" Cody said, eyes wide.

A few fellow patagotitans, displaying remarkable altruism, began stomping toward their friend. But more carnos whipped forward, snapped their jaws, and blocked the plodding Goliaths. The sauropods reared and bellowed and tried to push through. But after a few bites on the legs, the giants abandoned their comrade to his fate.

Finally it was all over. The wounded patagotitan crashed down, shaking the earth. The hungry predators had nearly decapitated their succulent prize.

The rest of the patagotitan herd moved on. There was nothing more they could do for their fallen brother. Bugling with grief, the sauropods thundered toward the trees. One patagotitan had fallen—the weakest of the herd, selected for death in nature's eternal Darwinian struggle. The survivors would live on, would perhaps in time evolve to become even larger and stronger. The arms race of evolution continued.

The surviving carnos did not pursue the herd. Why bother? They had slain one patagotitan—a banquet fit for a king. If they were lucky, the carnos would lounge around the carcass for days. They would eat and eat as the meat rotted and rotted, then finally waddle off with bellies ready to burst, leaving the festering remains for the scavengers. Most likely, the feast would not last that long. The smell would soon attract larger carnivores, perhaps even tyrannosaurs, and the carnotaurus pack would flee, losing their leftovers to somebody higher up the food chain.

Normally, Simone would never know all this. But Billy was explaining it to his sister, and she couldn't help but overhear. Darwinism, meet osmosis.

But right now the carnos weren't worried about any of that. All their troubles were forgotten. They feasted. The pack had lost three members in this battle. But the survivors ate well. They ripped into the sauropod, engorging themselves. Their hatchlings emerged from the forest, some not much larger than dogs, and leaped into the carcass headfirst, ripping away at the entrails.

"Eww, that is disgusting!" said Becky.

"They're eating its guts!" said Billy, eyes wide with morbid fascination.

Simone snapped back to reality. For a moment, she had forgotten about the astrolite, about herself. She was living the drama below, utterly captivated. Terrified, yes. Probably just as terrified as the dinosaurs in the fight. But yes, captivated. She understood why tourists paid top dollar to visit this world.

"It's so horrible," she said to Cody. "But there's something majestic and beautifully savage about it too."

"It's totally gnarly!" Cody agreed.

The holographic pilot smiled. "Ladies and gentlemen, welcome to Mintari."

CHAPTER THREE
The Fossil and Firkin

The astrolite flew onward, leaving the dinosaur banquet behind, gliding over the savage wilderness of Mintari.

In the distance, past blue mountains and grasslands, Simone descried a small village. Ha! How interesting. Simone knew Mintari had only one city—the famous Dinovia, home of the Rangers, an oasis of humanity on a planet of monsters. She had not realized there were villages too. You learned something new every day. She peered out the astrolite window, curious.

A few dwellings cluttered together among palm trees. The buildings all seemed humble, just clay huts, really. The only impressive structure was the circular wall that surrounded them. And the moat. And the electric fence. The village reminded Simone of the zoos you could still see in ancient movies. Back then, when some animals still lived on Earth, they were locked up. But here on Mintari the humans lived within the enclosure, and the dinosaurs roamed free. Simone wondered who lived in this village. Perhaps a few caretakers, more adventurous than most, had established an outpost far from the capital.

The pilot was back on the mothership, orbiting Mintari. But his hologram reappeared inside the astrolite. He was smiling under his white mustache.

"Ladies and gentlemen! Ahead you will see Dinovia, the only city on Mintari. Three hundred thousand people call Mintari home. Most of them live in Dinovia, safe behind the city walls. Your astrolite will take you straight to your hotel. We hope you enjoyed your flight with Galaxia Spacelines. Remember to check the astrolite mini-shop for your last-minute souvenirs."

Drones rolled forth with carts, offering Mintari baseball caps, coffee mugs, shot glasses, and of course plastic dinosaur toys.

Simone ignored the robotic salesmen. She blinked at the cluster of huts in the valley. This was the famous Dinovia City? *This?* No. Impossible. Simone had seen cities before. Cities were home to millions of people. Cities sported skyscrapers that glittered with lights, concrete canyons lined with shops, and enough neon to outshine a star. Why, there were football stadiums back on Cloventia that could engulf all of Dinovia City. It was hard to imagine an entire *culture* with only three hundred thousand people.

And yet a culture they had, and a civilization they were. Simone had never met a Mintarian. But she had seen them on television. They spoke with a rough accent, wore strange clothes, and worshipped reptile gods. Most Cloventians thought them backward. Just barbarians. Simone didn't know what to make of them. In some ways, they fascinated her more than the dinosaurs. How could a population so small—they could probably all fit into Simone's neighborhood back home—develop a unique national identity?

But of course, Mintari's human population had to remain small. The laws were strict. Only half a million humans were ever allowed on Mintari at any given moment. Just over half were locals. The rest were tourists. This planet belonged to the dinosaurs. The humans were here to observe and protect. Half a million, that was it. Any more and the ecosystem would collapse, and the dinosaurs would go extinct again.

Best to let them go extinct, if you asked Simone. But nobody asked her.

"Dude, do you think they have a rock scene?" Cory said.

"I'm sure Mintari is home to a variety of geologists studying the—"

"Rock *music*, dude. I packed my guitar. Maybe I can make it big on Mintari."

"We won't be staying in Dinovia long, Cody," Simone said. "Jurassic Joe doesn't live in the city. We're heading into the wild." She smiled thinly. "But first we'll check into our hotel and shower. You still stink of sheep."

The astrolite touched down on a dirt square, raising clouds of dust.

The tourist children squealed with delight. They were the first out the hatch, waving their dinosaur toys around. The other tourists followed, babbling excitedly. One balding man announced that he was heading straight to the nearest bar, and any dinosaur in his way could take a hike into a tar pit.

Simone remained in her seat, frozen.

Rattlesnake hefted his rifle across his back. He walked toward the hatch, paused, and looked back at her.

"Good luck, Ms. LaRue," the rawboned poacher said. "If you see Jurassic Joe, hand him this."

He tossed her something. Instinctively, Simone caught it.

She opened her hand. A bullet. The name "Joe Triplehorn" was engraved on it.

Triplehorn. There was that name again. That terrible memory that still ached deep inside her. Was this the same person as Jurassic Joe?

Simone felt light-headed. The terror threatened to overwhelm her. She pushed that memory down, then looked back up, intending to give Rattlesnake a piece of her mind. But the poacher was gone.

California Cody hadn't noticed the exchange. The long-haired cameraman was busy lifting his luggage, his cameras, and his guitar. He was a big guy, but he nearly crumpled under the weight. He wobbled toward the door.

"Coming, dude?"

Simone hesitated, still in her seat. "You don't suppose there are any dinosaurs out there, do you?"

"Don't think so, dude. We're inside Dinovia City. Totally awesome place! Protected behind stone walls, a moat, armed guards, and an electric fence powerful enough to stun a T-rex. Says so right here." He waved a brochure, then wobbled under the weight of his bags, tilted backward, and slammed against the bulkhead.

Simone gulped. "What about pterosaurs? They can fly over the walls, can't they?"

"No worries, duderino." California Cody grinned. "Brochure covers that. The pterosaurs learned to avoid the city. If they fly close, the Rangers on the wall shoot flares to scare 'em off."

"Go take a look for dinosaurs," Simone said. "Just to be sure."

"No problemo, dude." He stepped outside, carrying his supplies, then stuck his head back in. "Coast is clear! No dinos. Unless you count tourist kids in costume."

After sitting beside two annoying children for thirty-six hours, Simone wasn't sure that was much better. But at least no dinosaurs would rip her to shreds during her first five minutes on Mintari. They probably would at some point, but at least not right now.

She rose to her feet, bit her lip, and before her courage could abandon her, she stepped into the sunlight.

At once, she recoiled. Her heart burst into a gallop. Sweat drenched her. Dinosaurs! Dinosaurs everywhere! Hundreds of them! Cody, that dirty liar!

She took a shuddering breath.

No. No dinosaurs. It was just her anxiety and overactive imagination. Nothing but tourists wandering toward their hotel.

She looked around her. Clay buildings surrounded the dirt square. A few towers rose nearby, bells in their belfries. Perhaps lookouts for dinosaurs? But most of the buildings catered to tourists. There were a few greasy spoons. Brontosaurus Burgers seemed particularly popular; there was a line out the door. Cretaceous Cocktails was already open and full of revelers, despite the early hour. Dino's Bar & Grill thrummed with loud rock music. The sign above the door featured an allosaurus munching on a steak. The dinosaur's jaw was presumably meant to open and close, but a few sparking cables hung loose.

Some tourists were skipping breakfast and shopping for tour guides. T-rex Tours had several armored jippis parked out front. A local in a safari outfit was handing out brochures, promising to show tourists the best dinosaurs on Mintari. Not like Jurassic Jippis across the square, which apparently only knew the boring spots.

Simone had heard of jippis, but she had never seen one in real life. She peered curiously at the famous vehicles of Mintari. They looked like a cross between jeeps, pickup trucks, and bulldozers (vehicles Simone had seen only in historic films). The jippis boasted six big wheels with heavy treads. These babies could handle some rough terrain. Open-air cargo holds stuck out their backs, ending with sturdy tailgates and big exhaust ports. Cowcatchers thrust out their fronts—they looked sturdy enough to knock over dinosaurs. Some jippis sported horns on their hoods that would not shame a triceratops. For extra oomph, each vehicle boasted gaudy decals, featuring dinosaur scales, claws, and fangs. No two were alike.

Like the wide-brimmed ceratop hat or the double-barreled sleep-or-die, the jippi had become a symbol of Mintari. Children on Cloventia bought toy jippis, sometimes with Ranger action figures inside. You could usually find them beside the plastic dinosaurs.

While here, Simone hoped to see one of Mintari's famous tricopters too. Her cousin's kid, little Joey LaRue, had a toy tricopter with a remote control. It had once gotten stuck in Simone's hair, and it took scissors, a screwdriver, and lots of cursing to get it out. Apparently the Rangers' tricopters could only fly in an atmosphere. How quaint. Like a flying machine from the days of old. They couldn't even reach space, and even astrolites could do that. But their three rotors gave them extreme maneuverability and an iconic look. Simone looked around, hoping to snap a photo of one. Her cousin's kid would love it. But so far, no tricopters around, only jippis. Maybe Mintari's flying contraptions were just a myth. A good thing too. Little Joe's toy tricopter had caused enough damage.

"Place your bets, place your bets on the next Dino Derby!" a man cried out. He stood in a little kiosk by a parking lot. A hologram hovered above the wooden stall, showing jockeys riding dinosaurs in a circular track. The hologram fizzed and died. The man kicked a projector, and the translucent track flickered back to life. "Place your bets right here! Win big on the Dino Derby!"

Simone had heard of the Dino Derby. They broadcast it sometimes on Cloventia. The Rangers kept trying to shut it down.

They said it violated animal rights. But the Derby made enough money that Mintari's government kept it running. A real tourist attraction. At least it was better than the underground triceratops fights. Simone had heard of those too. Highly illegal and highly profitable. Matadors strutted into an arena, clad in shining armor like medieval knights. Armed with spears and swords, they battled triceratops to the death. Usually it was the matadors doing the dying. Simone shuddered.

"Ooh, look!" California Cody made his way toward the bookie. "Dino Derby! Gallimimus Gil is a hundred to one odds! Simone, can I borrow some cash?"

She pulled him away. "No betting on dino races!"

"But a hundred to one odds, dude! If we bet only a few clovers, we can—"

"I said no."

The cameraman crossed his arms, huffed, and sulkily watched the holographic derby.

"Grab your field guides!" chanted an old man with a white beard and a big ceratop hat. "Grab your Mintari field guides, only twenty clovers!" He pushed a wheelbarrow full of books toward Simone. "Welcome to Mintari, young lady! Care for a field guide? Full of all the latest dino details!"

The old man waved a book in her face. The cover featured a T-rex wearing a Hawaiian shirt and sunglasses.

"Grab your copy, ma'am! *The Mintari Field Guide: Everything You Need to Know about Mintari's Dinosaurs.* Over three hundred species in one book! Don't tour Mintari without it."

"Gnarly!" Cody said. "Does it have pictures?"

Simone paid the old man twenty clovers, buying a book, just to get rid of the old geezer. If there were pictures of dinosaurs, Cody could have it. She was not reading it. The oldster tipped his ceratop and went to harass other visitors.

The tourists were everywhere. They fluttered between the establishments like butterflies between flowers. It was easy to spot them. They indeed wore clothes as colorful as butterfly wings.

The local Mintarians were far more subtle. Some were here to sell their wares—books, toys, hats, you name it, they got it. But other Mintarians were simply walking about on their business, ignoring the tourists. They all wore simple safari outfits. Not much variation of fashion here. Simone guessed that wearing bright, colorful clothing wasn't the best idea on a planet full of predators large enough to swallow you whole.

Simone looked down at her own outfit. A blue dress with golden stars and moons embroidered with glittering thread. Practically a neon sign for a hungry dinosaur. SNACK HERE! DELICIOUS REDHEAD! What was she thinking?

"Cody, I don't know if I can do this," she said, voice trembling. "I should have turned down this assignment. I can't face this world."

The cameraman put his supplies down. He looked into her eyes. "Dude, listen to me. You are the toughest dude I know. When we were filming that battle in Liberia, I was so scared I almost crapped my pants. But you kept talking to the camera. You kept reporting as bullets flew overhead. You are one badass chick, Simone LaRue. If you could face Earth … dude, I *know* you can face Mintari. And I'm with you. As always. Dudes for life."

Simone wiped her eyes. "Dudes for life."

She hugged the tall young man. God bless him.

They hugged for a long time. A *long* time.

"Um, Cody? You can let go now."

"Oh. Right." He blushed. "Sorry, dude. Got caught up in the moment."

Footsteps padded. Simone looked up, tensing, expecting a vicious carnotaurus attack. But it was only Billy, the snot-nosed boy from the starship. He had broken free from his family and ran up toward her.

"Lady? Here. For you." He held out his plastic Jurassic Joe action figure. "I know you're scared of dinosaurs. Joe will keep you safe."

"Billy, don't bug the nice lady from TV!" cried his father. "Get back here."

Before Simone could refuse the gift, the boy shoved the toy into her hands, smiled apologetically, and ran back to his family.

"Sweet kiddo," said Cody. "But hey, why didn't I get a toy?"

"You're on the wrong side of the camera."

"Wait until I'm a rock star." Cody hefted his luggage. "For now, let's find a hotel. How about that one?"

He pointed. Many tourists were heading toward a wide, three-story building. Palm trees grew in the gardens. A sign hung above the gateway: THE TAR PIT: ONE-AND-A-HALF-STARS HOTEL.

"Cody, I don't think—" Simone began.

"Whoa, one and a half stars!" the cameraman said, captivated. "Decent! I've never stayed in a hotel with more than one star before. I bet they got mattresses and everything." He began heading that way. "You coming, dude?"

"We're not staying in a hotel, Cody," she said.

He froze. "But you said we can stay the night. You wanted me to shower, remember?" He sniffed himself, then winced. "Eww, gnarly. Not a bad idea to wash up. We'll chill out, spend some time in the hot tub, then head out into dino country tomorrow."

"I have another place in mind," she said. "We're still in Dinovia City, but it's not too early to start learning about Jurassic Joe."

They headed down the streets. The farther they moved from the central square, the dustier and narrower the streets became. The clay huts crowded closer together, one or two stories high. They had curved walls, no corners, and round windows. Brass pipes stuck out their domed roofs. Cycad trees cluttered between the huts, their fronds shading the cobbled roads. These were humble homes compared to the floating skyscrapers of Cloventia. But compared to the slums of Earth, hellholes overrun with cannibals and warlords and starving children, Mintari was paradise.

They were leaving the touristy area. Simone saw fewer summer dresses and Hawaiian shirts, more safari outfits. Soon all the tourists were but a memory. The locals glanced at her. One man, a mustachioed geezer in a rocking chair, wouldn't stop staring at Simone through his pipe smoke. Her cheeks grew hot. She stood out here—a Cloventian in a colorful dress and high heels, her hair like cascading flame.

"Dude, are we almost there?" Cody asked. He hefted his luggage across his back. With his Bermuda shorts, shaggy hair, and iridescent sunglasses, Cody stuck out like a colorful thumb himself.

"I don't know." Simone bit her lip and checked her map. "We're looking for a saloon called the Fossil and Firkin. According to legend, Jurassic Joe used to drink there."

"Can we hire one of the tour jippis to drive us there?" Cody asked, rearranging his camera straps.

Simone lowered her map. "Need help carrying anything?"

"No way, dude. You're Simone LaRue, star of *LaRue's News*, the eighteenth most watched program on *Gazette TV*. I'm the beast of burden."

"Actually, we dropped down to twenty-seventh spot," she said. "Just behind the live parliament broadcasts."

Cody cringed. "At least people still read your newspaper column, right?"

She nodded. "Oh, I'm sure all fifteen people who still buy paper newspapers regularly flip past the wanted ads."

Cody grimaced and nearly dropped one suitcase. "Okay, maybe carry one bag."

She was reaching for a piece of luggage when a dinosaur attacked.

It was a T-rex.

The monster lunged at Simone, jaws open in a deafening roar. The monster was about to swallow her whole. She screamed and stumbled back.

"Get outta here!" Cody said. He kicked the T-rex aside. The beast rolled across the dirt, then struggled back onto its feet. In an attempt to restore its dignity, the monster hissed, snapped its teeth, and fled behind a cart.

Probably not a T-rex, Simone realized. Now that she took a closer look, the dinosaur was no larger than a chicken. It even had feathers.

The old man on his rocking chair barked a laugh, puffing out smoke. He lowered his pipe. "Just a eoraptor, cheesecake. Pests around these parts. No more harmful than mice and not much bigger." He tapped his pipe. "If you can't stand a little eoraptor, you're on the wrong planet."

Simone cleared her throat and smoothed her dress. "Thanks for the tip." She tilted her head at the geezer. "Would you happen to know where the Fossil and Firkin is?"

The oldster leaned back in his rocking chair. "Might be I do, if you got your own tip to give."

She tossed him a coin. "A golden clover. Good enough for you, old-timer?"

Gold wasn't worth much on Cloventia. Lots of the stuff all around, mined on the nearby golden asteroids. But the old man's eyes widened. He bit the coin, then grinned, revealing toothless gums. "Good enough, cheesecake. You head down this road, take two rights, turn left by the big ole conifer, and you're there. Might head over tonight myself to spend some Cloventian gold."

Simone walked onward, trying to remember the directions. Cody walked a step behind, groaning under the weight of their luggage. Simone wasn't sure what to expect. What sort of saloon would Jurassic Joe drink in? It must be a seedy place. A rough sort of bar where wild men beat each other with pool cues. A place that made a biker bar seem like a girl scouts meeting. She imagined big, hairy brutes throwing one another out windows.

But when she found the place, she was pleasantly surprised. No drunkards lay sprawled outside. No bouncer glowered outside the door. No graffiti covered the clay walls. Like all buildings in Dinovia, this one lacked sharp angles. The windows were circular, the corners rounded. Adobe tiles covered the roof, and a cycad tree rustled in the yard.

A sign hung above the door, shaped like an overturned barrel spilling out bones. Words appeared on the barrel: THE FOSSIL AND FIRKIN.

A smaller sign hung below it from chains: LOCALS ONLY.

"Aww, man!" Cody said, dropping his bags. "We walked all this way and we can't go in."

Simone was already heading toward the entrance. "They just mean no tourists. We're not tourists. We're journalists."

"I'm not a journalist, I'm a rock star." Cody patted his guitar case, then wobbled and dropped a few suitcases. A group of eoraptors fled.

Simone shoved the batwing doors and entered the saloon.

At once, Simone tensed up and winced, ready to duck in case anyone threw a bottle at her. Surely a bar fight would be going on. Maybe even a gunfight. The Mintarians were known to be rough folk. And Jurassic Joe was the wildest among them, if half the stories were true.

No bottles flew her way. Simone relaxed and looked around. The Fossil and Firkin was surprisingly cozy. Embers glowed in a fireplace. Wagon-wheel chandeliers hung from the rafters. An old upright piano stood against the wall. The bar was carved from a great piece of live-edge wood, waxed and polished. The wood grain coiled like the surface of a planet, gleaming. Clay mugs hung above from hooks shaped like sauropod necks. Behind the bar, caskets of ale and spirits were stacked from floor to ceiling.

A holographic screen hovered above the bar, showing the Dinosaur Derby. Jockeys rode dinosaurs of all kinds, racing around a circular track. Crowds filled the bleachers, cheering. Lunatics! The track seemed to be located outside the city walls. You had to be crazy to go out there, if you asked Simone. A struthiomimus named Strutter was currently in first place. Gallimimus Gil was far behind. At one point, his rider fell off.

Nobody in the bar seemed to be watching the race. It was barely afternoon, but a few locals were already here, nursing clay mugs of ale. All eyes rose toward Simone. Like all Mintarians, they wore clothes in various shades of beige, khaki, and brown. To the last man and woman, they wore Mintari's famous ceratop hats. The hats reminded Simone of Smokey Bear, a deity from ancient

Earth mythology, worshipped as a protector of the forests. Some of the men sported magnificent mustaches, and the women didn't wear makeup. That was unheard of on Cloventia, where men were clean-shaved and a woman never, ever showed her true skin.

Simone froze under the stares. With her summer dress and makeup, she was clearly a foreigner. Judging from the looks they gave her, a peacock might as well have sauntered into the saloon.

A woman with curly white hair spat into a spittoon. "You're in the wrong bar, cheesecake."

Second time a Mintarian had called her that. Must be the local slang. The white-haired woman didn't make it sound too friendly.

The mustached men across the room glowered. All aside from one young man who gaped at Simone, his drink forgotten.

"She got real purty hair," he whispered. He shut up when a young woman, a wife or girlfriend perhaps, elbowed him hard in the ribs.

Simone was about to respond to the old woman, but just then Cody shoved his way through the batwing doors, tottering under his pile of luggage.

"Dude, this place is *de…cent!*" He dropped his suitcases with a shower of dust. "Not like that place we stayed on Earth. Man, this pub has windows and everything. *Cla…ssy.*" He whistled appreciatively. "Whoa. Look at that *skeleton!*"

Simone turned and felt the blood drain from her face. Great. Another dinosaur. At least this one was dead.

An enormous slab of stone stood along the wall, chained upright. A dinosaur skeleton was trapped inside. Some kind of theropod, roughly the size of a man. The neck was tilted back, the skull open in a silent scream. The *Mintari Field Guide* would probably tell her the species. Not that Simone cared. It was a monster. She knew that much.

"I know, dude, this is gnarly! I could live here." Cody finally noticed the dinosaur race playing above the bar. "Ooh, look! Dino Derby is on. And Strutter is leading! I knew I should have bet on him."

"You were gonna bet on Gallimimus Gil!" Simone snapped. Good old Gil had wandered off the track. Ignoring his jockey's pleading, the dinosaur was munching on a hedge.

A voice rose from behind the bar. "This saloon is for locals only. You'll want to check out the Tar Pit in the center of town. We don't have any gift shops here."

Simone turned toward the bar. An old man stood there, wearing a leather apron and glasses. His head was shiny and smooth like a bowling ball, but he made up for it with bushy white muttonchops.

"We're not tourists." Simone held out her hand. "My name is Simone LaRue. I'm a journalist for the *Cloventia Gazette*."

A big, bearded local approached. "A journalist! Hey, maybe you can write a story about this mole on my back." He turned around and began tugging up his shirt. "It looks just like a pachycephalosaurus."

"Sit down, Merl!" the barkeep said.

"But Barnum—"

"Sit down. The lady doesn't want to see your mole."

Mumbling about how his mole was a scoop, Merl returned to his beer.

Barnum the barkeep grabbed a rag and began cleaning a mug. He looked back at Simone. "Nothing ever happens here. You want a story to write about? You need to be outside the city walls. It's dinosaurs people come here to see. Not old bartenders."

Simone glanced toward the fossil. "Why a dinosaur skeleton? You live on a world full of living dinosaurs."

Barnum ran a rag along the bar. "The dinosaurs on Mintari were made in a lab. No, they're not genetically engineered.

I know. Nothing artificial about them. Time-casting lets scientists grab authentic DNA from the past. But they're still not the real deal, if you ask me. This fossil, now." He gestured with his chin toward the slab of stone. "That's an honest-to-goodness dinosaur. From Earth. Dug up from the ground. Ninety-five million years old. You won't find another one like it on Mintari. Not for another ninety-five million years at least."

He laughed at his own joke, which he had probably told ninety-five million times.

Simone took a seat at the bar. She placed her elbows on the polished wood, leaned forward, and fixed Barnum with a curious gaze. She saw herself reflected in the barkeep's glasses. A young woman, porcelain skin, flaming-red hair. Beautiful, yes. She was aware of it. She wasn't too humble to deny it, and she wasn't too proud to use it. She leaned forward a bit more, lips parting.

"I'm not here to write a story about dinosaurs. I'm here for a man. A man they call—"

"Jurassic Joe," Barnum finished for her. The old barkeep chuckled. "They still calling him that? Yeah, the young whippersnapper used to come by. He never drank much, but he did love my shepherd's pie. And he sure knew how to tickle the ivories. Nobody plays the piano much here anymore."

"I play guitar," Cody offered.

Simone shook her head at her cameraman, then looked back at the barkeep.

"I must say, that doesn't sound like the famous Jurassic Joe from the stories," she said. "On Cloventia, they tell of a rough, wild outlaw. I imagined he'd be guzzling whiskey, getting into fist fights, and smashing bottles over men's heads."

"Who, Joe? Ha!" Barnum grabbed another mug to clean. "Nah. He was always quiet. Kept to himself, mostly. Never said much, even in those days. Didn't get in trouble. Joe Triplehorn is good lad." He heaved a sigh. "A good lad. It was not right what happened to him. Not with his family. Not with his wife." He shook his head. "It was not right."

Triplehorn. There was that name again.

Simone thought back to the astrolite. Rattlesnake had given her a bullet with the name Joe Triplehorn written on it. She still felt it in her pocket, poking her thigh.

"So Jurassic Joe and Joe Triplehorn are the same person?" she asked.

Barnum raised an eyebrow. "You came all the way to do a story about him, and you don't even know his real name?" He snickered. "Jurassic Joe is what the tourists call him. Many of them still hope to find him on Mintari. They won't. He knows how to hide. And he's not ashamed of his last name."

Simone felt light-headed. Triplehorn. That name kept haunting her.

There was a Triplehorn family on Cloventia. A rich family. A family that sold hunting supplies across the Nyx system. A family whose daughter—

No. Simone winced. She dared not dredge up that memory now. Not here. That grief was still too real.

But she had to know.

"Joe isn't ... related to the Triplehorn family from Cloventia, is he?" she whispered. "To ... to Amissa Triplehorn?"

Barnum nodded sadly. "Amissa is his sister."

Simone felt faint.

Mutters and groans sounded across the tavern.

"She's a monster!" somebody said. "All Triplehorns are!"

"Tarry traitors, Clan Triplehorn!"

Somebody else spat. "I should fly over to Cloventia, march right into one of their stores, and punch those Triplehorns in their treasonous faces."

More and more mutters rose. A few people even raised knives. Maybe Simone would get her bar fight after all.

"Now, now, settle down, everyone!" Barnum said, holding up both hands. "There aren't no Triplehorns here in our saloon. The only Triplehorn left on Mintari is Joe, and you all know he's good folk. Got nothing to do with his family. Edna, lower that knife! Bruce, sit back down and holster your gun. Next round's on the house if you all simmer down."

That got them to sit down pretty quickly.

Simone took a few deep breaths, reeling. Was the universe playing some kind of cruel joke on her? Jurassic Joe, the man she sought, was the brother of Amissa Triplehorn? The same woman who had shattered Simone's family?

Her head spun. She struggled to breathe. Anxiety was wrapping its claws around her.

She forced her mind away from that terrible day. It would not do to break down in tears here in the saloon. She would figure this out. This mission was suddenly about more than tracking down a folk hero. A whole lot more.

To distract herself from the pain, Simone studied the crowd. For the first time, she noticed that everyone in the Fossil and Firkin sported a crest on their lapel. Each crest seemed to represent another dinosaur. She saw pterosaur wings, theropod teeth, raptor claws … but no triceratops. Not like the symbol she had seen on Rattlesnake's gun.

Those are clan crests, she thought. *And Joe's clan is shamed.*

She looked at Barnum. "What happened with Joe's family? How did Clan Triplehorn become … what they are?"

The barkeep looked over her head. He noticed that Cody was filming. The old man's expression hardened.

"I've said too much. You can have a meal. You can stay the night if you like. But no cameras. And no more questions."

The Fossil and Firkin offered three rooms to rent upstairs. Simone wasn't sure why. If the saloon was closed to tourists, who was renting the rooms? Well, apparently journalists and their cameramen. She rented one room, Cody the other. Paid for by the good folks at the *Cloventia Gazette*, God bless 'em.

The rooms were small and rustic. The bed frames were made from branches stripped of bark and tied together. An oil painting hung on one wall, featuring a T-rex and a triceratops locked in battle. Simone draped a towel over the frame.

Old Barnum sent up her dinner. Shepherd's pie. He cooked it himself. And it was heavenly. The meat was rich with gravy and mixed with fried onions, diced carrots, and peas. The mashed potatoes were creamy in the middle, crispy on top. Simone began to understand why Jurassic Joe spent so much time at the Fossil. She was ready to move in.

But the comfort food didn't comfort her for long. When she lay in bed and closed her eyes, she saw the monsters. Great winged reptiles screeched. Swift predators slashed into sauropod flesh. The beasts were everywhere on Mintari. Even inside her mind.

Simone opened her eyes. This fear of hers was ridiculous. Logically, she knew that. Was Mintari truly more dangerous than Cloventia? There were predators back home too. But they wore silken robes and prowled boardrooms. There were monsters there too. But they lurked in alleyways and shadowy bars. Simone had met her fair share of them.

Home was dangerous in its own ways. There were still nightmares that lurked deep inside her. There were still scars she kept hidden, memories she kept locked up. And Simone wondered if the *Gazette* had truly forced her on this mission. She could have refused. But she had accepted her assignment. She had flown here. Fled here. Dinosaurs and all.

What was it Rattlesnake had said? The two greatest predators were dinosaurs and men. The poacher was wrong. There was a reason the population on Mintari was capped. The dinosaurs, prodigious as they were, would not last a day on Cloventia. It was man—small, humble man, barely an ant by the great titanosaurs—who was the most vicious animal of all. The smallest germ could fell the mightiest behemoth, and so could men.

Lying in bed, Simone pulled the action figure from her pocket. She looked at him. Jurassic Joe. The toy wore a safari outfit made from real fabric, though the ceratop hat was plastic. The action figure carried a double-barreled rifle, presumably to shoot poachers with. The badge of the Mintari Rangers shone on the chest, shaped like a stegosaurus's dorsal plate. When Simone looked closer, she saw a smaller symbol on the plastic man's lapel. A tiny triceratops head. Crest of the Triplehorn clan.

"Who are you, Jurassic Joe?" Simone whispered to the toy.

She finally slept, holding the toy in her hand, and dreamed of theropods prowling the shadowy hallways of the *Gazette*.

In the morning, Simone dressed for a journey in the wilderness. Thankfully, she was not a complete airhead, and she had packed sensible clothes too. She pulled on shorts, a buttoned-down shirt, and a straw hat. She also packed away her heels and pulled on hiking boots. Her sister, who loved adventure, always used to say that hiking shoes could save your life in the wilderness.

God, I miss you, Elize.

Tears filled Simone's eyes.

"Not now," she told herself, wiping her eyes. "It's still too raw. Too painful."

Yet how could Simone not think of her twin sister? She saw Elize's face whenever she looked into the mirror.

She looked into the mirror now, studying the woman who gazed back.

Her red hair cascaded from under the straw hat, tumbling across her shoulders. Freckles spread across her pale cheeks. She had always endured a lot of ribbing over her skin tone. *You get sunburned standing in front of an open fridge! You're so pale you use chalk as makeup!* She had heard 'em all. Whenever she stepped out into Nyx's light, she turned red as a lobster, and more jokes would come. Facing the mirror, she spent a while applying industrial amounts of sunscreen.

When she was done, she just stood there for a moment, and a sigh rolled through her.

"Simone LaRue," she said softly to her reflection. "In over your crazy red head again."

She thought of her earlier life. Her life before the incident.

No, don't think about that now, she told her reflection. *You are no longer that woman. Some wounds do not heal, but that doesn't mean we have to pick at the scabs.*

She headed down to the common room.

Barnum was up already, polishing the bar yet again.

"We got a pot of coffee brewing," the old barkeep said. "I'll rustle you up some breakfast if you like. Eggs or flapjacks?"

"More shepherd's pie."

He looked up at her, then barked a laugh. "My goodness, cheesecake. You ain't but a slender little thing, but you eat like a sauropod."

She grinned. "It's good pie."

He brought her another helping along with a cup of steaming coffee. She added copious amounts of cream and sugar.

"Tell me, sir," she said when her plate was clean and her mug was empty, "where can I find Jurassic Joe?"

Barnum heaved a sigh. "I told you, my dear. No questions."

"Last one. I promise."

His face hardened. "Joe Triplehorn chose to live away from society. It was his choice. I honor it."

Simone leaned across the bar. "What if I can help him? What if ... well, what if he's lonely? What if, through me, he can tell his story?"

"Is that all this is about then?" Barnum said. "A story?"

Simone thought back to last night. To the reactions to the Triplehorn name. "No. Not only about a story. It's about broken families. About betrayal. About the sins of a father and guilt passed down to children." Her voice dropped to a whisper. "I know something about those things."

Barnum looked at her for a moment, and his face softened. There was something akin to pity in his eyes. No, not pity. Compassion. And Simone knew it wasn't for her. It was for a young man who used to play piano here. Long ago.

Finally Barnum looked away. He spoke in a gruff voice. "Mudge Mountain. Across Hell Valley. You can find guides outside the Tar Pit in the town square. Watch out for the hucksters."

"H-hell Valley?" Simone whispered. But the barkeep disappeared into the kitchen, leaving her with her empty mug.

Simone looked around the common room for Cody. Was the big, shaggy cameraman still asleep? Probably hungover. He had stayed up late—just to sample the local ale, he had told her. A few sips, nothing more. His raucous singing from downstairs had woken Simone twice last night.

She should wake him. Quite possibly, she would need to dump a bucket of ice water over his head. She was about to head upstairs when a voice spoke from behind her.

"So it's a tour guide you need?"

She turned around. A Mintarian leaned against one table. He wore a safari outfit, a ceratop hat, and a necklace of raptor claws. His skin was tanned, his eyes blue and sparkling. He flashed a smile so bright Simone swore she could hear a *ting!*

"The name's Terry. Triassic Terry, they call me." He held out his hand to her. "I know, I know, I'm not as famous as Jurassic Joe. But I'm making a name for myself. Tours are my specialty. I'd be glad to give you a private tour all the way to Mudge Mountain."

Simone tilted her head. "The barkeep said the tour guides are at the Tar Pit."

"The overpriced hucksters maybe. But I'm the real deal, cheesecake." He tapped a badge on his shirt. "See this? Triassic Tours. Says so right on the badge. Best tour company around. For the low price of only two hundred clovers, I'll show you the wonders of Mintari! If you want the best dino watering holes, we know 'em. If you wanna ride on pterodactyls, we'll strap you onto one. If you wanna ride a T-rex, well, find another guide, because I might be crazy, but I'm not suicidal." He winked. "I use that joke with every tourist. Never gets a laugh, but I keep trying."

Simone did laugh. The man was charming, she gave him that. "Thank you, Terry. But I don't need a tour. I just need a guide to take me to Mudge Mountain."

"Ah, that's easy then!" Triassic Terry grinned again, nearly blinding her with his pearly whites. "I'll do that for only one hundred and ninety clovers. What do ya say? All the other tour guides, well, they take big groups out. That means you'll spend days looking at dinosaurs with a bunch of snot-nosed little kids. I mean—I love kids. God bless the little tykes. You don't have one yourself do you? Ah, good. Terrible things, they are. None of them on our tour. Just straight to Mudge Mountain."

"I'll pay you three hundred if you take the path of fewest dinosaurs."

"Lady, you got a deal."

They shook hands.

Just then, Cody came trudging downstairs, rubbing his neck. "Dude." He groaned. "Do *not* drink Mintarian rum before bed. My head is still spinning."

She grabbed his arm. "Come on, Cody. We've spent enough time in civilization. We're heading into the wild." She turned toward their guide. "Terry? Take us to your jippi."

The tour guide lost his smile. "Slight problem there."

Simone frowned. "Is there."

He winced. "Best come outside and see for yourself."

They walked around the Fossil and Firkin to the parking lot. Several dusty jippis parked there. Among them stood a dinosaur.

Simone gulped. She struggled not to faint.

"What is *that*?" she said.

Cody leaned toward her and whispered, "It's a dinosaur."

"I know it's a dinosaur! What is it doing in the parking lot?" She spun toward Terry. "I thought dinosaurs weren't allowed in the city."

"*Carnivores* aren't allowed in the city." Triassic Terry flashed an uneasy grin. "Sorry, cheesecake. I see you're not too keen on dinos. But I can assure you. Rosetta is a sweetheart." He approached the dinosaur. "Aren't you, little baby?"

The dinosaur grunted and licked his hand. There was nothing little or babylike about her, if you asked Simone. Rosetta was enormous. Larger than a jippi. More like a tank. Standing on four legs, the dinosaur sprouted three horns longer than human arms, and her face ended with a beak. A very sharp-looking beak. The sort of beak that could crush redheads.

Most striking, even more than her size, was Rosetta's bony frill. It rose above her skull, as large as a dining room table, tipped with horns. But clearly this frill was not for defense. Unlike the frill of a triceratops, which was solid bone, *this* frill only seemed to have bones along its outer edges—like a window frame. Skin stretched over the bony structure like a drumhead. Not lumpy gray skin, which the dinosaur had across the rest of her body. The skin across the frill dazzled with blue, red, and purple patterns, as colorful as butterfly wings. When the wind blew, this colorful "drumhead" rippled, making eerie music. A warning sign to predators? A display for mates like a peacock tail? Simone didn't know. But that frill was oddly beautiful.

"Dude, this dino is gnarly!" Cody said, patting Rosetta's side. "Is she a triceratops?"

"No, mate." Terry shook his head. "See the colors on the frill? Trikes don't have those. They're both ceratopsians. Related. But my Rosetta is a—"

"Chasmosaurus," Simone said. She had finally dared open her *Mintari Field Guide.*

Terry's grin was blinding. "Yeah! You know your dinos, cheesecake. Indeed, my Rosetta is a chasmosaurus. They're a bit smaller than the trikes, but let me tell you, they're just as tough. My Rosetta can hold her own in a fight. I once saw her gore an allosaurus with those horns of hers." He kissed the dinosaur's beak. "Didn't you, cheesecake? You gored him good."

Rosetta grunted in agreement and stamped her elephantine feet.

Simone leafed through her book and gulped. "There won't be any allosaurs out there, will there?" She shuddered and closed the field guide. "They look awful."

"Of course not!" Terry said. "Not with Rosetta around. The allys know to fear her. They can spot the warning colors on her frill from miles away." He gave the colorful frill a few good pats. The skin wobbled. "Now hop on, cheesecake! We're going on dino-back."

Simone crossed her arms. "I am *not* getting on that thing."

Cody wobbled under the pile of luggage. "Can it at least carry our stuff?"

"We'll go with another tour guide. One who has a jippi. Terry, I'm very sorry. I know I promised to hire you. I'll pay you ten clovers for your trouble. Cody! Come on. We'll head to the Tar Pit."

Cody winced. The luggage straps were digging into his shoulders. "All the way back at town square?"

The poor guy looked exhausted. Not only from carrying everything. He was also badly hungover.

"I don't want your ten clovers," Terry said. "I want you to be safe. No other tour guide will cross Hell Valley. Not with them allys about. An allosaurus is large enough to knock over any jippi. But Rosetta here? They won't touch her. You're safest with me, ma'am, and that's the honest-to-goodness truth. If you want to reach Mudge Mountain and find Jurassic Joe, well ..." He waved dismissively. "Ah, forget it. I won't keep pushing ya. Best of luck, cheesecake. Now if you'll excuse me, I'll head back into the Firkin for another coffee."

Simone took a deep breath. "Wait."

Terry froze.

"Cody, load our stuff onto the dinosaur. You can ride with Terry."

The tour guide turned toward her, eyebrow rising. "What about you, cheesecake?"

"I spent good money on these hiking shoes. I'm walking."

If any dinosaur ever wandered around Cloventia, it would cause a panic. Even a runt like a eoraptor, who was barely larger than a chicken, would send thousands fleeing for their lives. Today a dinosaur the size of a tank lumbered through Dinovia City, and people barely noticed. One man stepped aside, never lifting his eyes from his newspaper. A couple of children paused from kicking a ball as the dinosaur thundered by. And those were about the strongest reactions Rosetta the chasmosaurus got.

Simone, who was walking alongside the beast, wished she could be so blasé. Her heart wouldn't stop racing. Just being so close to a living, breathing dinosaur made her tremble. She glanced at Rosetta.

The stocky ceratopsian plodded onward, her feet leaving deep imprints in the dirt road. She paused by somebody's garden to feed from some flowerpots, then lumbered onward, chewing on begonias. This was barely even a snack. Rosetta was truly enormous. Especially her head. Rosetta's skull was longer than Simone was tall. The bony frill rose behind the horns, dazzling with colors. The blue, green, and purple shades formed an abstract painting.

"Those aren't warning colors," Simone said softly. "That frill is for display. You're beautiful to attract a mate." She patted the dinosaur's scaly hide. "You've got your makeup on."

Simone suddenly realized what she was doing. Patting a dinosaur. She pulled her hand back, but oddly, her heart was no longer racing.

Cody looked down from the dinosaur's back. "Dude, you patted a dino! I'm proud of you. You ready to ride up here with us?"

And ... now her heart was racing again.

"Certainly not." She crossed her arms, raised her chin, and kept walking alongside the tanklike animal.

Finally they reached the city's defensive walls. Simone had to tilt her head all the way back to see the top. The houses in Dinovia were humble things built of clay, little more than huts. But this wall was a serious construction, even by Cloventian standards. Massive limestone bricks, each the size of a fridge, were stacked high. If Rosetta reared on her hind legs, she would still be too short to see over the top. Heck, even a brontosaurus might need a stool.

Simone pulled out her handy little opera binoculars. She had remembered to pack them, thankfully. She peered to the top of the wall. Armed men and women stood there, carrying double-barreled rifles.

"Are those Mintari Rangers?" she said.

Terry nodded. "Sure are. I almost became a Ranger myself, you know. But with a charming grin like mine, I figured I'm better giving tours than manning the wall." He winked and flashed his bright teeth. *Ting!*

"Jurassic Joe is a Ranger too, isn't he?" Simone said.

Terry shrugged. "Eh. Sort of. A rogue one. You see, Rangers generally live here in Dinovia City. Oh, they go out on ranges. They take their jippis and tricopters. Sometimes they even spend a night in the field—inside their armored vehicles, of course. Then they fly back home, report to their boss, and fill out paperwork. But Jurassic Joe, well ... nobody's seen him in ages. Most men would not survive fifteen minutes alone out the wild. Joe's been out there for fifteen years."

Simone gasped. "Could he be dead?"

Terry shook his head. "Not a chance, cheesecake. It would take a dinosaur with silver teeth to kill Joe Triplehorn."

"Whoa!" Cody said, eyes wide. "For real? Dude, is Jurassic Joe a werewolf?"

Simone thought back to the carnotauruses taking down the mighty patagotitans. She had a feeling regular teeth would do just fine, no silver needed.

They headed toward a towering gateway in the wall. A stone archway loomed, filled with heavy iron-banded doors. It all seemed rather medieval. Cities didn't have walls or gates on Cloventia. Not on Earth anymore either. Then again, the largest animal that could attack you on those planets was a house cat.

The Rangers on the wall waved. One Ranger pulled a lever, and the great doors swung outward, revealing a majestic view of ... a drawbridge, a moat, and a crackling electric fence. They took security seriously at Mintari.

The drawbridge creaked menacingly under Rosetta's weight, and Simone breathed in relief once they were across the moat. The Rangers on the wall pulled another lever, and a gate in the electric fence slid open.

And there it was.

Right ahead. Hell. Some could call the landscape beautiful, but Simone knew it was hell.

Grasslands spread toward flowering meadows, rustling forests, and mountains nearly lost in the distant haze. Back on Earth, paleontologists debated whether grass had existed during the original reign of the dinosaurs, but here on Mintari it grew in abundance. The faintest hint of sauropod necks rose through the mist, and pterosaurs circled above.

Simone paused and gulped.

"You can do this, Simone LaRue," she whispered to herself.

Trembling, she stepped out the gate, leading the way. The boys followed, riding the chasmosaurus.

The gate clattered shut behind them. Simone got the sudden impulse to fall to her knees and beg the Rangers, "Let me back in!"

Before she could embarrass herself, Simone walked down the dirt path, fists clenched at her sides, chin raised high. Grunting and pausing now and then to graze, Rosetta the chasmosaurus followed. They headed into the wild.

CHAPTER FOUR
Beasts in the Neon Jungle

Tobias Triplehorn, CEO of the largest hunting supplies company on Cloventia, did not tolerate fools lightly. And the man before him was certainly a fool.

"I gave you my answer, Mr. Triplehorn." The fool raised his chin. "The answer is no. My store has been with my family for three generations. Someday I'll pass it on to my son. I won't sell it. Not to you. Not to anyone. Good day, sir."

The man walked toward the door.

"One more thing, Mr. Fletcher!" said Tobias. "Before you go."

The man paused. He turned back and glared up at Tobias. "What?"

Tobias Triplehorn had built his office to include two levels. His chair rose on the higher level. His guests had to stand three steps below. He liked to stare down at his visitors. The chamber was so massive his voice echoed when he yelled at underlings. Some people joked that Tobias had built himself a throne room. Perhaps they were right. After all, had Tobias not built an empire? He had immigrated here with nothing but the dirt under his fingernails, a young bumpkin from Mintari. Now he was royalty.

He leaned forward in his chair. The leather creaked. The chair was upholstered with the scaly skin of a Tyrannosaurus rex. It was uncomfortable. It *should* be uncomfortable. An emperor should not sit easy on his throne.

"Mr. Fletcher, you own a small hunting supplies store, don't you? You sell … what was it? Compound bows?"

The rotund shopkeep raised his chin. "That's right. We sell the best bows in the business."

Tobias narrowed his eyes. "We shall see. Mr. Fletcher, I would like you to approach the table to your left. Please pull the sheet back."

The store owner huffed. "I've no time for your games, sir. I won't be selling my business, and that's that."

"Oh, I don't expect you to sell your store. Not anymore." Tobias smiled thinly. "Before you leave, humor me. The table please, Mr. Fletcher. Call it a parting gift. For your time."

Curiosity got the better of foolish Mr. Fletcher. He approached the table, pulled back the sheet, and his eyes widened.

"Do you recognize that, Mr. Fletcher?" Tobias said.

The storekeeper nodded. "One of our compound hunting bows. The Fletcher Shooter Classic. My father designed this one."

"Pick it up, Mr. Fletcher. And load an arrow. I suggest you move quickly. We're about to see how good your bows truly are."

A hiss rose from under the floor. The sound filled the cavernous room.

Mr. Fletcher froze. He glared up at Tobias. "What is the meaning of this? Do you think to scare me with parlor tricks?"

Tobias checked his diamond-studded wristwatch. "Please hurry, Mr. Fletcher. It only takes my pet sixty seconds to crawl from her enclosure into my office."

Fletcher ran toward the door. He grabbed and yanked the handle. Locked.

He wheeled back toward Tobias, face red. "What the hell sort of game are you playing, man?"

The fool was feigning anger. His cracking voice revealed his fear.

"Twenty more seconds, Mr. Fletcher. You claim you sell the best bows in the business. Better than Triplehorn bows? We shall see."

Again the hiss rose from below, filling the room like steam.

Fletcher's red cheeks went sheet white. He grabbed the bow. Fingers shaking, he loaded an arrow.

A hatch slid open in the floor. It was large enough to drop a piano into. An oily smell wafted into the room. Heavy breathing sounded in the shadows. Scales chinking, the creature slithered up from below.

Fletcher stumbled back, nearly dropping his bow.

A reptilian head rose through the hatch. An enormous head, covered in green scales. A head large enough to swallow a crocodile with one gulp. The gargantuan serpent slithered into the room. Her body was so wide that if a man dared hug it, his fingertips would not meet on the other side.

"Dear God, what is that?" Fletcher shouted.

Tobias poured himself a glass of Cabernet. He swirled the drink in the cup, letting the wine breathe. "Just a snake, Mr. Fletcher. I've named her Stella."

The creature emerged fully into the room, and the hatch closed below. It was a large room, but Stella filled it.

"That's no snake, man!" Fletcher cried. "That's a dinosaur. They're illegal on Cloventia, you Mintarian bastard. You know that!"

Tobias inhaled the sweet aroma of the wine. Almost ready for drinking now. Only fools drank wine and killed men too quickly. A good wine, like a good killing, needed to be savored.

"Oh, I operate entirely within the law, Mr. Fletcher. Don't worry. It's true that, like the dinosaurs, the titanoboa comes from millions of years ago. Like them, this magnificent species was restored with the miracle of time-casting. But it is not, in fact, a dinosaur itself. Only a very old snake. And a very large snake, as you probably noticed. Stella here is longer than a bus. She weighs thousands of pounds. Fear not! The floor is reinforced. You're perfectly safe. Well, from the floor breaking, at least. Whether you're safe from Stella or not, well … that depends on the quality of your product."

Fletcher fired his bow at the snake.

The arrow snapped against green scales the size of saucers.

Stella screeched, more in annoyance than pain. The sound was deafening. They could probably hear it across the entire building. Tobias could have soundproofed his office. He had chosen not to. He wanted his employees to hear.

The titanoboa thrust her great head toward Fletcher. The fool was busy loading another arrow, but his hands shook too badly. His arrow clattered onto the floor.

Not that it would have made much of a difference anyway.

Tobias leaned back in his chair, sipped the wine, and swirled it through his mouth. Ah, perfection. A lovely bouquet.

The titanoboa detached her lower jaw. Her gargantuan mouth opened wide, revealing teeth like daggers. But she would not use those formidable teeth today. No need to chew this meal. A man was but a morsel for such a prodigious beast. The ancient snake swallowed Mr. Fletcher whole.

Before he vanished down the gullet, he let out a bloodcurdling scream. Tobias hoped his employees heard that too.

The snake closed her mouth and licked her chops.

Tobias sighed. "You see, Mr. Fletcher, your bows are not very good at all. I'm doing your business a favor." He frowned. "Mr. Fletcher, can you still hear me? No? Oh, very well. I suppose you get the idea."

The fool was still alive, squirming and screaming inside Stella's belly. They usually squirmed for a while until the stomach acids did their work. Snakes, like Tobias, knew how to savor a kill.

Between sips of wine, Tobias lifted his telephone receiver. It was a historic artifact, constructed from beautiful brass and silver. Today many men had neural implants, could call one another telepathically. But Tobias preferred the elegance of an older, more civilized era. Technology created many conveniences. But the finer things in life were all old. Like this phone. Like the wine in his cup. Like the animal digesting her meal below.

"Amissa, dear?" Tobias said into the receiver. "I'm quite ready for your demonstration."

"Already, Dad?" came her voice over the phone. "The screams only started a minute ago."

"Poor Mr. Fletcher did not last long. Come now, Amissa, do not tarry."

"On my way."

Tobias hung up, sipped his wine, and leafed through the *Cloventia Gazette*. He was one of the few men on Cloventia who still bought the paper edition. Ah, Ms. LaRue had an article published today! Splendid. Something about the gang wars down in the sewage system below the floating skyscrapers. She must have written it just before her trip. A good piece. Pity they always buried her articles past the wanted ads.

"You are a fine journalist, Ms. LaRue," Tobias said softly, flipping the page. "You will serve me well on Mintari."

He was still reading the article when the door banged open.

"One dead snake, coming right up!"

Amissa Triplehorn strutted into the room.

She was a tall, striking woman in her thirties. Her chestnut hair cascaded down to her waist, and her eyes shone with blue fire. Her fans called her the most beautiful killer in the world. So did her enemies, for that matter. And she had millions of both. Amissa was the most famous—or infamous, depending on whom you asked—huntress in the galaxy.

She was decked out in Triplehorn gear today, all from the latest product line. Camouflage pants with magnetic buckles to hold a variety of blades. Boots with retractable claws for climbing and kicking. An armored vest with pouches full of bullets. A machete hung across her back, and in her hand, she held the latest Triplehorn bow. Artemis's Arch, they called it. Their new flagship product. A compound bow augmented with hydraulic technology, capable of delivering a bolt of kinetic energy that rivaled some grenades.

When Amissa saw the colossal snake, she grinned, licked her lips, and bared her teeth. Suddenly Amissa herself seemed reptilian. "Hello, Stella, my dear. I've been waiting for this moment since you hatched."

Stella spun toward her with a hiss. The titanoboa lunged, jaws opening for another meal.

Amissa did not flinch. In a single, fluid movement, she loaded an arrow into Artemis's Arch, drew the string, and fired.

The arrow—a shaft of steel wrapped in graphene—tore through Stella's upper jaw and pierced the wall behind. The arrow moved with such speed it ionized the air, leaving a trail of fire.

The titanoboa bellowed, a hole in her snout. But the arrow had missed the brain. Stella was still alive. She seemed to feel no pain, only fury. Gushing blood, she lashed toward Amissa, as quick as an asp, as deadly as a cobra.

Amissa grinned. She drew her machete, sidestepped, and swung the blade across Stella's striking head. Scales clattered onto the floor like coins from a split purse. The snake swayed. Amissa laughed, leaped onto the beast, and climbed the scaly body, working her way up toward the head.

Stella whipped her head from side to side, trying to shake off this pesky human. The snake had a perforated jaw, a gash across the snout, and a heavy meal in her belly. She needed this battle like a hole in the head. Which is exactly what she got.

Amissa planted her clawed boots firmly onto Stella's head, raised her machete high, then brought the blade down hard.

The mighty titanoboa, queen of the primordial jungle, crashed onto the floor, shaking the building. Amissa stood atop the corpse. She licked the blood off her blade, then tossed back her head and howled in victory.

"So dramatic." With his handkerchief, Tobias dabbed a bit of blood off his shoe. It had splashed far. "Do try to be more hygienic next time, Amissa. These shoes are worth more than your inheritance."

She spat and hopped off the dead snake. "The bow should have finished Stella off with the first shot. It doesn't work."

Tobias lifted his newspaper again and rustled the pages. "It works perfectly well if you aim it properly. You missed the brain."

"Didn't know your pets had brains."

"How droll." Tobias licked his thumb and flipped to the finance section. "Ah good! Triplehorn Incorporated stock is up. Your latest video, the one where you slew the mammoth, made quite a splash. If only you could avoid such splashes here in my office. The blood is everywhere."

"Dad, I'm tired of hunting mammoths. You know what I want to hunt. Why won't you let me—"

A muddled whimper sounded behind her. Amissa turned around, stared at the snake, and tilted her head.

"Oh yes!" Tobias lowered his newspaper. "I forgot. Amissa, be a darling and cut Mr. Fletcher out of the snake. I think he's learned his lesson, wouldn't you agree?"

"Dad, forget about snakes for a second, and listen to—"

He cleared his throat. "Amissa! I asked you to do a chore. Now do it."

She groaned, returned to the dead snake, and hacked at its scales with her machete. She gutted the enormous creature like a fish. Organs spilled onto the floor. So did poor Mr. Fletcher.

The man was still alive. It could have gone either way. Tobias supposed this way was better. Killing was good fun on frontier worlds, but after all, this *was* Cloventia. This civilization was a bit queasy when it came to murder. That didn't make much sense to Tobias, but well, as they said: When on Cloventia …

"Look at me, Mr. Fletcher," he said, rustling his newspaper.

Amissa grabbed the man's hair and yanked his head back. "You heard my pops. Look at him."

Tobias laid his newspaper across his lap, leaned forward, and squinted at the man. "My my, look at those burns across your skin. Stomach acid is such nasty business. But I assure you, Mr. Fletcher, this was merely a slap on the wrist. I own other pets too. Pets that do not swallow men whole. They rip them to shreds."

Mr. Fletcher was shaking. Hyperventilating. "I—I—I'll sell you the store! Take it. Take it! Oh God. You're insane! You're a lunatic! You—"

Amissa twisted his hair. "Watch your language. This is a place of business."

Tobias sipped his wine and returned to his newspaper. "Pleasure doing business with you, Mr. Fletcher. Daughter, darling? See our guest out."

His beloved daughter dragged the dripping Mr. Fletcher by the hair. When they reached the door, she sent him on his way with a kick.

"All right, Pops, I'm off to shower." She shook blood off her hands. "Got another photo shoot tonight. This time with the saber-toothed tiger I hunted last month. Got him stuffed and mounted nicely in the library."

"Amissa, one moment please."

She paused, one foot out the door. "What?"

"Don't stand in an open door while talking to your father, darling. Show some etiquette."

She snorted. "I'm an outback girl. I don't do etiquette."

Tobias rose from his seat. He knocked over his cup of wine. It shattered. Fury blazed through him. "You are Cloventian now! Do you know what the old families call us? Outlanders. Country bumpkins. Uncouth immigrants. To them, we're only Mintarians."

Amissa shrugged. "We *are* Mintarians."

"Not anymore!" Tobias shouted. "We're civilized now. Act like it!"

Amissa rolled her eyes. She affected an Old Money accent. "Very well, dear papa. Shall I powder my nose before hunting my next pachyderm?"

Tobias sat back down, taking deep breaths, struggling to regain control. "I do not want you to hunt another mammoth. Amissa, it's time we talk about our shameful past. About Mintari."

Tobias Triplehorn had been living on Cloventia for over forty years now. He had lost his rough Mintarian accent, and he spoke with the elegance of old Cloventian nobility. Instead of uncouth safari outfits, he wore flowing crimson robes embroidered with golden thread. He no longer squatted in a clay hut but lived in a mansion. If not for his surname, nobody would guess at his heritage. He had kept the name as a reminder—not for others but for himself. *I rose from the mud.*

Tobias had never forgotten Mintari. The memories still haunted him. The creatures that roamed Mintari also roamed the deep caverns of his mind. The monsters. Every night, he dreamed of what they had done. And he woke up trembling, fists clenched, jaw grinding.

He was a powerful man. He punished his enemies. He conquered boardrooms and skyscrapers in the urban jungle. He dined with presidents and devoured corporations. But at night, he was still a boy, running scared from dinosaurs.

He knew the beasts would always haunt his dreams. So he must turn the tide.

"Amissa, do you know how dinosaurs first came to Mintari?" he asked.

Standing by the slain snake, she rolled her eyes. "Oh God, Dad, another history lesson."

He overlooked her attitude. This time.

"Time-casting!" he said. "The greatest technological revolution since the spear. Actual time travel! But the technology, you see, has limits. We can only send small objects into the past.

No larger than a gnat. And we cannot bring objects from the past into the future. So how, do you ask, did the dinosaurs come into the year 3041?"

She heaved a sigh. "I didn't ask. Dad, I finished school long ago. Please stop the lectures."

"By sending back tiny electronic mosquitoes. We cast them back in time like fishermen casting lures. The little drones collected blood from dinosaurs, then burrowed underground. There they waited for millions of years until humans dug them up, recovered the DNA, and—"

"Dad, I'm leaving." She walked toward the door.

"Stay where you are, Amissa. Behave."

She let out a groan, tossed her machete onto the floor, and sat on the dead snake. "Fine, fine! Drone on with your history lesson."

"Around the same time, scientists discovered Nyx. A miraculous star system! A system with four Earthlike worlds, all ready for colonization. This is rare in the galaxy, Amissa. A true gift of fate. One planet—the very planet we're on now—our wise ancestors gave to humanity. A place for families fleeing the slums of Earth. The second planet they gave to modern animals—a world where tigers, lions, whales, and their friends can live free. The third planet we gave to the Ice Age creatures, and—"

"And Mintari to the dinos, yes, I know." Amissa yawned. "Can you tuck me in after my bedtime story?"

Tobias leaned back in his seat and steepled his fingers. "You've hunted many creatures, Amissa. Elephants, tigers, and bears on planet Thalia. Mammoths and saber-toothed tigers on planet Borealis. But you could never hunt dinosaurs. *That* planet is too dangerous. Even for you. Not only because of the vicious dinosaurs who roam there. But also because of the Mintari Rangers. They are organized. They are militant. They are brutal.

They hunt down poachers and shoot them dead." Tobias leaned forward in his seat. "Jurassic Joe is particularly ruthless."

Amissa shrugged. "Apple doesn't fall far from the tree. He is your son, after all."

Tobias leaped from his chair. Moving with shocking speed for a man of his age, he raced off his dais, grabbed his daughter by the neck, and squeezed. She sputtered, eyes bugging out, and clawed at his hand. He tightened his grip, baring his teeth at the huntress.

"Joe is no son of mine!" Tobias growled. "I have no son!"

He released her throat and shoved her back. Amissa fell to her knees, gasping for air.

"God, Dad, what's gotten into you?" She rubbed her throat. Amissa was fearless when it came to hunting beasts. But now Tobias saw the glint of fear in her eyes. He had often seen such fear in her mother's eyes.

"Joe betrayed our clan," Tobias said. "He shames us. He kills our customers."

Amissa glared at him between strands of her long brown hair. "You nearly killed *me*."

"Oh, don't be so melodramatic. You're not so easy to kill. I just saw you hack a titanoboa to death."

The young huntress grinned. "That *was* pretty amazing, wasn't it? Even for me."

"Walk with me, Amissa. The corpse is starting to stink."

As they left the office, Tobias signaled for a cleaning lady. The woman was busy dusting a picture frame in the corridor.

"Please clean my office, Dorothy," he said.

She nodded. "Of course, sir." She hurried inside. From the corridor, Tobias heard her gasp and drop her mop.

Robe rustling, he walked with his daughter down the corridor. Her boots left bloody imprints on the carpet, which cleaners quickly rushed forward to remove. Most offices today used cleaner drones. But Tobias Triplehorn liked the charms of the old world. To be on top, somebody must be at the bottom. On Mintari he had learned that no ecosystem could survive without a food chain. Tobias made sure he kept plenty of underlings around.

Along the corridor, soaring windows afforded a view of Neotropolis, capital of Cloventia. Tobias paused and admired the cityscape. Thousands of skyscrapers sprouted from floating platforms. Millions of cars flew back and forth like birds in an urban forest. Shadows cloaked the ground level where the working class toiled. The tunnels underground, places of poverty and despair not much better than Earth, were little more than myth. From up here, all you could see was neon, steel, and glass.

"I remember the first time I saw Cloventia," Tobias said softly. "I never imagined such a place could exist. I had never seen a building larger than a clay hut."

Amissa yawned. "Yes, and you walked ten miles to school every day. In the snow. Uphill. Both ways. Do you have any other large animals around I can kill? I'm getting bored."

"Soon you will kill the most magnificent beasts who ever lived," Tobias whispered.

Amissa's eyes widened. "Do you mean I'm finally allowed to ...?" Words failed her.

Tobias kept walking. Amissa followed, as eager as a pup. They reached a mezzanine that overlooked the main lobby of Triplehorn Incorporated. Employees were coming and going below. Little soldiers in his empire. Soldiers? They wore soft robes, and they had soft souls. They sold blades, guns, arrows, machines of destruction and bloodshed. But their soft hands did not wield them. At the end of the day, Tobias's soldiers were nothing more than salesmen. They did not understand the savage brutality of the hunt.

But Amissa understood. She had never liked wearing business robes. She would fall asleep in boardroom meetings. She would mock Cloventian princesses who tottered around in heels. She lived for the hunt. For the rugged outdoors. Tobias had worked hard to smooth his Mintarian rough edges. But Mintarian blood flowed hot. Amissa had perhaps been born and raised here in civilization. She had never even set foot on Mintari. But the wilderness ran in her veins. Her heart was as wild as that world of dinosaurs.

Her fans loved her for it. Goddess of the Hunt, they called her. Whenever she posed with a dead animal, millions of people took notice. Animal-rights activists hated her. Hunters worshipped her. Teenage boys hung posters of her on their walls. The bigger the animal she hunted, the more attention she got. And attention was good for business.

Tobias looked at the dinosaur skeleton that stood in the lobby. A real one too. Not a creature brought back to life through time-casting. An actual fossil, seventy million years old.

A triceratops.

It was the symbol of his clan. The origin of their name. On Mintari, every clan had a dinosaur that represented them. The people here on Cloventia didn't understand. To them, the fossil was a mere curiosity. His employees just walked around it, ignoring the bones. But Tobias had never forgotten.

"They killed your grandparents, Amissa," he said softly. "The dinosaurs."

Amissa lowered her head. "I know."

"I was there," Tobias said, voice barely more than a whisper. "I remember."

He was there again every night. Seeing those armored tails break his mother. Seeing those spikes impale his father.

His eye twitched. Some people believed that dinosaurs were only animals. They were not. They were monsters. And they must die.

"You proved yourself today, Amissa." His voice was suddenly hoarse. "You killed a titanoboa. You are ready. I want you to travel to Mintari. I want you to hunt dinosaurs."

Tears of joy flooded her eyes. She sniffed and hugged him. "Dad. Thank you. I've waited so long for this. I promise that I'll hunt the biggest dinosaurs for you. That ..." She frowned, wiped her eyes, and tilted her head. "Wait a minute. Why now? Don't tell me it's because of the titanoboa. I've killed big animals before. Mammoths, saber-toothed tigers, dire wolves—a bunch of beasts. What changed?"

Tobias raised an eyebrow. "Why look a gift horse in the mouth? I thought you'd be thrilled."

She inhaled sharply and bared her teeth. "I am! But I must know. Why now? For years, you forbade me from going to Mintari. Too scared of my little brother. I told you I don't fear him! But you worried. That he'd try to stop me. That it would be bad press." She barked a laugh.

"It would be. If the media learned that Joe Triplehorn, my own son, is protecting animals, is shooting at hunters, is fighting my own daughter ..." He sneered, the old rage filling him. "No. We cannot allow that. Some publicity *is* bad publicity."

"So why now?" she insisted.

A thin smile spread across Tobias's face. "Because now we have a secret weapon to wield against dear Jurassic Joe. You'll be quite safe from him."

He leaned closer, and he whispered into her ears.

Gradually a grin grew and grew across Amissa's face. "Simone LaRue? The girl we broke all those years ago?"

Tobias nodded. "The same."

Amissa tossed back her head and laughed. "Dad, you are a genius."

"I want you to kill many dinosaurs," Tobias said. "Take photos. Take videos. Post your kills on QuickFame. I want the galaxy to see. I want to inspire our customers. Amissa, every one of your fans must develop an appetite for dinosaur hunting. Mintari is a whole new business frontier."

Her eyes softened. She placed a hand on his shoulder. "Is this really about business? Or is this personal?"

"All business is personal, my dear. Anyone who tells you otherwise doesn't know a tarry thing about business. Now go! Pack for your trip. You leave tonight."

Late that night, only an hour before dawn, Tobias visited the family mausoleum. Built in the style of a Greek pantheon, the mausoleum stood on a grassy platform that floated high above the city—so high the air was thin, and even the tallest skyscrapers topped out below them. It was the closest you could get to actual heaven.

Two marble triceratops framed the gateway, the ancient guardians of Clan Triplehorn. Even here, so far from home.

Wearing white robes of mourning, Tobias entered the mausoleum. Two sarcophagi lay in the cold silence, side by side. They had died fifty years ago, but the pain still tore at Tobias. Tears ran down his cheeks.

"Mom. Dad." He fell to his knees. "Long ago, when I was a boy, I promised to avenge you." He clenched his fists. "I will keep my promise!"

When he finally left the mausoleum, it was noon. Nyx's light shone on the marble triceratops statues, and Tobias made a sacred vow. He would not rest until the only dinosaurs in the galaxy were made of stone.

CHAPTER FIVE
Kingdom of the Pterosaurs

"Will you tell that beast of yours to stop licking me?"

Rosetta the chasmosaurus had a tongue the size of a fire hydrant. Simone cringed, leaped away, and looked at her new safari outfit. Saliva drenched her. She cringed.

"What's that, cheesecake?"

Triassic Terry leaned out the howdah high above. The wooden structure was fastened onto Rosetta's back. Simone thought of elephants in the old Hannibal movies.

"I said—tell your dinosaur to stop licking me!" Simone cried up toward the howdah.

"Ah!" Terry grinned. "I heard ya this time. Sorry, cheesecake. Rosetta here likes to explore the world with her tongue. You sure you don't want to ride up here with us?"

"Ride a creature that could knock over a mammoth? No, thank you. I'll walk. At a distance."

Vainly attempting to brush the saliva off (but only getting her fingers sticky), Simone stepped farther from the dinosaur.

But not too far. They were out in the wilderness of Mintari. And there were plenty of creatures here who would do much worse than lick.

She looked around her. Cycads grew from the reddish soil. They looked similar to the palm trees at the Old Hawaii Lounge near the *Gazette* headquarters, an establishment she sometimes frequented. They made good mai tais. But these trees were much larger and thicker. And, of course, not made of plastic. Ginkgos grew farther back, their semicircular leaves rustling. You could not find such trees anywhere else. Like the fauna, the flora of Mintari had been restored from extinction. More gifts of time-casting.

Something rustled among some ferns.

Snorts and sniffs sounded.

"A predator!" Simone cried out. "Watch out, everyone, a predator!"

She hurried closer to Rosetta. The chasmosaurus, delighted to have Simone back, gave her an appreciative lick.

"For pity's sake!" Simone said, shoving the enormous tongue away. "This is not the time!"

The dreaded predator burst out from the ferns. It raced toward Simone, letting out a deafening roar. The monster's teeth flashed, prepared to rip into her flesh.

California Cody leaned out the howdah. "Aww, he's cute."

Simone, who was busy panicking, took a deep breath and a closer look. The "dreaded predator" was no larger than a turkey. Probably another eoraptor like the ones from the city. Or something similar, in any case. The mini-dinosaur let out another "deafening roar." Just a squeak.

"You all right, cheesecake?" Terry called down from the howdah.

"Of course I'm all right! I was just joking." She took a shuddering breath and smoothed her clothes, only getting more saliva on her hands.

A screech sounded above.

Okay—this one really *was* deafening. Simone was sure of that. Even the boys flinched. Even Rosetta, a dinosaur shaped like a tank, grunted and stomped the ground. Steam blasted out her nostrils.

It emerged from behind a cloud with another terrible shriek. A flying monster.

Simone screamed.

"Crikey, that's a big one!" Terry shaded his eyes with his palm. "Pteranodon by the looks of it. Female. You can tell by the brown color. Big old gal. And she's hungry."

Simone ran closer to Rosetta and clung to her scaly leg. The chasmosaurus swiveled her head around and gave her a lick.

The pteranodon swooped toward them, her beady eyes blazing. Big? The beast was colossal. Her wingspan was wider than Simone's apartment back home. The terrible beak opened wide, and Simone prepared to die.

The pteranodon scooped up the eoraptor who had startled Simone, gulped the little dinosaur down, then soared. Her beating wings blasted the hair back from Simone's face and nearly blew the howdah off Rosetta.

Leaning out the swaying howdah, Cody whooped. "That. Was. Gnarly! Dude, dude!" He looked down at Simone. "Did you see that? It was so close! Tell me you saw that."

"I saw it," Simone whispered, voice trembling.

"I think I caught it on camera," Cody said. "Everything was moving so fast. Dude, this planet is *totally epic.*"

Simone wanted to go home. Rosetta licked her comfortingly, slobbering all over her clothes. She was drenched by now. At least if Simone wet her pants in fright nobody would notice.

"Terry, dude!" Cody said, turning toward the tour guide. "How do those pterodactyls get so big eating little chickens?"

"That was a pteranodon, mate," said the tour guide. "Similar to a dactyl but bigger and meaner. That girl was just snacking. When she gets really hungry, she'll go after larger prey."

"Whoa!" said Cody. "You think she could eat a human? That would be *gnarly.*"

Terry nodded. "We're near Collini Cliffs. Also known as the Kingdom of Pterosaurs. You can find lots of human bones beneath those cliffs."

Simone gulped, wishing the boys would change the topic.

"There she comes again!" Cody said.

Simone looked up and winced. The pteranodon circled the sun, then swooped.

It all happened so fast Simone could barely react.

The beast reached out her talons, gripped Simone by the shoulders, and lifted her into the air.

"Crikey, she's taking her back to her nest!" Terry cried.

Simone screamed, kicking in midair. Her feet grazed Rosetta's howdah. The pteranodon beat her wings, carrying Simone higher. Rosetta reared, thrusting her horns up. Simone reached out, tried to grab the horns and cling on. Her fingertips just brushed one horn … and then the pteranodon gained altitude.

The ground dropped below her. Rosetta, an animal the size of a woolly mammoth, shrank and shrank. Cody was screaming something, but Simone couldn't hear him over the wind. The pteranodon held her in an iron grip, carrying her into the distance.

As the pteronodon carried her through the sky, something strange happened to Simone.

(As if being carried by a flying jippi-sized reptile weren't strange enough.)

She stopped panicking.

Oh, her heart still galloped. And her head still spun. But her *mind* was perfectly clear. A calmness like a still pond filled her. It was the same calmness she had felt during the Slum Wars on Earth, interviewing cannibal warlords as bullets flew overhead. The same calmness she had felt that day long ago on Cloventia, the worst day of her life—yes, she had been calm then too, and the grief only hit her later. It was the calmness they said pilots got as their planes went crashing down. The calmness those with the worst stage fright felt once they actually started speaking to the crowd. It was a sort of terror beyond panic. As if fear simply gave up, threw up its hands in resignation, and walked away in disgust, allowing the rational mind to take the wheel.

Simone was in mortal danger. She had no time for hysteria. She must act.

Words Elize had told her came back to her. "So long as you can take another breath, there is hope."

Her twin had not taken another breath that day. But Simone took a deep breath now. She was still alive. She must survive.

The pteronodon could have gulped her down by now. Her beak was certainly large enough. But instead, the reptile was carrying her toward a distant cliff.

Terry's words echoed in her ears. "Crikey, she's taking her back to her nest!"

All right now, Simone told herself. *Just hang on a little longer. The pteronodon will drop me into the nest. And then I run.*

The panic again. It was tickling her. The anticipation of horror to come.

She took deep breaths. So long as she could take another breath, there was hope. She took another breath. And another.

Her panic was still there but kept under control. Like putting a lid over a bubbling pot.

They flew closer to the cliff. And a mighty cliff it was. The sheer wall of stone soared from a ginkgo forest. Those trees were taller than sauropods, but beside this cliff, they looked like mere grass. A waterfall cascaded into a misty lake. High above, topping the cliff, cycads soaked up Nyx's warm rays. At least whatever sunlight made it through the clouds of leather wings. For here was the kingdom of the pterosaurs.

Thousands of the flying reptiles were here. Maybe millions.

They came in every size. Some were small pterodactyls and dimorphodons, not much larger than hawks or eagles. Others were the king-sized *Quetzalcoatlus northropi*, known as Q-pis among the locals. Here was a flying terror who stood taller than a giraffe, and its wingspan rivaled some planes. Large and small, they flew here, cawing, feeding, mating, fighting.

The pterosaurs had built a veritable city of nests, using twigs, rocks, mud, and the bones of their victims. Like in every city, some neighborhoods were nicer than others. The smaller, weaker pterosaurs nested below the cliff on the beach. The slums. The larger, tougher pterosaurs lived on the cliff itself, nesting in alcoves or on stone outcrops. The city center. The mightiest monsters lived atop the cliff, lords ruling from on high. The luxury district.

Their kingdom was not peaceful. They were a surly lot, the pterosaurs. Like humans crammed together into a small space, they didn't seem to get along. A few pteronodons were fighting over a carcass—it looked like a mutilated crocodile. Every once in a while, a pterodactylus dived toward a lake below, then rose with a beak full of fish, only for other dactyls to mob it, trying to grab the meal for themselves. Two pterosaurs with colorful horns were fighting on a stone outcrop, snapping their beaks and clanging their horns together. Perhaps males battling over a female?

A shadow fell. A gargantuan Q-pi was gliding above Simone. In its clawed feet, the giant held a juvenile sauropod. The little herbivore must have just hatched. He was no larger than a beagle, and fragments of shell still clung to his head. The sauropodlet mewled pathetically for his mother, long neck swaying from side to side.

Before the Q-pi could even sit down to eat, an impudent hatzegopteryx shot up. Simone recognized the species from her field guide. The flying beast was enormous—as large as a dragon from old legends. With a screech, the hungry hatzegopteryx snatched the wriggling sauropod from the Q-pi, then fled with its stolen meal. Soon the sky echoed with angry shrieks. The two flying reptiles clashed in aerial battle.

That's all Simone was here. Lunch. Just like the fish, the mutilated croc, and the sauropodlet. And sooner or later, a beak would close around her.

Soon enough, a hungry pterosaur noticed Simone. She supposed her fluttering red hair was hard to miss. The reptile came flying toward her, beak open in challenge, revealing rows of teeth. Simone wasn't sure what kind of pterosaur it was. But it was big. Just its beak was longer than her entire body. The terrible reptile flew closer, closer, eyes bugging out, beak opening wide to reveal its waiting gullet.

Simone let out an award-worthy scream. Call the Cloventian Film Academy. Give Simone LaRue the trophy!

The great beak snapped shut. Simone curled her legs in. The beak missed her by inches.

The pteronodon who held Simone let out an enraged screech. The big female was not going to give up her meal. She wheeled in the sky and snapped her teeth at the would-be thief.

The two ravenous reptiles snapped at each other. Beaks lashed. Talons scratched. Huge leathern wings whooshed through the air, buffering the pteronodon. Wind blasted Simone.

A screech pierced the sky. The pteronodon raised her claws in defense ... releasing Simone.

She fell.

She tumbled down, screaming. The pterosaurs still battled above. They didn't even seem to notice they had lost their snack. The cliff raced alongside Simone. Any second now, the ground would—

A pterosaur shot up from the cliff.

Talons grabbed her.

A beak the size of a canoe let out a deafening cry. Simone screamed just as loudly.

She recognized this pterosaur species. She had read about them in the field guide.

Tupandactylus imperator. They were hard to forget. Imperators were among the most colorful animals on Mintari.

Millions of years ago, back on old Earth, they lived in what would later be known as Brazil. And they fully embraced the carnival spirit. This imperator was a female, judging by her colors. She had a blue face, orange neck, and purple eyes. Her wings were the color of sunset. But her source of pride was the semicircular crest that rose atop her head like a sail. It was bright red with golden stripes. This creature liked to show off.

Great. As if flying ginger-eating reptiles weren't enough, this one also looked like a clown. Simone's two worst nightmares rolled into one.

The gaudy reptile carried her toward the cliff, whacking aside rivals with her wings. Mean claws tipped those wings, ripping into the flesh of any pterosaur that thought to steal the clown's meal. The wannabe food snatchers fell back, wings lacerated.

The imperator flew higher, victorious, toward her perch atop the cliff. Prime real estate. The colorful pterosaur flapped toward an elaborate nest built of bones and straw. Rib cages formed crude walls. A few of the bones buzzed with flies; there was still some meat on them.

As soon as I'm in the nest, I run for it, Simone told herself. She would head to the trees and hide among the branches.

The imperator soared, spun once in the sky, then began descending toward the nest.

Hungry screeches rose from below.

Simone looked down.

Baby imperators filled the nest. They were the size of pit bulls. The creatures opened their beaks wide, demanding food.

Simone let out an earth-shattering scream.

The mother imperator opened her claws. Simone tumbled toward the nest of hungry hatchlings.

Long ago, after the great tragedy of her youth, Simone suffered nightmares. Every night. For years.

In most of the nightmares, she replayed the terrible events of that tragic day. She woke up crying, still holding the dying Elize in her arms. Only to discover that her arms were empty. That her twin sister was gone.

But in some dreams, there was no blood. No snapping teeth. No screams. In those dreams, Simone was simply falling. Tumbling down and down into an abyss, plunging toward an unseen danger in the dark. She would always crash down onto a bed, wake up, and scream.

Falling through the sky today reminded Simone of those dreams. But this time there was no bed to catch her fall. Only the snapping beaks of baby pterosaurs. One hatchling shoved back its siblings and rose high, gullet open wide for food.

As she tumbled, Simone kicked wildly. One of her boots flew off her foot. It fell into the baby pterosaur's mouth.

At once, perhaps an act of instinct, the hatchling snapped its beak shut.

A second later, Simone crashed onto the animal, then tumbled off into the nest.

It was true. Hiking boots *could* save your life in the wilderness.

But it was too early to celebrate. Baby imperators surrounded her. The big one spat out her shoe. They all crept closer, snapping their beaks. They were smaller than Simone, but not by much. And those talons and beaks looked sharp enough to rip her apart. Their mother loomed above the nest, as large as a giraffe and infinitely more terrifying. With beady eyes, she watched her hatchlings learn to hunt.

Simone grabbed a bone from the nest. She swung it through the air like a club.

"Stay back!" she cried.

Then she noticed what kind of bone she held. A femur. A human femur.

Human skulls lay at her feet.

Oh God. Oh God. She was panicking. The nest was spinning. Her vision blurred.

A hatchling leaped at her. Simone screamed and swung the bone with all her might. The femur slammed into the hatchling's head, knocking the beast aside.

"That's right!" Simone shouted. "That's right, you little buggers! Stay back! Or I'll club you all."

She swung the bone madly. She walloped another imperator on the head, only for the femur to snap in two.

Something leaped at her from behind.

Simone crashed down, landing face-first in the nest's straw bedding. Something heavy pinned her down. A screech filled her ears. Wings beat against her. A hatchling! A hatchling had sneaked up on her.

Pain blazed across her back. The young imperator was pecking at her.

Simone grabbed a human skull and swung it over her shoulder. The skull thumped against the hatchling. Teeth flew through the air. The little monster released her, squawking in pain, and Simone leaped to her feet.

Her knees wobbled. She took a few stumbling steps, tripped over something, and fell down again. Her tailbone throbbed. She scampered backward, wriggling on her bottom, until her back hit a barrier. She had reached the rib cage that surrounded the nest. A rib *cage* indeed—a cage she was trapped in.

The hatchlings tottered toward her, their talons clumsy. A few still had eggshells clinging to their fuzzy bodies. They could not yet fly and barely walk. But they could feed. They were very good at that.

Simone sat with her back to the rib cage, weaponless. The hatchlings opened their beaks wide, baring rows of razor-like teeth.

That's when Simone noticed what she had tripped over.

An egg.

An unhatched egg.

That's my ticket out of here, she realized.

She leaped toward it.

A beak pecked her shoulder, drawing blood. A claw slashed her arm. But she managed to reach the egg, grab it, and lift it overhead.

"Stand back!" she shouted. "Back or I crush the egg!"

Brilliant, she told herself. *As if they speak Nyxian.*

But perhaps the imperators understood her tone, if not her words. The mother, who was still looking down upon the nest, let out a terrible cry. The hatchlings froze and retreated.

"That's right, stay back!" Simone said, holding the egg overhead. She looked up at the mother. "You too, cheesecake, or I'll turn your baby into an omelet!"

Cheesecake, huh? she thought. *I'm already dressed like a Mintarian, and now I'm talking like one. I just need to be eaten by a dinosaur to achieve the full trifecta. Not today, Mintari. Not today.*

She walked sideways, gripping her oval hostage, until she found an opening in the cage of bones. Egg held overhead, she stepped out of the nest.

The mother imperator leaned down, hissing. God, she was huge. Definitely big enough to gulp down a redhead.

"Back!" Simone cried. "Back or I'll drop your egg!"

She held the egg menacingly over the cliff. The lake churned far below.

The mother imperator let out a deafening shriek, blowing Simone's hair back and nearly sending her tumbling down to her death.

"Now I'm going to slowly walk toward those trees," Simone said. "Once I'm far enough, I'll put the egg down and—"

Wings beat.

A screech tore the air.

A pteranodon soared from a nest below, grabbed the egg right from Simone's hands, and flew off with the tasty treat.

The colorful imperator completely forgot about Simone. She beat her wings, racing after the fleeing egg-napper.

Simone ran.

She had only one boot on. She was bleeding from hatchling pecks. But she ran faster than she had ever run in her life. Maybe faster than anyone had ever run. Add an Olympic medal to her best scream award.

The pterosaurs battled above—one a mother protecting her egg, the other a hungry opportunist. They clawed and bit and beat their wings. Simone ran under the dueling giants and headed toward the cover of the trees.

Finally—after what seemed an endless marathon, but was probably just a quick dash—Simone reached the grove of cycads. She crashed to her knees among the trees, shielded by their canopy of fronds.

For long moments, she breathed heavily, waiting for her heart to stop pounding.

I'm alive. I'm actually alive. Miracle of miracles.

A hiss sounded ahead.

Simone froze.

Slowly she looked up. A little eoraptor stared at her, mouth opening to revealing tiny but sharp teeth.

"Oh, go to hell!" she shouted, pulled off her second boot, and hurled it at the chicken-sized theropod.

The diminutive dinosaur fled. Meanwhile, the pterosaur cries faded. Simone was safe.

And then the tears came. She trembled with trauma and relief. She was alive. She could breathe. She could take another breath and another and another—all those breaths denied to Elize. To her sweet twin who had died in her arms.

"I should have saved you," Simone whispered. "If only I were braver. I'm sorry, Elize. I'm sorry."

Footsteps shook the grove.

A rumble sounded ahead.

Something was charging toward her—something much larger than a eoraptor.

Simone rose to her feet. Her tears stopped flowing at once. She grabbed a rock and raised it, prepared to fight if she must. It seemed you never did get much of a break on Mintari.

Rosetta burst out from the trees, halted, and reared like a horse. Her bony frill flashed with brilliant blue and purple patterns. When the chasmosaurus brought her front feet down again, she shook the grove. Cycad fronds fell and a trunk cracked.

California Cody leaped off the animal's back. It was a long way down, but the shaggy-haired cameraman managed to land on his feet. He raced toward Simone and pulled her into his arms.

"Dude! Dude, you're alive. Thank God. I'm here, dude. I'm here to save you."

"Um, thanks, Cody. I appreciate it."

He stepped back, grinning. "Oh, by the way. Being snatched up by the pterosaur? Totally. Gnarly. I got most of it on camera."

Triassic Terry leaned out the howdah and grinned. "So, cheesecake, you wanna ride on Rosetta from now on?"

They headed east again, slowly making their way through the forest. Terry sat atop Rosetta's head, leaning against the dinosaur's colorful frill. Simone sat inside the howdah, huddling against Cody. In the distance, the forests swept into a misty valley, and beyond rose the silver mountain where a legend was said to live.

"Welcome to Marshwood Forest!" Triassic Terry gestured around him theatrically. "Named after Othniel Charles Marsh, one of history's greatest paleontologists. Over a thousand years ago, back on Earth, Marsh discovered the skeleton of a stegosaurus. Today, in these very woods that bear his name, the stegosaurus lives again."

Simone peered out the howdah, looking around the forest. She shivered. "I hope we don't see one."

Riding on Rosetta's head, Terry grinned. "Aww, they're harmless, cheesecake. It's the ceratosaurs you want to worry about. They live around these parts too. They eat stegosaurs."

"D-do they eat humans?" she asked.

Terry nodded. "Oh, they love any meat, especially if—"

"Dude, chill!" Cody said to the guide. "You're bumming her out. And me too." He patted Simone's shoulder. "You're safe, dudette. Don't worry. No dinosaur will get close to you. Not with me here."

"We're riding a dinosaur right now."

Cody tilted his head. "Dude, you're right. I forgot. Okay. No dinosaur other than Rosetta will get close."

Simone shuddered. Whenever she closed her eyes, she saw the terrible hatchlings again, snapping their beaks at her. "I hope we're almost at Mudge Mountain." She dropped her voice to a whisper. "Cody, I'm not sure how good a guide Terry is. He didn't seem bothered when that pterosaur grabbed me."

"Terry?" Cody whispered back. "He seems pretty harmless. Tactless, yes, but harmless."

"Maybe you're right," Simone said. "He just ... doesn't seem to care whether I live or die."

"I care," Cody said. "You know that, dude, right?"

Simone smiled and hugged him. "I know, dude. You've always cared. We've been through a lot together, haven't we?"

"Totally! We've had some gnarly adventures. But nothing like this! The way you fought off those dinosaurs? That was bitchin'! I wish I'd had a camera in that nest."

"Cody, next time a dinosaur kidnaps me, don't film it. Attack it."

"Oh. Right." He nodded. "Totally."

Simone hoped she'd reach Jurassic Joe soon. Between her cowardice, Terry's nonchalance, and Cody's ditziness, she'd feel much safer around a seasoned Ranger. It would be a miracle if they survived that far.

"Cody, do you still have that map?"

He nodded. "Totally do, dude. Let's see where we are."

The cameraman had picked up the map outside the Tar Pit. Locals were selling them for a handful of clovers. He unfolded it across his lap. The map was clearly drawn for tourists, and mostly for the kiddos. Cartoon dinosaurs roared on the margins. The volcanoes, trees, and canyons were all equally cartoonish. The volcano even had an angry face.

Simone tapped the map. "Here is Dinovia City, where we started. Here is Pterosaur Kingdom." She shuddered. "Now we're here. Past the cliffs. In Marshwood Forest."

Cody nodded, studying the map. "Once we're past the forest, we just need to cross Hell Valley. Then we're at Mudge Mountain. Where Jurassic Joe lives. Dude, we're almost there!"

"Just need to cross … Hell Valley." She gulped. "Assuming we even make it out of Marshwood alive. What was that predator Terry said lives here?"

The tour guide's voice came from outside the howdah. "Ceratosaurus, cheesecake! Nasty bugger. Huge teeth. Designed for carving through flesh. I once saw a pack take down a sauropod. They bit off his head."

"Whoa!" Cody's eyes widened. "That's gnarly! Can they bite off Rosetta's head too? Even with her horns?"

Simone leaned out the howdah. "Stop eavesdropping!" she said to the guide. "Both of you be quiet."

Thankfully, nothing had attacked them in Marshwood so far. So far. Riding a living tank with giant horns probably helped deter predators. Maybe, just maybe, Simone was safe. At the end of the day, though she hated to admit it, hiring Terry might have been a good idea.

She leaned back in her seat, hugged herself, and closed her eyes.

The hatchlings snapped their beaks at her. She could see their bloodshot eyes, hear their terrible caws …

Stop it.

Simone forced her thoughts away. She brought to mind her twin. She thought of Elize's cascading red hair, her laughing blue eyes, her infectious smile.

I miss you, Simone thought. *You were my other half. I'm half a woman now. I'm lost without you.*

In her mind, she imagined that she could hear Elize's voice. *I'm still here. I'm with you. I'm watching over you. I'm here.*

Simone didn't know if she believed in an afterlife. But whenever she thought of Elize, whenever she imagined her twin here, she felt soothed. The grief rose too, yes, and she missed her sister so badly she ached. But she also felt a loving warmth spread over her. Perhaps that was Elize's love, shining from a world beyond like sunlight through clouds. Perhaps Simone only imagined it. Whatever the case, she thought about Elize every day, keeping her alive in her memory.

When Simone opened her eyes again, Nyx was setting. Beams of red sunlight cascaded through the forest. Coos and caws sounded in the shadows. Ferns rustled. Somewhere in the distance, yellow eyes shone, then a creature hooted and vanished among the trees. Simone clutched Cody's arm.

She stuck her head out the howdah. "Terry! I thought we'd reach Mudge Mountain by nightfall. The map says it's just a day's journey."

Sitting on Rosetta's head, the tanned tour guide looked over his shoulder. "Sorry, cheesecake. They mean by jippi. My dear Rosetta takes her time." He patted the dinosaur's lumpy head. "Takes my baby girl two or three days to reach the mountains."

"Two or three days!" Simone blurted out.

Terry shrugged. "Slow and steady wins the race. Jippis go fast. Jippis get knocked over easily. Rosetta is slow but steady."

Simone sighed. She had barely survived her first day in the wilderness. Could she truly survive two more? She looked out the howdah at the rustling ferns and moving shadows. The sun was setting fast.

"Are there any way stations along the way? Maybe a tavern or nice hotel?" She smiled uneasily, daring to hope.

"Sorry, cheesecake, but this is dino country. We're spending the night in the great outdoors."

Simone looked at the rustling ferns and lumbering shadows. "O-out here?"

Even in the darkness, Terry's smile was bright. "Don't worry! I brought blankets."

They set camp among the trees. Simone didn't like the idea of sleeping in the woods. A predator could be lurking behind every tree and boulder. Then again, the next location on the map was called Hell Valley. So maybe Marshwood wasn't so bad after all.

She missed the slums of Earth. Sure, they were swarming with cannibalistic warlords and deranged cyborgs. But at least there were no creatures who could decapitate a sauropod.

Triassic Tours came with complimentary dinner, which Rosetta had carried in her saddlebags. Peanut butter and jelly sandwiches. As Simone ate, the boys built a campfire. They had nothing to roast, and the night was hot, but the fire would deter predators, Terry explained. Once she heard that, Simone put aside her sandwich and helped them stack firewood.

"Anyone for scary campfire stories?" Terry asked once they were seated around a crackling fire.

"No, thanks," Simone said ... just as Cody blurted out, "Totally!"

Apparently Cody was louder, since Terry launched into full theatrics. He even placed a flashlight under his chin for effect.

"You want a scary tale, do you?" he intoned dramatically.

"Nope," said Simone.

"Well, I'll tell you a tale!" Terry said. He probably rattled off the same show for anyone foolish enough to hire Triassic Tours. "A tale of the most dreaded dinosaur on Mintari. Some would say the most dreaded dinosaur who ever lived. King Ivan! The devourer!"

Cody whimpered and clung to Simone.

"Oh for crying out loud!" Simone said.

Terry leaned forward menacingly. The flashlight painted his face red. "You've all heard of Tyrannosaurus rex. The most brutal killer in history. But Ivan is no regular rex. He's bigger. Faster. Smarter. As smart as men. His scales are black as night, his eyes as red as the blood of his victims. They say he's a mutant."

"A *mutant*!" said Cody. "Whoa! Gnarly, dude! Can he shoot lasers from his mouth?"

Simone rolled her eyes. "Oh for the love of—"

"He doesn't need lasers," said Terry. "Ivan doesn't like to kill from afar. He likes to get close to you. Maybe in a dark forest like this one." He looked around theatrically, then leaned dangerously close to the fire. "And when you least expect it, he leaps out. He's as big as a whale, but he moves as silently as a shadow. You never see him coming. Before you know it, his mighty jaws close around you. If you're lucky, he'll swallow you whole. If you're unlucky, well ... those teeth of his. Terrible teeth. Teeth longer than my arm. But they're dull, you see. They're not sharp teeth. They're not designed for ripping flesh."

"Phew." Cody wiped his brow.

"They're designed for crushing bone," Terry said. "When teeth are thick and dull like his, they crush bones into powder. It hurts much more that way. Takes you longer to die. Just how Ivan likes it. You see, Ivan doesn't just hunt to eat. No. He hunts for pleasure. He enjoys inflicting pain. He enjoys the screams of his victims."

Cody's bottom lip trembled. He whimpered, grabbed Simone, and huddled against her.

"Oh for crying out loud, Cody!" Simone said. "It's just a tall tale. There're no such things as mutant T-rexes with superintelligence. Even I know that much."

Terry raised an eyebrow. "Maybe you should ask Jurassic Joe about it. He's met Ivan before."

"Whoa, and he survived?" Cody said. "Jurassic Joe is one certified tough dude."

"He survived, yes," said Terry. "But not his wife. Ivan devoured her. Joe saw it happen. They say his wife was pregnant at the time. That it drove Joe mad. That he fled into the wilderness, taking only his grief."

"Oh, how horrible!" Simone blurted out. "Is this part real? Not just a tall tale?"

"Oh, Ivan is real all right. Never seen him myself. But I've seen the tooth …" The tour guide paused for effect.

"The tooth?" Cody whispered.

Terry nodded. "Jurassic Joe carries one of Ivan's dreadful teeth. He wields it as a sword. He used that very tooth, plucked from the mouth of the beast, to stab Ivan across the snout! Ivan still carries the scar. He never forgot who scarred him. He still wants revenge."

"Whoa!" Cody whispered, eyes so wide they nearly popped out.

"One day, they say, Joe and Ivan will meet again. They will fight an epic battle atop the highest mountain on Mintari. If Jurassic Joe wins, he will usher in an era of peace, and carnivores and herbivores will live side by side. Yet if Ivan wins … all the land will fall under his dark domain, and evil will consume Mintari."

Cody gasped. "Whoa! Like, do you mean evil will literally *eat* the planet, or do you mean *consume* like metaphorically?"

Simone rolled her eyes. "I'm going to bed."

Terry switched off his flashlight. "Both of you should get some beauty sleep. I'll take the first watch. We'll take shifts. I'll wake you up for yours."

"We need to watch?" Cody said.

The tour guide nodded. "For dinosaurs."

Cody whimpered and hugged himself. "Ivan!"

"Fine, wake me when it's my turn," Simone said.

She crawled into her sleeping bag. It was the same sleeping bag she had used on Earth, sleeping in the trenches of the Slum Wars. Simone had always prided herself on being able to sleep anywhere. A lumpy hotel bed, a cramped starship seat, or even a war zone—plonk her down and she could doze off. Ah yes, sleeping—her greatest talent. Yet tonight sleep eluded her. She tossed and turned, and it seemed that no matter what she did, there was always some root or pebble beneath her.

Cody was soon snoring. Terry sat nearby on his dinosaur, smoking a pipe. Simone lay in sleepless misery. No, it wasn't the pebbles or roots. It was the hatchlings. Their terrible beaks still clattered in her mind. And every time a pebble jabbed her, she imagined it was their bite.

Why was she so afraid? She had survived the Slum Wars! She had walked across the killing fields of Mars! She was a foreign correspondent. She was not some pampered socialite who had never left the glittering skyscrapers of Cloventia. Why was this planet getting to her?

But she knew why. Of course she knew why. Because of what happened to Elize. Because of ... the incident.

That's what the police had called it. The *incident*. Such a sterile word. Not a tragedy that shattered a family, that tore Simone apart, that took her twin from her. An incident. Just another report. Another statistic. One sister dead. The other left with crippling zoophobia. No big deal. Move on to the next incident. And soon everyone forgot.

But not me, Simone thought. *I'll never forget you, Elize.*

Her twin smiled in her mind. Elize stood in a meadow, radiant in the sunlight. Her red hair billowed in the wind, and her eyes gleamed. Her freckles were a field of stars. And lying here in the dark forest, Simone no longer felt so alone.

She fell into a deep, dreamless sleep, and even the hatchlings did not torment her.

When she finally woke up, it was dawn.

"Huh?" Simone blinked, yawned, and rubbed her eyes. "Terry, you never woke me to watch?"

She looked around, blinking until her eyes came back into focus.

"Terry?"

Cody was sleeping beside her, holding a teddy bear.

Triassic Terry and his dinosaur were gone.

CHAPTER SIX
The Butchers of the Jurassic

Simone and Cody stood in the sunrise, looking at the camp.

"He took everything," Simone said. "Our luggage. Our cameras. Our money. Everything. All gone."

Cody's eyes widened. "Did Ivan do this? Dude, did Ivan eat Terry and Rosetta and our cameras?"

Simone slapped him on the head. "No, Cody! Terry did it!"

He tilted his head. "Terry ate his dinosaur?"

"Terry rode off on his dinosaur. With our stuff. Leaving us to die."

"Ah." Cody grinned and nodded. "That makes much more sense. I was wondering why Ivan would eat cameras." He frowned. "Whoa. I think Terry robbed us, dude!"

"Of course he robbed us!" Simone snapped. "Cody, try to keep up with—" She sighed. "Oh, I'm sorry. I shouldn't take it out on you. It's my fault. I'm the one who hired him. You'd think that after interviewing cannibal warlords, I'd be a little less trusting of humans, but there you go. Simone LaRue, as gullible as always."

"At least you didn't think Ivan ate the cameras," Cody said.

She looked at him, arms hanging limply at her sides. "Cody, if I weren't so terrified, I'd laugh."

"Don't worry, dude. We'll find our way back to Dinovia. So long as I have my trusty map, I—" He looked around. "Dude! He even stole my map! This is a total bummer."

Simone closed her eyes. How could she have been so stupid? The barkeep had warned her against hucksters. And Simone LaRue, sophisticated genius that she was, hired the first tour guide she ran across at the bar.

She checked her backpack. Terry had rummaged through it, taking her money. He had left the *Mintari Field Guide*. And thankfully, the conman had missed her SmartSphere. She had stuffed the round computer into a sock to keep it dry. Terry had not found it. Not that it was worth much anyway. Lots of people bought expensive SmartSpheres with all the bells and whistles. Simone, who was still paying off her journalism school loan, owned only the most basic SmartSphere. The peach-sized computer included a basic camera, a calculator, a few games, and that was about it. She couldn't even use it to call for help.

They were stranded.

"We'll go back to Dinovia," Cody said. "I'll find Terry and pound him! How dare he steal my map?"

"He left us here to die," Simone said.

"That too."

"Without Rosetta's protection, we're as good as dead." Simone sighed. "He gets the expensive cameras. We get eaten. The perfect crime."

"Yeah, well, he forgot one thing," Cody said.

Simone looked at him.

Cody stood, chin raised, armed crossed.

"And that is …?" Simone probed.

"You, of course! You're Simone LaRue, star of *LaRue's News*. You're famous. You're tough. You survived being kidnapped by a pterosaur! Which was totally gnarly. You're the most badass babe I know, and if anyone can get us back to Dinovia alive, it's you."

Simone smiled thinly. "You're not so bad yourself, buddy." She placed a hand on his chest and looked into his eyes. "But we're not going back to Dinovia City. We still have a story to cover. We're going onward. Eastward. To find Jurassic Joe."

"Alone?" Cody gulped. "With a mutant T-rex out there?"

"Not alone. We have each other. If you'll go with me."

The cameraman snapped to attention and saluted. "Always. To hell and back."

"Good. Because next stop is Hell Valley." She pointed. "East is that way. Let's keep going."

They walked through the forest. The ferns and trees rustled at their sides. Simone was barefoot, having donated her boots to the pterosaurs. Soon her feet were aching, but she pressed on.

There was no path. No landmarks. And their compass had been in their stolen luggage. But the sun rose in the east on Mintari—the opposite of Cloventia. Just like on good old Earth. They simply must follow the light.

That and survive the dinosaurs.

But Simone figured there were dinosaurs ahead and dinosaurs behind. She might as well go forward.

For the first mile, she kept jumping at every rustle of leaves. But they only encountered small animals. Furry cynodonts rustled among the bushes—little fluff balls, grabbed from the Late Permian, who would later evolve into mammals. Dragonflies the size of seagulls glided over rivers. Thankfully, the largest dinosaur they saw was about the size of a turkey. According to the field guide, it was a velociraptor, a harmless little thing. The feathered theropod ignored them. It was busy chasing a dragonfly.

Gradually Simone relaxed. Her thoughts strayed to Terry's campfire tale. Surely most of it was hyperbole. But was there a grain of truth there? Had Jurassic Joe truly lost his pregnant wife to a T-rex? To Ivan, a *mutant* T-rex?

There were so many legends about the man. Even on Cloventia he was a mythological figure. Hop online and the urban legends spread to the digital horizon. Maybe Jurassic Joe was just a myth. Maybe Simone was on a wild-goose chase. But if he was real, she would uncover the truth once and for all. She would understand the man behind the myth.

A grunt sounded ahead.

Simone looked up and froze.

A dinosaur. And not just a little feathered thing. A big one.

Her heart seemed to stop in her chest.

"Darwin's beard," she whispered.

The dinosaur was the size of a jippi. Rows of dorsal plates, each the size of a knight's shield, rose along its back. The head was surprisingly small for an animal so large. But the tail made up for it. That thick, long tail ended with four mean spikes. They looked like they could give Rosetta's horns a run for their money.

Simone didn't need her field guide to recognize this dinosaur. Every child on Cloventia knew it. Here was the iconic stegosaurus. Simone even remembered what the spiky weapon on its tail was called. A thagomizer. Named after the late Thag Simmons. And this dinosaur's thagomizer looked powerful enough to shatter a brick wall.

The stegosaurus was designed to stab, slash, lacerate, and poke. It was basically a big spiky bundle of *back off*. But despite its fearsome appearance, the dinosaur remained calm. It was peacefully eating some ferns. It didn't bother chewing. Stegosaurus had no grinding teeth like other herbivores. The dinosaur would place each fern in its mouth, then pull with its teeth, stripping off delicate leaves, and gulp them down. Despite the animal's impressive size, its neck was short, its head small. The leaves of the trees were unreachable. This formidable dinosaur had grown so large by grazing on humble ferns and berries.

Of course, *large* was a relative term here on Mintari. This stegosaurus would not fit into Simone's apartment back home. But one of the patagotitans—those gargantuan sauropods Simone had seen from the astrolite—could step on a stegosaurus. Granted, it would probably feel like stepping on a Lego.

Simone and Cody stood among the trees, gazing at the spiky dinosaur.

"Whoa," Cody whispered. "Dude, can I borrow your SmartSphere? I want to film this."

Simone's knees trembled, and her heart raced. But amazingly, she wasn't panicking. Only days ago, a mouse would have made her scream. Now she stood gazing upon a living, breathing dinosaur, and she was not fleeing in terror.

She handed Cody her SmartSphere. The camera was basic. Nothing like the expensive cameras Terry had stolen. But Cody started filming nonetheless. If anyone could get a good video from a cheap old SmartSphere, it was California Cody. The stegosaurus went about its business, munching on ferns and fruits, ignoring the two humans.

"This one isn't so bad," Simone said. "Not that I'd want that thagomizer swinging anywhere near me."

The stegosaurus grunted and took a few steps closer. But it wasn't attacking. It was simply moving to a fresh batch of ferns.

The dinosaur didn't even spare the two humans a glance. Whimpers came behind the feasting herbivore, and Simone's heart melted.

"Look, Cody! Babies."

Three stegosaurus hatchlings followed their mother. They were no larger than ponies. The stegotots moved under their mother's tail for protection, found a patch of ferns, and tucked in.

Simone took a step closer. A strange desire filled her to connect with this gentle mother. Maybe even to pat her.

Go on, Elize told her, smiling in her mind. Her sister's warmth filled Simone. Giving her permission to let go. To be brave. Yet still Simone hesitated. This was after all an animal. Gentle, beautiful, yes, but still an animal.

Forget about the so-called incident, Elize said. *Go pat this magnificent creature.*

Simone stepped closer, hand held out. The stegosaurus kept eating, allowing her to approach. Simone reached out her hand and—

A deep rumble sounded in the forest.

Simone scampered back.

The stegosaurus raised her head and emitted a low bellow. Her babies mewled.

Footsteps thudded in the distance. The trees swayed and leaves showered down. One trunk snapped and the ginkgo tree crashed down.

It burst out from the trees, howling for blood.

A predator.

The beast was enormous. As large as the stegosaurus, maybe larger. A big male, by the looks of him. He ran on two powerful legs with three clawed toes. His arms were short but tipped with scythe-like claws. A great horn thrust up from his snout like a rhino, and two more horns rose atop his scaly brow. Crimson scales covered his body, while a mane of yellow fuzz stretched along his back and tail. The monster bared rows of razor-sharp teeth.

Simone screamed.

She recognized this dinosaur. She had seen it in her field guide, and Terry had warned them that it hunted in these woods.

The dreaded ceratosaurus.

The horned theropod leaped toward the stegosaurus.

But the herbivore, who had seemed so peaceful moments ago, was not so tame when threatened. Especially not with babies to protect. With a furious cry, the stegosaurus swung her spiky tail.

The thagomizer lashed at the ceratosaurus. The predator leaped back, barely dodging the spikes.

Then, seeing an opening, the ceratosaurus lunged in attack. He was reaching for the stegosaur's flank. But the herbivore tilted, raising her dorsal plates like shields. The mighty predator's jaws, instead of finding meat, closed around one of the plates. The teeth punched through the bone. The stegosaurus howled in pain. The hungry predator bellowed, his teeth stuck in the plate. Trapped! He had bitten into bone and now he was stuck. His claws lashed furiously, carving through the stegosaur's flank, exposing a rib. Blood splashed the forest floor.

"No!" Simone cried.

Cody hushed her. He grabbed her hand and pulled her behind a mossy log. They hid, watching between ferns and mushrooms. The cameraman was filming everything.

The stegosaurus was still alive. Her babies were wailing. They could not survive without her. The mother swung her tail again.

This time her assailant was trapped. The carnivore's teeth were still lodged into the dorsal plate, holding him in place. The thagomizer plowed into the ceratosaurus. Four swordlike spikes drove into the predator's flesh.

The horned hunter bucked in agony, finally ripping out the stegosaurus's dorsal plate. For a moment, he stumbled, head tilted back, his teeth still embedded into the dislodged plate. Then he collapsed onto the ground.

The spike wounds bled across his chest. He was down for the count.

Simone breathed in relief.

But her relief was short-lived.

Two more ceratosaurs burst out from the trees, leaped onto the stegosaurus, and began biting and slashing.

The wounded mother fought hard, tail swinging. But she was losing blood. Her swings were slowing down. She managed to slash one ceratosaurus on the leg. But while she was doing that, the second theropod lunged, closed his mighty jaws around her neck, and chomped down hard.

The stegosaurus's eyes rolled back.

She thumped down onto the forest floor. Her tongue hung out.

Her babies mewled. They approached her, nudged her. But their mother was dead.

The two surviving ceratosaurs did not feed upon the mother. Not yet. Her skin was thick, her meat tough. There was a juicy appetizer to enjoy first. Licking their lips, they stepped toward the succulent babies.

"No!" Simone whispered, wishing there was something she could do. But she could only hide and watch.

A howl shook the forest.

Trees collapsed.

A male stegosaurus burst out from the foliage. He was larger than the predators, and the fury of the gods burned in his eyes. He charged and swung his tail, slashing one ceratosaurus across the flank. The dinosaur crashed down dead, gutted like a fish. The second horned carnivore quickly lost his appetite, turned tail, and fled.

Simone and Cody watched from behind the log. The male stegosaurus limped toward his mate. A gash from a ceratosaurus claw bled on his tail. Ignoring the injury, the spiky male nudged his fallen mate with his snout. Flies were already gathering over the female. The male nudged her a second time, then let out a mournful cry.

The hatchlings tottered toward their father and sheltered under his tail.

Gently, the father uprooted some ferns. But he did not eat them. He placed the ferns atop his fallen mate, nuzzled her, then woefully wobbled away. The stegotots followed, walking under their father's tail. They disappeared in the brush, leaving their dead.

Tears filled Simone's eyes.

I've known such loss myself, she thought. *Because my twin and I were prey. And Amissa was our predator. Amissa Triplehorn. And someday I know we'll meet again.*

"We should get going," Simone said.

Cody looked around. "Maybe we should wait a while. Make sure those predators are gone."

Simone gestured at the dead dinosaurs. Flies bustled over the corpulent corpses.

"These will attract scavengers. I want to be gone before they show up."

Cory paled. "Do you think Ivan is a scavenger?"

She grabbed him. "No, he only eats cameramen and gingers. Let's go."

Already they heard rustling in the bushes. Small, feathered raptors emerged. But they did not chase the humans. They leaped onto the meatier stegosaurus, shooed away the flies, and tucked in. Cody and Simone hurried onward through the forest.

Mintari was beautiful, yes, but hers was a feral beauty. The majesty of her dinosaurs shone upon a savage kingdom of predation and bloodshed. As Simone ran through the forest, she realized how small, how weak humans truly were. Without their technology, without their domestication and civilization, they barely climbed the first few rungs of the food chain. It was on Mintari that man was stripped bare of all pretenses and ambitions, revealed for what he truly was: a naked ape, afraid in the dark. It was in this Darwinian jungle that Jurassic Joe lived, a man who found a way to climb the rungs, not only to survive but to become a legend.

I should be writing this stuff down, Simone thought. *I'll put some of this into my article. If I survive.*

They walked through the forest for hours. Simone thought they were moving eastward, but with only the sun to guide them, it was hard to be sure. The sun always just seemed *up* to her. Cody claimed he could tell east from the moss patterns on the tree trunks. Something about how moss grew differently in the morning sun and evening sun. To Simone, it all just looked like moss. Worry grew in her that they were lost, that they would wander this forest until starvation, thirst, or a hungry dinosaur killed them. The last option seemed most likely.

Indeed, several times they heard rumbles, grunts, and heavy footfalls, and they hid under fallen logs or behind boulders. Once Simone even saw a ceratosaurus prowling in the distance, and she hid among ferns, heart pounding, until the horned predator wandered off.

Finally the trees of Marshwood thinned out. In the afternoon, Simone and Cody stepped onto a hilltop and beheld a grassy valley.

Cody nodded in satisfaction. "Hell Valley. We made it. I told you, dude. I know my way east."

Across the valley, maybe a day's walk away, rose Mudge Mountain. Home of the legendary wild man of Mintari.

Simone and Cody just had to cross an entire grassy valley. With no cover of trees. No places to hide. Two delicious humans in the open. For hours. What could go wrong?

It's suicide, Simone thought.

She gulped and almost returned into the forest. Then she remembered the theropods who hunted among the trees and the pterosaurs on the other side. There was danger everywhere on Mintari. The only exception seemed to be Dinovia City—if you ignored the hucksters and thieves. Maybe there was no safe place after all. She missed her apartment. She could be relaxing in her bath now with a mai tai, romance novel, and box of chocolates. But no, crazy Simone "Death Wish" LaRue just had to visit a planet of dinosaurs.

"Maybe we should stay in the forest until nightfall," Simone said. "Then move across the valley under cover of night."

Cody gulped. "Terry said that Ivan hunts at night."

"Ivan probably doesn't even exist." Simone patted her cameraman. "Just a myth."

"If Ivan is just a myth, so is Jurassic Joe."

"Touché. All right, Cody. I suppose predators hunt around the clock on Mintari. There's danger ahead and behind. At night and by day. Let's make a dash for it. The grass is tall. If we spot a predator, we'll crouch and hide."

"Maybe we should crawl the entire way," Cody said. "In case Ivan is awake."

"Sure, if you want to only reach the mountains by winter." She held his hand. "Come on, Cody. I'm the world's biggest scaredy cat. If I can do this, so can you."

They left the cover of trees, heading into the valley under the afternoon sun.

They called this place Hell Valley. But a grassy valley this size was more like Herbivore Heaven. As Simone and Cody walked across the grasslands, they were far from alone. Hundreds of dinosaurs roamed around them, feasting. Simone leafed through her dinosaur guide, and she recognized some of the species.

"Look!" Simone pointed. For a moment, wonder replaced her fear. "*Para … Parasau …*" She squinted at her guide. "*Para-sau-rolo-phus!* That's it. *Parasaurolophus.* What magnificent animals."

The *Para … Parasaurflufa …* something? Simone already forgot. She decided to call them parasaurs. The parasaurs were herding along a riverbank. Simone glanced down at her guide. They were a type of hadrosaur, also known as duckbill dinosaurs.

With their big bills, they plucked reeds and horsetails. They were heavy animals, roughly the size of elephants.

Their most striking feature, however, was not their size or hungry bills. It was the crests that grew from their heads, curling backward like pompadours. Those crests were as long as elephant trunks. While the dinosaurs' skin was greenish, their crests were bright red, yellow, and blue. Their purpose soon became apparent. A female parasaur, her crest a relatively tame yellow, approached a group of males with larger, showier crests. She waddled right up to the male with the biggest, most colorful crest, and they proceeded to mate.

"Cody!" Simone laughed. "Can't you give them some privacy?"

The cameraman crouched in the grass, aiming the SmartSphere. "Gotta capture the majesty of nature, dude."

They kept walking. Many other herbivores were here. Iguanodons lumbered through the tall grass, munching away. They were heavyset, scaly dinosaurs with a seemingly unending appetite. Their jaws were full of molars designed to chew, chew, chew. A handful of cycads grew along a watering hole, and the iguanodons placed their front feet on the trunks, stretched toward the fronds, and stripped them bare.

The iguanos were massive animals—easily the size of mammoths. But they were dwarfed by the sauropods who wandered the valley.

"Whoa! Dude!" Cody pointed at the long-necked titans. "Those are totally epic!"

Simone leafed through the *Mintari Field Guide*. "I'm not sure what kind of sauropod they are. I think ... yes!" She tapped a page. "Brontosaurus."

They were truly titanic. When one lumbered by, his feet shook the earth. Even Cody, a tall man, could walk between their legs without ducking. Their tails alone were as long as buses. Their necks put giraffes to shame.

The brontos were slow behemoths. A human could easily outrun them. Every step took immense effort for an animal this big. Understandably, they didn't move much. When a brontosaurus found a good spot, he planted his feet firmly on the ground, lowered his head toward the vegetation, and went to town. The neck swayed from side to side, sweeping across the grasslands. The head sucked up grass, bushes, ferns, anything it could reach. The animals were essentially living vacuum cleaners. Once the area was clear of vegetation, the brontosaurus took a few slow, lumbering steps, found a new grazing spot, and proceeded to vacuum up the vegetation there too.

"I always thought their long necks were for reaching the treetops," Simone said. "I was wrong. They're for grazing large areas from a standing position. It saves them energy. A creature this large can't afford to walk too much. The neck does most of the moving. Like an elephant's trunk." She watched in wonder. "Look at how much they eat! Everything about them is optimized for this one task. Eating."

"Like me at the buffet." Cody's stomach rumbled. "Speaking of which, I'm famished. I wish we still had Terry's sandwiches. Say what you like about that sneaky dude, but he made a mean PB&J sandwich. Do you think Jurassic Joe has peanut butter and jelly in his cave?"

Simone's own stomach growled. They had not eaten all day. She wasn't quite hungry enough yet to graze along with the herbivores, but another day or two and she'd be down on her knees with them, munching away.

They kept walking across the grasslands, giving the dinosaurs a wide berth. These were herbivores, true, but they were still dangerous. The herbivores of Mintari were no weaklings. These were no timid sheep. They wielded an array of spikes, horns, claws, and tails that could whip, club, or lacerate an enemy. On Mintari, herbivores were brawlers, just as deadly as carnivores. Simone and Cody kept their distance. If a herbivore so much as looked their way, they hid in the grass until it was safe to proceed. A territorial iguanodon could kill them just as surely as a hungry tyrannosaur. Herbivores they might be, but iguanodon thumbs sprouted claws as mean as any T-rex tooth.

They didn't dally long, however. The sun was moving westward, and Simone did not relish the idea of spending another night in the wilderness. They pushed on hard across Hell Valley. Cody's legs were longer, but Simone was probably more desperate and she kept up.

Finally, covered with burrs and bug bites, they reached the foothills of Mudge Mountain. The vegetation was thicker here, perhaps because the steep hillsides were hard for sauropods to walk on. Plant paradise. Ferns, brushes, and conifers covered the landscape. But farther east, the vegetation gave way to the soaring mountainside. Far above, the mountaintop shone with snow.

The sun dipped lower in the sky, sinking toward Marshwood Forest. The sunset painted the sky red, gilded the mountainside, and cast long shadows.

"Are you on that mountain, Jurassic Joe?" Simone said. "Watching us?"

Cody sucked his teeth. "It's a long climb, dude. But I figure Jurassic Joe would be living on the very top."

"Why is that?" Simone said. "For all we know, he lives at the bottom of the mountain."

Cody shook his head. "Not with Ivan roaming around. Safest up on the snowy peak. We can set camp tonight, and tomorrow morning, we can—"

A chorus of grunts and rumbles sounded behind them.

Simone turned around.

The herbivores were fleeing.

The crested parasaurs raced toward the distant forest. The iguanadons lumbered away as fast as their thick legs could carry them. Only the mighty sauropods, who stood in the grassland below the foothills, did not flee. They were too big for running. But they reared, stamped their feet, and raised their heads high, ready to fight.

Simone narrowed her eyes. "What is it? Do you see anything, Cody?"

They looked around, scanning the wilderness.

Nothing. No predators. Only ...

Then Simone saw it. She pointed at a patch of foxtails, bushes, and ginkgos. The vegetation was rustling. A creature was skulking. Maybe several creatures. And they were moving closer.

"It's Ivan!" Cody cried.

"Quiet!" Simone whispered.

But the cameraman's cry alerted the predators. They burst out from the brush, rumbling for meat.

Simone clutched Cody and let out a scream nearly as loud. She would definitely lose her voice before this trip was over.

It wasn't Ivan. But surely these creatures were just as horrible.

At first glance, they looked similar to T-rexes. But they were smaller. Only a quarter of the size, Simone estimated. Which was still bloody massive. Easily massive enough to eat Simone. Maybe just with a few bites instead of one. Their arms were proportionately longer than T-rex arms, and their hands sprouted scythe-like claws. Their teeth looked like a set of steak knives. Their skin was green and scaly, and spikes rose along their backs. Everything about these creatures seemed designed to stab, slash, or slice.

Simone recognized them from her book. Her heart nearly stopped.

"Allosaurus," she whispered. "The Butcher of the Jurassic. *Run!*"

They turned and ran up the foothills, heading through the brush toward the soaring mountainside.

The allosaurs bellowed behind them, chasing them among the trees.

Simone tripped over a root, screamed, and nearly fell. She managed to keep running. Cody ran at her side, eyes bugging out, his shaggy hair damp with sweat. When Simone glanced over her shoulder, the predators were closer. Darwin's beard, those dinosaurs were fast. They bounded easily over boulders, fallen logs, and bushes, charging toward the two humans.

Simone focused on running. Her arms pumped. She considered climbing a tree, but the conifers had smooth trunks. She would never make it. Hiding was no use. The predators would simply follow her scent. Her only hope was to reach the mountainside, climb the rocky slope, and hope allosaurs couldn't climb mountains.

The grumbles sounded behind her. Closer now.

Simone leaned forward, running with all her strength. She could not die here. Not after all this. Her side ached. Her lungs burned. But she forced herself to keep going.

You are Simone LaRue. You are a survivor. Run.

The trees and ferns parted ahead.

Another allosaurus burst out from among the brush.

The bushes rustled at her sides. Two more allosaurs leaped out from cover.

An ambush, Simone realized. *They herded us into an ambush.*

She skidded to a halt. Cody stopped running too, panting. Six allosaurs surrounded them. The predators no longer needed to run. Their prey was trapped. They closed in slowly, salivating.

We brought you back to life! Simone wanted to shout. *We humans restored you from extinction! This is how you repay us?*

She barked a laugh, and tears sprang into her eyes. A ridiculous thought. She was going to die now. Like Elize. Two sisters. Both killed by animals.

Cody lifted a rock. The tall cameraman snarled. His long hair was caked with leaves and dirt. Suddenly he seemed like some wild man of the mountains. He let out a howl and waved the rock menacingly.

"Get out of here!" he shouted. "I am a man! I am a predator! I'm not your prey. Get out of here!"

He hopped up and down, trying to make himself seem big and intimidating. Which was no easy task when surrounded by dinosaurs.

"Cody, no!" Simone cried.

He turned toward her. Tears were flowing down his cheeks. "I'll hold them off. Simone, run."

Then, with a howl, Cody charged toward an allosaurus. He hurled his rock with all his strength.

The rock hit the allosaurus on the chest, then thumped onto the ground. It did the dinosaur no harm. It was like a mouse throwing a pebble at a cat. Cody stood before the dinosaur, holding Simone's SmartSphere. Even now, he was filming.

Moving with lightning speed, the allosaurus lunged and closed its jaws around the cameraman.

"Cody!" Simone screamed.

The predator raised its head high, clasping Cody in its mouth like a dog biting down on a bone. The cameraman was still alive. Screaming. Kicking.

The allosaurus crushed him between its teeth. Another allosaurus ran up and bit at the dangling legs. A third joined the feeding frenzy. They gulped down chunks of meat, gurgling as they feasted.

A severed hand fell onto the ground.

It was all that remained of California Cody.

His hand was still holding Simone's SmartSphere. The round computer rolled to her feet. She lifted it, numb.

With his death, he created an opening in the circle of predators.

Blind with tears, Simone ran.

She ran between the conifers and ferns, heading to the mountainside. And the allosaurus pack followed. One human had not sated them.

The sun was almost gone now. Darkness cloaked the foothills, but they had her scent. And she could not outrun them.

One allosaurus leaped over a fallen conifer, landed in front of her, and hissed. Two more flanked her. They drew in closer, closer. Their teeth gleamed in the sunset, still red with blood.

Simone stood still and raised her head, waiting for the end. She would die standing tall.

I'll be with you soon, Elize.

A deep rumble shook the forest.

Not the sound of another allosaurus. This cry was even deeper. A rippling bass.

The trees shook.

The allosaurus pack hissed and recoiled.

With a trumpeting cry that rocked the mountain, a dinosaur burst out from the shadows.

A huge dinosaur. A dinosaur like a tank. Its head was bigger than a grand piano. Great stomping feet cracked boulders and snapped logs. Horns thrust forward like medieval pikes. The animal charged to battle.

Simone recognized it at once. An iconic dinosaur. Perhaps the strongest dinosaur on Mintari, rivaling even the mighty King Rex.

A triceratops.

When Simone was very young, her family had visited a museum of Earth culture. The museum floated among the skyscrapers of Cloventia, traveling the planet so that Cloventians everywhere could learn about their heritage. It had been five hundred years since the first Earthling colonists arrived on Cloventia, fleeing the barbarity of Earth. On the new world, they established a new civilization, one built on foundations of knowledge, cooperation, and excellence. A utopia.

It wasn't quite as successful as they had dreamed. Below the floating skyscraper, an underworld festered in the shadows. Nor was it always peaceful. Cloventia had fought a terrible civil war two hundred years ago, toppling the Sanhedrin and giving rise to the reign of the Silk Emperors. But in some form, at least, the founders' dream had come true. Cloventia was now a thriving planet. Far more industrious, cultural, and affluent than Earth. Billions of humans lived in privilege that Earthlings—those poor humans who remained behind—could barely envision. Cloventia was neon and wine and science. Earth was dust and famine and superstition.

Many Cloventians argued that they were indigenous, that they could not possibly be related to the cannibals, warlords, and dirty child soldiers of Earth, the ones they saw on the news. Sometimes on *LaRue's News*. Cloventians must be a breed apart. A breed of higher humans who had evolved right here. Some begrudgingly accepted that, perhaps, Earthlings and Cloventians shared a common ancestor. But surely they weren't the same *species*.

That always made Simone roll her eyes. And they said Earth was ignorant …

The Museum of Human History sought to enlighten Cloventians. To show them where they came from. One day, when Simone was eight or nine, the museum floated close to her home. She went with Elize and her parents to visit. They saw many historic artifacts from ancient Earth. The Statue of Liberty's head filled the lobby (the body had been lost in the biogenetic wars), and you could actually step inside it. Unfortunately, you could not sit inside Earth's first flying car. Too many teenagers used to make out in there, so now a steelglass cage protected the artifact. The *Voyager* spacecraft was on display too, one of the earliest objects humanity had sent into space.

One artifact that stuck in Simone's mind was relatively unimportant. Just standing there in the food court, abandoned between Happy Cow Shawarma, Dr. Nuggets, and Shakshuka Sheik. A bronze sculpture of a charging bull, larger than life. Apparently the bull had once stood outside the New York Stock Exchange. To this day, Simone didn't know what the New York Stock Exchange was. But as a child, the fierce statue dazzled her. The bull's head was lowered, his nostrils flaring, his horns ready to gore. For a long time, young Simone stood before that bull, hands on her hips, both fearing and challenging that bronze behemoth.

Today, when Simone saw the triceratops charge, she remembered that metal bull. Once more, she felt like that little girl in the museum, facing the majesty of a ferocious beast.

Of course, all of Mintari was essentially a museum. A planet-sized museum for creatures brought back from extinction. But this triceratops was no statue. No relic. He was alive. A big male. Bigger than that bronze statue. And he was furious.

He charged from the shadows, heading toward the allosaurus pack, rumbling for battle.

For a moment, the predators stood in place, uncertain whether to flee or fight. One moment was all the triceratops needed. Tons of horned fury bulldozed into one allosaurus.

The theropod never stood a chance. The triceratops was the size of a tank. His horns put the mightiest claymores to shame. Those dreaded horns crashed through the allosaur's green scales. The triceratops tossed his head back, raising the mighty predator overhead. An allosaurus weighed as much as a rhinoceros. And the triceratops lifted the beast on his horns, then hurled it through the air like a rag doll.

The allosaurus, this legendary Butcher of the Jurassic, was dead before it hit the ground. The corpse slammed down near Simone. She leaped aside, nearly crushed.

Four allosaurs still lived. And the trike's element of surprise was gone. The predators, working together, were a force to be reckoned with. The pack closed ranks. The carnivores bared their teeth and moved closer, ready to attack the mighty herbivore.

The triceratops pawed the ground, lowered his head, and snarled. He was ready for more.

The horned brute charged.

The allosaurs scattered, fleeing death by goring. One came at the triceratops from the side, hoping to bypass the terrible horns. But the triceratops was surprisingly nimble. His head swiveled around with remarkable speed, turning his horns toward the attacker. The allosaurus skidded to a halt. Too slow. A horn lashed it across the chest. Green scales flew through the night. Blood splattered the ferns. The allosaurus yelped and fell, chest ripped open.

The three other allosaurs lunged.

The triceratops reared and swung his head from side to side, struggling to keep them back. One allosaurus managed to close his teeth around the triceratops's bony frill. The carnivore tugged the frill, perhaps hoping to rip it off. The triceratops bellowed. The allosaurs gained heart, attacking with more fury.

A *boom* shook the forest.

Simone gasped.

A gunshot!

That was a gunshot!

The allosaurus released the frill and fell back, a feathered dart in its neck.

Through the darkness and terror, Simone had not seen it until now. But there he was. A man. A man was riding the triceratops!

The mighty herbivore stomped closer and knelt, lowering his enormous belly toward the ground. The man leaned down from above, holding out his hand.

"Get on!" he shouted, his face still cloaked in shadow. "There are more predators among the trees. Get on if you want to live!"

Simone grabbed the proffered hand.

The man pulled her onto the triceratops. This dinosaur didn't have a howdah. Not even a saddle. They rode bareback.

"Run, Dozer!" the man shouted. "Take us back home!"

The trike seemed almost disappointed. Simone guessed that an animal so strong never ran from a fight. She recalled something she had read in her book. The only animal T-rex feared was the triceratops. Tonight she saw why.

But then more allosaurs burst from the forest, their feathered crests standing on end. Their dreaded jaws snapped. And even the mightiest triceratops could not defeat an army.

Bellowing, Dozer ran between the trees. Branches whipped Simone. She clung to the shadowy man who sat before her.

An allosaurus leaped out from the shadows ahead, lunging toward the triceratops in a banzai attack. True to his name, Dozer bulldozed over the predator, first goring the butcher with his horns, then trampling him.

One thing was certain. On Mintari, you didn't have to eat meat to be tough.

The trike kept running. They emerged from the forested foothills onto the bare, rocky mountainside. For a dinosaur so large and bulky, the triceratops was surprisingly nimble. His massive feet clung to the mountainside, allowing him to propel his significant girth upward.

Simone looked over her shoulder, seeking the predators.

The allosaurs stood among the trees below, eyes shining in the shadows. They did not follow.

"Allosaurus is an ambush predator," said the man on the triceratops. His voice was deep and grainy. "They won't follow in open country under the moonlight. You're safe. For now. It was tarry foolish being out there alone."

"I wasn't alone," she whispered, and tears filled her eyes.

The man slapped the dinosaur's hide. The triceratops rumbled to a halt, grunting. Steam rose from his nostrils. The dinosaur knelt, lowering his gargantuan head toward the ground. The man slid off the dinosaur, then all but yanked Simone down with him. She nearly fell and broke her neck, but the man caught her, then placed her firmly on the ground.

They stood in the shadows. The man wore a wide-brimmed ceratop hat, and the moonlight did not touch his face. He ignored her, whispering to the dinosaur, soothing him, checking him for wounds. A gash was bleeding on Dozer's hide. The man reached into a pouch and smeared ointment into the wound. Dozer grunted and stamped his feet but took his medicine.

"Go back to your grazing, old friend," the man whispered, caressing the dinosaur's beak. "Go and feed and mate and heal. I'll call you back when the time comes."

Darwin's beard, that animal was enormous. The head alone was a good nine or ten feet long. The horns were a foot in diameter, tapering to sharp points. This gargantuan beast nuzzled the man, who seemed so small beside him, but it was clear who was master. With a quick look at Simone and another grunt, Dozer rumbled away into shadows.

The man stood among the trees, staring at Simone from under the shadows of his hat. The moonlight touched a tarnished crest pinned to his lapel. A triceratops head. A double-barreled rifle hung across his back, and a machete hung from his belt. No, not a machete—an enormous tooth with a hilt attached. A T-rex tooth.

"Who are you?" the man growled. "What the hell are you doing here?"

"My name is Simone LaRue, reporting for the *Cloventia Gazette*." She held out her hand. "And I came here to meet you, Jurassic Joe."

CHAPTER SEVEN
L'Enfant Sauvage

Figaro knew she was no ordinary dinosaur.

Most days, like today, it didn't matter much.

The pack had adopted her. Raised her. Defended her. So what if she looked different? She didn't have sharp pointy teeth. She didn't have any claws to speak of. She certainly had no feathers or scales, only black hair that grew atop her head. Oh, she knew she was different. That she looked more like some strange, bipedal mammal than a dinosaur.

Who cared? She was pack. She was loved. She belonged.

The day was hot, and the prey was thirsty. The herbivores must leave the cover of the trees and head to the watering holes. A good day for hunting. The pack raced across the plains. Figaro rode atop the big alpha male. Running on her own short legs, she would slow the pack down. But riding the alpha, she was as fierce as anyone in the pack. She bared her little teeth, and she raised her tiny fingernails in challenge. With her pack, she hunted.

The other hunters raced around her. The wind rustled their long red feathers. Their nostrils flared, inhaling the scent of prey. Saliva was already dripping between their teeth. Vicious teeth those were, serrated and long, optimized for slicing meat off the bone. Like Fig, the other hunters were bipedal. Each foot sported four sharp claws. Three of those claws ripped through the earth as they ran. But one claw, longer and sharper than the others, rose like a sickle. This claw was not for running. This claw they saved for slashing their victims.

They were achillobators. Predators the size of horses. Among the deadliest dinosaurs on Mintari. They were smaller than the big hunters like King Ivan, whom they feared. Smaller even than allosaurus, the Butcher of the Jurassic. But working as a pack, they were a force to be reckoned with. Figaro was proud to count herself among them.

Her own feet did not sprout claws, only stubby little toenails she sometimes nibbled when bored. But she did have a sickle claw of her own. She had ripped it off the cold, dead foot of White Feather, a huntress who had died battling an ankylosaurus. The claw was curved and longer than Fig's entire hand. Normally, she kept the weapon tucked into her belt—just a vine she had wrapped around her waist. But today Fig raised the claw overhead. So what if she looked different from other achillobators? She could kill as well as anyone. There was no room for weaklings in the pack.

The achillobator she rode gained speed, racing downhill toward the river. The land rose and fell around them. The wind whipped Figaro, fluttering the red feathers she had sewn into her hair. She tightened her legs around her mount. She resisted the urge to clutch a handful of feathers and cling on. She needed her hands for the hunt, and she dared not show weakness.

Among themselves, achillobators had no names. But Fig had invented names for them in her mind. The one she rode was named Red Scar. She had named him after the livid scar along his snout. Fig had given him that scar herself, carving through his scales with her sickle claw. He had tried to devour her that day. It had been winter, and they were all hungry. He came at her, jaws salivating. She could read his thoughts in his blazing eyes. *You are no bator! You are just food.*

She showed him what she thought of that. With a slash of her sickle claw, she had opened his snout from nostril to eye. Bleeding and whimpering, he knelt before her. *You are strong. You are pack.* She had scarred the beast that winter day, tamed him, made him her mount. Since then, she had ridden him on every hunt.

Red Scar's nostrils flared. The big alpha male tossed back his head. He gave three short yowls. The call meant that food was near.

The pack echoed his cry. *Prey! Blood! Flesh!*

Fig squinted, struggling to see in the sunlight. Her eyes were weaker than theirs.

There! She saw them!

A parasaurolophus family by the river. Fig licked her lips. Parasaurs were her favorite.

They were a type of hadrosaur. Duck-billed dinosaurs. The big herbivores heard the pack, raised their bills from the water, and bugled in fear. Unlike other dinosaurs, even other hadrosaurs, parasaurs did not vocalize using their throats. Instead, they blew air into elaborate crests that rose atop their heads. The air flowed like wind through a canyon, loud and eerie. They essentially had trumpets growing from their heads.

When she was very young, Fig had found parasaur crests frightening. They were longer than her entire body, bright red with yellow stripes, and they made awful sounds. But over time, she had learned that the crests were harmless. They were just color and noise. That was all. They were used for communication, intimidation, and display. Not as weapons. Harmless. In fact, Fig had learned to love parasaur crests. There was good meat on them for nibbling.

Her belly grumbled, already aching for the meal. Fig tossed back her head and let out three short cries.

"Yi! Yi! Yi!" *Prey! Prey! Prey!*

The parasaurs began to flee.

The pack howled and followed, their clawed feet ripping out grass and soil. They yipped for meat.

"Yip, yip, yip!" Fig cried out. *Meat, meat, meat!*

The parasaurs were panicking now. They were much larger than the achillobators. But the crested herbivores were no fighters. Big, dumb, and meaty. The perfect prey. Fig was already salivating. It had been a hard, long winter. Her limbs were stick thin, and her ribs pressed against her skin. Whenever she studied her reflection in still water, she saw a gaunt face, her eyes too large. But now spring was here. And the pack would put meat on their bones.

The bators ran faster. Bloodlust had seized them. Fig grinned and leaned forward as she rode, revealing as many teeth as she could. Her teeth might be smaller than her fellow pack members. But her heart was just as fierce.

The parasaurs fled toward the cover of the cycad grove. So predictable. They never learned.

The herbivores were almost at the trees when the rest of the pack pounced.

Five more achillobators burst from behind the trees, yipping for meat.

The parasaurs stopped running, reared, and blew more air into their crests. The clarion calls filled the grove, an eerie orchestra. The hatchlings crowded among the adults, mewling miserably. The parasaurlets were especially delicious.

Fig raised her sickle claw. It was time to kill.

With hungry shrieks, the pack of bators fell upon their prey.

It was Red Scar who drew first blood, biting the flank of a big male parasaur. The duckbill dinosaur reared, pawed the air, and lashed his tail. Fig ducked. The scaly tail swung over her head, rustling her hair. It had come close to crushing her skull. With a snarl, she leaped off Red Scar, vaulted through the air, and landed on the parasaur's back.

The herbivore bucked madly. Mad with hunger and the heat of the hunt, Fig drove her sickle claw into the parasaur's back.

The claw sliced through scaly skin and rubbery fat.

The parasaur howled and ran across the grass, wobbling on his two meaty legs. He was a big, juicy bull, weighing several tons. With sheer size and brute force, the duckbill barreled past Red Scar, breaking through the circle of bators. The crested duckbill ran across the plains, bugling in terror.

But Fig was still clinging to his back, riding the beast.

She grinned savagely, pulled her claw free, then drove it down again and again, tearing through scales. The living meat of the parasaur pulsed below the skin. Snarling, Fig pressed her face into the wound, grabbed a chunk of meat between her teeth, and ripped it out.

The parasaur yowled, still running. Fig climbed his neck until she reached the head. The dinosaur's crest rose before her, a blue trumpet taller than her. She wrapped her legs around the crest, then dangled upside down. Her short dark hair fell back from her grubby face. Clinging on with her legs alone, Fig slashed her claw across the parasaur's neck.

Blood spurted.

The dinosaur fell, shaking the earth.

Fig leaped off the corpse, tossed back her head, and howled in triumph. Hot blood dripped down her chin.

And she had almost thought herself a mammal! Like the little fluffballs that lived in the dirt! Ridiculous. Of course she was no mammal. She had red feathers strewn through her hair. She had a sickle claw. She was an achillobator, one of the pack. And today she had killed. She had taken down a giant.

The other bators were still fighting. Yellow Eyes, a fierce female, cornered a parasaurlet and lashed her sickle claw. The hatchling collapsed, belly slashed open. Red Scar and two other males took down a lumbering old cow, the matron of the herd. But only Figaro, the runt of the pack, had taken down a big bull in his prime. Hers was the greatest kill.

The other bators stared at her, yipping. They knew it. They bowed their heads before her.

They let the other parasaurs go. Achillobators were not mindless killers. It was not good to overhunt, to leave meat to rot. Rotting meat attracted dangerous scavengers. Better to let the others flee, breed, and return with more hatchlings another day.

This day, they had plenty of meat. This day, the pack feasted.

The rest of the pack joined the banquet. Not just the hunters but also the elders and juveniles. The youngest bators were so small Fig could cradle them in her arms, but their claws were sharp, and they carved off slices of meat and gulped them down.

One old male had only a handful of teeth left, and he must content himself with guzzling the soft entrails. He used to be an alpha male. Sad to see. Come winter, if he became too much of a burden, the old male would end up feeding the pack. Bators were not cannibals by nature. It was a last resort. But if times got tough enough, the pack would do whatever it must to survive. No meat was to be wasted. Not even grandpa.

Fig knew how precious meat was. But she was a picky eater. She had learned long ago to avoid some meats. Some parts of the prey, while good eating for the others, made her ill. One time, during a drought, the pack had stumbled across an old carcass. During lean times, bators were not above scavenging. They had swatted away the flies with their flightless wings, then buried their snouts into the old meat. Fig too. The other bators savored the well-seasoned meal. But Fig had lain for days in the nest, feverish, vomiting. Since then, she had learned what she could digest. Parasaur crests were good eating. So were fish. Old meat and offal made her ill. She would not touch them.

A soft stomach. It was another way she was different. Another weakness. She knew that physically, she was weakest in the pack. But not in every way. She was a slow sprinter, but she could run for longer distances. Her stamina put the others to shame. She was also the smartest, if she might say so herself. She was best at planning an ambush. Long after the others forgot, she still remembered the paths of the herbivore herds. Her hands were deft and her mind quick. She could cleverly use branches, vines, bones, and rocks to build traps. With a vine, stick, hooked claw, and worm, she could fish in the streams. She had even sewn herself a dress of red feathers that protected her soft skin. Nobody else could do such things. Nobody else could lift, manipulate, build. Just another way she was different. Little Figaro, the oddest achillobator who ever lived.

She looked at the pack. They were tucking into the duckbill dinosaur, stripping the meat off the ribs. Blood covered their snouts and dripped down their feathers, and their claws scratched through the earth.

Fig looked at the claw in her hand. It did not grow from her body. She held it. Another thing she could do that the others could not. Hold things.

What am I? she wondered.

The hunger had faded, clearing her mind. With her belly full, these pestering thoughts rose again. Lately, they never seemed to leave her for long.

She shoved them aside. Who cared? The day was hot, the eating was good. Fig leaned against a mossy boulder, nibbling on a parasaur crest. A true feast. Her favorite meal. She inhaled deeply, blew air into the crest, and heard the eerie sound emerge. She grinned. Ah, parasaur crests. They were so much fun.

That was when she saw it.

A figure on a distant hill.

Not a dinosaur. A figure that looked like her.

Figaro ran.

Her bare feet kicked up dirt. Her dress of feathers fluttered around her thighs. Heart pounding against her ribs, she raced toward the figure on the hill.

The rest of the pack did not follow. They were busy munching on the parasaur carcasses. Nothing short of a charging T-rex would move them now.

And it would probably take a charging T-rex to stop Fig. Her infamous curiosity, another trait that set her apart, roared inside her, propelling her onward. Running was costly in the wilderness. It burned precious calories, the currency of Mintari. You never knew where the next meal would come from. Dinosaurs ran for two reasons. To catch prey or escape predators. Nothing else was worth the cost of calories.

Fig ran for curiosity.

The figure stood there on the hilltop, watching her.

Fig halted a safe distance away, crouched, and raised her sickle claw. She stared, ready to fight or flee.

The figure on the hilltop stared curiously. Yes, this creature too was curious. Fig recognized the look in her eyes. Curiosity. An achillobator sometimes exhibited some inquisitiveness, but always in the hope of finding food, water, or a mate. Not curiosity for its own sake. That was what Fig saw in this strange animal's eyes.

Amazingly, this creature's spine was vertical. Like Fig's. She had never seen anyone else who stood upright. Many dinosaurs were bipedal. Bators were too. But their spines were always horizontal. Here on the hilltop—another animal that stood erect!

It was some kind of mammal, Fig suspected. A female cub, by the looks of her. But not like the little cynodonts who scurried underfoot. No, this wasn't just some fluffball. This mammal was bigger. As big as Fig. And her only fur grew from her head.

No, not fur, Figaro thought. A memory tingled her, and she touched her head. *Hair. Like mine.*

It was undeniable. This strange creature looked like her. The soft skin. The small teeth. The hands with five fingers and opposable thumbs. This stranger even held something—a furry carcass with dead black eyes. Fig had never seen a dinosaur able to hold anything. Bator hands were made for slashing, not holding.

The cub waved. "Hello. I'm Emily." She raised the furry carcass she held. "This is Mr. Stuffings, my teddy bear. Oh gosh, are you wearing a dress of feathers?"

Fig snarled. She crouched lower, prepared to pounce, and bared her teeth. She sliced the air with her sickle claw.

"Yip! Yip!" she barked. A challenge. She clawed the soil with her foot and growled.

The strange mammal tilted her head. "You're funny. What's your name?"

Fig let out a low growl. She snapped her teeth at the stranger.

Who are you? What are you?

She had so many questions, but she didn't know how to ask. So she only yipped and snorted and growled.

The cub held out her carcass. "Here, you can have Mr. Stuffings. You seem lonely. Do you live out here alone?"

A voice sounded from across the hill.

"Emily! Emily, get back here! No wandering off. Do you want a T-rex to get you?"

The cub looked over her shoulder. "Mom, there's a girl here!"

"Emily, get back here now! Do you want your father to come get you?"

A deeper voice sounded from the valley. "Let the girl play, Beverly."

"She can play once we're back at the hotel. Until then I don't like her leaving the jippi."

"You never give her any independence. She's seven years old, and you still mother her."

"Greg, can we not do this now? We came on this vacation so we can ..."

The voices kept going. Fig was amazed that she actually understood them. How could she understand the strange speech of these mammals?

Emily heaved a sigh. "I'm sorry. I have to go." She placed the carcass on the ground. "Here, Stuffings will keep you safe out here. My mom says that dino country is dangerous. My dad says she's neurotic." The cub turned to leave, then looked back. "Oh, before I go. What's your name?"

Fig stared at her blankly, saying nothing.

"Emily!" came the voice from the valley.

"Coming!" the cub said and ran off, disappearing down the far side of the hill.

Fig bounded after her. But on the hilltop, she heard grumbles and smelled smoke. Predators! Forest fire! At once, she crouched in the tall grass and stared into the valley.

No predators. No fire. The strangest dinosaur she had ever seen stood on the ground. It was made of some gleaming material like basalt or granite. Its six legs were round, and its eyes shone like two stars. Smoke rose from its backside.

Strangest of all—the dinosaur was hollow. Two more mammals, similar to Emily but larger, sat inside it.

"Emily, get into the jippi now!" said one of the larger mammals. The female, it seemed.

The cub hopped in. "Mom, I saw a girl. Honestly, she was right there!"

"Where is your teddy bear? Did you lose it? I swear, Emily, if you keep losing your toys, I will—"

"I didn't lose it. I gave it to the strange girl with feathers."

The big male mammal laughed. "She's got an active imagination, our little one, that's for sure."

The big female groaned. "I'm glad you find this amusing, Greg. I hope you're also amused when a T-rex eats us."

"No T-rex is going to eat us, Beverly. Calm down."

"Don't tell me to calm down! You got us lost. Why did I ever agree to this vacation? We could have holidayed at Blue Moon Resort again. Now we're lost in dinosaur country, miles away from the other tourists, only God knows where our guide is, and—"

"Beverly, I know exactly where we are. I got my GPS here, and—"

"GPS doesn't work on Mintari, Greg. This isn't Cloventia. There are no satellites."

"Well, my compass still works, and besides, I know exactly where we are. We just need to drive toward that grove of conifers, then ..."

Belching smoke, the hollow dinosaur—this *jippi*—rolled away on its round legs, carrying the bickering family away.

Fig remained on the hilltop, watching the strange mammals disappear in the distance.

But no. They were not strange mammals. They were familiar. Somewhere deep inside her, a memory flickered. Knowledge she had almost forgotten bloomed again like seeds after a long winter.

Humans.

Those were humans.

Fig trembled. Her head spun and her heart raced. Emily's question echoed in her mind.

What's your name? the cub had asked.

Tears flowed down Fig's cheeks.

My name. I have a name.

She opened her mouth, and for the first time Figaro could remember, she spoke. Just a single word. A word that shook her to her core.

"Fi-ga-ro."

The achillobators were still bumming around their kills, lounging in the sun and digesting their meal. Mostly likely, they would remain there all day. Instead of returning to the pack, Fig walked downhill and approached the river. The same river the hapless parasaurs had been drinking from.

Fig shooed aside frogs, parted the reeds, and leaned toward the water. Her reflection gazed back at her. Mud, bits of leaves, and parasaur blood covered her face. What a mess! She ducked her head under, scrubbed herself clean, then looked again. Ah, there she was.

She saw a round, gentle face. No scales. No fangs. Just soft skin like a newborn bator. Her eyes were large and brown. Black fur grew from her head instead of feathers. She often cropped it short with sharp stones, but it kept growing and falling over her eyes. No, not fur. Something called hair. She remembered. A memory from before time.

Yes. She looked like the cub on the hill. A little older, maybe a little larger. But so similar it scared her.

"Coo, coo?" she said to her reflection. A bator's inquisitive call.

Who are you, strange hunter?

She tilted her head. A breeze ruffled the red feathers strewn into her hair.

A girl, she thought, the word rising from somewhere deep in her memory. *A human girl.*

No. No!

She was an achillobator. A proud, fierce huntress. She was a little smaller, yes. A little different. But still a member of the pack.

She bared her teeth at her reflection and growled. There you go. See? Totally a fierce bator.

A fish swam by. She reached down, caught it, and gutted it on the riverbank. She ate the soft pink flesh. Fish was good food. Food she could eat without vomiting. She glanced around, made sure nobody was watching, and plucked some berries from a bush. She stuffed them into her mouth. Berries were a rare and secret treat.

Then she realized what she was doing. What kind of predator ate fruit? No self-respecting bator would eat berries! She spat them out, ashamed. Eating berries was something a human would do. Not her!

Fig vowed to eat lots of parasaur this spring. Fish was fine too. She would put some meat back on her skinny little bones. It had been a hard winter. But soon she would feel like a proper bator again. And all this human nonsense would go away. Maybe finally this year her feathers would grow, and she wouldn't need to collect fallen feathers and tie them onto her body.

Belly full, she bounded back toward the pack. They were still lazying around the parasaur carcasses, gnawing on ribs.

Ah, good. Fig raised her chin, feeling better at once. Fellow bators! Here was where she belonged. With her kind.

Lightning Foot, the fastest young male in the pack, and White Feathers, an albino, were battling over a wishbone. Half Tail, who donated half his tail to an allosaurus three springs ago, was snoring on a pile of bones. Four Tooth, the pack elder, was chewing on the softer tripe, doing the best he could with the four teeth he had left. An ankylosaurus had knocked out the rest, and they had never grown back. Fig doubted the old bator would last another winter.

She walked among them, collecting fallen feathers to add to her collection. She planned to tie a few new ones over her arms. Just until her own feathers grew in. Any day now.

A jarring *caw* disturbed her search. Crooked Wing rose from a carcass, snapping her teeth in challenge. Strands of meat dangled between her bloodied teeth.

"*Caw! Caw!*" Crooked Wing cried.

She was a large female, strong and merciless. If not for her crooked left arm, she might have led the pack. Bators mostly relied on their powerful back limbs. Their arms were shorter and thinner, covered with feathers, essentially forming flightless wings. They were used to seize prey while hunting. Crooked Wing had broken one of her front limbs last winter, tumbling down a mountainside. It had not healed right, leaving her with one crooked wing. Even the feathers on that limb were bent and bristly.

The bator blamed Figaro for causing the landslide, tumbling the first stones with her clumsy, clawless feet. A ridiculous accusation, of course. Fig could no more cause a landslide than a volcano eruption. But Crooked Wing considered Fig a runt, and what were runts good for other than scapegoating?

"*Caw!*" the big female repeated, glaring at Fig with her beady red eyes. She placed a talon on the parasaur carcass. That foot was massive and tipped with claws. The three smaller claws pierced the meat. The fourth claw, the sickle claw, rose in the air, ready to strike.

A clear message. *Mine. No meat for you.*

Fig was already full. She had only been looking for feathers, not meat. But she could not back down from a challenge. If she showed submission now, Crooked Wing would only escalate her torments. This wasn't just about meat. It was about the hierarchy of the pack.

Crooked Wing leaned across the carcass and snapped her teeth at Fig. The sickle claw twitched. The big bator leaned closer, growling. Her feathers bristled, making her look larger, more intimidating. Bloodlust filled her eyes.

A shadow darted.

Red Scar leaped forward. His jaws opened wide, displaying rows of serrated teeth. Strings of saliva dangled like harp strings. The big male let out a deafening screech.

The message was clear. *Do not touch the runt! She is under my protection.*

Crooked Wing whimpered and stepped back. The aggressive female lowered her head.

Figaro leaned forward, opened her own humble jaws, and roared.

"Ra! Ra!" she barked and snapped her teeth at Crooked Wing.

Back, back! Back or I'll bite!

Crooked Wing kept her head lowered. But she glared at Fig with venomous eyes. She bared her teeth, and a low growl rolled from her throat. Still showing some spirit then.

Fig drew the sickle claw from her makeshift belt, growled, and sliced the air. Crooked Wing looked at the ground.

"Gra!" Fig said. She stepped closer, roared again, and sliced the air. "Gra!"

Down!

Crooked Wing was sufficiently cowed. She rolled over, exposing her underbelly. The showdown was won.

Fig tucked her sickle claw back into her belt. Good. The big female knew her place.

I showed her, she thought.

Of course, it was easy to be brave when Red Scar stood behind you. The big alpha male nuzzled Fig with his snout, cooing softly.

I'm proud of you, little one.

Absentmindedly, Fig patted his scaly snout, running her fingers along the scar she had given him. The scar that had tamed him, turning him from her tormentor to protector. She had won another challenge today, taming another beast. But worry gnawed on Figaro like a young bator on a parasaur crest.

Red Scar was growing older. He would not be around forever to protect Fig. Sooner or later, there would be another power struggle. And while Fig was fierce and brave, she *was* the runt of the pack. She must keep fighting for her place. A runt's war never ended.

Sometimes achillobators tolerated a weak member. In the salad days of spring, when meat was plentiful and the weather warm, it was easy to overlook flaws. An elder who bit weakly might still remember the migration paths. An old female who could no longer lay eggs could perhaps still sniff out distant prey. Even a runt might have her uses—she could tend to the nest, groom for ticks, pull thorns from talons. But when the winters were long, and the hunger grew great, well … Figaro had seen it happen. The weak could end up as dinner.

She shuddered. Best not to spend too much time thinking about that. Fig was strong, and she would keep fighting for her place. She had no intention of ending up inside the bellies of her pack mates.

That night, they returned to the nesting grounds, bellies full. They dragged back some meat for the hatchlings and elders. The pack migrated every fall, finding a place to winter, then lay eggs in the spring. This year, they lived on a stone outcrop that thrust out from a mountainside. Here they had built nests from branches, moss, vines, and old feathers. Places to sleep. To lay eggs. To slowly digest a good meal. Bones lay across their lair, buzzing with flies.

It would have been nice to find a cozy cave. Especially during the winter storms. But caves were rare in the wilderness. When you did find one, there was fierce competition. The bigger predators—titans like giganotosaurus, carcharodontosaurus, or tyrannosaurus—monopolized the caves, and woe beheld anyone who encroached on their lairs. Achillobators were fierce. They were the terror of many. But they knew their place. They did not challenge the kings. One year, they had found a cave too small for the giants, only to find territorial raptors already inside. No. Caves were just not an option for a pack of bators.

But Figaro didn't mind living outdoors too much. She liked feeling the sun on her skin, and the rain soothed her. The winters were hard, but she collected many feathers for warmth, and she nuzzled among her pack when the snows fell, tucked under their wings. And on warm nights like tonight? This was happiness. She would much rather lie under the stars than inside some stuffy cave.

Everyone in the nesting ground had their usual perch. Their spot. The place they slept, mated, or hunkered down for winter. Location inside the nesting ground was strongly hierarchal and fiercely enforced.

The most desirable spots were nearer the mountainside. Soft moss covered the ground there. The mountainside shielded you from the wind. A few trees grew there, and their branches and errant roots whisked away the rain, preventing puddles. The pack reserved these spots for their eggs.

Fig kept her distance from those desirable parts of the nesting grounds. The mothers didn't like rival females approaching. Or anyone, for that matter. Last spring, an oviraptor had sneaked into the nesting ground and devoured three eggs before they crushed the little thief. Since then, the female bators had been extra protective. If Fig even looked at an egg, they would snap their teeth and slash the air. *Away, runt!*

Often, Fig wondered when she herself would begin to lay eggs. She was fifteen springs old, by her count, though she might be off by one or two. In any case—more than old enough for egg laying. But no matter how hard she tried, nothing happened. Maybe once her feathers finally grew in. Any day now, any day …

Fig walked to her own spot in the nesting ground. The spot was, on the surface, not particularly desirable. It was near the edge of a stony outcrop, exposed to the wind and rain. If the wind was strong enough, it could even knock you over the ledge. The sun beat down during the day without any shade. The ground was rocky and hard. But to Fig, this was the perfect place. From here, and only from here, she could look over her territory. She could see the rolling grasslands by day and the stars at night. From here, she could gaze upon Mintari, this land that she loved.

And Red Scar slept nearby. That was another benefit. The alpha male did not need to seek shelter from the elements like a roosting mother, elder, or hatchling. He chose this spot despite its discomforts. With this choice, he broadcast his strength. From here he reigned. Fig was honored to live at his side.

A yawn rolled through her, stretching her body from head to toes. It had been a long day. They were all tired. Red Scar fell asleep beside her, snoring, his feathered body rising and falling. Most of the other bators lay down to sleep too. As always, a few remained awake to keep watch. The pack had well-established shifts. The young females kept first watch. Then the young males. Then the elders—until dawn.

The alpha of the pack got to sleep all night. The perks of command. Red Scar perhaps forfeited a bed of moss under a tree, but he did enjoy sleeping all night.

Like always, Fig kept first watch with the other young females. She leaned against the sleeping Red Scar, soothed by the rising and falling of his chest. His feathers were soft and warm and the color of fire. Fig picked her teeth with a fish bone, watching the stars.

These were peaceful times for her. Her favorite times. Every night was different. Some nights the stars shone so brightly Fig thought she could reach out and touch them. Other nights lightning split the darkness and thunder boomed, and Fig nestled under Red Scar's feathers, peeking out at the sheets of rain. Some nights luminous ribbons of blue and purple danced across the heavens. Fig would sit here every night, watching, wondering.

So many questions filled her. What were the stars? Could they be the distant eyes of fallen achillobators? Where did lightning come from? She sometimes imagined that a great dinosaur lived above the clouds, casting down his fury in a storm. Her curiosity burned inside her. But how could she learn the truth? In her mind, she could pose these questions. But there was no one to ask. How did you ask a dinosaur a question?

Often, Fig suspected that she was the only achillobator who had such thoughts. The others seemed only concerned with earthly matters. Feeding, sleeping, mating, laying eggs, and repeating the cycle. They never watched the skies in wonder. They never gazed at their reflections, contemplating their identities. Tonight, watching the stars, her mind full of questions, Fig felt very alone.

The thought rose unbidden in the night.

A girl. I met a human girl.

She thought of Emily, the human cub on the hill.

She recalled seeing her reflection in the water. A soft face. No snout to speak of. No scales or feathers.

A human.

Impossible.

And yet in the darkness, the memories rose. Just vague images. Echoes. Whispers as soft as a bator's underbelly feathers.

Memories of her time before the pack.

Fig screwed her eyes shut, trying to banish those haunting memories. But something had happened today. She had met a human cub. She had heard humans speak—and understood them. Now, in the night, as the others slept, the memories rose.

The memories were few and vague.

Memories of a human.

A large human. Or maybe Fig had simply been very small.

She remembered the smells most. Smells of crushed berries and spices and herbs. She remembered sounds too. Chinking bracelets. Clattering necklaces of teeth and claws. Matted hair strewn with bells. Lips that chanted prayers.

Not much else. A face? Could she remember a face?

Yes. There it was. Big green eyes and painted cheeks. Just a wisp of memory. The wisp faded to nothing.

A woman. A human woman.

A mother? Was this Fig's mother?

She thought hard, trying to remember. The wisps rose again, wove into pictures in her mind, and she was a cub again. The woman was rocking her in her arms. Nursing her like a mammal. Nuzzling her and loving her.

A mother? No. Not a mother. Figaro somehow knew that. Remembered that. Not a mother. A guardian.

What had happened to her?

If I am a mammal, how did I …

And then she saw it.

Fig shouted in the night. Her cry was so loud that Red Scar awoke, snorted, and looked around. The other achillobators rose to their feet, feathers bristling.

But there were no predators around. Their nostrils flared but smelled nothing. They glared at Fig, snorted, and returned to their slumber. But Fig would get no sleep tonight. She trembled.

The memories. The girl on the hilltop had unlocked the memories. Now they flooded her.

She remembered.

She had been four years old. Yes, she was sure of that. Four.

They were in a hut in the woods, and a fire crackled among stones. Not a wildfire from a lightning strike or a summer drought. A fire the human had put there. A fire she could control. A fire to heat food and keep dinosaurs away.

But it had been a long winter. And the achillobators were hungry. Hungry enough to overcome their fear of fire.

Fig remembered. She could still see it. Their red eyes in the storm. Their claws tearing down the walls. Their toothy mouths opening wide.

Little Figaro had never seen such horrors. Not in all her four years. How she had screamed! The creatures from her nightmares had taken flesh. The achillobators broke into the hut, crazed with hunger. The old guardian tried to protect her ward. But the demons devoured the woman by her flames.

But they did not devour the child.

Softer memories filled her.

Snouts nuzzling her. Feathers draping across her. She rode a beast through the snow, clutching the feathers so tightly. A human cub in the wild. Taken in by the pack.

It had been many seasons since then. And Figaro sat on the ledge of stone in the night, no longer a little girl. Tears flowed down her cheeks. She looked at Red Scar, this proud dinosaur who lay at her side, growing older, weaker every winter. Her tears splashed his snout, and she stroked his feathers.

You spared me, she thought. *Why? You could have eaten me too. Or you could have left me for the scavengers. But you took me in. Why?*

And then another memory rose.

She remembered her favorite garment as a child. A hat woven with red feathers.

Fig lowered her head, trembling and crying.

You mistook me for a hatchling. But I'm not one of you. I'm not.

She looked up at the stars through the veil of tears.

"I ... am ... human."

Figaro pulled her knees to her chest and hugged her legs. She sat like that all night, gazing at the stars until the dawn dried her tears.

CHAPTER EIGHT
The Man on the Silver Mountain

Joe walked the narrow mountain paths, not pausing to see if Simone followed.

"Jurassic Joe?" Her voice rose from behind. "Jurassic Joe, sir? Can you please slow down?"

He did not even look over his shoulder. "It's almost midnight. The time when the megaraptors hunt. Keep up. Or join your cameraman in the belly of a beast."

"M-megarators?" she whispered.

He kept walking, a low growl in his throat.

Those foolish tourists! Coming here. Causing trouble. A lump filled Joe's throat.

He had killed today. Riding his triceratops, he had gored an allosaurus, slaying the theropod. Why? The predator had simply been doing what predators do. Hunting. Now it lay dead, and there was blood on Joe's hands.

I should have let the tarry woman be eaten, he thought.

"Sir? Please! I'm barefoot, and I think I sprained my ankle, and—"

He spun around, fuming, and glared at the woman. She stood on the narrow path, covered in dirt and old blood. She wore some ridiculous mockery of a safari outfit, probably purchased at some Cloventian high-fashion shop in a floating skyscraper. Mud caked her red hair, and weariness filled her blue eyes.

"What happened, cheesecake?" he growled. "Tossed away your high heels? Realized they slow you down when a dinosaur chases you?"

She crossed her arms and raised her chin. "For your information, mister, I was wearing hiking boots. A pterosaur ate them."

"Too bad it didn't eat you too. Keep up. Or maybe one will."

Joe had sent Dozer back into the forest. Triceratops were good at many things, but mountain climbing was not one of them. Turning away from Simone, Joe kept trudging up the mountain.

Nyx had set, but Hypnos and Thanatos, the twin moons of Mintari, lit the night. The snowcapped peaks shone like burnished silver above. Far below, shadows cloaked the foothills and sprawling Hell Valley. The mountain path was narrow and steep. It was not a proper trail, just a path he had carved over the years, stamping down dirt and kicking aside stones. He had walked this way countless times, and he moved confidently in the night. The tarry Cloventian was another story. She was making a racket. With every footstep, she sent scree cascading into the darkness. Every raptor on the mountain could probably hear her.

Why did I bother saving her? Joe thought. *I should have let nature take its course. Let the dinosaurs eat her.*

But he knew the answer. He still wore the badge on his chest. The badge shaped like a stegosaurus dorsal plate. Tar it, he was still a Ranger, even after all this time. His vows still mattered. He had sworn to protect life on Mintari. Even crazy redheads from another planet.

"Jurassic Joe, will you please slow down!" Simone called up from the shadows.

He snorted. "Would you ask an allosaurus to slow down? You're a long way from home, cheesecake. You're on Mintari now. You don't have servants to order around here."

"I am *not* some spoiled Cloventian princess! And I do not have servants. I'm a journalist. I'm—" She fell silent. "What was that?"

She froze and gulped.

A deep bellow echoed across the mountainside. It sounded like rolling thunder.

Joe glanced over his shoulder and grinned. "The megaraptors. They're the size of giraffes, their claws are the length of your arms, and they're excellent mountain climbers. I suggest you move fast, cheesecake."

She paled so much her freckles stood out like stars. She began to climb faster. "I told you already—my name is Simone LaRue. Not Cheesecake!"

"And my name isn't Jurassic Joe. Now *keep up.*"

The megaraptors howled again.

The princess hurried up.

Of course, the megaraptors didn't hunt this high up the mountain. Not much to eat up here aside from the odd pachycephalosaurus, and those dome-headed dinos were good at headbutting predators (and often one another) and sending them crashing down the mountain. So the raptors stuck to the foothills, where they prowled the darkness for slumbering iguanodons. But their cries often echoed up the mountainside, sounding eerily close. Best if the woman thought they were snapping at her heels. Maybe she'd walk faster.

Tarry tourists. They were nothing but trouble. If Joe had his say, none would be allowed on Mintari. He didn't like other humans period. And clueless Cloventians, stumbling over themselves in the wilderness, were the worst. The governor said the tourists brought in money. That they funded the Mintari Rangers. If you asked Joe, the tourists were more trouble than they were worth.

It was midnight when they reached the cave where Joe lived.

From the outside, the cave was unremarkable. They were far above the tree line, and nothing but some scrub grew here, stubbornly clinging to the mountainside. Caves were prime real estate on Mintari. Joe had claimed this one as his own. Many dinosaurs would have loved to move in. The opening was too small for a rex, but a pack of raptors would be comfortable here, even this high up. For a mountain-loving pachycephalosaurus, this cave would be heaven.

To deter them, Joe had installed steel bars across the cave opening. A few bars were bent where a domehead had headbutted them. Another bar was scratched where a raptor had clawed it. But the fortifications had held.

Simone looked at the dents and dings on the bars. She gulped. "Did dinosaurs do that?"

"No. These marks were made by redheads I left outside my cave because they kept asking too many questions."

She rolled her eyes. "So clever, Jurassic Joe. You enjoy tormenting redheads, don't you?"

"I told you!" he growled, reaching into his pocket for his key. "My name isn't Jurassic Joe. Tarry foolish name the tourists use. Half the animals on Mintari aren't even from the Jurassic period. They're Cretaceous dinosaurs."

"Well, excuse me, Mr. Joe Triplehorn." She placed her hands on her hips and raised an eyebrow. "Better?"

"It would be better if you had never shown up."

He turned the key, then cranked a winch. The bars slid upward like a portcullis. He stepped inside.

The woman did not follow.

Joe paused, his back to her. He took a deep breath.

"Well, are you coming inside?"

Her voice sounded behind him, soft, almost timid. "I'm not sure. I'm wondering if I'll be safer with the raptors."

Joe spun around, a growl on his lips. But when he saw her face, his anger flowed away.

She was scared. Not of dinosaurs this time. But of him.

All his fury melted like snow down the mountainside.

"I won't hurt you," he said. "I saved your life just a few hours ago."

She still didn't step inside. "For all I know, you saved my life so that you could take me home and stick me in a cage."

Now the old anger came back, just a flicker. "Fine! Stay outdoors. I'm closing the gate. Step back or step forward. Just don't stay in place or you'll get crushed."

He began turning a second winch, this one inside the cave. The portcullis began descending.

The woman hurried inside, and the metal bars slammed shut behind her.

"Well, I made my choice," Simone said, standing inside the cave. "Where's my cage?"

Joe snorted. "Your cage is back on Cloventia. Whatever little apartment you princesses trap yourselves in, far from the wilderness, floating above a sea of concrete and neon—that's your cage."

A crooked smile found her lips. "Says the man who lives behind steel bars."

Joe snarled at her. "You have a sharp tongue. Has anyone ever told you that?"

"And a sharper pen. I'm here to write a story about you, Joe Triplehorn. So be nice."

He barked a laugh. "It'll be a cold day in hell before I give you an interview. You can stay the night. That's it. Tomorrow morning, I'm calling the Rangers to pick you up. Make yourself comfortable, because at dawn, you're out."

She looked around the cave, and her eyes widened. "Darwin's beard! This is a nice place. Not what I expected."

Joe walked toward the fireplace and began poking the embers. "Don't touch anything."

A nice place. Yes. It was. *She* had made it a nice place. Mina. Back then, the cave had been just a way station. A place to rest on ranges. To spend a night. Joe never imagined he would spend fifteen years here.

He froze, poker in hand, as sudden pain stabbed him. Yes, it was fifteen years since Mina had died, and the pain never left him. How many years since he had even talked to another woman? Joe had lost count.

He didn't want this Simone LaRue here. This was his home. Mina's home. He shouldn't have brought her.

"Well, well." Simone placed her hands on her hips, and that infernal eyebrow of hers rose again. "Mr. Triplehorn, your home is downright cozy! A rug on the floor. A crackling hearth. A bed topped with blankets. And—"

Simone let out a scream.

Joe cursed. He unslung his weapon from across his back. He never went anywhere without his sleep-or-die. The rifle had two barrels. One for shooting tranquilizer darts at dinosaurs. The other for shooting bullets at hunters. He swept the rifle from side to side, seeking danger.

"What is it?" he growled.

She pointed a trembling finger. "A d-d-dinosaur. Inside the cave."

She clung to him, shaking.

Joe lowered his gun with an eye roll. "Oh, for crying out loud, lady! You almost gave me a heart attack."

"A dinosaur!" She gripped his arm so tightly it hurt. "Look!"

He groaned. "That's just Vinnie. My pet. He's just a velociraptor. He's harmless. For pity's sake, cheesecake, from how loud you screamed, I thought there was a tarry allosaurus in here."

The velociraptor looked at them, tilted his head, and cooed. Vinnie was roughly the size of a turkey. Blue and green feathers grew across his body. His tail flicked behind him, bristling.

Simone wouldn't release her grip on Joe's arm. "Nice try, mister. But I've heard about velociraptors. They're vicious predators."

He wrenched his arm free. "Ya hear that, Vinnie? You're a vicious predator. Maybe act like it and catch a mouse now and then." He barked a laugh and looked at Simone. "You've watched too many movies, lady. Velociraptors are no more harmful than dogs."

"I'll have you know that I'm terrified of dogs." She raised her chin. "Of all animals, in fact."

"I got bad news for ya, cheesecake. You're on the wrong planet."

"I know," she said softly. "Trust me, I know."

Joe frowned. She had lost somebody to the allosaurs. A friend? Maybe Joe had been too harsh on her. He could almost hear Mina's voice in his mind.

Be nice, Joe! She's scared, grieving, and alone. Show some compassion.

Joe's anger faded. But then he remembered the battle. Having to gore an allosaurus. To kill one of the dinosaurs he was sworn to protect. Because of this woman's stupidity. Any flicker of compassion he had felt faded.

Vinnie sensed his turmoil, as he always could. The velociraptor leaped onto Joe's shoulder, cooed softly, and nuzzled him. It helped. It really did. Joe ruffled the raptor's feathers.

"Look at you, vicious predator," Joe mumbled, burying his face in the soft blue feathers. "Can't even kill time, can ya, buddy?"

Simone watched from a few steps away. A shaky smile shone on her face like Nyx shining through the clouds after a storm. "You're different with Vinnie. You show him your softer side. You're not as wild as they say, are you?"

He glowered at her. "What were you expecting? A lair strewn with human bones? That can still be arranged."

She took a step closer, smiling crookedly. "You don't scare me, Joe Triplehorn. You're a softie. I can tell. You act like a tough dinoboy, but deep down, you—"

"You know nothing about me!" He bared his teeth. "Your quaint little observations might fool your readers, cheesecake, but they don't fly here on Mintari. I suggest you keep your mouth shut."

Vinnie hissed at her and snapped his teeth.

She backed away, raising her hands in a placating gesture. "All right, all right, boys. I won't pry for dirty details." She winked. "Yet."

"The only thing dirty here is you, cheesecake. You're covered in more mud than a sauropod's foot."

Joe returned to the fireplace. He added a log and busied himself with stoking the fire. Meanwhile, Vinnie plopped himself down on the rug and began pecking at his feathers, looking for mites.

Standing by the fire, Joe closed his eyes and tightened his jaw. The pain was like dinosaur claws inside him.

She's pretty, he thought. *Beautiful, even. Ah, who cares? She probably uses her looks to get what she wants. She won't get anything from me.*

Simone looked around the cave, hands on her hips. "You know what this cave needs? A name. How about ... Dino Den. No, that's silly. The Burrow! No, too big. Maybe the Cozy Cavern? Too sappy."

"My cave doesn't need a name," Joe muttered.

"Sure it does. I know." She smiled wistfully. "The Last Home Hollow. That's the name."

Joe rolled his eyes. But he had to admit the name fit. This was something of a last home for him. A place he had come to hide in. To die in.

"Nice place, the Last Home Hollow." Simone wandered around the cave, touching everything. "Beautiful crystals. Did you find them yourself? Ooh, a dinosaur egg! I hope it's fossilized. It is fossilized, isn't it? It better not hatch while I'm here. And is that—" She gasped. "Is that a *T-rex skull?*"

She ran toward the back of the cave. Until now, shadows had cloaked the area, but with Joe rustling the fire, new light filled the cavern, illuminating the enormous skull.

Joe had been living on Mintari for thirty years, and he still marveled at the sheer size of a T-rex. The skull in his cave was as long as a man was tall. The teeth were like bananas, thick and dull. Not sharp teeth for slicing meat. Lesser predators had sharp teeth for slicing. The T-rex had teeth for crushing bones. Joe had seen such teeth crack the frill of a triceratops—and that bone was as thick as a wall.

He carried such a tooth as a sword. Though the tooth he carried was much longer than the ones on this skull. The skull in his cave, fearsome as it was, had belonged to an ordinary T-rex. The tooth hanging from Joe's belt came from the jaws of King Ivan himself. A mutant. A freak. That T-rex was bigger, meaner, and still very much alive. Out there in the dark. Somewhere.

Simone reached the skull and gasped. "You turned it into a chair! How clever! And morbid."

The skull's jaws were open wide. The top part formed a backrest. On the inside, the skull was upholstered and topped with cushions.

"Don't sit on it," Joe said.

She shuddered. "As if I would voluntarily step into the jaws of a T-rex." She gingerly touched one of the teeth, then pulled her hand back as if bitten. She looked at Joe. "I never pegged you as a man to keep trophies of dead animals."

"I didn't make this chair. I confiscated it from a poacher. The man was an Earthling. Some hotshot general. Came to Mintari to kill something bigger than other Earthlings. I put a bullet in his neck."

Simone stared into his eyes. "I know the type. I've been to Earth. I saw the Slum Wars."

"Well, he's dinosaur coprolite now. He shot the T-rex, chopped off its head, and made this chair. He planned to take it back to Earth, to make it his throne." He looked at the enormous, morbid armchair. "It makes me sick to look at. I don't know why I kept it. I should get rid of the tarry thing."

Simone stepped closer to him. She hesitated, then touched his arm. "Maybe you kept it because of what happened. Because of what a T-rex did to—"

"Watch your words!" Joe growled, leaning closer to her, teeth bared.

She paled and took a step back. "All right. Sorry. I probed too hard."

He grabbed her arms and glared. "Let me tell you something, cheesecake. You mind your own business. You pampered tourists. I had to kill a dinosaur because of you. I had to gore that allosaurus and leave him for the scavengers. That blood is on your hands, not mine." He shoved her back. "I'm going to bed. At dawn, you're outta here."

Tears welled up in her eyes. Joe didn't care. He turned and stomped away.

Simone stood by the T-rex skull, watching him step deeper into the cave. The shadows were dark there. But she could just make out a bed. Joe climbed into it and lay still.

What an awful man.

So much for the legend. Jurassic Joe was supposed to be a hero. Instead, she found a brute. Venom filled every word he spoke. He was no better than his sister! Just another cruel

Triplehorn. Simone doubted she could sleep tonight. There was a good chance he'd slit her throat.

Then again, she thought, *he did save my life.*

He had ridden in on his triceratops. Had saved her from the allosaurus. He had taken her in for the night.

He was a brute, yes. But there was kindness to him too, she thought. And there was pain. So much pain. What could drive a man to live out here in the wilderness?

No. He was not like Amissa. Not like the woman who … who …

Simone's eyes dampened. No, she was not ready to relive that memory. Not here. Not now.

Her belly gave a sudden growl.

She was hungry. Ridiculous! She was trapped in a cave with a wild man of the mountains, dinosaurs roamed outside, her beloved cameraman was dead—and she was worried about her belly. But there it growled again.

"Have you got anything to eat?" she called to the shadows.

Joe did not move on his bed.

"I'm going to look for food!"

Again he did not acknowledge her.

Simone sighed. She walked around the Last Home Hollow, exploring the cave. Maybe he had something to eat. She would just nibble a little. It wouldn't be stealing, would it? He had invited her in! Surely his offer included room *and* board.

Well, maybe it was stealing. But she was famished. Surely it wasn't a crime for a starving woman to steal some bread?

There were several chambers in the cave, all with craggy, curved walls. Simone walked around, exploring, looking for the kitchen.

As she passed by a stalagmite, she paused. A framed photo hung on the stone pillar. A photo of a young woman.

Smooth black hair. Dark almond-shaped eyes. She wore scrubs and had a stethoscope around her neck.

Triassic Terry's stories returned to Simone.

"His wife," she whispered. "Ivan the T-rex killed her."

Guilt filled her. Was she intruding on something private? A ridiculous thought for a journalist. It was her job to dig! But the pain she had seen in Joe's eyes ... Simone had seen such pain on Earth. Seen it in the eyes of the survivors of the Slum Wars. People who regretted surviving. Who had lost everything to the machine guns, the cannibals, and the roaming cyborg killing squads.

She turned away from the photo.

"Food," she whispered. "I wanted food."

Sniffing, she detected the whiff of something good. Following her nose, she entered a chamber deeper in the caves. Jackpot! She found shelves of canned goods, flour, sausages, preserves, lentils, dried fruit—enough supplies to last for months. Funny. She didn't imagine that canned pork and beans grew on trees out here. Clearly Joe visited Dinovia City sometimes. Not completely wild after all, was he?

A caw sounded behind her.

Vinnie burst into the pantry, hissed, and bared his teeth.

Simone screamed and stumbled back, hitting a shelf of cans. The cans clattered down around her. It made an unholy racket. A sack of flour burst open with a puff of white.

Simone stood there, frozen in terror.

A moment later, Joe rushed into the pantry, his face red with fury. His fists clenched at his sides.

"Um ... sorry?" Simone said. She could feel herself blushing. And when somebody as pale as her blushed, she turned as red as a tomato. "Caught with my hand in the cookie jar."

She looked down at a jar of pickles. It had shattered.

"Or pickle jar, at least," she whispered, wishing the ground would swallow her.

Joe advanced toward her, fists raised. Simone took a step back. She grabbed one of the fallen cans and raised it as a weapon, prepared to bonk him on the head.

Joe took one step closer, murder in his eyes ... then started to laugh.

Simone blinked at him. "Excuse me, are you completely insane?"

He laughed harder. "Look at you! You got flour in your hair."

She held out strands of her red hair, examining them. At least they had been red. They were now white with flour.

"Oh, for crying out loud!" she said. "Joe, I'm sorry. I'm honestly so sorry. I'm a klutz. A schlemiel. A nincompoop. You can toss me into the jaws of a megaraptor. I deserve it."

He was still laughing. "No. It's my fault. I should have offered you dinner. Be careful! You're barefoot and there's glass on the floor."

He lifted her, carried her out of the pantry, and set her down.

"I'll buy you more food," she said. "Please don't murder me."

He heaved a sigh. "I'm not going to hurt you, Ms. LaRue. It's not your fault. None of this. People don't understand Mintari. Don't understand the delicate balance of this world. They stumble around the planet, and dinosaurs die. People die."

Simone lowered her head. "I'm sorry for everything. Not just for the food. You're right. I don't understand Mintari. I thought that if I could survive Earth, then a big nature reserve would be a piece of cake. But I blustered about, an ignorant foreigner, causing trouble wherever I went. Now dinosaurs are dead. And my cameraman is dead. He was more than my cameraman. He was my friend. A good friend." Tears flowed down her cheeks. "I can't even bury him. There isn't even a corpse to bring back to his family. Those animals, they ripped him apart."

"They did what dinosaurs do," Joe said, but there was no anger in his voice. There was compassion. "Don't blame a dinosaur for doing what a dinosaur does."

Simone looked up at him, tears in her eyes. "How can you love dinosaurs? They're monsters. They killed my friend. They killed ... your wife."

She ended with a whisper. And she regretted those words at once. He had warned her to mind her own business. Not to pry. She expected him to rage, maybe even to strike her. But his eyes were soft.

"They're animals. They do what's in their nature. It's humans who can tell good from evil—and who choose evil. Dinosaurs have hurt me. But humans have hurt me more."

She hesitated, then reached out and touched his cheek. "How have humans hurt you?" she whispered.

He stepped back from her. His face hardened. "We'll clean up this mess tomorrow. Get some sleep. There's only one bed. But you can sleep in the T-rex skull. If you curl up, it's comfortable enough."

She gulped. "I'm not sleeping inside a dinosaur's mouth!"

"It's the skull or the floor."

"The floor."

"Very well. Good night, Ms. LaRue."

He turned and left the pantry. Simone stared at the shadows where he had vanished. "Good night, Mr. Triplehorn."

She tiptoed out the pantry and looked at the upholstered T-rex skull. Not a chance.

She snatched a few pillows from inside the terrible jaws, then lay on the rug. The fireplace crackled, the smoke rising through a hole above. Simone yawned. She was bone tired. Despite the horrors of the day, she wanted nothing more than to sleep.

But there was one more thing she must do.

She tiptoed toward the edge of the cave. The bars were closed, protecting them from dinosaurs. But when Simone held out her SmartSphere, she got a signal.

Cloventia was several light-minutes away. There was a delay. But she could still make a call home.

She called Cody's parents.

They appeared on-screen. A lovely couple in their fifties. They were having breakfast when Simone called. Orange juice and poached eggs.

And she told them. About their son dying. About there being no body left to bury. Several minutes later, as the signal came back to her, she saw them break down. They wept. And Simone wept with them.

That night, she found no rest in slumber. All night she dreamed of the allosaurus attack. But in her dreams, the dinosaurs were not devouring Cody. It was Elize who died between their teeth.

CHAPTER NINE
Predators

Tobias Triplehorn stood on the rooftop of Triplehorn Incorporated headquarters, high above the floating city. He paused for a moment, holding his shotgun, admiring the view. The sight from the rooftop always took his breath away.

Neotropolis, capital of Cloventia, sprawled below him like a sea of neon. Five hundred years ago, when the first humans arrived to colonize this planet, it was nothing but fields of clover as far as the eye could see. Today the only things growing on Cloventia were houseplants, and even most of those were plastic. They produced some food in labs, but they imported most of it from Dagon, the massive farming planet that orbited Nyx with them. Cloventia herself was too beautiful to tarnish with farmlands. Humanity had created a wonder here, not only taming the wilderness but slaying it, building upon its corpse a paradise of light. Cloventia had become a synthetic planet, a monument to modernity.

"Man has always sought to slay nature," Tobias said softly. "Since Saint George slew the dragon, we've been slaying beasts. That is why I founded Triplehorn Incorporated. To carry on this legacy of triumph."

Standing nearby, Isaac Carmichael chuckled. He was a big, beefy man. His silk robes shone with electric embroidery. He held a shotgun with his big, jeweled hands.

"Well, you're certainly out-slaying me today!" the big man boomed. "What's the score now? Fourteen doves to me, sixteen to you?"

Tobias smiled thinly. He could be beating the man a hundred to fourteen by now. But it was unwise to beat him too severely. Isaac Carmichael was the editor of the *Cloventia Gazette*, among the largest media companies in the Nyx system. Tobias sold guns and arrows and blades. But he knew that the pen was mightier than the sword. And the *Gazette* owned a whole lotta pens. Tobias was still a new shareholder. It took time to grease the wheels.

"I believe you are correct," Tobias said. "Fourteen to sixteen. Maybe you'll catch up this turn. Ready? On three. Two. One."

Tobias opened the cage door. Ten more doves fluttered out and took to the sky.

Doves were expensive on Cloventia. Tobias imported them all the way from planet Thalia. Each one cost more than a nice dinner at *La Maison Volante*. Normally Tobias tested his weapons on sparrows, which were cheaper, smaller, and harder to hit. But to entertain the editor of the *Gazette*, a few fat and beautiful doves were well worth the cost.

The animals flew slowly. Tobias had clipped their wings in just the right way, allowing them to still fly—but clumsily.

Carmichael thrust out his bottom lip, raised his chin with a jiggle of his jowls, and aimed his shotgun. He closed one eye, the one with the monocle, and placed the butt of the shotgun against his ample belly. With a finger that twinkled with rings, he pulled the trigger.

The shotgun boomed.

The pellets flew out.

The doves kept flying.

"Goddammit all!" the editor blustered.

Tobias had secretly implanted little electrodes inside the doves' heads. Pretending to adjust his tie, he tapped a hidden button. Three doves fell from the sky, dead. They vanished into the neon sea below.

"Ah, looks like I got a few after all!" The editor chuckled. "Jolly good show. Why, looks like I'm ahead of you now, Tobias. Seventeen to sixteen. I seem to be getting the hang of this hunting business."

Tobias smiled thinly. "You're a natural, Mr. Carmichael."

Yes, doves were expensive. But far more costly were shares in the *Cloventia Gazette*. Five hundred years ago, when Cloventia was still a fledgling colony, the *Gazette* had begun as a simple newspaper. Printed on actual paper. Today the *Gazette* controlled so much more. Holographic streams. Music labels. Virtual reality worlds. The company even owned QuickFame, the largest social media network on the NyxNet. The same network where Amissa pleased her millions of fans.

Most importantly, Mr. Carmichael owned a young journalist by the name of Simone LaRue.

Tobias licked his teeth, loading his shotgun. He remembered the young LaRue. There used to be two of them. Twin girls. They were never apart. At least until that unfortunate incident with the dog. Tobias would see them at his daughter's school, feisty little redheads. One was now buried in the lower levels beneath the neon sea, the place they dumped trash, toxic waste, and the bodies of the poor.

The surviving LaRue would serve Tobias well.

I sell many weapons, he thought. *Guns. Bows. Blades. But the greatest weapon in the galaxy is a beautiful woman.*

He released more doves.

He fired.

He missed. He could have hit them all, of course. But he chose to miss.

"Ah, bad luck!" Carmichael said. "Looks like I'm still ahead."

Tobias smiled a tight smile. "You're a natural, Mr. Carmichael."

The big man placed a meaty, heavily jeweled hand on Tobias's shoulder. The touch disgusted Tobias, but he kept his smile.

"Toby, old boy, you've shown me a good time today. I'm glad to have you on our board of directors." He barked a laugh. "With the amount of shares you're buying, you'll soon own more of the *Gazette* than I do."

"I would not dream of it," said Tobias. "I'm merely a humble investor. Of course, if you do need to raise more money … my coffers are always open."

His coffers were almost empty. Buying eleven percent of the *Gazette* had ravaged them. Tobias had drained his life savings for this. But his fortune had purchased more than just a media company.

It purchased a beautiful redhead.

"How is our Ms. LaRue doing?" he asked, trying to sound casual. "Is her trip to Mintari going well?"

Carmichael's face fell. "Toby, old boy, I meant to talk to you about that. I had a talk with the lawyers. Planting hidden recording devices is a legal gray area. Espionage, they call it."

Dammit all!

Fury flared inside Tobias. The fool had talked! Now Tobias must track down those lawyers. Make sure they kept their mouths shut. It would be messy business. If they refused to cooperate, the pits below the neon sea might gain a few more bodies.

Tobias forced his rage down. Feigning nonchalance, he raised his eyebrows. "Espionage, sir? No." He forced a laugh. "I'm merely concerned about my son. That's all." He heaved a sad sigh.

"Young Joe Triplehorn has disavowed me. He refuses to see me. He won't even call me. But if Simone can reach him, could let me know he's okay, my burden would feel a little lighter. I'm simply worried about my boy."

Carmichael licked his lips nervously. "I understand, Toby. I do. Such a terrible thing—for a son to renounce his father." He cleared his throat. "Don't worry. We won't say more of this. I assure you, Simone LaRue is a fine journalist. One of my best. She'll find your boy." He slapped Tobias on the back. "Now— looks like there are still a few doves in the cage! What say we go for one more round? The loser pays for dinner."

They shot a few more doves.

A few carcasses fell into the neon sea. A few lucky birds got away. Once they were far enough, the implants in their heads would detonate. Tobias didn't want too many loose birds around.

After all, birds were the offspring of dinosaurs. And Tobias had vowed to wipe the dinosaurs off the face of the galaxy.

I will smite them down like an asteroid, he vowed. *For you, my parents. This is all for you.*

Carmichael shot his final bird, laughed uproariously, and slapped Tobias on the back. Hard.

"Well, Toby, old boy, looks like I won. Beginner's luck, huh?"

Tobias forced a tight, twitching smile. "Looks like dinner is on me. Grilled doves, perhaps?"

Amissa Triplehorn was no stranger to hunting.

She had slain a woolly mammoth with a simple compound bow (the Artemis's Arch, 15,999 clovers at all Triplehorn stores).

She had taken down a grizzly bear with only a hunting knife (the Triplehorn Tactical Blade, only 999).

In a daring feat, she had slain an entire pride of lions. She had needed a shotgun for that one (the Triplehorn Slugger, 19,999 clovers, financing available), but it was still one for the record books.

Her fans loved it.

Whenever she posted a video of herself slaying an animal, millions watched. Sometimes billions. Whenever she posed over a kill, triumphant, the photo spread across Earth and Cloventia. Teenage boys hung posters of her on their bedroom walls. Teenage girls aspired to be like her—as beautiful, as rich, as deadly.

Her father ran Triplehorn Incorporated. He was the company's heart, soul, and mind. But Amissa was the face. Who could resist a woman so beautiful and deadly?

Amissa appeared in the company commercials, her chestnut hair flowing in the wind, her blue eyes narrowed with concentration, her arrows flying true. She smiled from billboards, one boot upon the corpse of an animal. There was even an Amissa Triplehorn virtual reality game (*Goddess of the Hunt*, only 199 clovers). Players controlled a virtual Amissa, hunting elephants, lions, and bears.

She was the most famous huntress in the galaxy. But she had never killed a dinosaur.

Not with her big brother and his Rangers running around. Jurassic Joe was ruthless. Amissa knew this. He had murdered many hunters. Some had been her friends. She had seen the body bags come home to Cloventia. She had attended the funerals.

Her fists clenched. "You murdered people, big brother. To protect lizards you murdered men. But your little act of defiance against your clan is over." Her face split in a grin. "If you try any of your games on me, I will shoot you down like a dog!"

The flight attendant cleared her throat. "Excuse me, ma'am. This is a family flight. And you're yelling."

Amissa blinked and looked around.

Oh. Right. She was still on the starship. She had forgotten. Rows of seats stretched around her, full of tourists. Her thoughts sometimes took hold of her, carrying her to another realm.

"Get lost!" Amissa snapped at the flight attendant. "Or I'm going to buy this spaceline and demote you to scrubbing the toilets. Go! Wait." She grabbed the woman's arm. "First serve me coffee. Then go."

When she was sipping her coffee, Amissa pulled out her SmartSphere. She tapped a few buttons, and a hologram burst out from the circular computer. A grin spread across her face. She took another sip.

"What was it you called that LaRue girl, Dad? A secret weapon?" She laughed. "Brilliant."

Triplehorn Incorporated made and sold many weapons. Compound bows. Blades. Guns. But the greatest weapon they wielded, it seemed, was a beautiful redhead.

"Simone LaRue," Amissa said. "You were a brat in high school. But you've become such a good little servant."

She could see the gullible ginger in the hologram. The so-called journalist was sleeping soundly, completely unaware. She was curled up on a rug, her head on a pillow. Her red tresses spread out around her. The crackling fireplace painted her porcelain skin a golden hue.

"Look at you," Amissa hissed. "You were so proud of your looks when we were schoolgirls. Always prancing around."

She licked her teeth and fingered her hunting blade. "Once I'm done using you, maybe I'll carve up your pretty little face."

The stewardess cleared her throat. "Excuse me, ma'am, but all weapons must be stored in the overhead compartment in a sealed bag during the—"

"Get lost!" Amissa snapped. "Or I'll drive this blade into your heart!"

The stewardess fled like a frightened bird to join her flock. The spaceship staff crowded together, whispering among themselves, sometimes tossing glances at Amissa. She overheard snippets.

"She threatened me with a knife ..."

"... don't you know who that is? Her father is ..."

" ... worth a billion clovers ..."

Amissa shook her head in disgust. Flying in a commercial spaceship, even in business class, was demeaning. Other rich Cloventian families had private spaceships. Why should she debase herself by flying with the masses?

But the flock of stewardesses was wrong. Clan Triplehorn was not worth a billion clovers. Not even close. Bribery was expensive. Greasing the wheels of power came with hefty costs. The clan was in debt, sinking deeper every day. Just recently, Tobias Triplehorn had sold the family's resort on Emerald Orbital Ring. And to make things worse, the taxman kept nipping at their heels, demanding more, more, more.

But Mintari was a goldmine. If Amissa could defeat the Rangers, then open up the planet to hunting, the clovers would flow. And Amissa would have her private starship. She vowed to hire these same stewardesses. She would make their lives living hell.

She looked back at her SmartSphere. Simone LaRue was still sleeping soundly, unaware she was being watched.

"Pops, you are a genius," Amissa said.

Last year, Triplehorn Incorporated had purchased a substantial amount of shares in *The Cloventia Gazette*. It had emptied the clan coffers. But Tobias Triplehorn now had a seat on the board.

Amissa caressed the hologram that hovered above her SmartSphere, pretending to caress Simone's freckled cheek. "You work for me now, precious little sweetheart."

Simone was completely oblivious. What a fool! No idea she was being watched! No idea she was just a puppet! And Amissa was pulling the strings. Clan Triplehorn now owned eleven percent of the *Gazette*. That gave them special access. Using the shareholder codes, Amissa had personally entered the *Gazette* warehouse, had bugged everything Simone was taking to Mintari. The cameras. The microphones. The computers. All of it was constantly streaming everything to Amissa.

Most of the equipment was lost now. That pea-brained cameraman got himself devoured. What was his name? California Cory? Cary? Something ridiculous like that. Half his gear was now rattling around inside an allosaurus's belly. Still transmitting too. And it was not a pretty sight.

But Simone had saved one device—her personal SmartSphere. Just a humble little computer, no larger than a peach. Primitive compared to the latest model, which Amissa owned. But Simone's SmartSphere, old and cheap as it was, still had a camera and microphone. The circular computer rested right beside Simone now, and Amissa watched her sleep.

"So beautiful," she whispered. "So innocent. Did you think I forgot what you did?"

She remembered that day. It was long ago now. Amissa closed her eyes and dug her fingernails into her palms as the memories flooded her.

They had been only sweet sixteen. Just innocent little flowers blooming for the first time. Well, Amissa had been more of a thorn than a flower. Even then she had been spiky. But the LaRue twins? Daisies. Both of them.

Amissa had never cared for the pair. They came from a poor family. They did not belong at Clover Heights Academy. Let the lower classes remain below the neon sea! The lower levels were where they belonged. In the grime. But sometimes Clover Heights plucked up some dregs. Tried to nurture them. To save them from the underworld. If you asked Amissa, it was ridiculous.

Oh, she had made sure the twins knew they did not belong. She knocked over their milk cartons. Once she framed them for cheating on a test, had nearly gotten them expelled too. But the twins clung on. Like leeches. So vain! So proud of their red hair! Always fluttering around, flirting, flaunting their looks.

Until that fateful day when Amissa met them outside of school.

She had brought company. Her dog, Boomer, growled on his leash. He was a genetically engineered pit bull and a big one too. Such dogs were outlawed on Cloventia, but when your father was Tobias Triplehorn, the law made exceptions.

She had not planned to *kill* one of the twins, of course. Just to scare them a little.

Boomer barked on command. He bared his teeth. But Amissa held him back on his chain. Her dog never touched the girls. Not a hair on their precious ginger heads! Was it her fault that Elize LaRue fled into traffic? The girl was an idiot. She deserved to get run over. Boomer never hurt anyone.

But Clover Heights Academy blamed Amissa. Of course they did. All Simone LaRue had to do was bat her eyelashes, toss her pretty red hair, and put on a show. Oh, how Simone had cried her crocodile tears! How her lips had quivered! *Please, headmaster, please ban Amissa Triplehorn. She killed my sister.*

Rubbish. But the headmaster had bought the act. And Amissa was expelled. If not for her father pulling strings, she might have ended up in juvie too. Charged with manslaughter. Ridiculous.

Worst of all—they had put Boomer down.

Poor, precious Boomer. The dog had done nothing but bark. And because of Simone LaRue, he was dead.

"One day very soon, I will make you pay, sweet slum princess," Amissa whispered, staring at her sleeping rival. "But until then, you are mine."

Amissa flew her own astrolite down to the planet.

The Galaxia Spacelines mothership could not enter an atmosphere. Normally, people shuttled down in small, cramped landing craft. Included in the price. But Amissa wouldn't be caught dead in one of those tin cans. She had brought her own astrolite from home, thank you very much. During the long flight between planets, her astrolite had waited in the hangar bay.

Her clan did not yet own a private starship. But she sure as hell could afford an astrolite.

The flight had been long and wearisome. Thirty-six hours trapped in her seat, suffering the indignities of rude stewardesses, snot-nosed tourists, and meals she wouldn't feed her dogs. There wasn't even a NyxNet connection, allowing her to escape into virtual reality. Amissa would have stayed in the hangar bay, hiding inside her astrolite. But they shut down life support in the hangar until arrival. And her astrolite only contained enough air for an hour or two. What a nightmare!

But the ordeal was over. Now she was back in her astrolite, a sleek machine she had named *Huntress*.

Finally, after all these years of dreaming—there it was below her.

The promised land.

Mintari. A world of dinosaurs. A hunter's paradise.

She had slain many deadly beasts. Tigers. Hippos. Mammoths. But nothing could compare to dinosaurs. Here were the most magnificent animals in history. The most dangerous predators. The grandest of herbivores. A cornucopia awaited below.

Amissa checked her makeup, brushed back her hair, then pointed her camera at herself. She clicked a button, initiating a live stream, and smiled at her millions of fans.

"Hello, fellow hunters! This is your girl, Amissa Triplehorn, reporting in from the sky of Mintari. Yes, my dear Tripletots, I'm finally here. And it is spectacular." She pointed the camera out the windshield. "Look."

The astrolite glided over a lake and grassy valley. Sauropods were wading through the water. The beasts were truly titanic. Amissa had thought that mammoths were large. One of these sauropods could step on a mammoth. When they saw the astrolite fly overhead, the sauropods raised their ridiculously long necks and brayed.

Amissa clutched her rifle, her fingers tingling.

"Look at them, my Tripletots! Aren't they magnificent? This species is *Brachiosaurus altithorax*. If the astrolite window could open, I would shoot one for you now." She laughed. "But we must be patient, Tripletots. I'll make sure to face them up close, to show you their true grandeur—from the ground—before I take one down. I can barely wait. I know you're eager too."

Her likes and comments came flooding in. Hundreds of thousands of fans were watching her live stream. They flooded her with love. Every second, more comments poured in.

"Go get 'em, Dino Huntress!"

"Queen Amissa, slay!"

"Can't wait to try out the new Triplehorn rifles."

"Gorgeous!"

Of course, the usual trolls were there too. The animal-rights activists were having their usual meltdowns, uttering their pathetic little threats.

"Murderer!"

"How could you possibly kill such beautiful animals?"

"How would you feel if somebody hunted you?"

"Die, you monster!"

Amissa blew a kiss to the camera. "And this is for my haters. I love you too. Someday you'll become Tripletots as well. *Mwah!*"

She winked. More hearts flooded her video. Along with much more hate. She basked in them both.

She pointed the camera outside again. She flew the astrolite over a canyon. Cycads grew on the canyon's edges, and a river snaked through the deep gorge. Hundreds of pterosaurs bustled there. They nested on the canyon walls, swept down to catch fish from the river, and fluttered among the trees. Amissa zoomed in.

"Look at those!" she said. "Simple pterodactyls. Not much larger than me. I'll let these ones live. I plan to find the mighty quetzalcoatlus, a flying reptile large enough to swallow a human whole. According to legend, the beating of its wings brings storms. That is the pterosaur I plan to hunt."

Her live stream flooded with comments.

"Can't wait!"

"Shoot yourself, not a beautiful animal!"

"Kill the quetz, kill the quetz!"

"Somebody needs to hunt you!"

Amissa pointed the camera at grasslands. "Look at those. A herd of herbivores. Triceratops?" She zoomed in. "Nope! Only two horns. A herd of nasutoceratops. I would love to mount one of those skulls on my wall."

"Mount your own head."

"Killer Queen!"

"T-rex, T-rex, T-rex!"

Within seconds, that last comment got hundreds of likes. Soon hundreds of her followers were posting the same thing, over and over.

"T-rex, T-rex, T-rex!"

Amissa laughed, turned the camera toward her face, and blew her fans a kiss. "Yes, I hear you, Tripletots. You want me to hunt a T-rex." She grew serious. "A Tyrannosaurus rex is the deadliest predator that's ever lived. The most ruthless killer evolution has ever produced. Do you think I can truly do it?"

"I hope a T-rex kills you!"

"You got this, babe."

"T-rex, T-rex, T-rex!"

Amissa pouted. "Well, if you don't think I can do it …"

"You can do it, baby!"

"You da best!"

"Don't let the haters get you down."

"Eat her, T-rex! Team T-rex!"

Amissa wiggled two fingers in an imitation of a T-rex's arms. "Well, Tripletots, you'll have to wait and see. My astrolite is landing now. See you later, my lovelies! Kisses!"

She kissed the screen and shut off the live feed. Nearly eight million views this time. She would have to bump those numbers up. Once she got a few dinosaur carcasses to pose with, she would be getting a hundred million live viewers.

She looked at her tablet. Simone LaRue was still sleeping. A private show for one.

Dawn had risen. Behind the redhead, in the shadows, Amissa could now see it. A bed. A man waking up.

Amissa grinned. "Hello, big brother."

Most visitors to Mintari landed in Dinovia.

It was the only city on Mintari. If you could call it that. The place was built like a prison. A moat, towering walls, an electric fence, and guard towers defended the humans within. Most Mintarians cowered within those walls, fearful of dinosaurs. Pathetic. Weren't Mintarians meant to be tough?

Not only the locals sheltered within the city walls. Tourists and even poachers stayed in Dinovia's hotels. They liked their soft beds, their breakfast buffets, and the safety of stone walls around them. When they felt adventurous, they left the city in armored jippis, then rushed back to their feather beds at night.

Cowards.

Amissa was different. She was made of tougher stuff. She had no use for a city full of weaklings. She landed her astrolite in the wilderness. If Joe could survive out here, so could she.

She had to admit it. Jurassic Joe was no weakling. He was like her. Strong. A fighter. Grudgingly, she gave him this respect.

It's too bad you chose to fight on the wrong side, brother, Amissa thought, slinging her rifle across her back.

She hopped out of her astrolite onto the soil of Mintari. Grasslands rolled toward conifer forests and beyond them blue mountains. A river snaked in the east, gleaming under the sunlight. Flowers rustled around her boots, and the song of crickets filled the air. A flock of pterodactyls glided across the blue sky.

Amissa tilted her head back, inhaled deeply, and sighed. Fresh air. The smell of flowers and grass. You didn't get that on Cloventia.

Amissa tossed her SmartSphere into the air. The plum-sized computer hovered before her, filming her.

"I'm here. And it's beautiful." She smiled, eyes closed, and tilted her head back, letting the wind play with her hair. "I love the great outdoors. People think that hunters hate nature. That we destroy nature. But I know that's not true. I love nature with all my heart, and it's here where I feel most at peace. It's here that I can connect with my ancestors, my past, and my soul. It's here that I can be one with the universe. We are predators, we human beings. We've always hunted—ever since the first human lifted a rock and hurled it at a deer. Here, I'm connecting with what it means to be human."

Holograms of little emojis floated out of her camera. Mostly they were hearts. Her fans loved it. And they loved her.

Amissa made sure she was beautiful for them. She had worn her favorite hunting outfit today. Camouflage pants, snug enough to accentuate her curves. A tactical vest, low enough to reveal some skin. Her long brown hair fluttered in the wind, and her makeup was perfect. Yes, she was putting on a show for the fans. But she had spoken the true words in her heart.

"Nature is where I belong," she said. "Where I feel strong."

Snorting sounded behind her.

Amissa spun around, and her heart soared.

Dinosaurs.

Amissa didn't need her field guide. She had spent years studying dinosaurs. Learning their names. Their habits. Their vulnerabilities. She recognized this species at once.

"Look, Tripletots!" she whispered. Her camera still hovered nearby, filming everything. "Amazing! I only landed a few minutes ago. And already I see a beautiful family of nodosaurs."

There were four. A mother and three juveniles. They trundled forward, coated in heavy armor and spikes. Their thickly armored heads dipped down to feed on ferns.

"Beautiful!" Amissa whispered. "They don't fear me. With so much armor, they don't fear predators. Nodosaurs lived across North America throughout the Jurassic and Cretaceous periods. They're a type of ankylosaurian dinosaur. Look at all those spikes and armored plates!"

She stepped closer. Her camera hovered behind her. The mother dinosaur looked up, grunted, and puffed air from her nostrils. Amissa took a step back.

"She's a fierce one!" she whispered to the camera. "She's protecting her hatchlings. Even fully grown, nodosaurs are small for dinosaurs. This one is about the size of a hippopotamus."

Comments came flooding in. They floated above the camera like wisps of steam.

"Aww, she's cute."

"Shoot her, shoot her!"

"Don't you dare harm her!"

"Beautiful babies. I want one!"

Amissa barely paid any attention to the comments from fans. She crouched in the grass and leaned forward, examining the animal. The nodosaur was now munching on grass.

"These animals are small. But look at how they evolved to survive! They're built like a tank, low and thick and covered with armor. Those spikes across their backs and sides could cause some serious damage. And see their coloring? Brown and yellow spots. That's camouflage. Consider that fact, Tripletots. An animal wearing so much armor, with such fierce weaponry, still needed to evolve camouflage. That's how dangerous some of the predators on Mintari are."

Amissa plucked some ferns and held them out. The baby nodosaurs approached. One began to eat out of her hand.

The comment section exploded.

"Awww, cute!"

"Hungry little fella."

"Watch out for mommy!"

The adult nodosaur stomped closer. She opened her mouth in an angry roar. Her spikes thrust out like scythes, and she raised her tail menacingly. That tail was a formidable weapon—muscular, fast, and covered with spikes.

Amissa's heart burst into a gallop. She stepped back from the hatchlings.

"Easy, girl. Easy. I just want to show you to my viewers."

The mama nodosaur grunted and pawed the earth. Her deadly tail swung from side to side.

Amissa had faced animal mothers before. Once she had battled a grizzly bear protecting her cubs. Back then, Amissa had thought the grizzly a monster. A true terror of claws and fangs. Now she realized how small and weak grizzly bears actually were.

The nodosaur was bigger, covered in armor, and sprouted spikes that could put a rhino's horns to shame. Evolution had built a tank. And when a living tank growled at you, it was a little intimidating, Amissa had to admit. Even she, the great huntress, the slayer of many beasts—even she was taken aback.

She forced down her fear.

Control yourself. You are an apex predator. You can defeat this beast.

"Nodosaurs survived for tens of millions of years, facing the toughest predators nature ever produced," Amissa told her followers. "They survived in a world swarming with allosaurs, megaraptors, and even T-rexes."

The armored dinosaur burst into a gallop, charging at her.

"But they never faced me."

Amissa's heart raced. Her hands were slick with sweat. Her knees shook. The tanklike dinosaur was charging right at her, bellowing for her death.

With trembling hands, she managed to raise her rifle and fire.

She was firing the Triplehorn Dinoslayer, a new rifle specifically designed for dinosaur poachers. A bullet the size of a shot glass blasted forth at hypersonic speed, rippling the air. It slammed into the charging dinosaur.

Amissa had aimed for the head. But the slug went too high and slammed into the nodosaur's armored back.

The Dinoslayer could shoot through brick walls. The slug shattered the animal's armor. Bony spikes flew through the air.

But the dinosaur still lived. She kept charging.

Amissa inhaled sharply. Impossible. Impossible! This gun could take down a mammoth!

Bellowing, the nodosaur lunged at her.

Amissa rolled aside, heart pounding. A scythe-like spike slashed her thigh, tearing her pant leg, scratching her skin. Not a deep cut. Tarry close though. Could have easily carved off her entire leg.

Comments hovered over her floating SmartSphere.

"Woo, go dino!"

"Team Nodosaur! Get her, Nody!"

"Amissa, you got this! Slay, queen!"

The dinosaur was big, heavy, and tough. But also slow and dimwitted. The dinosaur ran several more steps before realizing she had missed Amissa. Grunting, the nodosaur made a U-turn, pawed the earth, then charged toward Amissa again.

"Go, Nody!"

"Fight fight fight!"

"This is barbaric. I can't watch."

"A hundred clovers on Nody!"

Amissa wanted to run. Every instinct in her body screamed to flee, to reenter her astrolite, to slam the door shut.

No.

Not her. Not Amissa Triplehorn.

She cocked the gun, loading another bullet.

The dinosaur charged closer. Closer. She was a second away, and the spikes thrust toward her, and—

She pulled the trigger. The *boom* deafened her. Amissa flew backward and hit the ground.

Had the nodosaur gored her? Was she dying? Her ears rang. Her head spun. She glanced down at her body.

No blood. She was unhurt. In her haste, she had failed to shoulder the Dinoslayer properly. The recoil had knocked her onto her backside. She blushed, feeling like an amateur. But at least she was alive.

A groan sounded ahead.

Amissa pushed herself to her feet. The nodosaur lay before her, a mountain of armor and spikes. The bullet had entered the dinosaur's head.

The mythical animal looked up at Amissa with one eye, gave one last grunt, and died.

Amissa placed her foot on the dinosaur's head, raised her rifle overhead, and howled in victory.

Her fans went wild. Holograms of clapping hands spun in a tornado around her camera.

Amissa struck a few poses. She turned her back toward the camera, looked over her shoulder, and blew a kiss. She climbed onto the dead dinosaur's back and flashed a V sign. She compared the length of her arm to one of the nodosaur's spikes. The photos would circulate across QuickFame for days, racking up millions, maybe billions of views. Her haters would help spread the photos. Their fury multiplied her publicity.

A ticker symbol flashed above her camera. Triplehorn Incorporated stock just went up three percent.

Whimpers sounded behind the corpse. The baby nodosaurs were nudging their mother. The camera captured it all—the whole tragic affair.

Amissa stared gravely into the camera. "This is the brutal reality of nature. Nature can be beautiful, peaceful, even inspiring. But nature can also be cruel. Sometimes even the strongest animals meet their match. These babies, only recently hatched, will have to survive without their mother. If they're strong, they will pass on their DNA to the next generation. If they're weak, nature will select them for death. This is the reality of the great Darwinian struggle that has shaped nature for billions of years, giving rise to the dinosaurs. And to us. This is Amissa Triplehorn, your Dino Huntress."

She gave a scout's salute—one of her trademarks—and ended the feed.

Her subscriber count shot up by twenty thousand.

For the first time, she had killed a dinosaur. A small one. There would be many more.

She knew that her brother would hear of this. Jurassic Joe would hunt her like she hunted dinosaurs. A smile twitched her lips, and she gripped her shotgun with both hands.

"Bring it on."

That night, Amissa parked her astrolite on a forested hilltop, covered it with vines and leaves, and secured herself inside. The hull was thick enough to withstand atmospheric entry. No dinosaurs were getting through. As for the Rangers, well … a few cowboys driving around in jippis, peeping through binoculars, were not going to find her.

Normally on a hunt, she slept outdoors under the stars. Not on Mintari. Everything on this planet was trying to kill you. Sleeping inside the astrolite it was.

She peeled off her hunting clothes, wincing as the fabric brushed her bruises. Her father had beaten her a week ago now, but the bruises were still raw. She had deserved it. She had talked back to him. The pain taught her to respect the CEO of Triplehorn Incorporated.

She looked at herself in the mirror. She was still beautiful, she thought. Even with the bruises. Even in her thirties.

Oh, Amissa knew she was still young. Many hunters were older than her. But for a QuickFame Queen, she was aging. On QuickFame, fans wanted to see youth and beauty. Amissa took care of herself. Her hair was long, brown, and lustrous. Her makeup was always impeccable. She trained daily to stay in shape. But she could not stop the ticking of the clock. When she hit forty, game over. The fans would move on to the next hot young huntress. And Amissa would be left to rot.

She must do something great by then. She must hunt a true monster. Not just little dinosaurs but a true titan. On QuickFame, your fame came quickly, but it also left just as quickly. During her time in the limelight, Amissa would make her mark.

After lying down in bed, she unfolded her SmartSphere. But this time she did not activate the camera. She did not take selfies or stream a video to her fans. She pulled out an old photo. A photo from three decades ago.

The photo showed herself as a baby. Joe, a somber boy of nine, was holding her.

It was the last time they had seen each other. After that photo was taken, their mother fled Cloventia. She took Joe with her to Mintari. And she left Amissa behind.

Tears splashed the old photo.

"You left me," Amissa whispered. "You and mother. You left me to a man who beats me. You abandoned me."

Rage.

Rage flowed through her, drying her tears. She clenched her fists.

"I'll make you pay," she vowed. "You thought you could return to Mintari without me. But I'm here now. And this whole tarry planet will burn."

Another sob fled her lips. Outside in the night, dinosaurs grunted and shuffled and slumbered. Inside her astrolite, Amissa Triplehorn closed her eyes and wept.

CHAPTER TEN
Mudslinging and Megaraptors

The smell of cooking woke Joe up.

His eyes snapped open. Judging from the light shining between the cave bars, it was just past dawn.

He normally slept throughout the morning, rarely waking up before noon. Why wake up any earlier? He used to be an early bird. Back when Mina was here, they would wake up at dawn. But since she was gone, Joe found fewer and fewer reasons to wake up early. To wake up at all. Sometimes he spent all day in bed.

Sleep was better than waking hours. Sleep brought some relief from the grief and loss. Sometimes Joe wanted to sleep forever.

But now the smell of cooking filled his nostrils, pulling him from bed. He rose, grumbling, and rubbed his eyes.

"What's going on?" he muttered.

He dragged himself out of bed. He had slept in his clothes again. Khakis, a tan buttoned shirt—the uniform of a Mintari Ranger. He had even slept with his ceratop hat. He passed his hands over his clothes, absently smoothing out wrinkles. How long had it been since he'd washed the uniform? Perhaps he should change into a fresh one. Maybe trim his beard. Maybe wash. There was a woman in the cave, after all.

Ah, who cared? So what if he was a bit disheveled? He was a man. A Mintari man. Mintari men were meant to be a little dirty. What was he, some kind of Cloventian sissy? A soft lad who showered daily, shaved his beard until he looked like a boy, and splashed himself with perfumes? If the woman didn't care for wrinkled clothes, a scruffy face, and musky odor, she could buzz back to Cloventia. The sooner he got rid of her the better.

He sniffed, smelling the food again. Meat. And eggs.

He shuffled toward the fireplace. Simone stood there, her back to him. She wore no pants, but an oversized, buttoned shirt hung halfway down her thighs. *His* shirt. Her red hair cascaded down to the small of her back.

"What the hell are you doing?" he snapped.

She turned around. She held a frying pan topped with eggs and sausages.

"Cooking breakfast."

"That's my food," he said. "And my shirt."

She shrugged. "Do you want me cooking breakfast in my muddy safari outfit?"

"I want you out of my house."

She pouted. "Aww, big tough Jurassic Joe is grumpy when he's hungry. Sit down! I'm serving you breakfast."

"I'm not—"

"Sit down!" She pointed at the table.

Joe sat down with a grumble. "I was saving those sausages."

She smiled. "For me? How sweet."

Simone rummaged along a shelf, found some clay dishes, and placed them on the table. She ladled the food onto the plates. She had also found the coffee. A pot was brewing. She had even fed Vinnie. The velociraptor was munching on sausages from his bowl on the floor.

Joe just stared at his plate. But Simone tucked in.

"I'm famished." She stuffed eggs into her mouth. "Mmm. Wish you had some pepper, but I think I did a good job."

"Did you use the eggs from the top shelf?"

She nodded. "Sure did." She scooped up another mouthful.

"Those are velociraptor eggs."

Vinnie whimpered.

Simone paled, gulped, and winced. "I'll stick to the sausages." She lifted one on her fork. "Don't tell me this is dinosaur meat."

Joe said nothing.

Simone looked at him. "Well?"

"You didn't want me to tell you."

Simone blinked, then shrugged and bit into the sausage. "I'm better off not knowing how the sausage is made. I think that's true for all sausages."

Joe still did not touch his food.

"You don't have to do this, you know," he said.

"I know." She sliced through the sausage. "The woman cooking for the man? So old-fashioned."

"I mean you don't have to be here at all. In this cave. On this planet. I'm not giving you a story." He growled at her over his plate. "You can take your tarry camera back to Cloventia and cover the latest celebrity scandal. That's all you journalists care about it, isn't it? You're all scavengers."

"Whoa, whoa, dinoboy, you haven't even touched your eggs yet. Please at least try the food before you eviscerate my career."

Joe didn't have an appetite. He wanted to grab the knife off the table and stab something. Why had she come here? He was happy enough on his own. Okay, not happy, but he found his ways to forget the pain. Like sleeping. Drinking. Shooting poachers. A redhead who stole his clothes, ate his food, and pried into his business was not part of that equation.

A voice spoke in his head, soft yet admonishing. *Be nice, Joe. She's nice to you.*

It was Mina speaking. Probably just a figment of his imagination. But she spoke to him daily.

She's a buzzard, he replied to her. *All journalists are. This whole breakfast routine is just flattery. A way to loosen me up.*

Mina smiled. *Or maybe she's just hungry and made enough food for two? Eat, Joe.*

Simone was watching him, her blue eyes soft.

He glowered at her. "Why are you staring at me?"

"You're just ... not what I expected."

He grunted. "And what were you expecting, cheesecake?"

"A hero. I saw a boy on the flight over with a Jurassic Joe action figure. On Cloventia, I saw Jurassic Joe posters. There was even a cartoon for a season. The mythical hero fights bad guys, helps damsels in distress, and teaches kids to say no to drugs."

"I do fight bad guys. I shoot poachers. And I saved your backside. As for kids, well ..."

I almost had a kid, he wanted to say. *Until Ivan devoured my pregnant wife.*

But he could not bring those words to his lips. Often, even to this day, he thought about his child. A girl. They had done the ultrasound. She was a girl. She would have been fifteen now.

His eyes stung. Vinnie seemed to sense his pain. The small theropod padded under the table and rubbed against Joe's legs. His blue and green feathers were soft and soothing.

To hide his pain, Joe lowered his head toward the plate and began to eat.

"Ah, there you go." Simone smiled. "Big tough dinoboy needs a big breakfast."

"Do you ever shut up?" he grumbled between mouthfuls.

Her smile grew into a grin. "Not until I get what I want."

Joe stared at his food, trying to ignore her. So she was pretty. Beautiful, even. So what? So she cooked him breakfast. Big deal! He didn't want her here. He would call the Rangers headquarters right now. They'd send someone to pick her up in a jippi.

He pushed his plate aside.

"Sorry to disappoint you, Ms. LaRue. Thank you for breakfast, but I'm calling you a cab."

He patted his pockets, looking for his communicator. Where was the tarry thing? He had left it around here somewhere. He rummaged around his shelves, pushing aside empty bottles of booze. Where the hell was it?

Mina spoke in his mind again. *When I was alive, you would never remove your communicator from your belt. Only when you slept, and even then, it was on your nightstand.*

Joe shoved aside some fossilized dinosaur eggs on a shelf. *So what? That was years ago. I was young and uptight, that was all. I'm more mature now. More laid-back.*

His wife was silent.

As he was searching, his hand knocked into something.

A framed photo fell. He caught it before it could shatter.

His last photo of Mina. She was pregnant and beaming. Joe stood beside her. No white streaked his temples back then. His uniform was freshly ironed, his beard neatly trimmed. And he had to admit—his belt was a few notches wider now. That young, innocent man was beaming, his hand on Mina's belly.

Fifteen, he thought, throat constricting. *You would have been fifteen now, little girl.*

"She was beautiful."

A voice from behind. Joe spun around to see Simone.

"Are you sneaking up on me?" he snapped. "Mind your own business."

She stepped back, going very pale. "Sorry," she whispered.

"There it is." He put the photo back and snatched his communicator from the shelf. "I'm calling the Rangers to get you now. Hopefully they toss you off the planet. I—"

He froze, staring at his communicator.

Five missed messages from Fort George, the Rangers headquarters.

All were marked urgent.

He read the first message.

Joe. We need you. Your sister is on Mintari.

"You're not coming with me." Joe stomped down the mountain, his sleep-or-die slung across his back. "Get back into the cave."

Simone hopped after him on one foot, pulling her boot on. No, not her boot. One of Mina's boots, which she had found in the cave. They were the same size.

"You already locked the gate!" Simone cried. "I can't go back in."

He tossed her the key. "Here."

She tried to catch the key while hopping on one foot, wobbled, and fell. Scree cascaded down the mountain, and she yelped.

Joe kept trudging down the path. "Will you be quiet? You'll alert every tarry raptor on the mountain."

Vinnie raced after them. The little velociraptor was no larger than a beagle, but he fashioned himself a Ranger too. He let out a little cry.

"I don't mean you!" Joe said. "I mean the megaraptors."

Vinnie puffed out his feathers and let out a little screech. Simone squeaked in fear. The journalist managed to pull both boots on, and now she was struggling to button up her safari shirt. All while racing after Joe. The wind blew off her straw hat, and when reaching to catch it, she faltered and nearly tumbled down the mountainside. Vinnie had to catch the back of her shirt and pull her to safety.

Simone screamed. "Your dinosaur bit me!"

"He saved your backside. Vinnie, you have orders not to save her again. Now get back to the cave, lady!"

"Have people ever told you that you're abrasive?"

"I mostly stay away from people. I wish you did the same."

Joe walked faster, trying to ignore her. His heart shook in his chest.

Amissa. Here on Mintari.

The greatest huntress in the galaxy, she called herself. That she was not. But she *was* perhaps the most famous huntress. Even Joe, who lived in a cave, kept hearing about her kills. Rangers, tourists, other poachers—they all talked about her.

Five rocky planets orbited Nyx. Two belonged to humans: urban Cloventia and rural Dagon. Three planets belonged to animals. Using time-casting, scientists sent robotic mosquitoes into the past, collected DNA samples, and recreated extinct animals in modern times. They gave planet Thalia to the victims of the Holocene extinction event. Rhinos, elephants, lions, dodos—all those animals humans had driven to extinction in modern times. The second planet, Borealis, they gave to Ice Age animals.

Until now, Amissa had kept to Thalia and Borealis. She delighted in hunting bears, giraffes, mammoths, pandas, and a thousand other creatures big and small. When animal-rights activists condemned her, she only laughed, blew them a kiss, and winked.

But until now, despite all her fame, Amissa had stayed away from Mintari.

Something changed.

Now she was here. On Joe's turf.

His communicator beeped. The Rangers were all sending messages back and forth. Amissa was doing another live stream.

Joe paused on the mountain path. He stared at his communicator's screen, disgust roiling in his belly.

Amissa stood with one foot on a dead nodosaur's head. Grass rustled around her, and mountains soared behind her. Joe recognized the place. Laramidia Fields. Only fifty kilometers southeast from here.

He had not seen his sister in years. She had not changed much. She was thirty-three now, but she still looked the same, youthful and beautiful. She could have passed for twenty. Probably using a good dose of filters and definitely a lot of makeup. She had always been vain.

She looked into the camera, speaking gravely.

"I know that many people condemn what I do here," Amissa said, broadcasting her words to her millions of followers. "I get the hate mail. The death threats. But these so-called animal-rights activists are ignorant. They sit in their cozy little apartments, living in cities built on animal graveyards, judging people like me who live in nature. I don't hate nature. I'm restoring the natural balance. Nature chose dinosaurs for extinction. Scientists played God, recreating these ancient animals in their labs. I'm simply doing what is natural. What humans have done since the dawn of history. Hunting."

Rage flowed through Joe. His hand shook around his communicator. He nearly crushed the little device.

Simone rushed up to him. She caught the last bit of Amissa's words.

"What a load of garbage!" Joe said.

Amissa seemed to be staring right at him through the screen. A thin smile touched her lips. "Are you watching me, my brother? If you are, I would like to tell you something. I will keep hunting. I will keep showing the beauty of nature to my fans. And if you or anyone else tries to stop me …" She leaned forward and grinned. "You are welcome to try."

Joe stood there, head spinning, teeth grinding.

Simone reached into her pocket for her SmartSphere. It was a cheap SmartSphere, but it still included a hover option. When Simone tossed the circular computer into the air, it floated between her and Joe.

"Is there anything you would like to say to your sister, Joe?" Simone said softly.

He nodded.

Simone tapped the floating SmartSphere, turning on the camera app. It began to record him. Live.

Joe stared at the lens.

"Listen to me, Amissa Triplehorn, and listen well. You know who I am. You know what I do to poachers. Leave this planet now. Or I will do what Rangers do."

On her own live feed, she looked up and smiled in delight.

Joe gripped Simone's floating camera and nearly crushed it while shutting it off.

"There, you have your sound bite," he snapped at Simone. "Happy? Now get back to the cave! I've got a poacher to shoot."

He stomped downhill, already regretting losing his cool. He had allowed the journalist to manipulate him. From now on, he hunted in silence.

When he reached the foothills, Joe climbed onto a boulder, stuck his fingers into his mouth, and let out a loud whistle.

He stood, watching the forest.

Simone froze at his side, pale. "Don't forget the megaraptors!" she whispered. "You'll alert them!"

"Good! Maybe they'll eat you."

She crossed her arms. "Not funny, Mr. Triplehorn."

Vinnie let out a cackle that sounded almost like laughter.

Joe wasn't worried about attracting predators. They didn't respond to whistles. The only animals that whistled around here were archaeopteryxes—feathered dinosaurs who, on Earth, eventually evolved into birds. The archies were small, quick, and fled easily, and the big predators rarely bothered hunting them. So no, Joe wasn't worried about attracting anyone with his whistles. And in case any predators did come near, Joe took extra precautions.

Simone, who had been preoccupied with pulling on her clothes, finally seemed to notice his "extra precautions." She sniffed, frowning.

"Something stinks around here."

Joe nodded. "It's T-rex urine." He pulled a bottle from his pocket. Amber liquid swirled inside. "Want some?"

She gagged and took a step back. "Disgusting! Don't tell me you drink that stuff."

"What?" He frowned. "Of course not. I splash a few drops on my boots whenever I leave the cave. Raptors recognize the smell. It terrifies them. And they keep away from my trail."

Simone snatched the bottle from him and began dousing her boots. Mina's boots.

"Hey, hey, go easy on that stuff!" Joe said, pulling the bottle back. "Just a few drops are enough. This is hard to come by."

"I can imagine," Simone said. "I don't want to know how you got it."

Joe scanned the foothills. "Come on, where are ya?" He whistled again.

A rumble sounded in the forest. The trees rustled and bent. And there he came, charging through the woods.

Dozer the triceratops.

Simone had ridden the dinosaur before. But she still gulped, gripped Joe's arm, and hid behind him. Joe didn't scoff. He had to admit: the sight of a triceratops bearing down on you was terrifying. Right up there with a tyrannosaur's open jaws.

But Dozer would not harm them. The burly dinosaur ran up the hill, reached them, and reared. Even when standing on four legs, he was so big that his beak was higher than Joe's head. And when he stood on his back legs, Dozer was truly a titan. He was bigger than a woolly mammoth—several tons heavier and far more muscular. His horns were a foot wide at their base, tapering to deadly points.

Dozer didn't fear the smell on Joe's boots. A triceratops feared nothing.

Dozer knelt and lowered his head, forming a ramp. Joe grabbed the trike's horns, yanked himself up, and climbed onto his back.

"Get back to the cave!" he told Simone and kneed the triceratops.

"It's called the Last Home Hollow!" she said.

But Dozer was already rumbling downhill.

Simone, who remained behind, gave a loud whistle.

Dozer froze, turned around, and lumbered toward her.

The journalist stood there on the hill, pale and shaky. But she managed to smile. "He's well trained."

Joe felt the blood rush into his face. He clenched his fists, staring down at Simone from atop Dozer's back. "Stop calling him back!"

Snorting contentedly, Dozer knelt beside Simone. He seemed to like the redhead. She grabbed the dinosaur's lumpy hide and began climbing up.

"Okay. If you take me. Wh-whoa!"

Joe kneed the trike again. Once again Dozer rumbled downhill. Simone yelped, nearly fell, but clung on. While the dinosaur animal was bounding through the forest, she managed to climb and sit behind Joe.

"That was a dangerous stunt, you know!" she told him. "I could have fallen off and been trampled."

Joe nodded. "You would have been safe in the cave."

She rolled her eyes. "Joe Triplehorn, you are insufferable."

"Great, you finally realized it. Maybe now you'll leave me alone."

A rumble sounded in the depths of the forest. Just a random dinosaur minding its own business. Simone gulped, wrapped her arms around Joe, and squeezed.

"Never gonna leave you," she said.

"Loosen your grip, at least."

"Not gonna."

"You're crushing me."

"Don't care."

He groaned. "Just go away!"

"Don't wanna."

They rode on through the foothills until they reached Hell Valley. The grasslands spread into the distance. Morning mist still clung to the valley, hiding the forest beyond. In the distant haze, one could make out the blurred forms of grazing sauropods.

"Do you know where Amissa is?" Simone asked.

Joe nodded. "Laramidia Fields. About a day's ride from here."

"A day's ride! Mr. Triplehorn, you need to install an engine on this triceratops of yours."

"I don't do engines. I don't drive jippis. I don't fly in tricopters."

Simone frowned. "Don't the other Rangers use technology?"

"They do. Good for them. I don't."

"But if it takes you so long to get anywhere, how do you stop poachers?"

"Sometimes they get away," he admitted. "That's the cost of my philosophy. Ms. LaRue, my job isn't just to shoot poachers. That's part of it, yes. But not the soul of it. Do you know what my real job is?"

"Hopefully not to butcher redheads and turn them into sausages."

He ignored the joke. "My real job is to preserve the purity of Mintari's wilderness. So I try to avoid anything that can disturb nature. So I live in a cave. And I ride a dinosaur." He glanced over his shoulder at her. "And no, I don't hurt redheads."

She smiled and leaned against his back. "You sound like one of the Mintari shamans. I've heard about them. Humans who don't live in Dinovia. They live in the wilderness and worship dinosaurs as gods."

"My mother is a shaman," Joe said. "She raised me. I got it from her. But I chose a different path." His voice dropped. "Different from both my parents."

The old pain stabbed him.

His father. His sister. They were predators. Worse than any dinosaur.

Riding behind him, Simone placed a hand on his shoulder. Her red hair tickled his cheek. "We all become our own people. My parents grew up below the neon sea. On the lowest levels of Cloventia. Right on the planet surface. My mom was a cleaner, my dad a mechanic. They had never been to the floating skyscrapers." Her voice was so soft Joe could barely hear. "I left them down there. I climbed."

Joe looked over his shoulder at her. Her eyes seemed to be gazing at a distant memory. Another trick? Just acting, trying to play on his sympathies?

Don't fall for it, he told himself. *She just wants a story. That's all you are to her. A scoop.*

"We are nothing alike," he said.

She met his gaze steadily. "More than you realize, Mr. Triplehorn."

"You don't know what it's like," he growled. "When your family betrays you. When someone you love dies. You're nothing but a buzzard, here to scavenge for some scoop so you can keep climbing your neon towers. So you can leave your family deeper in the muck. You're more like Amissa than like—"

"Amissa murdered my sister," Simone said.

Joe shut his mouth.

Simone stared at him steadily, not even blinking. Her freckled face flushed, her fingers trembled, but her gaze did not waver.

"What?" Joe whispered.

Simone nodded. "That's right, Mr. Triplehorn. Something you didn't know about me. When I said we are alike, I meant it. I—"

The foliage parted.

Dinosaurs burst out from the trees.

Simone screamed.

"Megaraptors," Joe muttered. "Great."

There were five of them. Despite their name, they bore little resemblance to small, harmless theropods like velociraptors. The megaraptors were more closely related to T-rexes. They were smaller than their gargantuan cousins but still a force to be reckoned with. From snout to tail, a megaraptor was as long as a school bus.

Small theropods like Vinnie sported feathers. It kept them warm. The megaraptors were just large enough to have lost their feathers. Their skin was scaly and brownish green. They snarled, baring rows of serrated teeth. Their arms were longer than a T-rex's and tipped with claws. More claws sprouted from their feet, curved and sharp and longer than Joe's forearm.

The pack surrounded them. They inched closer, not yet attacking, sizing up their enemy. Vinnie hissed but the big predators barely noticed him, no more than a man might notice an angry field mouse. Dozer grunted, reared, and swung his horns from side to side. The megaraptors hissed and clacked their jaws, hesitating. A triceratops was nothing to trifle with even for a pack of five butchers.

Simone clutched Joe. "How did they find us? You said the T-rex urine would mask our scent!"

Joe sniffed. He frowned, sniffed again. "Do I smell sausages?" He grabbed her pack and ripped it open. "What the hell?"

Simone paled. "I ... I thought I'd pack us lunch."

Joe groaned. "Tar it, lady! You drew them right to us."

The megaraptors inched closer, unable to resist the intoxicating scent of sausages. They were lean and hungry after a long winter, and even Dozer did not deter them. Their sickle claws rose. They licked their chops, salivating.

Trembling, Simone tossed the sausages at them.

"Here, eat it!" Her voice trembled.

The sausages slapped onto the ground. The megaraptors ignored them. Who wanted crumbs? They had a larger meal in mind.

"These aren't dogs you can buy off with treats." Joe unslung his sleep-or-die from across his back. "You really screwed us over this time, lady."

"I'm sorry," she whispered.

One megaraptor lunged, mouth opening in a hungry howl. Simone screamed.

Joe fired his sleep-or-die.

The rifle had two barrels. One for sleep. One for die. He fired the left one—sleep. A tranquilizer dart slammed into the megaraptor's chest.

The beast reared, howling in rage. Tranquilizers took a few moments to kick in. Rangers normally used them to sedate wounded dinosaurs before tending to them, not to stop charging predators mad with hunger. A dart in his chest, the megaraptor continued its attack.

Little Vinnie, bless his heart, launched himself into battle. He bit the megaraptor's ankle. The big theropod didn't even notice.

Dozer swung his horned head toward the charging predator. And a massive head that was. It was ten feet long, and it weighed almost two tons. Its three horns thrust out like medieval pikes, and the bony frill rose high, forming a barrier of thick bone. This massive head—the finest defensive weapon nature had ever produced—moved incredibly fast. Triceratops had ball joints in their necks. It let them swing their heads in every direction at breakneck speed—without actually breaking their necks. These ball joints, it was said, were the most perfectly spherical objects nature had ever created in an animal.

The megaraptor perhaps ignored Vinnie. But it was impossible to ignore a furious triceratops. Seeing that gargantuan head wheel toward him, the theropod shrieked and fell back. A wise decision. Those horns could gore a T-rex. They would make short work of a megaraptor.

But four more megas were here. And they lunged at Dozer from the sides and back.

A trike put all his armor on the front. Not like an ankylosaurus, who spread his armor across his entire body. A triceratops was virtually indestructible from the front—his skull could withstand blows that would shatter even the fearsome ankylosaurus. But his sides and back were exposed. And the megaraptors knew it.

One sank his teeth into Dozer's tail. Another raptor lashed her sickle claw, ripping into Dozer's flank. The triceratops bellowed in agony.

"Run, Dozer!" Joe cried.

The trike lowered his head and bolted forward.

With massive force, Dozer plowed into one megaraptor. His horns tore through scaly flesh.

Dozer kept running. For a few seconds, he carried the raptor impaled onto his horns. Then the triceratops tossed his head, hurling his foe. The gored carnivore slammed into one of his fellow raptors. Both predators collapsed.

But three more megaraptors were running in hot pursuit. The smell of blood emboldened them.

Joe slung his rifle over his shoulder. Simone ducked, and he fired another dart.

The dart hit a raptor. The predator shrieked and fell back.

Two other megaraptors leaped forward.

Dozer swung his tail, knocking one back. The second raptor—an old male with one eye—landed on Dozer's back.

Simone screamed, clinging to Joe.

The carnivore dug his claws into Dozer's flesh, climbing the triceratops. The one-eyed raptor opened his jaws above Simone. Those jaws were as long as the woman was tall. They could devour her with one or two bites.

Joe tried to load another tranquilizer dart. But just then, another raptor came at Dozer from the side. The triceratops swiveled his head around, goring the animal. One of Dozer's horns carved deep into his foe's flank. Joe bounced on Dozer's back, dropping the dart. Tar it!

Riding Dozer with them, the one-eyed raptor loomed over Simone, salivating. The hungry carnivore leaned down to feast.

Simone reached into Joe's pack, pulled out the bottle of T-rex urine, and hurled it at the enormous predator.

The bottle hit the raptor's teeth and shattered, spraying the amber liquid everywhere.

Like all dinosaurs, the megaraptor was slave to his instincts. And one of those instincts was to avoid T-rexes. The smell alone repulsed them. The one-eyed raptor shook his head wildly, inhaling the scent of his nemesis. T-rex meant danger. T-rex meant *run*. The predator released Dozer, fell off the triceratops, and fled into the bushes.

That was the last of them.

Vinnie cackled, snapped his teeth at the fleeing raptors, and strutted around. *Take that!*

One megaraptor had fled. Two lay wounded behind Dozer, gored and bleeding out. Two more were succumbing to the tranquilizers. One swayed and fell with a *thud*.

"Halt, Dozer," Joe said.

The triceratops lumbered to a halt, moaning. The big dinosaur was wounded. Blood ran down his flanks and tail. He had suffered a bite and several gashes from the terrible sickle claws. But he was still standing.

Joe leaped off the dinosaur, landing on his feet. Simone followed, not quite as gracefully. She landed awkwardly, wobbled, and fell down hard on her backside. Thankfully a patch of grass cushioned her fall.

"Are you all right?" Joe said to her. He couldn't hide the annoyance from his voice.

She sat on the grass, legs sprawled out before her, drops of T-rex urine clinging to the rim of her straw hat. She looked miserable but she nodded. "I'm all right."

Joe turned toward Dozer. The big dinosaur moaned. He took a few more steps, then curled his legs and sat down hard beside Simone, shattering a fallen log like it was a twig.

"Poor Dozer," Simone said, struggling to her feet. "Is he hurt badly?"

Joe ignored her. He approached the wounded triceratops and stroked his beak.

"It's all right, big boy, it's all right," Joe cooed. "You're fine. You're fine."

The enormous herbivore moaned and licked his hand. Joe examined the trike's wounds. A megaraptor had sunk his teeth into Dozer's tail. Other raptors had slashed him along the ribs.

Triceratops perhaps lacked bony armor on their bodies. But their skin was thick, scaly, and hard. The megaraptors had done some damage, ripping the skin, even reaching the flesh beneath. But thankfully, they were all flesh wounds. The predators had not reached any internal organs. The wounds were painful, no doubt. But dear Dozer would overcome.

"Is he dying?" Simone whispered.

"He'll live," Joe said. "He's a tough old boy. It could have gone a whole lot worse."

He opened his pack and rummaged through his medical supplies. At times like this, he missed Mina more than ever. His wife had been a paleonarian. A dino doc. Joe had no formal education, but he had picked up a lot over the years.

You taught me well, Mina.

He splashed antiseptic into the wounds. Dozer leaped to his feet and bellowed. The sound shook the forest.

"Calm down, boy, calm down!" Joe had to spend long moments stroking the animal's beak. He didn't want to tranquilize Dozer if he didn't have to.

Finally Dozer settled down again. It was impossible to stitch dinosaur skin. But Joe screwed in a few steel bolts to hold the thick, lumpy skin together. Old Ranger trick. Dozer grumbled and grunted but let him work.

"Can I help?" Simone said.

"You've done enough."

Joe taped long bandages onto the wounds. He patted Dozer's beak and gave him something for the pain. He hugged the trike's head and whispered into his ears.

"Thank you, friend. You saved my life. Again."

Simone stood by silently, watching.

"Joe," she finally said. "Joe, I'm sorry."

He turned and began walking uphill, leaving Dozer to rest.

Simone hurried after him. "Joe? Where are you going?"

"To find the megaraptors."

Simone gasped. *"What?"*

"There are wounded megaraptors up there. I'm going to treat them too. Stay here. Out of my way."

He walked uphill, rage simmering inside him.

Joe, that's unfair, Mina said in his mind. *Why are you so mean to the woman?*

He dug his fingernails into his palms, stomping among the ferns and ginkgo trees. Dozer's blood left a trail through the forest.

She drew the predators to us! he answered in his mind. *Now dinosaurs are hurt.*

Mina sighed. She seemed so real in Joe's imagination. As beautiful as the day he met her. And as the day he lost her.

She didn't know, Mina said. *She just packed food.*

She also stole your boots, Joe answered silently.

Joe, you're not really angry at Simone, are you? You're angry at your sister.

Joe gritted his teeth. *We'll discuss this later.*

He trudged uphill, the rage like raptors inside him. He had not wanted this. Any of this. He had been happy enough in his cave, alone with his misery. No, not alone! He had Dozer and Vinnie. Who needed more? Now these two women from Cloventia were here. Simone and Amissa. A journalist and a huntress. Now all hell was breaking loose. Now dinosaurs were hurt.

He reached the first wounded megaraptor.

The enormous predator lay on her side. A young female.
The length of a bus, with a head the size of a recliner, she struck
an imposing figure—even while lying still. When she saw Joe, the
megaraptor finally moved. Her sickle claw twitched, a weapon the
length of a Roman sword. But the dinosaur would not harm him
now.

Dozer had plowed into the megaraptor like a true
bulldozer. The theropod was bleeding from her side—the work of
Dozer's horns. Her left leg was broken.

"She won't live long like this," Joe muttered to himself.

Vinnie bared his teeth and hissed. *Let her die!* the little
raptor seemed to say.

"We must heal her. She's a dinosaur of Mintari. Same as
you, Vinnie. Same as Dozer. She deserves life."

Joe aimed his sleep-or-die. He fired. A tranquilizer dart
jabbed the megaraptor in the neck. The wounded beast found
enough strength to rumble and hiss. But soon she began to calm,
to grow sleepy.

Now Joe could tend to the dinosaur. First, just to be safe,
he pulled rope from his pack and bound the megaraptor's jaws
shut. Some Rangers did not take this extra precaution. Some
Rangers died young.

When the dinosaur was secure, Joe examined her wounds
more closely. They were bad. The worst was the broken leg. If a
megaraptor could not run, she could not hunt. If she could not
hunt, she would die.

"You'll need help setting that bone."

The voice came from behind him.

Joe spun to see Simone standing there.

"I told you to stay with Dozer. Why do you keep sneaking
up on me?"

She placed her hands on her hips. "Well, good luck setting
the bone by yourself. The femur is longer than your body."

She turned to leave.

Joe closed his eyes and took a deep breath, trying to calm himself.

"Fine," he said.

She looked over her shoulder. "What's that?"

"Fine. Help me set the bone." Another deep breath. "Please."

She smiled. "Mr. Jurassic Joe! Did you just say the magic word? My, my, I think I'm taming the beast. Maybe next I can even teach you how to make the bed." She hid her mouth behind her palm. "I saw the state of your linens."

"I'm regretting this already," he muttered.

They worked together, him pushing, her pulling, finally setting the bone. Joe found a sturdy branch, and they made a makeshift splint, securing it with rope. Hopefully it would not shatter once the megaraptor awoke.

"Is this how you heal all your dinosaurs?" Simone asked. "Like this in the field, using ropes and sticks?"

"How else should I do it?" He began cleaning the megaraptor's cuts.

"In a proper clinic! With medical tools. With real splints or casts, not branches."

He snorted. "And how do you suggest we transport a dinosaur to a medical clinic?"

She bit her lip. "A giant ambulance? Okay, dumb suggestion. An airplane?"

Joe stapled the deeper cuts. "See any runways around here, cheesecake? This is Mintari. We don't have planes large enough for dinosaurs. There are a few paleonarians who make house calls. They fly out in tricopters to the field. I already checked. They're all on other calls."

"A few paleonarians?" Simone said. "Like a few hundred?"

"Three," Joe said.

"Three hundred?"

"Three."

Simone's jaw dropped. "Three dino docs. For an entire planet. With billions of dinosaurs on it."

Joe placed bandages over the cuts. The megaraptor was still sleeping soundly.

"Mintari has a population smaller than your neighborhood back home, cheesecake. And not nearly as much money. We do what we can with what we've got."

Simone blinked. "But … the tourism industry! It must bring in a fortune."

"Most of that money goes toward importing food from Dagon. No farmlands on Mintari. The land belongs to dinosaurs, not tractors. Importing food from another planet gets expensive."

Simone heaved a sigh. "It's no wonder Amissa and other poachers run free here."

Joe paused from his work. He looked into her eyes. "Not entirely free. I still hunt them. At least—I was hunting poachers before you drew a pack of megaraptors with your sausages."

She flinched. "I said I'm sorry. How much more do you want me to apologize, Joe? Or will no amount of groveling appease you?"

He packed his things. "I'm going to look for the other megaraptors."

He walked through the forest, following the trail of Dozer's blood. Simone followed silently. Vinnie cantered alongside them, pausing every now and then to snatch a dragonfly.

Not far away he came across another wounded megaraptor.

Simone gasped and covered her mouth.

This one was in worse shape. Joe saw that at once. Dozer had gored the carnivore deep into his gut, probably slicing up

internal organs. Two ugly gashes bled on the megaraptor's belly.
The predator lay on his side, breathing heavily. Already flies were
bustling in the wounds.

Joe aimed his sleep-or-die.

"Joe?" Simone said. "Joe, you forgot to load a tranquilizer
dart."

He pulled the trigger.

This time he fired from the right barrel. A bullet drove
into the megaraptor's head. The dinosaur died instantly.

Simone jumped. "Joe, why?" she whispered.

He wheeled toward her, upper lip peeling back. "Never
had to put a dog down, princess?"

Her face flushed. Something seemed to snap inside her.
Her own upper lip rose in a snarl. "I've had enough of this. I told
you I'm not a princess. And I'm not a cheesecake. And I'm not
someone you can just keep insulting."

"Don't like it? Get lost. Get off my planet."

"It's not your planet, dammit! Who do you think you are?
You're just some hermit who lives in the forest and pretends to be
a hero. You're no hero." She snorted. "You're nothing but a
drunk, cranky, middle-aged loser who can't face his own pain. So
you take it out on others. Guess what, buddy. We all have our
traumas. But we don't all spend our lives sulking over it. Oh, sure!
You love dinosaurs. You're a great protector of nature, blah, blah,
blah. Maybe that's just because you don't know how to handle
another human being!" She stepped closer, eyes narrowing. Blue
fire blazed in those eyes. "You know what I think, Joe
Triplehorn?"

"Watch your words," he said.

"I think you're no different from your sister. Just another
human who came here to play with dinosaurs. Oh, she's a
huntress, and you're a Ranger, but at the end of the day, you both
shoot dinosaurs."

He raised his hand to strike her.

She did not flinch. "Go ahead, Jurassic Joe, hero of Mintari."

With sheer force of will, he lowered his hand. But his anger only grew. "And I suppose you're different, is that so? At least I protect dinosaurs." He pointed at the corpse. "This one did not have to die! You drew it with your sausages. Just like you attracted the allosaurs with your whining. Several dinosaurs dead because of you!" He barked a laugh. "You're doing a better job than Amissa. She's only killed one."

She scowled. "Yes, okay! I don't know what I'm doing here. I'm a foreigner. I'm blundering about like an idiot. But if you lived in the city like a normal person, I wouldn't be out here!"

He rolled his eyes. "If I lived in the city, cheesecake, you wouldn't give a damn about me." He stepped closer to her. "Admit it. You liked the idea of some wild, unwashed mountain man. Somebody unlike the soft, perfumed men you know from Cloventia. You wanted to meet the rugged Ranger. Didn't you? Had dreams of romancing the beast?"

She gasped. "How dare you, Joe Triplehorn! If I ever dreamed about you, it would be a nightmare. You're insufferable."

"You're a pest!"

"You're a rude, obnoxious brute!"

Joe laughed mirthlessly. "Maybe I am. But I was better off without you. Since you came here, predators have been attacking me, my pet trike was wounded, and you ate the dinosaur eggs I was hoping to hatch!"

"Well, I got T-rex pee all over me!" Simone shouted, gesturing at her clothes.

Joe stared at her, fists clenched. He looked at her wet clothes, then into her eyes.

Then he started to laugh.

She blinked at him. "Are you laughing at me?"

He nodded, laughing harder.

Simone glared at him, hands on her hips. She knelt, lifted a handful of mud, and tossed it onto his face.

His laughter died at once. He stared at her, face covered in mud.

Simone kept glowering, chin raised, hands on hips. Then she guffawed. And then she was laughing uncontrollably.

Joe grumbled, scooped up mud, and tossed it onto her. It splattered across her face.

Simone gasped, got mud in her mouth, and began to cough and spit. Which only made Joe laugh again. Until she threw mud in *his* mouth. Soon they were slinging mud at each other, scoop after gooey scoop of the stuff, until Simone finally slipped and crashed down, covering her entire body with mud. Joe laughed until she grabbed his leg and pulled him down with her.

They lay in the mud, covered from head to toe. Slowly their laughter faded.

Joe turned his head and looked at her. She looked at him.

Joe spoke softly. "A long time ago, when all humans lived on Earth, our ancestors found dinosaur bones. For thousands of years, they told stories about those bones. They thought they were mythical dragons, beasts who could blow fire and challenge the gods. Some thought the bones belonged to giant humanoids who roamed the ancient lands of chaos. They believed their ancestors, great heroes, slew those monsters and buried the bones."

Simone smiled. "So dinosaurs are responsible for the legends of dragons and giants."

"Then, when the era of science began, humans believed dinosaurs to be a failure of nature. They described dinosaurs as lumbering, tubby, slow-witted buffoons. Evolutionary dead ends."

Simone pouted. "It's not their fault the asteroid hit them."

"But they're only animals," Joe said. "They're enormous. They're majestic. They're incredible. But they're only animals.

Same as we are. They're like us. They want to protect those they love. They're scared of dying or getting hurt. They're scared of being alone."

Simone's eyes softened. She caressed his cheek. "You're not alone, Joe."

He looked at her, seemed about to say something. Then he pushed himself to his feet. "Let's get back to Dozer. Amissa is still out there. Killing dinosaurs. And I'm going to stop her."

CHAPTER ELEVEN
Runt of the Pack

The parasaur meat was spoiling.

Not much was left anyway. The achillobators had eaten most of the carcasses in the field. They had dragged some back to the nesting grounds—a rib cage, a few severed limbs, a tail. The meat would feed the expectant mothers, who were still brooding on their eggs.

While the pack gnawed around her, Fig remained hungry. She had learned that she could not eat meat more than a few hours old. This meat was a few *days* old. The flies bustled. Maggots were already hatching inside. Her fellow bators did not mind. They would eat until every scrap of meat was gone, then stack the clean bones around their nesting ground, urinate on them, and mark their territory. Figaro could help stack bones and mark territory, but she would not eat meat once the first fly appeared.

Another way I'm different, she thought, hugging her flat belly. A funny underbelly with no feathers, with a little round scar in the middle. She was so hungry. She had not eaten since the day the meat was fresh. Not unless you counted some berries, roots, and seeds she chewed on when nobody else was looking. Her stomach growled. But she remembered all too well the illnesses of her childhood. She sat, leaning against the stony mountainside, trying not to waste too much energy. She watched the others.

The entire pack was here. Lately, they spent most of their time in the nesting grounds, hunters and mothers alike. They all

259

needed to protect the eggs. By old customs, the rotten meat was for the nesting mothers only. The hunters ate in the field. But every once in a while, a hunter would get peckish, grab an old bone, and gnaw on it, using their serrated teeth to carve off whatever meat remained. Hunters were ruthless beasts, but they were not above scavenging or stealing.

Crooked Wing was especially ravenous, stealing several ribs from the jaws of hungry brooders. The big huntress had no mate, had laid no eggs. She was growing restless in the nesting grounds, and stealing entertained her. One of the expectant mothers, a young female named Long Tail, was lazily picking at a parasaur rib. Crooked Wing stomped up to her, snatched the bone right from her mouth, and crushed it between her jaws. Long Tail hissed, rose from atop her eggs, and snapped her teeth at the big thieving huntress.

Crooked Wing screeched, slashed her sickle claw, and sliced several red feathers off Long Tail. After that, the young mother obediently shared her meals. Her top priority was for her eggs. After laying them last moon, Long Tail was weak. The calcium in her body was depleted. She could not risk a fight with a strong huntress like Crooked Wing. Even if she must go hungry.

Fig, who watched the confrontation, waited for things to settle down. Then she tiptoed forward, snatched Long Tail's lost feathers, and wove them into her dress. Fig grew no feathers of her own, so she relied on those the others shed. Every once in a while, the feathers Fig collected wore out, fell off, and fluttered away on the wind. Fights were good for replenishing her garment.

Crooked Wing returned to her own perch, gnawing on the stolen bone. She was six years old, well into her prime breeding years, and her lack of eggs embittered her. Unlike the little turtles Fig liked to study by the river, achillobators could not lay unfertilized eggs. Only when mated would a female bator perform this sacred duty. And Crooked Wing had not laid eggs since breaking her wing in the landslide. Since then, no males competed for her. She was deformed. Strong, yes, but not a healthy female.

Fig thought that silly. Why not breed with Crooked Wing? She was the biggest, strongest female in the pack, and her hatchlings would be great predators. A crooked limb would not pass to hatchlings! It was the result of an injury. Not a deformity in the blood. Fig understood this. Why couldn't the others? The male achillobators were creatures of instinct. The spirits of the soil and sky had given them wisdom. But sometimes their instincts failed. To the males, an imperfect female meant imperfect hatchlings. Babies who would be born weak, deformed, and die in the cruel wilderness of Mintari. They had no way of knowing that an injured wing would not pass on to offspring. They simply knew Crooked Wing was deformed and therefore not good for breeding. And so the big female remained barren.

And I am barren too, Fig thought. No males ever competed for her, no matter how many feathers she adorned herself with. She had tried performing mating dances once, copying the other females, but the males only snorted and turned away.

I too am deformed, Fig thought, looking down at her body. She was much smaller than the other bators. Not much larger than a yearling. Her limbs were skinny and brown. She had five toes on each foot, not four, and no claws grew from them, only weak little nails that Fig would sometimes bite short. While the other bators groomed their feathers, searching for mites and ticks and other parasites, Fig would be there, a foot pulled to her mouth, using her tiny little teeth to bite off her toenails.

As the pack bummed around the nesting grounds, Fig kept thinking about it. The way she looked. The cub on the hill. A human cub.

A cub who looks like me, Fig thought. *I am a human. I am ...*

She tried uttering the word again, struggling to spit out each syllable. "Fi—ga—ro!"

A few bators raised their feathered heads, stared at her, and snorted. What strange sounds was this underfed, raggedy bator making? She was clearly a freak. A runt. They should drive her out of the pack. On the other hand, Red Scar protected her. And she helped mark territory and arrange bones, and she sometimes nested on eggs while the mothers were away. She was a runt. But she was pack. The bators lowered their heads. Just another eccentricity from little Figaro, the weirdest bator who ever was.

Yes, a weird one. And not only because of how she looked. But how she thought. How she seemed to lack even the most basic instincts. How she tormented herself with questions that rattled around and around her mind.

She needed to understand. What she was. What her memories meant.

I'm human. Yet I'm pack. I understand the pack. And the pack welcomes me. But I look like a human. I have human memories. I'm confused.

She did not think these thoughts with words. She thought with images, emotions, broad concepts. But she remembered some words too. She had understood the girl and her parents. She had lived among humans once. And she wanted to understand.

She made a decision.

She was still weak after the winter, still scrawny, unable to run for long without weariness. There were scabs on her arms, and she kept pulling lice out of her hair. After the next hunt, once she put some meat on her bones, she would regain her strength. Then she would be ready. Strong and fierce with spring's meat and berries inside her, and she would go out there. She would track down these strange bipeds with no feathers or scales. And she would find out who she was.

Berries. Yes. Fig ate those too. Secretly. Shamefully. No self-respecting achillobator would eat berries. That was what herbivores ate! The next step was eating leaves. Fig hadn't stooped as low as leaves yet. But sometimes she did sneak away, collect berries and nuts and roots, and stuff her cheeks.

The guilt filled her afterward. She would scrub her face and hands in streams, hiding the juice. The fruit called to her every day. For a long time, she had felt broken. Shameful. Weak. But now she understood her cravings better. Humans must be herbivores. Or perhaps they were omnivores like the tiny feathered raptors who sometimes scurried among bushes, creatures no taller than Fig's knee. If she was indeed human, that must explain her strange cravings.

Yes, she *was* a human. She had to be. Often Fig was almost entirely sure. But then night would fall, and she would curl up with Red Scar, and the pack breathed deeply around her, a sound as soothing as waves, and the feathers were so warm … and Fig felt like an achillobator through and through. Part of the pack. Forever.

After five days, the parasaur meat was all gone. The bones formed new walls for the nesting grounds, covered with urine to deter oviraptors or other egg-snatchers from approaching. And the hunters went out again.

Mintari was full of prey. Countless herbivores roamed the forests, mudflats, and floodplains. They climbed the mountains and swam in the lakes. Among themselves, the herbivores fought for territory. Stegosaurs and ankylosaurs stuck to the forests, where they munched on low-growing ferns. Many hadrosaurs herded along riverbanks, guzzling foxtail reeds, bits of rotten wood, and insects. Some sauropods extended their ridiculously long necks to the treetops, while others swept their heads across the plains, inhaling grass and shrubs. The horned ceratopsians grazed along scrublands and hills, devouring massive quantities of palms, cycads, and ferns. Sometimes, before spring gave forth enough blooms, the herbivores fought for food. Usually they each kept to their own territory, preferring chewing over fighting.

Predators did not like fighting either. Like herbivores, carnivores just wanted to stay alive. They avoided confrontation whenever possible. When given a choice, they hunted the youngest or oldest herbivores, those would not put up a fight. Easy prey. Over time, the predators of Mintari had established their territories, their own pecking order. The massive predators like the tyrannosaurs and carcharodontosaurids preyed on big, meaty prey, even hunting old or juvenile triceratops (though even they avoided the big male trikes). The small raptors preyed on insects, little mammals, and eggs. The spinosaurids kept to the marshlands, while the pterosaurs grabbed fish from rivers and lakes. Few predators dared attack the giant sauropods—unless they were desperate. Even mighty T-rex feared the enormous patagotitan, supersaurus, and argentinosaurus. Sauropods were not to be trifled with. Their tails and massive feet were strong enough to crush the biggest predator.

In this Darwinian hierarchy, midsized predators struggled to find a niche. They were too big to live off eggs, amphibians, and insects. Too small to attack the big ceratopsians, ankylosaurs, and stegosaurs. Those spikes, clubs, and horns could do serious damage. Achillobators found themselves in this unfortunate "midsized predators" group, alongside competitors like sinraptors and megaraptors. Crammed midway up the food chain, it was a daily struggle to survive. A small meal wasn't very filling. A big meal meant competing with big predators. Not an easy niche.

But they made do, hunting hadrosaurs (Fig's favorite), the odd gallimimus if they could catch one (and those dinos were *fast*), sometimes even juvenile or old iguanodons (a dangerous endeavor—their spiked thumbs had eviscerated quite a few bators). When meat ran low, the bators were not above scavenging, eating the old bones and gizzards a T-rex might leave behind as scraps.

But there was one particular herbivore that achillobators loved most.

The magyarosaurus. The smallest sauropod on Mintari.

Most sauropods were gargantuan. They were as long as whales. They lorded over the planet, fearing nothing, true titans who could crush mountains. Magyarosaurus was a sauropod too. It had the long neck, the round body, the healthy appetite. But it was tiny. A dwarf sauropod. A typical magyarosaurus was no larger than an achillobator. If Fig stood on her tiptoes, she could peer over one's back.

Fig didn't know why magies were so small. But she knew they were delicious. Once you cracked through their armored skin, you found soft red meat. If Fig ate that meat within the first few hours, she didn't even get sick.

Maybe they were so small because they lived on an island. They could not swim, leaving them trapped in their little habitat. Thankfully, bators *could* swim. Today the pack headed into the water. Magy Island awaited.

They weren't great swimmers by any means. They could only paddle awkwardly. Every once in a while, a bator would sink to the bottom of the lake. But with their powerful feet, they kicked themselves back up to the surface, gulped down air, paddled a short distance, then sank again. Like that, hop by hop, they could cross the water.

Swimming burned a lot of energy. More than running on land. That was good. The big boys like T-rex simply didn't bother coming here. Why waste energy swimming to an island if only dwarf sauropods lived there? Not worth the effort. The spinosaurs were powerful swimmers, but they lurked in the marshlands. As a result, not many predators even bothered attacking the isolated magies.

But the bators did. For them, if they were willing to put in the effort, the island always promised a tasty, filling meal.

Figaro was probably the best swimmer in her pack. She didn't even sink. She stayed afloat for the entire swim, moving her skinny brown limbs like some aquatic spider. It filled her with pride. She was perhaps the slowest runner in the pack, but by golly, she could outswim even the powerful Crooked Wing.

She reached the shore of Magy Island first.

As she waded through the rushes, bugs bit her, adding to the many bite marks on her arms and legs. She shoved aside tall reeds, reached solid ground, and sat down on the grassy bank. At once she began a grooming routine, looking for any bugs, leeches, or other parasites she might have picked up on her journey.

Grooming was a ritual among achillobators. And an essential one. Fig feared bugs. Everyone in her pack did. Bugs could lay eggs inside you. Bugs could sap your strength. Bugs could kill you within a year.

Ticks were the worst of a bad bunch. Bators groomed themselves religiously for ticks, and they had taught Fig this skill. She had seen bators bitten where they could not reach. Once bitten, powerful predators weakened, thinned out, lost their feathers, and were finally abandoned by the pack. They died slow and miserable deaths, diseased and withered and feverish. The pack's greatest enemy was not triceratops with his terrible horns, not the stegosaurus with his spiky tail, not even T-rex with his huge teeth. It was the humble tick.

Even their mating dances were all about ticks. Raise the wings! Flap the tail! Crane the neck! Left foot up, right foot up! These beautiful dances were not only about impressing a mate with one's dexterity. They revealed body parts for inspection. If a potential mate saw any tick hiding under wing or tail, it was game over. No breeding. Only a slow death ahead.

Fig had become the best groomer in the pack. Her slender fingers seemed made for parting feathers, her sharp eyes were good at inspecting skin, and with her flexible limbs, she could reach the toughest spots. She had picked many ticks off achillobators. It was, she suspected, one of the reasons they kept her around despite her oddities. With her strange, clawless fingers, she had saved many lives.

This year, her nimble fingers would work hard. Winter had brought relief from the scourge of parasites. But with spring, the bugs were out in numbers, hiding in tall grass, in puddles, in ferns, even in the flesh of dead herbivores. Fig knew what the other bators had taught her. She must remove the ticks quickly. Before they could infect her with their terrible wasting curse. If you caught them fast enough, you were fine. Sitting on the shore, she inspected her body.

"Ack!"

She let out a sound of disgust. A leech on her calf! She twisted and pulled it off, ripping some skin. Fig gagged and stuck out her tongue. She hated leeches. They were disgusting, but thankfully, they were rarely deadly.

The other achillobators finally made it ashore, weary after their long swim. They climbed onto the grass, shook the water out of their feathers, and—

"Ack!" Fig cried, louder this time. Bator heads spun toward her.

A tick! A tick on the back of her neck!

She could not see it. But she felt it. She recognized how it felt under her fingertips. She twisted her fingers, careful to pluck the tick off without crushing it. Crushing a tick could leave the legs inside your skin—along with their disease.

She looked at her fingers. Yep—a tick all right. She shuddered and tossed it away. She had caught it fast enough. Before it could infect her. Had she not groomed herself after her swim, she would have languished, reduced to skin and bones, too weak to eat, to run. Her joints would calcify, and finally some scavenger would come pick on her still-living flesh.

The other achillobators, perhaps inspired by Fig's gruesome discovery, began to groom themselves too. But suddenly, halfway through the ritual, Red Scar raised his head and stared westward—toward the center of the island. One by one, the other bators removed their snouts from their feathers. Their nostrils flared. Their muscles tensed, and they crouched, taking position to pounce. A few bators salivated.

Fig sniffed the air. She smelled nothing. That was normal. She had accepted long ago that her sense of smell was lacking. The other bators were constantly sniffing around, detecting scents she could not. She was their fingers, and they were her nostrils.

Red Scar gave a long, slow sniff ... then inched forward, skulking low to the ground. The others followed, their underbellies grazing the ground. Bushes and ferns hid their progress. Fig crawled on her stomach, parting ferns and grass. Grasshoppers bustled around her. Hopefully no more ticks or leeches. In her right hand, she gripped her sickle claw, the gift of a dead bator. The claw was longer than her hand, harder than granite, sharper than any thorn. If Fig applied enough force, she could disembowel a herbivore or slice its windpipe.

A snake slithered toward her. Fig's heart lurched. But it was only a simple brown snake, going about its business. Harmless. She let it wriggle under her belly and slither on its way.

Fig had learned which snakes could kill a bator. Had this snake sported yellow stripes, she would have leaped away in fear. As it was, she kept crawling.

Finally even Fig smelled it. A rich, meaty aroma.

Prey animals.

The bators moved slowly, nostrils flared. They were just small enough to hide in the bushes. That was fortunate, for their red feathers offered poor camouflage. They had evolved them on a different world, in a time when they were dominant, an apex predator in their environment. Here on Mintari, they must rely on sneakiness. But their red coloring still offered some advantages. The color served a purpose similar to the yellow stripes on a venomous snake. *Beware me, I bite!* Useful when you were small enough for a sauropod to accidentally step on.

Fig crawled closer, rose to a crouch, parted the tall grass … and there they were.

Her mouth watered.

A magyarosaurus herd.

The small predators were peacefully munching on ferns and cycads. They were a little larger than bators, which meant they were much larger than Fig. But for sauropods, they were tiny. Laughably so. They couldn't even reach the higher branches. Fig could easily walk between the legs of a normal sauropod. Even standing on tiptoes, stretching her arm upward, she wouldn't reach their underbellies. But she stood eye level with a magy.

They were sort of adorable, Fig had to admit. Unfortunately for them, also delicious.

"Yip, yip!" Red Scar cried. *Time for attack!*

The pack pounced.

Fig pounced with them, howling, twisting her face into a fearsome mask.

The magies started and cried out in terror. Juveniles ran between the legs of their mothers. It was a small herd, only twenty or so dinosaurs. They turned to flee … only to run into ambush. Crooked Wing had led another group of bators around them, cutting off retreat. Leaping from the grass, Crooked Wing and her gang yapped and snapped their teeth.

The idea was to trap their prey and stir panic. Not yet to pounce. They must choose a good target first. Magies were perhaps small sauropods, but they still outweighed the bators. A lashing magy's tail could still break a leg. A broken wing could perhaps be tolerated; Crooked Wing was living proof of that. But a bator with a broken leg could not hunt. They were as good as dead. The pack would feed brooding mothers and chicks, but nobody would take pity on a cripple.

So the pack carefully considered. That big magy bull looked dangerous. He huffed and reared and swung his tail through the air. Too risky. The magy mothers protected their hatchlings. Everyone knew that made them dangerous. But there—an older cow, slow and lumbering. Her meat would be a little tough. But she would be easy to kill, and the other magies would not risk their lives to save her.

Red Scar pointed his snout toward the old mag, then yipped, giving the signal.

The pack swarmed.

They leaped onto the old sauropod, biting and clawing. Crooked Wing bit into the magy's neck while Long Tail tore at her flank. Even Fig participated. She hugged the magy's leg and bit into the rubbery skin. Her tiny teeth didn't even draw blood. Ah well, she tried.

Within moments, the old cow was down.

As expected, the other sauropods fled. Working together, the magies might have saved their old comrade. But rescue attempts could go wrong. Some healthy magies might die. Juveniles could be trampled or orphaned. Young females might be left without a mate, never to lay another egg. The cold reality of survival on Mintari dictated that they must leave a sauropod behind. The herd fled, crying out in anguish.

The achillobators did not follow. They had felled a one-ton sauropod. Small compared to the big long-necks on the mainland. Some of those titans could weigh a staggering hundred tons. But even this dwarf sauropod provided ample food for the pack. They feasted.

This was a successful day. They had crossed the water without anyone drowning, avoided battles, ate well, and the weird little runt pulled out their ticks with her slender fingers. A good day. A day they survived. Any day you survived on Mintari was a victory.

Fig ate with gusto, bloodying her face. Then, while the others gnawed on bones, she wandered the island, picking berries and dates. She even found some tasty grains and some crunchy tubers. The others were too busy eating more meat to notice. When Fig knelt by the water to drink, she gazed again at her reflection. A small face. A face without scales or snout. Skin that had been so pale throughout winter, which was now tanning brown in the sun. Black hair which just kept growing, which she cropped short using sharp granite shards. Strange eyes. Eyes with white around the irises. Curious eyes. Human eyes.

Today she had eaten well. Today she was healthy, which she so often was not. There were no ticks on her body, her muscles were lean but strong, and she was ready to take a journey.

To find out the truth.

To find more humans.

She set out that same day.

The pack would remain on the island overnight, gnawing on bones. Tomorrow they would return to the nesting grounds with leftovers for the brooding mothers. Fig couldn't wait that long.

Clouds were gathering. Rain might soon fall. And she had tracks to follow. It must happen today.

As the rest of the pack lounged by the carcass, nibbling and relaxing in the sun, Fig tiptoed toward the water. A few steps away her heart began to race. A few steps more and her legs began to shake. A few steps after that and her head spun.

I must go back. I can't do this.

She took a shaky breath and thought of the girl on the hill. She remembered those vague images of a woman in her past. She must do this. She must.

Fig started to run. She ran until she reached the shore and dashed into the lake. The chill water soothed her, calmed her heartbeat, and steadied her spinning head.

I can do this. I'm strong enough. I'm a huntress. A fighter. A proud female of my pack. I can survive a quest on my own.

She began to swim back to the mainland.

Often Fig would wander away from her pack to find berries, but never too far. Today, for the first time, she would leave the pack beyond earshot. She might get lost. Might never find them again. Might die in the wilderness.

What a fool she was, swimming out here! What a silly quest! She had to turn back. She must rejoin them. She was pack!

She was not a human. She was a bator! Small and featherless, perhaps, yes, but she was one of—

No. Figaro, no! Keep swimming. Keep going!

She tightened her lips and kept swimming, leaving the island behind.

Just for a while, she told herself. *Just until I find out who the humans are. The pack will keep returning to the same nesting ground all spring. I can find them again. Once I have my answers.*

That soothed her. This was just like another trip to find berries. Just a longer trip, that was all. And instead of berries, she would find answers.

She was climbing onto the mainland, careful to avoid the ticks and leeches in the reeds, when she noticed that a bator was swimming after her.

Fig stared at the lake. The dinosaur was coming from the island. When his snout rose from the water, she recognized him.

Red Scar. Leader of the pack.

He was the only one following. The others were probably still bumming around the carcass, too full to move. But Red Scar was swimming vigorously.

"Gak, gak!" Fig cried, pointing at the island. *Go back! Go back!*

He snorted and ignored her command. What kind of alpha took orders from the runt?

The bator stepped onto the shore, shook water from his feathers, and stared into her eyes. *I'm coming with you.*

She pointed at the island. "Gak! Gak!"

He took a step closer to her. *No way.*

Fig groaned in frustration, stamped her feet, and snapped her teeth. He must go back! She would be gone for days. If Red Scar abandoned the pack for that long, a challenger would arise. Crooked Wing especially had been gunning to lead, testing Red

Scar again and again—nipping at his legs, tugging out his feathers, biting his tail, constantly probing for weakness.

"Gak!" Fig said. She bent her arm, an imitation of Crooked Wing, and bit the air.

Red Scar understood. He snorted and took a step closer to Fig. *Even so, I go with you.*

"Gak, gak!" Fig insisted. She spun around and marched away from the shore, heading across the grasslands.

And the big old bator followed. Stubborn, loyal fool!

She kept walking, chin raised, ignoring him. He wanted to follow? Very well. Fig would run. Bators were fast sprinters, but they could only run short distances, soon exhausting themselves. Fig was slow, but she had more stamina. A year ago, she had fallen into a river, and the current had pulled her far from the pack. Fig had jogged all morning, finally catching up with the others, and still had enough energy to join them on a hunt. No bator could do that.

She burst into a run, heading over the floodplains. She knew these lands. She had been roaming these parts all her life. Every hill, every bend in the river, every distant mountaintop marked her location. She did not need to rely on scents like a bator. She painted maps in her mind. Without claws, fangs, or much muscle, Figaro relied on her wits to survive.

Were all humans like her? Weak, soft, with useless noses? Did they too rely on brains instead of brawn? Could they too run for long distances, moving slowly but steadily? One more question she must answer.

She was several hours away from the hilltop where she had seen the girl. If tracks were still there, she could follow them. Find out where the humans lived. Find answers about herself. Her past. Where she came from. Fig had no memories of hatching. No idea where her mother had nested on her brood of eggs.

Where did I hatch? What kind of nesting grounds do humans inhabit? Do I have sisters and brothers? Have they laid eggs already?

So many questions! They rattled around her mind. She kept running.

For a while, Red Scar loped alongside her, easily keeping pace. But after a while, the big bator began to slow down. He was easily five times her size, and carrying that much weight wasn't easy, even for a big strong male. With his thick coat of feathers, he was also more prone to overheating. Figaro was barely larger than a hatchling, her limbs slender but strong, and her dress of feathers billowed loosely, cooling her off. She kept running, leaving him behind.

Good.

Fig kept running. After a while, she had to stop. Even she had reached her limit, and she clutched her side, panting. She looked behind her, and she no longer saw Red Scar. She had lost him. Maybe he would return to the pack, maintain his leadership, and when Fig returned in a few days, she would still find a home.

The race had exhausted her. Yes, she had eaten well these past few days, but she was still weak and scrawny after winter. Maybe running had been a mistake. She looked around for nuts, fruits, maybe a crunchy grasshopper or two, but she found nothing. Hungry again and light-headed, she kept going. The hill she sought rose alongside a river where she had caught fish and eaten berries before. Hopefully she would find dinner there.

This was the life of an achillobator. Constantly hungry. Constantly seeking food. Herbivores had it easy. Grass, shrubs, trees—they grew everywhere on Mintari. Herbivores had to skip the odd meal, especially in winter, but they rarely starved to death. A predator was free and strong, but a predator was always outracing starvation.

Clouds gathered, hiding the sun, and Fig lost track of time. It must be late afternoon when she finally saw the river and hill. A few parasaurs stood along the riverbank, drinking from the water. They looked up, startled, when Figaro approached. Their crests gleamed in the sunlight, purple and blue. Fig salivated. Parasaur crests—her favorite food. But they were big dinosaurs, significantly larger than achillobators. It took a pack to bring one down. The crested duckbills certainly did not fear a human cub. They went back to drinking. Fig left them alone. She wasn't taking on six adult parasaurs on her own. Not even for a taste of their delectable crests.

Belly grumbling, Fig climbed the hill where she had met the girl. The humans had departed inside some strange, hollow beast they called a *jippi*. A dinosaur with round legs that puffed smoke out its backside? Ridiculous! Fig must have imagined it. Maybe while searching for berries, she had accidentally touched one of the dangerous red mushrooms. Those sometimes made dinosaurs lose their minds, yap at invisible enemies, and whimper at every shadow.

Yet when Fig climbed downhill, she saw the oddest tracks she had ever seen. Long, solid tracks. Not footprints. Tracks from the weird round legs of the smoky creature. The tracks looked like two snakes. Had that hollow dinosaur without a head devoured the humans? The girl had entered it willingly. Like an animal entering a nest. Maybe it wasn't a dinosaur at all. Maybe it was some kind of nest. A nest that could move.

Fig shuddered. Humans were unlike any dinosaur she had ever seen. No, they weren't even dinosaurs. They were barely even animals! What were these strange creatures?

What am I?

She began following the tracks. They stretched across the grass and ground. Even somebody like her with a useless nose could follow this trail.

At least until it started to rain. Which it did. Heavily.

No. No, no, no!

Figaro yipped in frustration. This was what she had feared. Rain. Cursed rain! The bane of any tracker. Even achillobators, with their powerful noses, struggled to follow tracks after rain.

With angry yowls, Fig raced after the fading tracks, trying to follow them as best she could. She could still see them. The tracks were deep. The rain filled them, forming two little streams. Good, good!

She ran, arms pulled tight to her chest like a sprinting achillobator. The rain kept falling, washing the mud from her hair. Wind buffeted her. A few of her feathers, which Fig had painstakingly collected and woven into a dress, came loose and fluttered away. She paused, yipped in anger, and chased the feathers. She caught a few, but the others scuttled far off-trail.

She stood in the rain, considering. She needed that coat of feathers. She could not grow her own, and without feathers, what kind of bator was she?

A human. I am human. Or think I am. I must find out.

Oh, let the feathers fly! She still had plenty on her dress. She ran onward through the rain, following the tracks.

Only she could barely see the trail now. The rain kept splattering down, coating the long narrow tracks with mud. Lightning flashed. Thunder rumbled.

"Yoeeeee!" Fig cried. "Yoooeeeeee!"

A bator's cry of annoyance. Mud was sluicing over the tracks, burying them. Fig scampered onward, hunched over now, moving on all fours, trying to sniff for the tracks. She had seen bators moving like this. It didn't work. She smelled nothing. Oh, curse her tiny nose!

Lightning split the sky. On a distant hill, a tree burst into flame. A second or two later, the thunder pounded into Fig. She yowled to the sky.

"Yeooo, yeoooooo!" *Bad, bad!*

She lowered her head to the ground, sniffing, caught a whiff of something ... something like tar. Her eyes widened. A scent! A track!

She scampered forward on all fours, her nose pressed to the ground. The whiff of tar again ... but it was softer already.

She kept going, tracking her prey through the rain as lightning flashed and thunder boomed. Sniffing, the scent got stronger, thicker, meatier. Somewhere deep in her mind, Figaro realized that made no sense. Why would the scent grow *stronger* as the rain kept falling? But she was intoxicated. She was a predator on the hunt, single-minded. She moved along, sniffing on hands and knees.

Until she found herself sniffing a clawed foot.

A foot with three claws. Two claws that gripped the ground. One claw that rose into the air, longer and sharper. A sickle claw.

So that explains the smell, she thought.

Fig stumbled backward, slipped, and landed on her backside. She gaped up, her heart galloping. For a split second, she had dared to hope. Perhaps she had simply run into an achillobator? But no. This was something different.

The dinosaur stood in the rain, staring at her with yellow eyes. A big male. Smaller than giants like tyrannosaurs but still bigger than an achillobator. He was probably ten, maybe even twenty times heavier than Fig. He stood on powerful talons, his flightless wings sprouted mean claws, and fangs filled his elongated jaws. Brown and white feathers coated him, slick with rain. He emitted a tarry stench.

Fig recognized this species. She had run into them before. They were the archrivals of the achillobators, competing in the same ecological niche. Everyone in the pack feared and loathed them.

A utahraptor.

The utahraptor let out a low growl and licked his chops.

Raptors normally moved in packs. But sometimes young, strong males struck out on their own, searching for females. They were dangerous, violent, and always hungry. And Figaro was small, weak, and alone. The perfect prey.

The raptor took a step closer, salivating in the rain. Blue scales rippled across his snout. Fig gave him a name in her mind. Blue Snout.

Sitting in the mud, she raised her sickle claw. It trembled in her hand.

A shriek pierced the storm.

But it didn't come from Blue Snout. It came from behind Fig.

Red feathers flashed through the rain. A big, powerful figure vaulted over Fig and slammed into the raptor.

Fig leaped to her feet. Red Scar! He had followed her!

The two feathered dinosaurs slammed together with a *crack*. They fell backward and hissed.

"Yip, yip, yip!" Fig cried, jumping up and down. Red Scar was here!

The two dinosaurs charged again. Lightning flashed, illuminating their bared teeth and swiping claws. They snapped and snarled and slashed, but so far, they cut only feathers, not flesh.

While jumping, Fig dropped her sickle claw. Brilliant. She knelt and felt around in the mud, never removing her eyes from the fight.

"Yaooo, yaooo!" she cried.

Red Scar and Blue Snout circled each other in the mud, growling. As Fig watched, a chill flooded her belly. It seemed an unfair fight. Red Scar was smaller, older, slower on his feet.

The two species were close relatives—they were both dromaeosaurids. While utahraptors were larger and stronger than achillobators, they still competed within the same ecological niche. Both species were midsized predators, dwarfs to tyrannosaurs, giants to velociraptors. In this middle weight category, they preyed on the same herbivores. That made them mortal enemies. Like rival siblings, the two species often clashed. Here in the mud, these two great warriors would fight one more battle in their ongoing war.

Thunder boomed. Where was that tarry claw? Ah, there! Fig raised it from the mud. The sickle claw gleamed in the lightning. It was longer than her hand, curved, and sharp.

The two deadly predators stepped back, then charged again, howling. Red Scar stretched his neck forward, trying to reach Blue Snout's neck. But the utahraptor was faster. The bator's teeth snapped down on only air. Sidestepping, Blue Snout lashed his sickle claw. With a sickening *rrrrip*, the claw tore through Red Scar's side. Feathers fell into the mud. Blood splashed.

"Yaoooooo!" Fig cried.

Within a split second, her terror blazed into fury. She leaped forward, slashing her sickle claw through the air.

Blue Snout was not expecting this weak mammal cub to attack. Certainly not with a claw this size. The raptor took a step back. But he was too surprised to defend himself properly. With all her strength, Fig thrust her sickle claw down. The weapon ripped into Blue Snout's shoulder, tearing out a chunk of flesh.

The raptor gave a deafening yowl. But he did not retreat. The beast leaned forward, jaws open, ready to slay this impudent little mammal.

Fig stumbled back. The jaws widened before her, large enough to bite her in half. She hurried farther back, but the raptor moved so fast, and—

With a furious screech, Red Scar slammed into the raptor's side, knocking the larger dinosaur into the mud.

Before Blue Snout could recover, Fig lashed her claw again. She ripped out a chunk of those blue scales along the snout. She pulled her hand back before the raptor could bite it off.

The raptor yowled, leaped to his feet, and snarled. Blood dripped down his muzzle.

Red Scar and Fig circled him, each raising a sickle claw, slashing the air.

"Yrrr, yrrr!" Fig said, teeth bared, and moved in closer.

Blue Snout had enough. This wasn't worth it. He was bleeding, he was outnumbered, and there wasn't enough meat on this scrawny mammal anyway to fill his belly. He had mistook the little creature for a herbivore. Clearly she was some unfamiliar predator. He would avoid her kind in the future.

The utahraptor fled, bleeding and hungry. He would live to fight another day.

Fig took a shaky breath and turned toward Red Scar. The bator stood in the mud, the rain washing the blood from his wound. The raptor had sliced Red Scar across his flank. Thankfully, it looked like a flesh wound. Once the rain stopped, Fig would look for the special blue maggots that cleaned wounds of infection. The pack knew how to find them in fallen logs. The wound would heal, and the achillobator would have two scars to his name.

He looked at her, tilted his head, and sniffed. *Are you hurt?*

Fig did a full turn, letting him inspect her, then cooed. *I'm fine.*

Then she could not help herself. She hugged the bator, crying softly into his feathers as the rain fell. He draped his long snout across her slender shoulder, comforting her.

"Yeeeooo, yeeeeoooowww," she purred. *I love you.*

By evening, the rain eased to a drizzle. Fig found a patch of fallen logs and branches. The rain brought out the special blue maggots, and she placed them into Red Scar's wound. The bator flinched and hissed. It hurt. But Red Scar knew it would heal him. He was the one who had taught Fig this skill.

After treating the wound, Fig looked for the tracks, but they were gone. The sun was almost gone too. The last red light of sunset was fading to a deep blue tinged with gold. There was no good place to sleep out here. They eventually found a flat slab of rock, safe from bugs that moved in the mud. They lay down, and Fig buried herself in his feathers, feeling warm and safe. His steady heartbeat lulled her into sleep. She was glad he was here.

CHAPTER TWELVE
Skull Swamp

After recovering for a while on the ground, Dozer was back on his feet, munching on ferns. The megaraptors had done a number on him, but it would take more to keep the triceratops down. A few flies bustled around his bandaged wounds, but Dozer was good at turning his head, snorting at them, and blowing them away.

"He's eating!" Simone said. "He must be feeling better."

Joe stroked the dinosaur's enormous one-ton head. "Dozer here spends most of his time eating."

The dinosaur ignored him, munching away. The bandages were still securely in place. The trike had lost blood but not enough to slow him down for long.

"You ready to keep going, boy?" Joe whispered, patting his friend. "Or do you need to rest?"

The dinosaur grunted, gulped down his mouthful of ferns, and pawed the dirt. He was ready. Simone was worried about riding him in this state. But Joe reassured her. For a triceratops, carrying two humans was nothing. They might as well be two sparrows.

"We'll cut east across Hell Valley, make our way through Skull Swamp, then reach Laramidia Fields," Joe said. "That's the last place Amissa was sighted."

Simone cringed. "S-skull Swamp?"

Joe nodded. "There are skulls among the branches of the trees there. Legend says that a monster lives in the water. That he decapitates his victims and hangs the skulls on branches as trophies."

She shuddered. "That's just a tall tale. The kind hucksters like Triassic Terry tell around the campfire." Her voice dropped to a whisper. "Right?"

"Maybe," Joe said. "I've seen the skulls myself. Could just be the remnants of an old flood, tossing dead dinosaurs onto the trees. Maybe the bones of the bodies fell back into the water, and only the skulls remained in the branches. Or maybe ..." He smiled wryly. "A monster."

"The only monster I want to catch is Amissa," said Simone. "And she's the worst monster on Mintari. Let's go."

As they rode onward among cycad trees, Joe thought back to Simone's words. She had spoken them just before the megaraptor attack.

Amissa murdered my sister.

He wanted to ask for more details. But he kept silent. The time did not feel right. He did not want to probe into her past. No more than he wanted her probing into his.

Maybe I was wrong about her, Joe thought. *Maybe she's not just here for a story. This is personal for her.*

Or maybe Simone had lied. Maybe this was just a sick joke. A trick. If he found out she had lied, that she was using Amissa against him ...

Joe felt sick. He pushed that thought out of his mind. For now, he would give her the benefit of the doubt. But no, he did not trust the journalist.

Joe Triplehorn did not trust anyone.

Other than dinosaurs, he thought.

He patted Dozer's frill. The bony shield was as thick as a house wall and far sturdier. For ten years now, Dozer had been his shield. His companion. His friend. Joe had been at his lowest, lying drunk in a field, a widower drinking himself to death, too broken to even get up and walk. A pack of predators had approached. Joe had been too drunk to even determine the species. He kept lying in the grass, cradling his bottle. Let them eat him. But Dozer had charged up, had sent them fleeing. The triceratops had saved Joe's life. In more ways than one. Since then, the two had been inseparable.

Joe looked at Vinnie. The little rascal was loping alongside the trike. True to his name, the velociraptor was a speedy beast. Much faster than a triceratops. Every once in a while, Vinnie ran ahead, then returned with a lizard or cynodont in his jaws. Sometimes he darted into the bushes to catch a dragonfly. Velociraptors were perhaps the deadliest predators on Mintari. Luckily for other dinosaurs, they were too small to kill anything bigger than a sparrow. Vinnie was no larger than a beagle.

You've been here for me too, Vinnie, Joe thought. *For a long time now.*

Humans had hurt him. Humans had betrayed him. Given half a chance, Simone would betray him too. Joe knew this. How could he ever trust another human? No. He could not. He would keep his trust only in dinosaurs. Simone was here for the ride. But as soon as he could, he would send her packing.

"Are there lots of predators around here?" Simone whispered, unaware of his thoughts. She rode behind him, her arms wrapped around his waist.

Joe nodded. "You're here, aren't you?"

"Ha ha, very funny. You know what I mean."

"This is Mintari, cheesecake. There are predators everywhere. Keep an eye open."

Simone gulped and tightened her arms around him, almost crushing him.

He cringed. "Loosen your grip!"

"Not gonna."

Daniel Arenson

As he struggled to breathe, Joe was keeping a lookout. He always did. And he knew Vinnie wasn't darting ahead every moment just to catch bugs. He was scouting their path.

"It's dangerous business, roaming around Mintari," Simone said. "You have to be crazy to do it."

"Nobody's ever accused me of being sane," Joe said.

A pterosaur sailed overhead, shrieking. Simone yelped. She tightened her grip around Joe even more, almost snapping his ribs.

"Shoot it!" she said.

"Relax! It's just a pterodactyl. It won't hurt you."

Simone was trembling. "One carried me off once. To its nest."

He looked over his shoulder at her, frowning. "A pterodactyl carried you? *Pterodactylus antiquus*?"

"Some kind of pterosaur. It was a ..." She leafed through her field guide. "*Tupandactylus imperator*, I think. A big one. Colorful. She placed me in her nest." She shuddered. "I'm scared."

Joe shook his head and whistled softly. "You're lucky to be alive, Simone LaRue."

"I do not recommend the experience." She smiled wanly.

"I've flown on a pterosaur before," Joe said. "Long ago."

Her eyes widened. "Did one grab you too?"

"Not exactly. Now be quiet. We're entering spinosaurus country. We don't want to attract them."

Her trembling intensified. "S-spinosaurus?"

He nodded. "Yep. Big fellas. Even longer than a T-rex."

She whimpered. "Wonderful. I miss the Slum Wars."

They rode in silence for a while. The grass rose as tall as a man. But riding the trike, the grass didn't even reach Joe's feet. Sauropods grazed in the distance, their necks sweeping across the fields like vacuum cleaners, sucking up grass. Parasaurs congregated by a river to munch on reeds. A few reared and blew air through their colorful crests, filling the valley with music. A pachycephalosaurus herd gathered by some cycad trees to breed. The churlish herbivores sported domes of thick bone atop their heads. Those domes were even thicker and harder than a triceratops frill. Two domeheads raced toward each other and butted heads, competing for a female. The *crack* reverberated across the grasslands.

Dozer rode onward, the two humans on his back, while Vinnie raced ahead through the grass. Finally Joe spoke again.

"I've heard of the Slum Wars. And I don't get it." He shook his head. "Humans fighting humans. For what? A few more square miles of dust."

Simone leaned her head against him. "We don't all have the luxury of a cave."

Joe snorted. "A cave is luxury?"

"For the people of Earth, it would be. I've seen children starving in the desert, too weak to even bat away the flies. I've seen child soldiers with guns taller than their bodies. At night, their warlords place them in cages. Sometimes they make them fight for sport. A cave would be luxury for them."

"That sounds awful," Joe said. "I can't even imagine living like that. You're right. I am lucky. It's no wonder humans left Earth for Cloventia."

Simone smiled wanly. "The same thing happens on Cloventia. On the lower levels. Deep under the neon sea. There are children on Cloventia who live under bridges and inside huge machines. They scrounge through landfills to survive. I was one of those children. I got a scholarship to Clover Heights Academy. I made my way out. Most of the Grunge Children, as they called us, were not as lucky."

"Clover Heights," Joe said. "That's where my sister studied."

"She did. And she made my life hell."

Joe tapped Dozer's frill. The dinosaur snorted, rumbled to
a halt, and began munching the tall grass. Joe twisted around to
face Simone on the trike's back. She looked at him. She had
washed her face and hair in a nearby creek, though mud still caked
her clothes.

"Earlier, just before the raptors attacked, you said
something." Joe stared into her eyes. "You said that Amissa
murdered your sister."

"She did."

"What happened?"

Simone lowered her eyes. A tear trailed down her cheek.
"Not now, Joe."

"I'm sorry. I told myself I wouldn't pry into your
business."

"It's all right." She placed a hand on his knee. "I'm just ...
still in pain. It was many years ago. But it still hurts."

"It was fifteen years ago that I lost my wife," Joe said.
"Some pain never leaves you. You just carry on through it. Every
day." He laughed mirthlessly. "I haven't always been great at
carrying this burden."

She held his hand. She looked into his eyes again. "If you
ever want to talk, Joe, I'm here. I meant what I said earlier. You're
not alone."

"Talk to you?" Joe said. "Or to the readers of the *Cloventia
Gazette?*"

"I won't publish anything you don't want me to."

He smiled thinly and nodded. "Sure."

"You don't trust me." Simone heaved a sigh. "I can't
blame you. But the offer stands."

Joe almost told her. About the night King Ivan had
devoured his pregnant wife. About the long, lost years after that,
years of shadow he could barely remember. About how Mina still

spoke to him after all these years. About his family betraying him, betraying all of Mintari.

But he could bring none of it to his lips. No, he was not ready to trust her. Or any human.

"Come on, let's keep going," Joe said. "Amissa is fast, we're slow, and it's still a long way."

Dozer moved slowly but steadily like a tank rumbling across the wilderness. They cut east across the grassy valley, and by afternoon, they reached Skull Swamp.

Even Rangers feared to enter this place. But cutting through the swamp was the shortest way to reach Laramidia Fields, where Amissa was running wild. Joe would risk it.

The great Gould River flowed from Mudge Mountain, watering the meadows and forests. Here in the lowlands southeast of Hell Valley, the river flooded the plains, creating a swamp. There was no solid ground. The best one could hope for was deep mud. The water soaked up minerals from the soil, turning greenish and brackish. Moss and ooze draped boulders, tussocks, and logs. Mangroves grew like ancient soldiers of wood and leaf, their roots rising from the water like stilts. A volcano rumbled in the distance, belching smoke. The air was hot and soupy, glimmering with floating green spores.

Dozer trudged through the mud, grunting and coughing. The trike wasn't happy. He preferred roaming along grasslands or low hills. This was not his natural habitat. The mud rose past his knees. Sometimes the mud gave way to mossy water, and he splashed his way through. The triceratops seemed miserable, but at least he found many ferns to eat. Joe kept checking Dozer's bandages, making sure they were tightly sealed. The last thing he wanted was this green water infecting the wounds.

Joe had never realized how slow triceratops were until now. He needed to catch his sister. He tried to tell himself that he was a tortoise chasing a hare, and that slow and steady won the race. But he felt more like a snail chasing a cheetah.

He was probably just being stubborn. Riding around on a triceratops like some crazy dinoboy. If he used a jippi or tricopter like the other Rangers, he'd be facing Amissa by now. He could fly over the swamp instead of trudging through it. When he was a younger Ranger, he would sometimes take a tricopter. Before these long shadow years. Maybe he should embrace technology again. But tar it, what was the point of Mintari if you filled it with machines? It might as well be Cloventia in that case. This planet should be kept pristine. A nature reserve. A place for dinosaurs to live free of human interference. He was only here to protect the planet from other humans, and every day, he struggled to keep his footprint minimal. Ironically, that gave other humans an edge. To defeat them, he must become one of them.

"Joe!" Simone gasped and clutched his arm. "What's that?" Her voice trembled. "Darwin's beard! It's so awful."

Joe looked into the distance. A smile spread across his face. "Nothing to worry about. They're gentle giants."

Simone trembled. "Those claws. They're huge." She clung to him tighter. "That's the ugliest dinosaur I've ever seen."

Joe's smile grew into a grin. "Tourists always say that about them. Simone, meet the therizinosaurus. I call them therizins for short. They're famous for having the longest claws of any dinosaurs. In fact, of any animal that ever lived. On average, each claw is four feet long. But they can grow five feet or longer."

Simone blenched. "Great. An animal with Simone-sized claws."

The Rangers always laughed about how tourists reacted to therizins. Visitors described them as goblins, demons, nightmares. Joe didn't think they were that bad. But he understood where tourists were coming from. They had all heard of T-rex, triceratops, brontosaurus, stegosaurus—the classics. But most tourists had never heard of therizinosaurus, and its appearance shocked them.

A therizin was the size of a T-rex. But it looked nothing like the famous predator. Nor like any other dinosaur, for that matter. Its underbelly was gray and warty, while its back sprouted shaggy feathers. The neck was long and skinny. The head was small and beaked. It walked on two legs, stooped over like a gargoyle, potbellied and hunchbacked. But most bizarre were those horrid claws, the longest nature had ever produced.

Simone whimpered. "I hate them."

Joe laughed. "They're harmless. Herbivores."

Her eyes widened. "Those ugly brutes with claymore claws are herbivores?"

"Yep. They use the claws to grasp branches and pull down the leaves. Watch."

Three therizins were moving ahead through the swamp. They were so tall that the mossy water barely reached their knees. The bizarre dinosaurs reached toward the treetops, hooked leafy branches with their enormous claws, and pulled the meals toward their beaks. One of them was using its bizarre hands to scoop up vegetation from the swamp, filter out the water, and snack.

"They look like a cross between a turkey, sloth, and goblin," Simone said. "And they're the size of dragons. I never knew such a dinosaur existed. You don't see those at the gift shops." She laughed uneasily. "I guess they wouldn't make good toys. Nightmare fuel."

"They're gentle creatures," Joe said. "Proof that you can't judge a book by its cover."

"Or a dinosaur by its claws." Simone curved her fingers in a mimicry of claws, then smiled and rested a hand on Joe's shoulder. "Or a mountain man by his manners."

Vinnie cackled something that sounded almost like a laugh. The velociraptor was riding on Dozer with them. The swamp only reached the trike's underbelly, but Vinnie would have drowned.

Dozer waded through the water, moving closer to the towering oddities. The trike had to test each step. The water was shallow here. But just to their left, Joe knew, it sank into the depths of the Gould River. One could tell where the water was shallow based on its color and the vegetation. Mangroves grew from the shallows. A coating of moss marked the deeper waters. Nyx was inching toward the horizon. Joe hoped they could leave the marshlands before nightfall.

He knew there was a terror that lurked here. He did not relish spending the night.

As Dozer rode closer, the therizins paused from eating. Atop their slender necks, their little heads swiveled toward the intruders. The clawed herbivores snorted and groaned, but they seemed more curious than hostile. After all, it wasn't every day one saw a triceratops trudging through a swamp. Especially not one with two strange mammals and a velociraptor on its back.

"We must look as strange to them as they look to us," Joe said.

Simone brushed back her hair. "I don't look *strange*. Well, maybe now I do, covered in mud and dinosaur pee, riding a triceratops. All right, I'm a weirdo."

The therizins returned to their meal. With claws like forklifts, they scooped up plants from the water and stuffed their beaks.

"I guess they're not so bad," Simone said. "I wouldn't want one as a pet, but—"

A dinosaur burst out from the water.

A huge dinosaur.

Jaws opened wide, dripping water and algae. That mouth could eat a human with one bite. The monster let out a deafening rumble. Waves of bass shook the swamp.

Simone let out a scream almost as loud.

Joe's heart burst into a gallop. It was just what he feared.

A spinosaurus.

"Dozer—run!" Joe shouted.

This was a foe beyond them. Joe knew it. The trike did too. Grunting, Dozer moved as fast as he could, splashing through the water.

Joe could not help but watch. His morbid curiosity compelled him. One almost never saw a spinosaurus and lived. It was likely Joe himself would not live to tell this tale.

The monster reared from the river. Normally Joe would never think of any dinosaur as a *monster*. But he made an exception for spinosaurus. It was among the largest predators on Mintari, rivaling the mighty T-rex for title of king.

The spinosaurus was lighter than a T-rex but longer. From nostrils to tail tip, it was as long as a sperm whale. And far meaner than Ahab's nemesis. The dinosaur had a snout like a crocodile, long and full of nasty teeth. The teeth were smaller than those of a

T-rex, but a spinosaurus had far more of them. The skull was enormous, longer than a man was tall. The carnivore walked on two legs, but unlike a T-rex, it had long arms tipped with terrible claws.

Many dinosaurs were large and fearsome on Mintari, but spinosaurus boasted a unique feature. Rows of spikes taller than men rose along its back. Scaly skin stretched between these spines, forming a sail. Most of the animal was green, but the fearsome sail was red as blood. The color meant this one was a male. The sails were primarily used for courtship, but a spinosaurus could also lurk underwater, then rise in a surprise attack, impaling his victims upon those spikes.

Fortunately for the terrestrial dinosaurs of Mintari, spinosaurus did not roam the land. Like a croc, he stayed in rivers and marshlands. Unfortunately for Joe and Simone, they were now in his element.

The beast reared from the water, as tall as a three-story building, rumbling for blood. The therizin family cried out in terror and burst into a run. But they were clumsy creatures, potbellied and slow. The spinosaurus leaped onto one of the gangly herbivores. The hungry carnivore closed his mighty jaws round his victim's neck.

With a single bite, the spinosaurus severed the therizin's head. With a swipe of his claws, the hulking predator tossed the head into a tree, where it lodged itself among branches.

Watching from Dozer's back, Simone cried out in horror. Even Joe recoiled. He had heard of such things—but never seen it in real life.

To make things worse, the spinosaurus did not even feed on his victim. Apparently he was not hungry. The therizinosaurus had simply been in his way. The towering predator splashed through the water—toward Dozer and the humans on his back.

The triceratops waded away, moving frustratingly slow. Dozer didn't seem happy about running from a fight, but he obeyed Joe.

"The spinosaurus is not hunting," Joe said. "He's territorial. The male spinosaurus beheads his victims and places the heads among the mangrove branches to deter others. Apparently it also impresses females."

"Yes, I'm very impressed," Simone said. "Does this mean the dinosaur will just chase us away instead of eat us?"

"Hopefully. I don't have much experience with spinosaurs. I thought the skull collections were just a myth, to be honest."

"Wait. *Hopefully?*" Simone gulped.

The spinosaurus gained speed, bellowing. Algae and moss dripped off his scales. Strings of saliva dangled between his bloodied teeth. Dozer ran as fast as he could, splashing through the mud. The trike could move with surprisingly fast speed on land, outrunning any human sprinter, but here he floundered. The spino loped after them, seeming almost to grin.

"What kind of monster is this?" Simone shouted. "Dinosaurs are only animals! What kind of animal displays severed heads as trophies?"

The spinosaurus moved closer. His claws swiped through the air, spraying moss. His mouth opened wider, revealing his gullet.

Joe aimed his sleep-or-die. He fired a tranquilizer dart. It slammed into the spino, but the dinosaur didn't even notice. He kept chasing, moving closer, closer, only steps away now.

"Make for that hill, Dozer!" Joe shouted.

"The hill, the hill!" Simone cried.

Joe fired again. This time he did something he hated to do. He fired a bullet at a dinosaur.

Scales shattered on the spino's chest. Blood poured. The spiny beast howled. He was hurt but still in the fight. If anything, the gunshot only made him angrier. He gained speed. His claws swung through the air, just missing the fleeing triceratops.

Joe fired again. The spino yowled but kept going. The bullets did not seem to bother him too much.

Joe glanced ahead.

The hill was still far.

He looked behind him.

The spinosaurus was closer. His claws lashed again, missing Dozer by only a meter or two.

They had to fight.

"Dozer!" Joe shouted. "Turn and charge!"

One would assume that Dozer, a dinosaur who outweighed two African elephants, would be slow on his feet. But despite its bulk and sturdy build, a triceratops could move with surprising speed and agility. Within an instant, Dozer spun a hundred and eighty degrees, bringing his horns to bear on the charging spinosaurus.

The spino reared in the swamp, halting his chase. The semiaquatic killer just barely avoided impaling himself on Dozer's menacing horns.

The trike would not let his foe off the hook so easily. With an angry grunt, Dozer charged. Massive as he was—and Dozer would make a mammoth look puny—he was smaller than the spinosaurus. But he raced right at that predator without hesitation. Triceratops horns could punch through a car, shatter a house wall, and even take down a T-rex. The burly behemoth feared nobody. Dozer drove his horns into his enormous spiny enemy.

Normally, the horns carried the force of twelve tons of Dozer moving at high speed. But in the water, the trike was slower, and his horns carried less kinetic energy. The tips pierced the spinosaurus. But just the tips. The predator snorted, swung his claws, and knocked Dozer's head aside. The spino's mighty claws left gashes across Dozer's frill.

The trike bellowed in agony. The pain only fueled his fury. He reared in the water, bellowed, and shoved with his back legs, lunging at his foe. His horns slammed into the spinosaurus again. This time, unleashed at close range, the attack carried more force. The horns cracked through scales. Blood darkened the water.

Blows from triceratops horns would kill most dinosaurs. But the spino stayed standing—and attacked. The predator closed his jaws around Dozer's frill. The teeth scraped across the bone. The spino tugged the bulky armored head, trying to yank off the frill, to find soft flesh, to decapitate the trike.

Joe, riding on Dozer's back, found himself facing the spino's scaly head. The snout was longer than he was tall. Human and spinosaurus stared into each other's eyes.

Joe aimed his sleep-or-die.

He could shoot a bullet into the spino's eye. He could slay the beast.

Instead he loaded another tranquilizer dart. He fired it between the spino's eyes.

The dart sank through the scaly skin, releasing its soothing liquid. This close to the brain, it worked fast. Within seconds, the huge predator began slowing down.

The spinosaurus moaned. His jaws loosened, releasing Dozer's frill. The predator stumbled back, splashing through the swamp. His great spine wilted like a deflated sail.

Dozer reared and prepared to charge again.

"Halt, Dozer!" Joe said.

The trike looked over his shoulder at Joe. He growled. *I want to fight!*

"Easy, Dozer, easy," Joe said. "Let him live."

The spinosaurus wobbled on his feet, dazed. Two tranquilizer darts stuck out from him. He bled from horn wounds. The mighty predator turned away, slunk into the river, and vanished underwater.

Joe shut his eyes and exhaled in relief.

He had met a spinosaurus and lived to tell the tale. Few men were this lucky. Or women.

It was then he realized that Simone was no longer holding him. And she hadn't screamed in his ear in a while either.

He looked behind him.

She was no longer sitting on the triceratops.

His heart seemed to shatter in his chest. No. Surely the spinosaurus hadn't gotten her. Oh God, it couldn't be.

"Simone!" he shouted. "Simone!"

"Right here!" The cry came from below.

Joe turned around, and there she was. Sitting in the mud a few paces away.

Thank God.

Joe exhaled in relief. But he hardened his expression. Better not show her any feelings. Journalists fed off feelings like a spinosaurus feeding on flesh.

"What are you doing down there?" he snapped.

"Your triceratops dropped me!"

"You were supposed to hold on."

"You need to get seat belts on that thing!" she said, shoving herself up.

"Your arms are tighter than any seat belt." He rubbed his ribs where her arms had crushed him.

He pulled her back onto Dozer. At once, those viselike arms wrapped around him, crushing him.

Dozer's tail was bleeding, but Joe dared not linger here long enough to treat the wounds. More spinos lurked in these waters. The poor trike would have to suffer for a little longer.

"If we move fast, we can be out of the swamps by nightfall," Joe said, patting Dozer on the frill. The spino's teeth had cut grooves into the armor. It probably hurt like hell. "Just a little longer, old friend. And we'll be safe."

Dozer snorted and continued wading through the water. They passed by mangroves whose branches held dinosaur skulls like lurid Christmas ornaments. Nyx dipped lower in the sky, and the sunset seemed to paint the skulls with blood.

CHAPTER THIRTEEN
In Laramidia Fields

The sun was gone and the twin moons glowing when they reached Laramidia Fields.

Some called it the most beautiful place on Mintari. The flatlands sprawled toward distant mountains. Flowers and ferns carpeted the land. At night, the flowers were closed, but at dawn they would bloom again, filling Laramidia Fields with color and sweet aromas.

As they left Skull Swamp behind, they breathed easier. Partly because the air was fresher; cool breezes scattered the soupy swamp air. But mostly because they left the kingdom of the spinosaurus. Joe loved dinosaurs more than anything in this world. But that was one dinosaur he hoped to never run across again.

At least Joe, Dozer, and Vinnie were breathing easier. Simone was trembling.

"What's wrong?" Joe said.

She looked around the moonlit fields. A shudder ran through her. "What horror awaits us here?"

Joe looked around. "Um, flowers?"

"There's gotta be some horror. At Collini Cliffs, a pterosaur grabbed me and almost fed me to her hatchlings. In Hell Valley, allosaurs ate my cameraman. In Marshwood Forest, a ceratosaurus nearly gulped me down. At Mudge Mountain, megaraptors nearly tore me apart. And in Skull Swamp, a spinosaurus almost mounted my head on a spike. Every spot has a monster. What lurks here?"

"Don't worry, cheesecake, you're safe," Joe said. "The only predators here sleep at night."

"And at dawn?"

"We'll worry about the giganotosaurus at dawn."

She stiffened. "The *what*."

"I said don't worry about it."

Her cheeks flushed, and she opened her mouth, seeming ready to argue again. But then Simone squinted and leaned forward.

"There." She pointed. "Look. Is that dinosaur sleeping?"

Joe saw it. Some type of ankylosaur, judging by its spiky armor. He checked his communicator. This was the spot. The same coordinates where Amissa had streamed her video.

They rode closer and dismounted. Simone's eyes dampened, and she covered her mouth. Joe stared at the corpse. A few eoraptors, miniature omnivores even smaller than Vinnie, were eating the dead dinosaur. Joe shooed them aside. They scattered and hissed among the grass.

"A nodosaur." Joe's fists clenched at his sides. "The one we saw Amissa shoot in her video."

"Where's the head?" Simone whispered.

"She took it as a trophy. At least the spinosaurus eats the bodies. Amissa just leaves them to the scavengers." He ground his teeth. "Tar it, we're too late. If I had a tricopter, we could have gotten here in time. We—"

"No." Simone put a hand on his chest. "Even in a tricopter, it would take time to fly over the swamp. Amissa would have been long gone. There was nothing you could do."

Joe placed his hand on the dead nodosaur. The animal was the size of a rhinoceros. Small for a dinosaur. But big or small, every life here was precious—from the grandest sauropod to the smallest raptor. Joe closed his eyes and whispered into the wind.

"Go back now, child of Mintari. Go back to the soil from which you came. In the warm embrace of the world, you will bring forth new life. The energy in your body will feed the grass that grows and the trees that reach toward the sun. Flowers will bloom where you fell, and the rain will wash your blood away. You will be reborn. Rest now, child of life. We will always remember you, for you will never die."

He stepped back and opened his eyes. Tears glistened on Simone's cheeks.

"That was beautiful," she said.

"An old shaman's prayer," Joe said. "One my mother taught me long ago."

"She sounds like a wise woman."

Joe looked at her. Her face glowed white in the moonlight, and her normally fiery hair seemed like burnished silver. Her eyes were two blue moons like the twin moons above. She touched his hand, her fingertips electric.

Joe pulled back. "We should make camp. We'll continue in the morning. Amissa hasn't posted any new videos today. Once she does, we'll pinpoint her location and keep chasing her."

Simone nodded. "All right. Camping. Out in dino country. What could go wrong?"

Joe allowed himself a smile. "You're safe, Simone. For tonight, you're safe. I promise."

They left the corpse, walked across the meadow, and reached a gurgling stream—a tributary of Gould River. Several cycads grew along the water. A good place to make camp. Simone looked at the water in concern, but Joe assured her that spinos couldn't fit into a stream so small.

First things first, Joe bandaged the bite wounds on Dozer's tail, then tended to the grooves on his frill. He patted the old trike.

"You've been through a lot today, friend. Get some rest."

The scarred triceratops snorted and thumped down onto the grass, shaking the trees. Soon the dinosaur was snoring. Normally trikes slept standing up. But poor Dozer was so exhausted he conked out on his side. Vinnie had spent all day running around. The velociraptor curled up among Dozer's legs, seeking safety. Soon the feathered theropod was sound asleep. Joe looked affectionately at his two friends.

"Some guards you are," he said, but he was smiling. For a long time, he had been lost, alone. Without Dozer and Vinnie, he would not have made it. There weren't pets. They were family.

When he looked around for Simone, he didn't see her. He frowned. What the heck?

Then he saw it. Simone was bathing in the stream. It was perhaps too small for a spinosaurus, but it was just the right size for her. She had waded in with her clothes on, and she was busy washing out the mud. She dunked her head under, scrubbed her hair, then came up for air.

He frowned and stood on the riverbank. "What are you doing?"

She looked up from the water. "Dancing the Charleston, of course." She splashed him. "Bathing! What does it look like?"

"It's a cold night. Get out of there. You'll freeze."

"I'm covered in mud and dinosaur pee. I'm washing myself."

Joe rolled his eyes. "I swear Cloventians are so pampered. They can't go a day without—"

He yelped as she grabbed him and pulled him into the stream. He crashed into the water.

"Simone!" he cried out. "What the—?"

"You're bathing," she said. "I've had enough of you being some wild mountain man. You're washing and then I'm cutting your hair."

"Like hell!"

"Your hair is too long."

"Who cares? You can't even see my hair. I always wear a hat."

"You have so much hair it's going to knock your hat off." She splashed him again. "Now shut up! You'll get water in your mouth. Bathe!"

He tried to climb out of the water. She pulled him back in. Once more, she splashed him.

"Bathe!" she commanded, standing hip-deep in the water.

"Fine," he muttered and began scrubbing the mud off his face. "For God's sake. Next you'll have me wearing makeup and perfume like a Cloventian."

"Oh, sorry, macho Mintari man. I forgot that real men don't eat quiche and never bathe."

"What the hell is quiche?"

She rolled her eyes. "You wouldn't like it. There's no meat in it."

"I don't only eat meat. I eat potatoes too. That's a vegetable."

"Oh dear me, you'll be wearing a dress next, Jurassic Joe. Be careful." She splashed him. "There's mud in your hair. Take the hat off and wash it."

"A Ranger never removes his ceratop hat."

She snorted. "Oh please. Even you dinoboys must remove your hats sometimes. To clean your hair, at least."

"Fine. I'll clean my hair, but you ain't cutting it." Joe removed his ceratop and began rinsing out more mud. "I can cut my own hair."

She squinted at him. "The evidence would suggest otherwise. I packed toenail scissors. I'll cut it properly."

He stared at her as if she were insane. "You packed toenail scissors on safari?"

She shrugged. "In case my toenails grew too long."

"And you didn't pack a gun."

She tilted her head. "Why would I need a gun?"

He sighed. "Well, you certainly know your priorities. If I were you, I'd—"

Movement caught his eye. He shut his mouth, reached into the stream, then rose holding a wriggling fish. A big one too.

Simone took a step back from the squirming, scaly fish. "Is that some kind of dinosaur fish?"

Joe grinned. "This is dinner."

Not long later, they sat drying by a campfire, eating the fish. The smell woke up Vinnie, and they shared the meal with him. Dozer woke up once, guzzled down half a tree, then went back to sleep.

When they were done eating, Joe and Simone leaned against Dozer, picking their teeth with fish bones. They were still wet and not ready to sleep. Not until the fire was done drying their clothes.

Joe looked at Simone. The firelight painted her skin gold, and her red hair seemed like an extension of the flames.

"Thank you," he said. "For the haircut and beard trim."

She looked at him and smiled. "Least I could do after you saved my life. About a hundred times so far. I probably owe you at least another ..." She counted on her fingers. "Two haircuts."

"One was enough." He stroked his neatly cropped beard. "It's too short. Dozer won't recognize me."

Simone stared into the crackling flames for a while. Crickets chirped and the stars shone. Finally she spoke softly, not removing her eyes from the fire.

"I was only sixteen when my sister died. She was my twin. My other half. The person I loved most in the world. We even had a secret language, and it breaks my heart that I'm forgetting it."

"I'm sorry," Joe said. He didn't know what else to say.

"We were only sixteen when she died. I'm thirty-one now. Next year, I'll have lived half my life without her. And I don't know how to handle that." A tear rolled down her cheek. "The courts said it was an accident. But I know that Amissa murdered her."

"What happened?" Joe said. "When it happened, I was already living on Mintari, estranged from my family."

Simone kept looking at the flames, lost in memory, seeming almost afraid to look away. "Amissa tormented my sister and me throughout school. She was two years older, a senior, rich, popular. She hated us. She hazed us ruthlessly. The usual stuff—stealing our lunch, shoving us into lockers, dunking our heads into toilets. Good times. Even worse, she spread gossip. Mean gossip. She made our lives hell. All because we came from below the neon sea. She deemed us unworthy of Clover Heights Academy. So she bullied us relentlessly. One day, she showed up with her dog. A big pit bull. Genetically modified and trained to be mean. She just wanted to scare us, Amissa later claimed in court. But I tell you, that dog was going to rip us apart. Elize fled onto a floating road ... and was hit by a car. She died in my arms."

Joe lowered his head. "I'm very sorry. I'm disgusted by what my sister did."

"Since then, I've been terrified of animals. Any animals. Be they dogs or dinosaurs." She finally looked at him. "When I met you, I could not understand how you could love dinosaurs. To me they were monsters. Like the dog that killed my sister. But I think I understand now. I see how you, Dozer, and Vinnie are a family. I see how beautiful Mintari is. Well, maybe not the predators. But that nodosaur was beautiful. And I understand why you do what you do."

"No you don't," Joe said.

Her eyes narrowed. "I don't?"

"I love dinosaurs," Joe said. "They are noble, magnificent creatures. They are miracles of nature. I love taking care of them. Being around them. Dedicating my life to them. To me, dinosaurs are a blessing and a joy. But that's not why I'm a Ranger."

She tilted her head, her red tresses bouncing. "Tell me. Why?"

"Because of my family. Who they are. What they do." He tapped the pin on his lapel. "Do you see this silver triceratops head? The crest of my clan. Clans are the lifeblood of human society on Mintari. Every clan is built around a core of a wealthy family, but they expand to include staff, friends, neighbors, brothers-in-arms. A big clan can include over a thousand people. Clans become an identity. A source of pride. For generations, the Triplehorns proudly displayed this symbol. Every clan on Mintari chose a dinosaur to represent them. The dinosaur symbolizes the clan values. For centuries, the Triplehorns embraced the values of the triceratops. We were strong, but we used our strength for defense. We were noble, but we remained down-to-earth. These are the qualities the triceratops embodies. Until my father, the clan chief, threw it all away. He abandoned Mintari. He betrayed this world. And he used the triceratops as a symbol for his company. A company that sells weapons to poachers."

Joe clenched his fists. He began to tremble.

"I can't even imagine how that feels." Simone placed a hand on his shoulder.

"My mother fled him." His voice caught. "I was only a boy. I was born on Cloventia to a family of Mintarian immigrants. The floating skyscrapers were all I knew. Yes, Simone. I too come from your neon world. My mother fled back to Mintari, taking me with her. I was nine. Back on this world, my mother withdrew from society, becoming a shaman in the wilderness. I became a Ranger. My father was killing dinosaurs, so I vowed to protect them. Until ... until one of those dinosaurs killed my wife. My pregnant wife."

He lowered his head, the pain overwhelming him. Simone embraced him.

Joe continued in a low voice. "Mina died fifteen years ago. The same year your sister died. King Ivan did it. The mutant T-rex with black scales."

"And yet you still love dinosaurs," she whispered.

He nodded. "Dinosaurs do what dinosaurs do. I don't blame them. Predators hunt because it's in their nature. But humans ... humans know good from evil. My father and sister chose evil."

Simone embraced him. "But you chose good. You're rude. You're grating. You're as stubborn as a stegosaurus. But you're good."

"There's more to this story." Joe looked into her eyes. The fire reflected in them. "I never met my paternal grandparents. They died before I was born. They lived on Mintari. And dinosaurs killed them."

Simone gasped. "Not Ivan!"

"No. This was before Ivan was even born. A herd of gastonias, of all things. They're another genus of ankylosaur, similar to nodosaurs. They got spooked by a predator and ran. They trampled over my grandparents. Just an accident. But my father never forgave dinosaurs. To Tobias Triplehorn, these animals are all monsters. For years, he hated dinosaurs, feared them, loathed them. He left Mintari because he could not tolerate the animals that killed his parents. And Simone ... I think he founded Triplehorn Incorporated as his twisted revenge against dinosaurs."

"Revenge against dinosaurs!" Simone said. "But they're only animals."

"To my father, they're monsters. He delights in selling the guns that kill them. The name Triplehorn, which was once so noble, has become synonymous with poaching. Mintarians see my crest and spit on me. They hear my name and curse it."

Her eyes softened. "You can take the pin off. You can change your name."

"No. I'm proud of Clan Triplehorn. Its legacy stretches back for centuries. It's one of the oldest families of Mintari. A Triplehorn was on *Darwin's Ark*, the first starship that landed here from Earth five hundred years ago. I vowed to someday restore my family name to honor."

Simone leaned her head against his shoulder. "Well, you've already converted one person."

Joe smiled wryly. "I suppose you'll put all this into your article."

She leaned back, looking into his eyes again. "Not if you don't want me to."

"Write it," he said. "Let them read it. Let Cloventia know what I'm doing here. I always wanted privacy. But Amissa won't give me that. She already talks to her followers about me. So let them hear my side of the story."

Simone leaned forward and kissed his cheek. "Thank you for sharing your story, Joe Triplehorn."

"Thank you for sharing yours, Simone LaRue."

She yawned. A huge yawn that stretched her entire body. Joe was infected at once, and he too began to yawn. They lay down on the grass. The breeze was cold, and they had no blankets. She wriggled closer to him, and he wrapped his arms around her.

She smiled sleepily, eyelids fluttering. "Are you hugging me, Jurassic Joe?"

"No!" he grumbled. "Just keeping you warm. It's a cold night."

She nuzzled closer. "It's cold …"

He fell asleep with her hair tickling his chin, his arms around her. He slept deeply, and for the first time in years, he did not suffer nightmares.

At dawn, beeping awoke him.

Joe blinked and looked around, still dazed. He saw blue sky, a gurgling stream, and a flowery meadow. For a moment, he could not remember where he was. Simone was still asleep in his arms, her head against his chest. She had drooled onto his shirt. Lovely.

The beeping sounded again.

He frowned and pawed around for his communicator. He found the small device lying in the grass beside him.

It was flashing. An urgent alert.

Joe looked at the little screen, and his heart seemed to stop in his chest.

"Dear God," he whispered.

Simone mumbled, opened her eyes, and blinked groggily. "What is it?"

"Amissa is recording another video," Joe said. "She's about to kill the largest dinosaur on Mintari."

Amissa stood by the nest of hatchlings. Her SmartSphere hovered before her, streaming her to billions of people across the Nyx star system.

"Howdy, Tripletots. This is your girl, Amissa Triplehorn, also known as the Dino Huntress. I hope you enjoyed my video yesterday, showing you a beautiful and rare nodosaur. Today I have something even more amazing for you. Yes, Tripletots, I'm not holding anything back. Today I will hunt the largest dinosaur that ever lived."

With a twirl of her fingers, she spun the SmartSphere toward the nest.

Twigs, leaves, and straw filled a bowl dug into the earth. Hatchlings cooed inside, no larger than lapdogs. They were adorable little things, Amissa had to admit. Their necks were long, their eyes huge, their feet too big for their tubby little bodies.

Holographic snippets of text floated around the camera—comments from her fans.

"Aww, cuties."

"Babies!"

"Biggest dinos? Yeah sure."

Amissa knelt by the nest. "These are sauropodlets. Baby sauropods. They were only born this morning, and they're so small you could carry one in your purse. But these adorable little hatchlings will become the largest animals to ever live on land. Their species: *Supersaurus vivianae*. A titan among titans."

She paused for effect. Her fans began a heated debate. She knew they would.

"Supersaurus—biggest dino ever!"

"Sorry, not the biggest dinosaur. Argentinosaurus is heavier."

"Supersaurus is longer than argentinosaurus. Therefore bigger."

"Sauroposeidon is taller than both. Fail!"

"Longest counts as biggest! It's length, not weight or height."

"Don't hurt the babies!"

"Where's Mommy?"

Amissa stroked one of the hatchlings. "This little guy only weighs a few kilograms. But soon he'll start to eat. And he'll gain an incredible forty kilograms a day. That's my weight." She winked at the camera.

The comments erupted.

"Sure …"

"You wish."

"What is that in pounds?"

Amissa plucked blades of grass and fed the sauropodlet. "This dinosaur will not reach his full size until he's thirty. Older than I am now." Another wink.

More comments exploded.

"Mm-hmm."

"Sure …"

"You wish!"

Amissa cleared her throat and continued speaking. "When fully grown, this tiny dinosaur will weigh a hundred tons. The weight of ten T-rexes. That's right, Tripletots. This dinosaur will be ten times the size of a T-rex. Only the blue whale was larger than the supersaurus. On land, this giant reigns supreme."

"Kill something already."

"I love you, Amissa! My queen!"

"Beautiful animals, beautiful huntress."

"You're a murderer!"

Amissa left the nest and walked across the grass, stirring wisps of fog. Her astrolite was parked nearby, barely visible in the morning mist. She hopped down into an enormous footprint, then climbed out and kept walking. She added a little sassy sway to her gait. After all, the camera was hovering behind her. She must put on a good show. From the astrolite, she retrieved her bow, turned toward the camera, and posed with the weapon.

"Artemis's Arch. The deadliest compound bow money can buy. Only 15,999 clovers in all Triplehorn stores." Amissa kissed the bow. "Let's see if this baby can bring down giants."

"Not a chance."

"An arrow against a supersaurus? Good luck!"

"Murderer!"

"I'm calling the Rangers right now."

"Die!"

Amissa strode purposefully back toward the nest. The sauropodlets were still cooing inside. A few tried to rise, but their legs buckled, and they flopped back down. Within a day or two, they'd be big enough to walk and graze. Right now their mother was off collecting food. This was normally a vulnerable time for the hatchlings. Today it was a vulnerable time for Mom.

Footsteps shook the earth.

A rumble sounded in the distance.

Amissa and the camera both faced the sound. A figure was moving through the mist. A towering figure. A colossal dinosaur was lumbering forth.

The mist parted.

The beast emerged.

The fans went wild. Thousands of comments exploded around the SmartSphere.

Amissa did not read them. She stood, gaping, lost for words. She had seen wonderful, terrifying animals before, but none had ever taken her breath away. Until now.

The supersaurus loomed above her. From head to tail, she was larger than Christ the Redeemer, the ancient statue from Brazil that now floated on Cloventia. Her legs were like the columns of cathedrals. Her neck soared like an ancient obelisk. Her head seemed to gaze down from among the stars. In her mouth, she held an uprooted sapling—food for her young. If Amissa stood on her tiptoes and stretched up her arm, she still would not reach this dinosaur's underbelly. This being was like the nephilim of old, towering and unearthly.

Tears streamed down Amissa's cheeks. She had never seen anything so magnificent. To kill such a beast—it would be her life's greatest achievement. It would be so beautiful.

"Beautiful," she whispered, eyes wet. "It's so beautiful."

The supersaurus stomped closer. Every footfall left deep imprints in the soil. Amissa tightened her lips. With shaking hands, she raised Artemis's Arch.

Shooting such a beast in the body would be useless. Even with a modern rifle. But a shot to the head—right through that tiny brain—would bring the giant down. Amissa could only imagine the sound such a titan falling would make. It would be like killing a god.

She nocked an arrow.

The supersaurus hurled down the uprooted tree.

Amissa leaped aside, never getting the chance to fire her arrow.

It was just a sapling, but it was taller than Amissa, and the trunk was thicker than her arm. The tree slammed into her, knocking her to the ground. Leaves fluttered through the air. Amissa groaned in pain.

She shoved aside branches, drew her bowstring, and—

A foot came plunging downward.

Amissa rolled. The foot slammed down beside her. It left a footprint larger than a bathtub.

She leaped to her feet and aimed her bow again.

A *boom* shook the air.

A blast of air hit her. Amissa stumbled back, dazed. Her ears rang.

What the hell just happened? she thought. *Did a bomb go off?*

She shook her head wildly, returned her finger to the trigger, and—

Another boom shook the air. A shock wave knocked her down. Then she understood what was happening.

The supersaurus was whipping her tail through the air. She was swinging that tail so fast it broke the sound barrier. Those were sonic booms. Same as the crack of a whip—but much louder.

A third time the tail swung. This time it was coming right at her.

Amissa ran and ducked. The tail swung over her head, breaking the sound barrier again. The sonic boom deafened her. The tail tip slammed onto the fallen tree, shattering the trunk into a million pieces. It could just as easily shatter Amissa's bones.

Dear Lord! Amissa thought. Maybe she had underestimated this beast. She had thought it a mere herbivore. Big, yes. But still just a tame prey animal. Essentially a giant cow. What a fool she had been! Now Amissa felt smaller than ever. Even worse, she had the terrible feeling that the supersaurus was toying with her. A cat toying with a mouse.

The dinosaur flicked her massive tail again. Amissa leaped aside, stumbled into a footprint, and crashed down.

She lay on her back inside the footprint, staring up at the giant.

The supersaurus raised her foot, prepared to flatten her.

Amissa did not run. Lying on her back, she aimed Artemis's Arch.

The foot came plunging down.

She fired.

A steel arrow drove into the sauropod's foot. Artemis's Arch, the most powerful compound bow on the market, fired arrows with enough force to shatter bones. The dinosaur yowled and stumbled backward. Blood dripped from her foot.

Gotcha!

Amissa leaped to her feet, nocked another arrow, and drew the bowstring. She would try to hit something more critical this time. The dinosaur was flailing her neck around in pain. The head kept moving. Amissa could not aim properly. A head shot seemed impossible. But the torso was a massive target, and if she could hit an artery, even shoot deep enough to damage an organan . . .

She squinted and—

The tail swung her way.

She leaped aside. The tip of the tail caught her bow, hurling it mightily.

The bowstring snagged her arm with terrifying force.

Amissa flew through the air.

For a disorienting few seconds, she was tumbling through the sky.

She crashed down and hit the grass. Hard. She lay there, moaning. Her bow was gone. She moaned in pain, tried to rise, could not.

Her arm blazed with searing white agony. Broken. The bowstring had yanked her arm so powerfully the bone had snapped. She winced, tears in her eyes, nearly blind with pain.

The supersaurus thundered toward her. Amissa had only a handgun left. One of her arms was useless, bent at an odd angle. With her other hand, she drew her handgun and fired.

Again. Again. Again.

Bullets plowed into the sauropod's chest.

The dinosaur reared, bleeding, still alive. The bullets only infuriated her. Her feet rose high in the air, and Amissa knew the dinosaur would stomp her dead.

A siren wailed.

A tricopter streaked through the sky.

Yellow and green lights flashed.

The Mintari Rangers were here.

As Amissa lay on the ground, moaning in pain, the Ranger tricopter flew rings around the supersaurus. Its siren blared, and its lights flashed. The enormous dinosaur bellowed and swung her tail, trying to swat the tricopter away.

A Ranger leaned out the tricopter, aimed a double-barrel rifle, and opened fire.

Watching from the grass, Amissa gaped. A Ranger shooting a dinosaur!

Then she understood. The Ranger was firing a sleep-or-die. A rifle that could fire bullets from one barrel, tranquilizer darts from the other. The Ranger in the tricopter was tranquilizing the sauropod. They probably wanted to subdue her so they could treat her wounds. Pathetic!

Amissa had run into so-called animal lovers before. They were all hypocrites. They claimed to hate hunting, but they bought meat from the grocery store. Some claimed to be vegetarians, but they ate produce grown on the destroyed habitats of a billion slain animals. They claimed to love nature, but they lived in cities of steel and glass. Cities built on animal graveyards.

Amissa was the true nature lover. Because she *respected* nature. She did not eat meat butchered on a factory farm. She hunted her own meat. She did not fly a tricopter around a sauropod, shooting from the air. She faced the beast head-on. On the ground. Using nothing but a bow and arrow. She was part of nature. Not above it. It was what the Rangers would never understand. They saw themselves as gods. She saw herself as a predator.

Bleeding from bullet wounds, an arrow in her foot, several tranquilizer darts in her neck, the supersaurus stumbled toward her hatchlings. The elephantine legs were wobbling. When she reached the nest, the sauropod let out a heartbreaking howl. Wobbling, she sat down hard, cracking the earth, and coiled her neck around the nest. The sauropodlets whimpered and nuzzled their groggy mother.

The Ranger tricopter descended, blasting back the grass with its three rotors. Rotors. How quaint. Like a relic from a time gone by. The antique Mintarian vehicle thumped onto the grass.

Two Rangers leaped out. They wore that ridiculous uniform of theirs. Tan buttoned shirts. Campaign hats. Badges on their chests shaped like stegosaurus plates. These ones even wore shorts. What kind of paramilitary force wore shorts?

"Great, the boy scouts have arrived," Amissa muttered, pushing herself to her feet. She winced. Her arm hung at an odd angle. Her vision swam with tears, and the pain pounded through her.

One of the Rangers, a lanky man with a bushy goatee, rushed toward the tranquilized sauropod. He was carrying a medical kit.

The second Ranger, a woman with dark skin and green eyes, drew her sidearm and approached Amissa.

"Drop your weapon—now!" the Ranger shouted.

Amissa realized she was still holding her handgun. She kept holding it. "I do not recognize your authority, Ranger!" she shouted. "According to the Nyx Accords of 2798, recreational hunting is allowed on all Nyx worlds."

"You can argue that in court," the female Ranger said. "Drop your gun! Now! Or I will shoot!"

Amissa glanced over her shoulder. Her SmartSphere was still floating nearby, recording everything.

"Emergency flare!" she said.

Quickly, Amissa looked away. The SmartSphere blazed with blinding light. The feature was meant for emergencies. The light could be seen from space, they said. It shone as brightly as the sun. Within a second, the sphere drained its battery and thumped onto the grass, dead.

But for that one second, the Ranger was blind.

And one second was all Amissa needed. She raised her handgun. She fired. A perfect shot between the Ranger's pretty green eyes.

The woman crumpled, dead before she hit the ground.

Good thing the camera battery is dead, Amissa thought. *Wouldn't be good for my fans to see that.*

It was the first time she had killed a human. She felt … hollow. She wasn't sure how to feel. She would process this later.

There was another Ranger nearby. The one tending to the supersaurus.

Amissa turned toward him. He was kneeling by the snoozing sauropod. The man looked stunned. His eyes flicked toward his dead comrade, then to Amissa.

"I don't have a gun," he whispered. "Please. I'm unarmed. Don't hurt me. Please. I have a wife and k—"

Amissa pulled the trigger.

Blood sprayed the sauropod.

The Ranger collapsed.

Amissa began to shake. Her head spun. She nearly dropped her gun. And it wasn't just the agony of her broken arm.

I just killed two people. Oh God, I killed humans.

The pain flared. She yelped. With the adrenaline wearing off, the agony came roaring in. There was a medical drone inside her astrolite. It could heal her. But before setting her bone, it would sedate her. And she needed her mind clear. She had to think, to think …

Two bodies at her feet. Tar pit! Could her father sweep them under the rug?

Amissa Triplehorn had been in trouble with the law before, of course. Quite a few times. Hunting animals was a legal gray area. Then there had been that incident with the LaRue twins. And the time the authorities raided one of her side businesses, accusing her of tax evasion. All those times, the Triplehorn lawyers had gotten her out of trouble. But this was new. This was killing humans.

They'll accuse me of murder, she thought. *Not even self-defense but murder!*

Suddenly she wished her SmartSphere *had* been recording. Then they would see. She had defended herself! The Ranger had pulled a gun on her!

She took deep, shaky breaths.

Calm yourself. You are Amissa Triplehorn. The heiress of an empire. Act like it.

She should get rid of the bodies. Bury them or burn them. Then she laughed at how ridiculous that was. She was on Mintari! Scavengers would show up any moment now. Within hours, the wildlife would eat everything, even the bones. And if anyone did find the bodies—well, good! Let it be a lesson to them.

"If you hunt me, I will shoot you down," she hissed. "I am not prey. I am a predator."

Speaking of which …

She glanced toward the supersaurus. The enormous animal lay on the ground, sleeping. It looked like a beached whale. Still tranquilized.

Amissa found her compound bow nearby. Still in one piece. Good. Sadly, she couldn't use it with one broken arm. Instead, she aimed her handgun at the sleeping sauropod. A bullet through the brain should do the trick. But then she lowered her gun in disgust. There was no triumph in slaying a sleeping giant. She had come to Mintari as a huntress, not an executioner. She was done here.

Her fans would be disgusted. Well, too bad. Besides, her camera was out of batteries. What was the point of killing something if you couldn't take a photo?

One last thing before she treated her arm. She filled the Rangers' abandoned tricopter with bullets, destroying the engine. It would never fly again.

Finally she stumbled into her astrolite, the *Huntress*.

"Drone!" she shouted hoarsely.

The little squid-like drone hovered toward her. His camera lenses widened like shocked eyes. "Mistress, you are hurt!"

She grimaced. The pain was really coming in hard now. "You need … to set the bone. To … cast … But first—pain …"

The drone already knew her preferences for drugs. He hovered closer. One of his metal tentacles injected her with a potent sedative. Her pain flowed away. She leaned back in her seat. As he set the bone and wrapped her arm in a cast, Amissa did not feel a thing.

Soon she was flying again, floating over the clouds. Leaving Mintari's largest dinosaur behind. Alive.

The Rangers had ruined her hunt. She knew who had sent them. Joe. Her brother was behind this.

"You will pay, Joe Triplehorn." She shoved down the throttle. Her astrolite raced over the grasslands and hills. "I've killed Rangers now. And I can kill again."

CHAPTER FOURTEEN
Lost Child

The tracks were gone. The rain had washed them away like the blood off Figaro's face. She stood on the muddy floodplain, scrawny and hungry and lonely. Just an orphan. One girl lost in a big world full of predators. She had hoped to find the other girl. Emily. The girl who had parents, who spoke so nicely. But now Fig worried she would never find another human. That she would remain alone forever.

As if he could read her thoughts, Red Scar nickered beside her. Fig hugged his neck.

No. I'm not alone. I have you.

They spent the morning by the river, catching fish. Fig was normally good at fishing, but today she was distracted. Whenever she caught a fish, it slipped from her hands. But Red Scar was excellent at it. He would stand on the riverbank for long moments, staring at the shallow water. Then, fast as lightning, he'd dart underwater, then come up with a fish wriggling in his claws. He gulped down a few himself and offered one to Fig. Fish were good eating if eaten fresh. They never disturbed her sensitive stomach.

While she ate, Fig considered her steps. The jippi's tracks were gone. She had sniffed all over, and even Red Scar had added his powerful nostrils. But there was no scent left. Fig could return to the hilltop where she had met Emily. Maybe the girl would come back. But that sounded unlikely. Emily's parents had spoken, and oddly, Fig had understood them. Understood that they were off track. That they would not return to this hill.

I understood their language because I once lived among humans, she told herself.

It had been many years ago, but some vague memories remained. Words. Her name. And a blurred image of a woman with matted hair, painted cheeks, and chinking bracelets and necklaces.

A shaman, Fig thought. She remembered that word too. *Shaman. A wisewoman.*

The shaman had not been her mother. Fig was sure of that. Every day, Fig remembered more. Today she remembered the shaman telling her stories. Stories of finding her in the forest, an orphan babe. The shaman had been like the achillobators. A caretaker.

And Fig remembered the day the shaman had died. The day the bators killed her. They would have killed Fig too. But she had worn a headdress woven with red feathers. Perhaps the bators had mistaken her for one of their own, an odd hatchling. Perhaps it was a simple instinct. See red feathers, do not attack. Fig didn't know.

That was ten winters ago now. Or was it eleven already? Fig had only a vague concept of numbers. Bators had no use for numbers, but Fig often counted things like berries, fish, and seeds. She could count up to twenty using her fingers and toes, and she thought that she was fourteen, maybe fifteen now. Was that old? How long did humans live? Or bators, for that matter? Fig remembered meeting Long Tooth ten years ago, when he had been young and strong. Now he was old and slow, his red feathers gone to white. Fig must be an old woman now.

Before I die, I must find more humans. I must! I can't die with all these questions.

Emily had traveled with parents. Fig had lived with a shaman. That meant humans were not solitary. There would be more somewhere, congregating. Maybe some even moved in herds. There would be …

It hit her like lightning.

The memory was so powerful Fig fell onto her backside, splattering mud everywhere. Red Scar started, lowered his head, and sniffed at her. Fig barely saw him. The memory, long suppressed, flooded over her.

A pack, she thought. *There was a pack of shamans.*

The images floated before her. A hill in the night. Three snowcapped mountains on the horizon. A henge of stones etched with strange runes. The twin moons shone like eyes, full and bright, filling the runes with light like liquid silver. Many shamans, as many as Fig had fingers and toes, stood within the henge, hands raised, worshipping the eyes of the night. They wore dinosaur skulls atop their heads, and strings of claws and teeth jangled around their necks and wrists. Fig could hear their chanting, see the glow of the runes, feel the chill wind of night.

The memory faded. Fig blinked. She was back on the floodplain and it was daytime again. The memory had seemed so vivid. Like a waking dream.

I was there, she thought. *I was only a hatchling. I heard them chant.*

Red Scar sniffed her, nuzzled her with his snout. Fig ruffled his feathers.

We need to find three snowcapped mountains, she wanted to tell him. *A hill with a henge of stones.*

But he understood no human language, and she had forgotten how to speak. She could only say one word. Her own name. Fi-ga-ro. Yet they could communicate in the language of bators. It was less complex. But perhaps she could make him understand.

"Yeeooooowww!" she said, gesturing north where she knew that tall mountains rose. "Haroooo harrrr!" *There, there! Travel there!*

Red Scar snorted and pointed his snout south. "Garrrr harroooo!" *Pack there, in the south!*

Fig had no proper snout to point with, but she did her best with her little nose. "Garrrr harrrroooo." *My pack is north.*

Red Scar pointed his snout at his body, then toward the south, then to himself again. "Garrrrr." *We are your pack. I am your pack.*

She hugged him, cooing. *I know. I love you. I know.* "Garrrr harrooo." *But I must go north. I must see.* "Yip yip. Yip?" *Come with me?*

He growled, eyes narrowed, fierce and ready to fight. *Always, little one. Always. We are pack.*

She nuzzled him. *We are pack.*

They headed north toward the mountains. Fig's memories guided her, a map in her mind. She needed to find three mountains. A hill with a henge. And a pack of humans.

She didn't have much time.

In her memory, the shamans met when the twin moons were full. Fig often gazed at the stars and moons, tracing their celestial journeys. She had learned their patterns, could predict their movements. To Fig, the lights of the sky were old friends, and she always knew when to expect them, where they were going, when they might leave.

When the constellation shaped like a sauropod shone over the eastern sky, the oily fish swam upriver to spawn, and they were easier to catch than ever. When a constellation shaped like a frond shone in the sky's zenith, the dinosaur eggs were almost ready to hatch. The bright light she called Dawn's Eye shone over the horizon throughout winter, but only before dawn, and every night it moved a little more toward the north. The twin moons each danced their own dance, one silver and one blue, sometimes moving apart, sometimes intersecting. But only rarely did they shine side by side like two unblinking eyes.

Tonight would be such a night. A night the two moons danced together. Tonight the shamans would gather.

Fig must hurry. She ran but slower than usual. Weariness tugged on her bones like vines. She had eaten a fish for breakfast, but running quickly burned off the energy. And she was still too scrawny after a hard winter. But she kept going. She could not tarry, not to hunt or gather. By nightfall, she must find the henge.

Red Scar snorted, lowered his head, and nudged her thigh with his snout.

"Hyu? Hyu?" Fig tilted her head.

He crouched and tilted toward her. *Ride me.*

Fig shook her head. She looked at his wounds. "Heooooo." *You're hurt.*

"Ap, ap!" *I'm strong.* He rustled his feathers and snorted. *Ride me!*

Fig wanted to refuse again. The old bator was still recovering from fighting the utahraptor. He needed to take it easy for a while. But Fig relented. She was so hungry, so weak. Reluctantly she climbed onto his back. He was several times her size. Normally he could carry her with ease. Now she felt his weariness, the stiffness in his muscles moving between her thighs. But he walked onward, confident and steady. She rode him like she did during a hunt. To direct his path, she tugged on his feathers. A tug on his right side—move right. A tug on his left side—move left. They had been using this system for years.

Fig knew where she was going. Every step stirred new memories. She recognized this meadow. When she had been only a hatchling, the shaman had taken her here, explained to her which flowers could be used for healing. Fig had forgotten the names of the flowers, but as she ran among them, the smells seemed so familiar. They triggered feelings of warmth and care and safety.

Beyond the meadow, she saw them now, rising from the mist. Three mountains topped with snow. She was heading the right way.

As the day went by, no dinosaurs harassed them. At noon, an iguanodon herd rumbled by. They were hefty herbivores, probably twenty times larger than achillobators. The green, scaly giants were always hungry. They could munch down a forest within days. They generally kept to what they did best—eating. But if disturbed, they could become deadly. Iguanodons weren't just big and powerful. Terrible claws grew from their thumbs. The other four fingers were stubby, used for grabbing vegetation. But the thumbs rivaled any weapon on Mintari. Big predators like tyrannosaurs preyed on iguanodons. But the bators feared them and gave them a wide berth.

Bators were pack predators, and Red Scar and Fig were now alone. Without the pack, they could not set an ambush, could not catch big prey. They must content themselves with grabbing bugs, snails, and little lizards. Finally at afternoon, they stopped by a stream to drink. They caught no fish, only frogs. Figaro hated eating frogs. They were slimy and the meat jiggled and jumped in her mouth. But she forced herself to eat one, grimacing all the while. She nearly threw it up, but with sheer force of will, she kept the meal down. Today strength mattered. She must keep running. The frog gave her another few miles.

By nightfall, she saw the hill.

The henge crowned the hilltop like stubby horns. The moons shone above, one blue and one white, two unblinking eyes watching over Mintari.

Fig tugged Red Scar's neck feathers. The achillobator slowed to a halt. They stood in the dark valley, gazing up at the henge. The wind ruffled Fig's hair and dress of feathers. The hill seemed so much smaller than she remembered. In her memory, it was almost a mountain. But this had to be the place.

I remember. I was here before.

She dismounted and stood before the bator. Red Scar tilted his head and made little clicking sounds. *Aren't we going onward?*

Fig growled low in her throat. *Not yet. Wait. Watch. Be careful.*

They stood for a while in the darkness, side by side, two companions. A pack. The breeze rustled the grass and their feathers, and the moons rose higher above.

When the moons reached their zenith, they heard it. Chanting from the hilltop.

The moonlight illuminated the henge of stones. The runes glowed. From behind one stone, a figure appeared. Small. Mammalian. Bipedal.

A human.

Red Scar tensed, and his eyes narrowed. A low growl rose in his throat. He was confused, scared. Fig stroked his feathers, soothing him. They remained hidden in shadows, watching.

The lone figure danced on the hilltop, head tilted back, hands raised to the moon. She sang. She worshipped the light. The wind caught her hair, and it streamed like a silver river in the night.

As Fig watched, tears flowed down her cheeks. The song was beautiful, and it stirred so many memories and feelings. Her caretaker had sung that tune. Fig did not understand the words. They were old words. Words in the tongue of another world. But she understood what the music meant. This was a song about the night and the stars that traveled dark roads. A song about spring's dawning and the looming heat of summer. A song of great titans who walked the plains, roamed the forests, and soared on the wind. A song of life. Fig could listen to it forever.

The constellations roamed the sky, the moons dipped behind the mountains, and the song ended. The woman on the hill stepped out from the henge. She stared down into the dark meadow, raised her hand, and called out: "Hello there, friend!"

Fig was so shocked she fell into the grass.

She saw us! She'll hunt us! Hurt us!

Red Scar sensed her fear. He growled and bared his teeth.

"I mean you no harm!" called the woman. "Come join me, friends. I have food to share."

Red Scar growled louder. The dinosaur was confused. Fig could almost read his mind. Was this small mammal on the hill a threat? Why did she smell like Figaro, his small pack mate? Why had they come here?

Fig stroked the bator's feathers. She made little chattering sounds in his ear. *Stay here. I'll inch closer. Remain in the tall grass.* It was a signal they often used when hunting. Achillobator language revolved around hunting, mating, surviving. They had no words for a situation like this. But Red Scar understood. He crouched lower in the grass, staying put.

Fig found herself walking toward the hill. For a predator on Mintari, every calorie counted. Every step burned energy, so every step must be weighed in advance. A predator fought hard for her calories and conserved them jealously. But Fig walked onward, spending those precious calories. She was not drawn by hunger. She was not seeking higher ground during a flood. She was not looking for a mate or a place to lay eggs. Curiosity drew her. It was for curiosity that she spent the currency of survival. Curiosity had always set her apart.

On the hilltop, Fig walked between the henge stones. They towered around her. Each stone was the height of a T-rex. How did they get here? Could somebody have moved them? Figaro had never seen anyone but herself able to lift and move objects. A few herbivores knew how to grasp branches and pull them to their mouths, but that was about it. Figaro, meanwhile, could lift branches, rocks, feathers, and old claws. Her strange grasping hands were another oddity in the pack. Had some dinosaur with huge hands lifted these stones, placed them here, then etched runes into them?

The woman waited there, smiling. Fig had not seen a smile in over a decade. But that gentle curve to the mouth shot signals of meaning through her. She had never learned human body language and facial expressions. She was born knowing it. The way a bator could understand scents in urine, Fig instinctively understood a smile. It was one gesture in a language all humans knew. The woman was smiling. Nonthreatening. Welcoming.

Fig approached her. But she paused a few steps away.

"Hello there." The woman kept smiling. "How are you, friend?"

A beam of moonlight fell upon the woman. Fig's eyes widened. She took a step back.

She wasn't human at all!

The two looked nothing alike. Fig had short black hair. The woman's hair was long and the color of old bones left in the sun. Fig had soft, smooth skin like the underbelly of a hatchling. The woman had wrinkled, weathered skin, and three big moles grew on her cheek. Fig had dark eyes like pools of tar. The woman had eyes as blue as summer sky. Fig stood straight like a tree trunk, while the woman was hunched over, leaning on a third leg. No, not a third leg but a stick! How bizarre.

The woman seemed to sense Fig's confusion. She laughed. "Yes, this is what happens to you when you grow old. It'll happen to you too someday."

Fig frowned. She understood part of that. The words tickled old memories. Yes. Old. That was a word she understood. The woman was old. She must be at least twenty. Maybe even thirty! If Fig's calculations were correct, by age twenty, achillobators began to slow down. By thirty they could barely walk anymore, and the pack must leave them behind. Would Fig look like this old, wrinkled woman once she reached her twenties?

This *was* a human. An old human.

Sudden fear filled Fig, though she could not explain why. Her knees shook. She crouched at once, raised her fingers like claws, and hissed.

Stay back! I bite!

The woman's eyes softened. "Oh, you poor, lost child. You've been alone for a long while, haven't you?"

Fig crouched lower, keeping her knees raised but her elbows on the ground. Ready to pounce. She hissed louder, teeth bared.

I bite! Be careful!

Her insides trembled. Fear pounded through her. Her hackles rose, and she growled low in her throat. Her hand tightened around the dull end of her sickle claw.

The woman stepped closer. Her necklace of claws and teeth clattered, and a cloak of feathers fluttered across her back. Not *her* claws! Not *her* feathers! Claws collected from the ground. Shed feathers gathered from the wind.

She's like me, Fig thought.

"My name is Lifa," the woman said. "What's your name?"

Crouching on all fours, Fig stared at up her, teeth bared, eyes narrowed.

Fight! screamed one voice inside.

Flee! shouted another.

Those were a bator's instincts. And Fig found herself replying in the language of humans.

"Fi-ga-ro."

Trembling seized her. She dropped her sickle claw, fell to the ground, and began to weep.

"Fi-ga-ro," she repeated, tears falling. "'Ame … Fi-ga-ro."

Clouds gathered, hiding the moons, and rain began to fall like her tears. Lifa knelt beside her, wrapped her in her arms, and soothed her. "Come, lost child. Tell your friend to follow. A dry burrow awaits you with food and warmth and love. My sweet lost child, you are no longer alone."

The old woman walked through the tall grass, and Figaro followed. Even hunched over, leaning on a cane, the woman moved briskly. The raindrops clung to her feathery cloak and shone in the moonlight like ten thousand crystals.

Red Scar followed too, but he kept a safe distance, eyes narrowed, muscles tense. He was still uncertain of the stranger. He knew this was a mammal, potential prey, with meat that smelled like good eating. But he also knew this strange old woman was similar to Fig, and Fig was pack. Confusing. Red Scar followed, not attacking but not lowering his guard.

If the old woman was concerned about a carnivorous achillobator following her, she showed no sign of it. She hummed a tune as she walked, and her blue eyes sparkled.

Once, many years ago, a shaman like this tended to me, Fig thought. *The bators devoured her. She should be more careful.*

Fig herself was still on guard. Who was this Lifa? Was she truly a friend? Or was she an enemy of the pack? Fig did not know. But the woman had answers. The woman was like her. Older, wiser, but still human. Fig kept following.

They walked for a while, leaving the grasslands and entering the forested foothills of the tall mountains. A northerly wind dispersed the clouds, the rain faded, and fireflies danced among the trees. Red Scar was fascinated. He snapped at the fireflies, trying to catch them in his mouth. He wasn't hungry, just playing. Fig looked at the swirling, luminous lights in wonder.

Brighter lights shone ahead. Fig narrowed her eyes, and her heart raced. Lifa was walking toward the lights, but Fig paused. Lights—in the forest! Near the ground! Not small, gentle lights like fireflies either. Bright ones!

Achillobators feared fire. Every dinosaur did. Light near the ground could mean flame. Red Scar saw it too. He tensed, abandoning the fireflies, and growled.

"Haoo, haoooo!" he called to Fig. *Flee! Flee!*

Lifa turned toward them. "Don't fear the lights, friends. Only my porch lanterns. They can't hurt you."

Fig didn't understand those words. What was a *porch*? What were *lanterns*? What were *friends*?

"Ha-roooooooeeee!" Fig yowled. *It will burn me!*

Lifa shook her head. "Don't be scared, lost child. You're safe. You're safe."

Fig understood the woman's tone. Soothing. Comforting. She kept following.

They reached the oddest nest Fig had ever seen. This was nothing like a dinosaur's nest. Branches were arranged in a dome the size of a sleeping iguanodon. Mud filled the gaps between the branches, forming crude walls. Grass, moss, even flowers grew across the roof. From above, it probably looked like a simple tussock. But from up close, Fig saw signs of habitation. There was an opening to the burrow, partly concealed behind branches and vines. And of course—there were the lights.

Several dinosaur eggs hung from the branches like fruit. The eggs were cracked open, but there were no hatchlings inside. Instead, fire burned inside the eggs!

Fig hissed, snarled, and pawed the earth. But the fire wasn't spreading. The eggs kept it contained.

"Don't fear," the woman said. "They're only lanterns."

Fig growled at the flaming eggs. She scampered back, raised her sickle claw, slashed the air, and howled. Red Scar crouched low, hissing, ready to flee.

"Hold on, hold on!" Lifa said. She approached the eggs one by one, blew on them, and the fire vanished. Shadows cloaked the forest.

It was like a great weight lifted. At once, both Fig and Red Scar calmed down.

Lifa pulled back the cover of vines and branches, revealing the doorway.

"Come in, Figaro," she said. "Your friend will feel trapped indoors. He can wait outside the hut. He'll feel better under the sky. Will you tell him that?"

Fig thought she understood. She held Red Scar's snout and cooed softly. *Stay.*

He purred. *I'll stay. I'll guard.* He huffed and snorted. *Call out if you need me. And I will break this nest apart.*

Leaving the achillobator, the two women crawled into this "hut."

A few more lights shone inside. Fig trembled but tolerated them. Her curiosity overcame her fear. This was the strangest nest Fig had ever seen. Crystals, circles of twigs, and feathers hung from branches above. Embers glowed in a pit. More fire! Fur pelts covered the floor and hung from the walls. The place smelled strange. There was no scent of urine here to mark territory. She smelled herbs, flowers, smoke. Transparent bulbs—they looked like dewdrops the size of Fig's head—stood in alcoves, full of leaves.

Fig wanted to flee. This was a strange place. Dangerous. Fire! Fire that could burn!

Another memory. Herself as a little girl. Curled up on fur pelts, sleeping by a fire. This was how human nests looked. Humans somehow did something no dinosaur could. They tamed fire. How could mammals so weak and small wield such power?

Weariness draped across her. Fig couldn't help it. She yawned. She had so many questions to ask, so much to explore. It was all overwhelming. She plopped onto the rug, feeling safe and warm. She curled up like a bator and slept.

She awoke the next morning and found herself alone in the hut. Lifa was gone.

Sunlight spilled through round holes in the walls. Somewhere deep in her mind, Fig remembered seeing such holes. There was a purpose to them. A word for them. Windows! That was it. They jogged a memory from her childhood. She had been three, maybe two years old, looking through a window at the rain.

In the morning light, Fig looked around the room. The rugs were not actually fur, she realized. She had mistaken them in the shadows. They were woven from countless slender threads, forming elaborate designs. Fig knelt and ran her hand along the fabric, fascinated. She had never seen anything like this! Fabric. A rug. Yes, more memories.

This was not a nest. That was the wrong word. It was ...

Home.

The word shot through her. This was a home.

She tried to say it. "Haoooooo!"

She had not spoken human words since she was four. She was a little rusty. She cleared her throat, stamped her feet like a bator preparing for a charge, and tried again.

"Hooo—rrroooo!"

Close enough. Best she could manage for now. Human words were strange. Bator howls, hisses, and growls made much more sense.

With perfect timing, her belly gave a loud growl. Fig realized she was famished. Where was Lifa? Did she have food to share? Fig sniffed around, seeking something to eat. Were there any carcasses lying around? Any bones to chew on?

Singing distracted her. It came from outside. Lifa must be out there.

Scratching her belly, still yawning, Fig shuffled toward the door. On the way there, in the corner of her eye, she glimpsed—

A girl! Another human girl!

Fig stopped in her tracks. Her heart leaped. She spun around, stuck out her finger like claws, and bared her teeth, ready to fight.

The girl snarled right back at her, fingers raised as if she wielded claws.

The two girls faced each other, eyes locked, teeth bared. They sized each other up.

She's feral too, Fig thought.

The girl facing her was short and scrawny. Her limbs were tanned brown and covered with scratches and scabs. Her face was round, her hair short and dark. Her eyes were the color of blackberries. Most shockingly, she wore a patchwork of red feathers over her skinny frame.

Bator feathers.

Fig stepped closer, sniffing. The girl stepped closer too, also sniffing. Fig hissed. The girl hissed. Fig drew and lashed her sickle claw. The girl lashed her own sickle claw.

Fig stumbled back in shock. The other girl stumbled back too. It was like looking into water. But much, much clearer! It was a reflection. But not the smudgy reflections Fig had seen in lakes and puddles. Those were barely more than shadows. This was ... amazing. Shocking. So real. Instead of looking at water, she was looking at ... what?

She reached forward, hesitant. Her reflection reached toward her. Their fingertips touched. But instead of feeling a fingertip, Fig felt something like hard, cold stone.

Magic, she thought. *Amazing!*

She relaxed, did a little twirl, and examined her reflection. She had never seen herself so clearly.

Well, I'll be, she thought. *Am I pretty?*

Such a silly thought, yet it popped into her head nonetheless. Perhaps, like curiosity, it was another innate human instinct. Vanity.

Well, enough vanity for now. Fig left the magical reflective surface, ducked through the doorway, and stepped outside.

In the daylight, Fig got a better view. A garden surrounded the hut, lush with flowers, aromatic herbs, and fruit trees. A fence woven of branches surrounded the place, similar to the piles of bones achillobators placed around their nests. Odd-looking dinosaurs pecked for seeds in the yard, clucking and scratching the ground. They were even smaller than eoraptors and grew toothless beaks. One of these bizarre dinosaurs sported a red, fleshy crest. It stood on the hut's roof and let out an ear-piercing *cock-a-doodle-do!* Funny little dinos, whatever they were. Red Scar might have devoured them, but the achillobator was away now, perhaps hunting for bigger prey. He sometimes went out on his own before dawn, and Fig knew he would return.

The singing came from a nearby stream. Fig padded over, her bare feet stepping on clover and moss. Lifa knelt by the stream, singing softly. Flowers bloomed throughout her long white hair, and butterflies fluttered around them. As she sang, Lifa reached into the water and pulled out a wicker basket. Fig gasped. Several fish floundered inside!

Lifa turned from the water, smiling. "Are you hungry for fish, little one?"

Fig's stomach growled.

"I take that as a yes." Lifa stepped over the clover toward her. "Figaro, do you know how to scale and gut fish? You can help me to …"

Her voice trailed off. Her smile faded. She stepped closer to Fig, eyes narrowing.

Fig just stood there, arms at her sides. She tilted her head. "Harrooo?"

Lifa reached out a wrinkled, pale hand. She brushed back Fig's hair. "By the moons, look at you. My eyes don't work well in shadows anymore. Now that I see you in daylight, you look just like …" She pulled back her hand as if stung. "How old are you, child?"

Fig tilted her head the other way. "Hawooo? Aeerrrrrr." *What?*

"How many springs have you lived?" Lifa's voice was soft. "Do you know?"

Ah, Fig understood. She nodded. She tapped all ten fingers, lifted one foot, and tapped four toes. She hesitated, thought for a moment, then tapped the fifth toe.

"You're fifteen," Lifa whispered. "You were born the year that …" Her voice trailed off, and for a long moment, she gazed into the distance. Then she sighed and smiled. "Come now. Help me prepare the fish."

They sat down in the yard among the flowers. Butterflies and dragonflies fluttered all around. A pile of embers glowed here among stones. Only yesterday, embers would have terrified Fig. Now when Lifa sat by the embers, Fig joined her without hesitation. The old woman had the magic to tame fire. Indeed, she tossed a few sticks onto the embers, and they ignited. What a wonderful thing! To control fire! Even the mightiest tyrannosaurs could not do that.

Lifa placed down the basket and took out a fish. Fig's stomach growled again, and her mouth watered. She snatched the fish from Lifa and bit deep, ripping through the scaly skin until she found the soft pink flesh. The juices filled her mouth. Delicious!

"Fig, wait." Lifa pulled the fish from her mouth.

Fig bared her teeth and hissed. *Mine, mine! Back down! I bite!*

Lifa leaned back. "Don't worry, Figaro! I'm not trying to steal your food. I want to show you something. Okay? Look what I'm doing."

The old woman took a strange, straight claw from her belt. She ran it across the fish, removing scales. They flew every which way. Fig ducked and hissed as the scales flew overhead. Next, Lifa cut the fish open, reached inside, and pulled out the guts, which she tossed into the fire. They sizzled.

Fig yowled. She was wasting food!

"That part isn't for eating," Lifa said. "You're a human girl. You must eat like a human."

Fig yowled and pointed at her belly. *Hungry!*

"Wait!" Lifa said.

The old woman stuck a skewer through the fish, further mutilating the poor thing.

Fig mewled and made a grab for it. *Give me! Give it to me raw and wriggling!*

But Lifa pulled the fish away and kept working. She tore a few herbs off a nearby plant, crumbled them over the fish, and squeezed a strange yellow fruit onto the meat. The woman had clearly gone insane. Then, as a final insult, Lifa held the fish over the fire. It began to sizzle.

Fig whined in protest. The fish was ruined! Why did Lifa do this?

Without waiting for an invitation, Fig reached into the wicker basket. She grabbed another raw fish. Still alive and flopping. Mmm. Perfect. Fig salivated.

Lifa tried to take the raw fish from Fig.

Thief! Mine! Fig pulled the fish back, snarling and snapping her teeth. *Don't you touch my fish! I'll bite your fingers off.*

Fig bit into the fish, spat out scales, and swallowed the soft pink flesh. She licked her lips. Yum.

Lifa sighed. After a few moments, she pulled the first fish off the fire. The ruined, mutilated fish. It steamed and sizzled and smelled strange. Not a bad smell. But a smell Fig could not describe. Oddly, her mouth watered.

The old woman blew on her seared fish, took a bite, winced, blew on it again, then handed it to Fig.

"Try it cooked."

Fig sniffed at the cooked fish suspiciously, then raised her nose. She stuck out her tongue in disgust. "Blah!"

Lifa burst out laughing. "Try it!"

Fig sniffed again. All right, she had to admit. It did smell good. The smell of herbs, citrus fruit, and cooked flesh intoxicated her. More magic!

Fig took a tiny bite. Just a nibble really. It was …

A sigh flowed through her. Her eyes rolled back. She nearly collapsed.

It was delicious. It was the tastiest thing Fig had ever eaten. It made every other meal in her life seem bland.

"Good, huh?" Lifa said.

Fig snatched the entire cooked fish and devoured it, almost choking on a bone.

"Here, I'll teach you," Lifa said.

For a while, the two women sat together in the yard, cleaning, gutting, seasoning, and cooking fish. Fig made a mess of it. Whenever she tried to scale a fish, she just got scales in her hair. When she tried to season a fish, she put grass on it, and Lifa had to pluck the grass off and show her the right herbs. When Fig tried to cook the fish, she nearly burned herself. Lifa had to grab her wrist and pull Fig's hand away from a pretty ember. But somehow they got more fish cooked, and they shared the meal.

While they worked, Lifa kept looking at Fig. Sometimes she would stare at her intently for a long moment, then look away. The old woman then got very quiet.

There are thoughts inside her mind, Fig realized. *Same as there are thoughts in my mind. She's not like a bator who is driven by instinct. She's like me. She thinks. She remembers. She ponders. I wish I could read her thoughts, but I can't, no more than I can smell a bator's scent markings.*

Fig could think these thoughts. But she didn't know how to put them to words. She could understand the language of humans well enough. But speaking was beyond her.

Fig tilted her head. "Arooo?" *What's wrong?*

Lifa smiled thinly. "I'm just thinking. You remind me so much of someone I knew ... long ago. And of someone else I still know."

Fig tilted her head the other way. "Who?"

Lifa blinked, then laughed. "Figaro! Did you just talk?"

"Hawwwhooooo!"

"Try it again. Like before. You said 'Who?'"

Fig nodded. "Who? Who … Fi-ga-ro?" She tapped her chest. "Who Fi-ga-ro?"

Suddenly Lifa had tears in her eyes. This sometimes happened to Fig too. The salty wetness in her eyes. It never happened to bators.

"You have the same eyes," Lifa whispered. She brushed back strands of Fig's dark hair. "Your eyes have epicanthal folds. Those are rare on Mintari. A woman I knew had such eyes. A woman named Mina. She died fifteen years ago. The year you were born."

Figaro hugged herself. "Mi-na? Mi-na? Fi-ga-ro?"

She began to tremble. What was this woman saying? Was … was Mina her mother?

"Mi-na? Mi-na Fi-ga-ro?" She tapped her chest. "Mi-na Fi-ga-ro? Arrrrroooo! Arrrooooo!"

Her emotions were taking over her. Her words became excited howls.

One of the little feathered dinosaurs was clucking nearby. Lifa had referred to them earlier as *chickens*. Figaro darted toward the chicken and pointed at it. "Mi-na?" She pointed at an egg. "Fi-ga-ro?"

Was Mina my mother? Did she lay the egg I hatched from?

Lifa heaved a sigh. "You better come inside, Figaro. There's something I must show you."

In the daylight, Lifa's house bloomed. Grass rustled across the roof. Vines draped over the earthen walls, heavy with flowers and berries. Even the branches that formed the framework seemed alive, twisty and knotty and still covered with bark. Lifa parted the curtain of vines and stepped inside. Fig followed.

Lifa rummaged through her alcoves, moving aside crystals, raptor teeth, jars of dry herbs, pots of living herbs, bundled feathers, river stones, and other sundries. Finally she produced a strange object Fig couldn't begin to understand. She had never seen anything like it, had no frame of reference. She blinked and tilted her head.

"Come, sit beside me by the fire," Lifa said.

They sat on the rug. It was soft like grass, but Fig felt antsy. She wasn't used to being indoors. She lifted her foot to her mouth and began gnawing on her toes, a nervous habit.

Lifa patted the strange object. "This is an old photo album. From twenty years ago. Since I've decided to live alone in the forest, it's kept me company."

Fig scratched her head. "Awroo? Foo? Foo?" *What was a photo album?*

Lifa opened the book. Fig leaped to her feet and scampered back. She hit the wall, rattling the mugs and jars, and hissed. There were people trapped inside the book! Little people no larger than bugs! She crouched, ready to attack, and growled.

"It's all right, Figaro. They're photos. Not real people. Come, sit. Take a look."

Fig snarled and hissed and dared not approach. More magic! But then she remembered looking at the reflective surface, seeing herself there. Was this book like that? A strange illusion?

She didn't like this world of humans. She wanted to leave the house, to run into the forest, to find Red Scar. That's where she belonged. Where things made sense. With the achillobators.

With her pack. Suddenly she was trembling, and tears ran down her cheeks.

I should never have come here. I don't understand this world. I'm scared. I'm so scared.

Lifa wrapped her in her arms, and suddenly the fear flowed away. Figaro had never been hugged before. It felt right. It felt warm. It felt so wonderful. The best thing she had ever felt.

"Fi-ga-ro?" she whispered. *Who am I? What am I?*

They sat by the fire, and Lifa held her and stroked her hair until Fig calmed. Finally Fig dared look at the photo album.

Lifa tried to explain what photos were. Most of the explanation went over Fig's head. But it seemed like a way to trap a copy of a person, not the actual person. Sort of like reaching into a pond and trapping the reflection. Once Fig realized those weren't actual living people, just reflections trapped in time, she was no longer afraid.

Lifa flipped through the pages and settled on a photo of a woman. A woman with long black hair. With dark eyes.

Fig squinted, scrutinizing the photo. Then her eyes widened. It was her! Another reflection! Wasn't it? It looked like her. A *lot* like her. But older. Stronger. Not ridden with lice and gaunt after winter. The woman in the photo had longer hair than Fig, and she wore strange fabrics, not just a dress of feathers.

Fig tapped the photo. "Fi-ga-ro?"

"This is Mina," Lifa said.

Figaro leaped back. "Mina. Mina! Mina!" She trembled. "Fi-ga-ro? Egg? Egg? Mina Fi-ga-ro egg?"

She trembled. Was this her mother? Was this woman in the photo her mother?

Lifa smiled sadly. "Humans don't lay eggs, dear. We give birth to live young. Mina was pregnant when she died. It was fifteen years ago. You look exactly like her. We all thought that her baby died with her, but ..." She shook her head. "Maybe I'm getting ahead of myself. Maybe it's just wishful thinking. Maybe I found you, and I saw her, and I dared to hope …"

Fig trembled. Her mother. The woman in the photo was her mother. And she was dead. Tears gathered in Fig's eyes.

Questions raced through her mind like a pack of raptors. How had her mother died? Who was the shaman with dreadlocks who had tended to her long ago? Where were all the shamans she remembered from childhood? Did only one remain—just Lifa?

She pointed at the photo of Mina. "Haoo? Haoo?" *What happened to her?*

Lifa's eyes darkened. "It was Ivan who killed her. They call him the King of Mintari. A black T-rex. The shamans claim he is a dark god."

Fig gasped. "Ayyyvum?"

The old woman shuddered. "His very name is cursed."

A memory pulsed through Fig. Many years ago, she had seen a gargantuan dark predator on a hilltop. Only a shadow with red eyes. Fig had thought it a dream. The apparition still haunted her nightmares. Could that have been Ivan, the dark god? The terror that slew her mother?

Fig wanted to ask more about this dreaded T-rex. But then a realization hit her. She leaped up and pointed at Lifa.

"You! Lifa! Lifa … give bir … Mina?" *Are you Mina's mother?*

"No, Mina is not my child," the old woman said. "I'll show you my child."

She flipped to another page.

This page showed a photo of …

Fig leaped back, bared her teeth, and howled. "Yaaaooooo!"

A cry of challenge. She was scared and ready for battle. The person in the photo was not human! There was fur on his cheeks! His shoulders were broader than human shoulders. He looked taller. Stronger. Wilder. Another species! Similar to human, eerily similar. But dangerous. Enemy! Predator!

Lifa looked up in shock, eyes wide. But then her face softened. "You've never seen a man before, have you?"

Fig considered. A man. What was that? An adult human male? She had seen one from a distance once. The man driving the jippi. Emily's father. But the man in the photo was different. Bigger. More dangerous. Fig shuddered.

"Don't worry, child," Lifa said. "He's human like you. This is Joe Triplehorn. My son. Your father."

Fig stared at the shaman, silent. She wasn't looking at the book anymore. Those were only reflections. People she had never known. Here before her stood a real, living woman. A human woman. Her grandmother.

Fig nuzzled the woman with her tiny snout. She did not know how to hug. But Lifa wrapped her in her arms and soothed her as she wept.

CHAPTER FIFTEEN
The Titans of Mintari

By the time Joe reached the supersaurus, there was nothing he could do.

Dozer plodded closer. Joe and Simone rode on his back, staring.

"Oh God." Simone covered her mouth. "Oh my God. What happened here?"

Joe stared with dark eyes. "The supersaurus fell asleep. By day. Alone. And sealed her fate. We're too late."

Most sauropods did not sleep alone. Part of the herd always kept watch. But sometimes eggs were late to hatch. The herd roamed on, desperate for enough food to replenish their massive bodies. And the mother remained behind with her hatchlings. While she tended to them, she would remain awake, ever vigilant. If she must sleep, she would keep one eye open, and so much as a snapping twig would awake her.

But this supersaurus had tranquilizer darts in her. And bullet wounds that still bled, sapping her strength. So she had sunk into a deep slumber, neck coiled around her nest.

And the predators had seized their chance.

"What are those?" Simone whispered, trembling.

"Sinraptors," Joe said.

They covered the supersaurus like crabs on a dead whale, feasting.

They were large predators. As long as school buses. As tall as a bungalow. But atop the supersaurus, they seemed small. It was a kingly banquet. Three sinraptors were here, gorging themselves.

Dozer grunted and stomped closer, furious. He swung his head from side to side, displaying his horns. The three sinraptors turned from the sauropod carcass. Blood covered their snouts and dripped between their teeth. They hissed at the triceratops, and their claws rose menacingly, threatening lacerations.

Stay back, herbivore! they seemed to hiss. *This is our meal. Beware we do not eat you too.*

"Oh God!" Simone suddenly blurted out. "The Rangers … Oh God."

Joe saw them. Two Rangers down on the grass. He wasn't sure if they were alive, but he couldn't check. Not yet. If he climbed off Dozer, the sinraptors would pounce.

Riding the triceratops, Joe raised his sleep-or-die. He fired into the air. The *boom* shook the plains.

The sinraptors screeched and clawed the soil. Simone squeezed Joe like a vise. He couldn't blame her this time. When three predators the length of buses screeched in fury, it could unnerve the strongest Ranger, let alone a Cloventian journalist.

He fired into the air again. And again. Dozer reared, legs kicking, and then lowered his head to the ground, front legs bent, horns pointing forward. Ready to charge. Sinraptors were big, heavy predators. But the triceratops probably weighed more than all three put together. And his horns dwarfed their claws.

The sinraptors hesitated for a moment, considering. Predators were not bloodthirsty killers. Hunting was risky business. Even for giants like a T-rex, let alone creatures only halfway up the food chain like sinraptors. Every confrontation could result in broken bones, lacerations, even death. When they could, they preyed on the young, the old, the weak. Sometimes a predator risked a fight. When the hunger was bad enough, they took chances. But these sinraptors had already eaten quite a bit.

Battling a triceratops and a gun-wielding Ranger was simply not worth it. Not for just a few more bites.

The sinraptors retreated, racing across the grass and vanishing among the trees. Their pride was hurt but their bellies were full, and that was what mattered.

Joe dismounted Dozer. For a second or two, he faced a choice. Who should he check on first? The hatchlings in the nest? Or the Rangers? Dinosaurs or humans?

Joe preferred the company of dinosaurs to humans. That was no secret. But right now he ran toward the fallen Rangers. They were his top priority. As much as he loved dinosaurs and mistrusted humans, he must check on them first.

But like with the supersaurus, it was too late.

"Dead," he said. "Both of them."

Simone rode closer and stared from atop Dozer. Joe expected her to break down, but she seemed oddly cool around the bodies. Of course. She had covered the Slum Wars. Clearly she was no stranger to death.

"The sinraptors didn't do this," Simone said. "Bullets did."

"Amissa." Joe felt sick. "So she's graduated from poacher to murderer." His lips twisted in disgust. "My murderous sister."

Leaving the bodies, he walked toward the sauropod nest. The mother supersaurus had died with her neck curled around the nest, trying with her last breath to protect her offspring.

Joe's breath shook in his chest. His eyes stung. The hatchlings were dead.

"The raptors tore them apart," he whispered, voice hoarse.

Simone dismounted and came by him. Tears ran down her cheeks. "Oh, Joe. I'm sorry. I—" She gasped. "Darwin's beard! Joe, come over here! Look!"

A pile of branches and leaves in the nest was rustling. A tiny head—no larger than an apple—stuck out from the leaves.

Big yellow eyes blinked. Joe knelt and cleared away the branches. A sauropodlet wobbled into his arms and licked him.

"A baby supersaurus," Joe said, cradling the animal. "A boy."

"He's so small!" Simone said.

"You're not scared?"

She shook her head. "No. Not anymore." She knelt and stroked the hatchling. The sauropodlet licked her hand.

"He only weighs a few pounds now," Joe said. "But he'll become a giant. Like his mother."

Simone smiled, tears in her eyes. "Can he survive without his mother?" She caressed the baby's head.

"A mammal would die, but a baby sauropod does not drink milk. He eats leaves. And this one is eating already."

Even as he cradled in Joe's arms, the baby stretched his neck toward the branches in the nest and began munching leaves.

"We should name him Clark," Simone said.

Joe raised an eyebrow. "Why Clark?"

"Clark Kent. Superman. Because he's a supersaurus."

Joe frowned. "Who the hell is Superman?"

She rolled her eyes. "Didn't you study second millennium mythology at school? Don't bother answering. You were probably busy flying pterodactyls into volcanoes to rescue trapped dinosaurs."

"Something like that."

Simone laughed as Clark the sauropodlet nuzzled her hand, maybe looking for more food. She handed him another leafy branch.

"Can I hold him?"

Joe placed the dinosaur in her arms. Simone held the hatchling. She laughed. "I'm holding a dinosaur. I'm actually holding a dinosaur and I'm not wetting myself with fear." Tears fell as she laughed. "I can't believe it. Clark, you are amazing. Can we keep him?"

Joe shook his head. "No."

"But you kept Dozer and Vinnie!"

At the sound of their names, Dozer snorted and Vinnie cackled.

Joe snorted. "I didn't keep them. They're not my pets. Those two just stuck around. But Clark is different. He's going to grow big. Real big. Too big to be around humans. We need to find his herd. And return him to his kind."

"Good thing supersaurs are the biggest dinosaurs on Mintari," Simone said. "They can't be too hard to find."

A Ranger tricopter smoldered nearby. Amissa had filled it with bullets.

To hold me back, Joe thought.

If he had a working tricopter, would he abandon his convictions, use modern technology on Mintari?

To catch her—perhaps. She was not just killing dinosaurs now. She was killing fellow Rangers. He would do whatever it took to stop her. But it was a moot point. The smoking tricopter beside him would never fly again.

He glanced at Simone. She sat on the grass, cradling Clark, laughing as the little dinosaur nuzzled her. The breeze billowed her flaming-red tresses, and her eyes sparkled in the sunlight. Yet even as she laughed, the shadow of sadness filled her eyes. She was a twin in mourning. One half of a whole.

This wasn't the first time Amissa killed humans, Joe reminded himself.

He needed to find her, to stop her. He needed to return Clark to his herd. But before he could do those things, he must bury his fallen brother and sister.

He didn't have a shovel. But he did have a bulldozer. With his mighty horns, Dozer quickly dug two graves.

Simone approached, solemn, still cradling Clark in her arms.

"Shouldn't we take the bodies back to Dinovia City?" she said.

"There is no cemetery in Dinovia City. Mintarians bury their dead outside the walls. We come from soil. And to soil we return."

A Mintari Ranger almost never removed his hat. Not even during sleep. The wide-brimmed ceratop hat, reminiscent of old Earth's park ranger hats, was a symbol. A source of pride. Practically a religious headdress. But sometimes one could remove it. For example, when a crazy redhead insisted on cutting your hair. Or when you were burying fallen comrades. Joe took off his hat.

The wind in his hair, he carried the bodies into the graves. He knew these Rangers. He had fought with them. Shared meals with them at the Fossil and Firkin. They had been at his wedding. Before he covered them in soil, he paused. He hesitated. Then he nodded.

He pulled out his communicator. "I must call their families."

He waited until the tricopters arrived from Dinovia, their rotors raising clouds of dirt as they landed. The grieving families stepped out. They were weeping, shocked, crying out. A child clung to her mother. "Is Daddy gone?" A husband fell to his knees and cried to the sky, voice torn.

Then more tricopters landed, and Rangers emerged. Dozens of Rangers, come to pay their respects to fallen comrades. Joe served in their order, but he rarely met the others. He was a solitary Ranger, a rogue. And he realized how little in common he had with his peers.

It was hard. Not just the deaths. But being in a crowd. Joe had not been among so many humans since Mina had died. He felt trapped. Surrounded by predators.

A few Rangers came up to him, patted him on the back.

"Thanks for calling, Joe."

"Joe, it's good to see you, buddy."

"What has it been, fifteen years?"

But other Rangers shot him venomous glares. Joe still wore a triceratops crest on his lapel. Crest of his clan. The same crest that appeared on the guns Tobias Triplehorn sold to poachers. Likely, the gun that had murdered these Rangers had borne the same crest.

One Ranger spat at Joe's feet. "Go to hell, you son of a bitch."

Another Ranger cried out: "Traitor!"

One even glared at Joe and said, "You killed them. I know it."

A few mutters of agreement passed among the Rangers. Their eyes shot daggers.

Joe looked away.

Simone approached him, eyes soft. She put a hand on his arm. "Are you all right, Joe? Do you want to leave?"

He shook his head. "We stay until they're buried."

Simone held his hand and leaned against him. "I'm sorry, Joe. To see fellow Rangers hate you ... I understand now why you live in the mountains."

"They don't hate me," Joe said. "They hate my clan. I understand. This is my burden to bear."

"But it's not your fault!" she said. "They hate you because of what your family did!"

"Yes, my family did this," Joe said. "And I've vowed to restore my family honor. So I must be here."

Simone nodded. She held his hand. "And I'm here with you."

As Dozer refilled the graves with soil, Joe spoke softly to the dead.

"Go back now, children of Mintari. Go back to the soil from which you came. In the warm embrace of the world, you will bring forth new life. The energy in your bodies will feed the grass that grows and the trees that reach toward the sun. Flowers will grow where you fell, and the rain will wash your blood away. You will be reborn. Rest now, children of life. We will always remember you, for you will never die."

He climbed back onto Dozer. And he rode onward, leaving the graves. The others stared after him, and even those Rangers who had spat and cursed were now silent.

Vinnie loped alongside the triceratops, dipping down now and then to snatch a bug. Simone rode behind Joe. This time she was not crushing him with her arms. In her arms she carried a sleeping sauropodlet.

Tracking down the supersaurus herd was easy. After all, they were among the largest dinosaurs on Mintari. If not *the* largest. They left footprints you could lie down inside. Not to mention a trail of denuded trees, flattened bushes, and piles of dung the size of cars.

Yes, tracking them was not a problem.

Dozer moved slowly and steadily, munching on grass as he plodded along. The trike still needed time to recover from his injuries, but the cool air and fresh vegetation would help him heal. Joe too needed this time in the open, far from the crowds, from the glares and mutters. The funerals had unnerved him. More than he realized. Not only the loss of his fallen comrades—but the hatred of comrades who still lived.

He did not blame his fellow Rangers. He understood. He blamed his family.

The sins of my father passed on to me, he thought. *I must expunge them.*

They rode on through the wilderness. In the afternoon, they spotted the towering necks of sauropods ahead.

They found the herd.

The supersaurs were roaming across the grasslands in their eternal pursuit of food. They moved slowly, plodding along with all the time in the world. Every few steps, they stopped, lowered their heads, and swept their necks from side to side, vacuuming up plants.

They were nature's ultimate eating machines. Everything about them served this ultimate purpose. Eat a lot. Move a little. Grow bigger. Eat some more. Their long necks allowed them to reach a huge amount of food without spending calories on walking too much. They didn't even waste energy on chewing. They stripped leaves off bushes, sucked up grass, and simply gulped it down. Instead of chewing, they swallowed rocks along with their meals. The rocks were known as gastroliths. They rubbed against one another inside their bellies, grinding their food like pestles and mortars. They were not only Mintari's greatest eating machines but also the laziest creatures around, saving calories wherever they could.

The sauropods barely registered Dozer approaching. The triceratops was large and powerful enough to intimidate a T-rex.

But the supersaurs merely glanced his way, then resumed eating. They were so large they feared nothing. Even the greatest predators feared taking on a supersaurus.

But my sister killed one, Joe thought. *Indirectly, at least. These animals can whack aside a T-rex with their tails. But humans can kill them. They say Mintari is a world full of monsters. But we are the real monsters.*

Simone, who was riding behind him, gazed at the herd with huge eyes. She cuddled Clark closer to her. The sauropodlet was hiding under a blanket, only his apple-sized head sticking out.

"It's hard to believe that little Clark will ever grow so big," she said.

"Oh, he'll grow all right. These animals can gain the weight of a human every day."

Simone gasped. "Clark will be bigger than me tomorrow?"

"Soon he'll make Dozer seem tiny."

Dozer snorted. It sounded almost like a laugh. Sometimes Joe swore that the trike understood more than just a few basic commands.

When they got closer, he halted the triceratops, and they dismounted. Joe and Simone tilted their heads back, gazing up at the towering herbivores.

"It feels like being back on Cloventia, staring up at skyscrapers," Simone said.

"These are the skyscrapers of Mintari."

Simone placed the bundled sauropodlet on the grass, then pulled off the blanket. Clark rose onto his wobbly feet, looked up at the herd, then back at Simone. He tottered closer to her and nuzzled her.

Joe smiled. "You imprinted on him. He thinks you're his mother."

"That's so sweet. But I don't think I can handle a baby who'll be bigger than me by the weekend." She kissed Clark on the top of his knobby little head. "Go join your family. I'll be here for you. Always. And maybe we'll meet again."

The sauropodlet hopped back into her arms. She placed him onto the grass. But he jumped right back onto her.

The herd noticed the hatchling. Massive sauropods lumbered closer. One titanic female lowered her head toward the humans. She sniffed, her breath so powerful it ruffled the grass and billowed Simone's hair. The sauropods were so big it boggled the mind. You could ride a horse between their legs, and the dinosaurs wouldn't notice. It was hard to believe that Clark would someday be so large.

Simone paled and trembled, but she conquered her fear.

"Go on." She nudged Clark toward the inquisitive female.

Clark wobbled toward the adult supersaurus. The gargantuan herbivore sniffed him, nearly sucking up his entire body into her nostrils. Clark hopped around her head, curious.

A few other sauropodlets stepped closer. They were bigger than Clark. More like Dozer's size. Still very small for sauropods. Clark hesitated, looked at the other sauropodlets, then looked back at Simone.

"Go on," she whispered. "Join your friends."

Clark ran, wobbling and falling, then rising again, joining the herd. Soon he was waddling around between the adults' feet. The dinosaurs moved so slowly the hatchling had no trouble keeping up. Within moments, Clark joined them in doing what sauropods did best. Eating.

Joe's communicator buzzed. He checked the screen.

Fury exploded through him.

"Amissa!" he howled to the sky.

Simone started. Dozer and Vinnie swiveled their heads toward him. Even the sauropods paused from eating—which was a big deal for them.

Simone approached hesitantly. "Joe?"

His hands shook. His eye twitched. "She's in my cave. In my home. She's going through my things. And showing the world."

Amissa strutted around her brother's cave, whistling appreciatively.

"My, my, Jurassic Joe. Sweet digs! You pretend to be some rugged mountain man. But this cave is adorable! Like an old lady's cottage."

Her arm was in a sling, and her supersaurus hunt had failed, but her spirits soared. Her SmartSphere hovered before her, connected to her QuickFame account. The camera was filming everything. This was good content. As Simone LaRue would say—a scoop. The redhead thought herself a serious journalist. Ha! Amissa's video streams got a hundred times the views.

"Yes, Tripletots, it's true. This is the home of the infamous outlaw Jurassic Joe. Let's take a look, shall we?"

The cave was large and comfortable. A rug hid the floor. Ocher paintings of dinosaurs covered the walls, similar in style to caveman paintings on old Earth. There was even a fireplace. Curious crystals, clay mugs, and leather-bound books filled alcoves carved into the cave walls. A driftwood bed stood among stalagmites, topped with pillows. Shadowy tunnels led to deeper rooms where soft lights glowed.

From the outside, the place looked humble. Just a hole in the mountain, blocked with steel bars. But after Amissa had picked the lock and stepped inside, she found a homey haven.

"Aww, this place is so cute!" Amissa said. "Just needs a few doilies, and my grandmother would love it."

She checked her QuickFame comments.

"Hey, lay off him. This is a great man cave."

"Yeah, this place rocks."

"Cool! Is that a real dinosaur claw on the shelf?"

"Damn, I'd live here."

Amissa cursed inwardly. This wasn't working. Should she keep trying? Portray Joe as a homebody, not the rugged outdoorsy type? Nah. The viewers weren't buying it. If anything, this was making Joe look *better*.

She needed another angle. There had to be something in this cave. Some real dirt. Something to destroy his reputation. Millions were watching. She better dig up something.

She sniffed and detected a familiar scent. Following her nose, Amissa walked down a short tunnel and found a pantry. Her eyes widened. Ah, she knew it! Here was something better.

"Look, Tripletots! Look at what Jurassic Joe eats. I see sausages! He pretends to love animals. But he's a meat eater. And a hypocrite!"

This was a little better. Got more of a reaction. Comments flooded the feed.

"How dare he eat animals!"

"I bet they're dinosaur sausages."

"So what? Let him eat meat! I'm eating a sausage right now."

"He's a murderer! No better than you, Amissa."

"Um, you know meat eaters can still love dinos, right?"

A mixed reaction. Better than nothing. This was half-decent dirt. Amissa could spin this. Embarrass him a little. Still—

this would not deliver a killing blow. She had to find *real* dirt. Something that would *destroy* Joe. This was war. And in war, narrative beat bullets. Every time.

This was not just a war against her brother. She planned to crush Joe, yes. But also to crush *all* the Mintari Rangers. She would discredit them, demoralize them, and finally disband them. And then this planet would be hers. She would flood Mintari with a million hunters. And each hunter would carry a gun from Triplehorn Incorporated.

Her father would not live forever. Someday, maybe soon, Amissa would take over. Her father had built a kingdom. But she would rule an empire.

Outside the pantry, she found something new. It hung from a stalagmite. A photo of Mina.

"Aww, look at this." She pointed her camera at the photo and zoomed in. "Do you know who this is, Tripletots?"

"She's pretty."

"She's hot!"

"Who is she?"

"Joe's wife," Amissa said. "Mina Clubber."

Stunned silence from the comments. Then an eruption of fury.

"The terrorist's daughter!"

"Who?"

"Her dad was Chief Clubber!"

"The killer!"

Amissa smiled thinly. "Yes, my fans. This is her. Daughter of Chief Ganzorig Clubber. Some of you don't remember. But I do. I was only a little girl. But I remember it so well ..."

It happened years ago. Amissa was only a youth, growing up on Cloventia. Joe was living on Mintari, already old enough to call himself a man, to join the Rangers.

The siblings barely knew each other. Amissa had been only a baby when her parents split up. Her mother had run off to Mintari, taking Joe with her. He had been nine. Amissa remained behind, abandoned, motherless. Throughout her childhood, she always asked about Mintari. Always wanted to know what became of her mother and brother.

So she remembered that day. The day in her youth when Mintari came on the news. A big story. *Gazette TV* was discussing it nonstop. A starship of hunters had flown to Mintari, armed with the guns her father sold. And somebody on Mintari had shot the starship down. Chief Clubber, they called him. A local warlord. He shot down that starship with a missile, and he killed thirty hunters. He also killed the starship crew. A pilot. A helmsman. A navigator. Dead simply because of who they ferried.

Amissa remembered her father's fury. He was Tobias Triplehorn, patriarch of his clan, and he demanded satisfaction. The Cloventian government must do something, dammit. Chief Clubber must be brought to justice! Cloventia must attack Mintari! This was war! Tobias fumed and raged and prowled his penthouse, banging his fists. He used to drink too much back then. Fine wine only, but too much of it. He ranted on and on about Clan Clubber, how horrible they were, a bunch of brigands and barbarians. The feud spread. Across Mintari and Cloventia rose voices that demanded war.

By Christmas, things were finally calming down. Tobias could even manage a full day without mentioning Chief Clubber and his missile. Then, on New Year's, came more news from Mintari. The final insult.

Tobias Triplehorn's eldest son ... was marrying Chief Clubber's eldest daughter.

Joe and Mina were getting married.

To Tobias Triplehorn, it felt a spit in the face. A punch to the gut. An intolerable disgrace.

Many across Cloventia felt the same. To this day, Cloventians remembered the name Clubber. The warlord who shot their starship down.

"Yes, my friends," Amissa said, showing them the photograph. "Jurassic Joe married into the murderous Clubber clan. Thankfully, the dissident Mina Clubber died long ago. Clearly Joe still loves her. And hates Cloventia."

QuickFame exploded with activity.

"He's a traitor to Cloventia!"

"Bomb Mintari!"

"Down with dinos!"

"Wait, who is Mina Clubber again?"

"Some terrorist's daughter, I dunno. Anyway, she's hot."

All right. Amissa was amassing a decent pile of dirt here. The grizzled, rugged Ranger lived in comfort. The animal lover ate meat. And best of all, the so-called noble hero loved a terrorist. Well, a terrorist's daughter, at least. Not a bad haul, all things considered. Three strikes. A treasure trove of hypocrisy.

But Joe was not yet knocked out. Amissa still needed that home run. The *real* juicy dirt. The coup de grâce. There had to be something …

She wandered deeper into the cave, heading toward a back room.

Her eyes widened.

Jackpot.

A grin spread across her face.

Joe was going down.

Standing in Laramidia Fields by the supersaurus herd, Joe held his communicator, watching Amissa's live stream. Unable to stop it. His hands shook in anger. His jaw clenched. Simone stood at his side, but she could not soothe him.

Amissa was rifling through his home. Invading his privacy. Mocking his wife. Tarnishing his reputation.

And now she had found it. She pointed her camera right at it.

"Look, Tripletots!" she said, using that ridiculous name she gave her fans. "Do you see what I see? A T-rex skull. Authentic. Converted into a recliner."

The camera zoomed in. Millions of people saw it. The toothy jaws were wide open, filled with upholstery and topped with pillows. Turning a dinosaur skull into furniture? Shameful. Joe still remembered the day he had shot that poacher, confiscated the trophy. Why the hell had he kept the tarry thing?

"Do you know what this is?" said Amissa. "A hunting trophy!"

The comment section exploded.

"Cool chair!"

"I want one."

"Wait a minute—Jurassic Joe has a hunting trophy?"

"Jurassic Joe has a hunting trophy!" Amissa announced to her millions of viewers. "Oh, the hypocrisy! Joe keeps claiming he wants to save dinosaurs. To stop poachers. To kill hunters. And here in his very house—the severed head of a T-rex! Gruesomely upholstered into a chair. Yes, Tripletots. Jurassic Joe, the famous Ranger … is a trophy hunter!"

"The tarry skull is not mine, and you know it!" Joe barked into his communicator.

But his words just appeared as one more comment beneath the video, drowning within a second under the barrage.

He tried again. "It belonged to a poacher! I confiscated it!"

His comment drowned at once. Nobody noticed. More comments sped by.

"Jurassic Joe is a hypocrite!"

"Joe, I'm ripping your posters off my wall!"

"My kid ain't getting a Jurassic Joe cake for his birthday, I can tell you that much."

"Smashing my Jurassic Joe action figures now!"

Joe growled and shut off the communicator, disgusted. He looked at Simone. "There's gotta be something you can do. You're a journalist, right?"

She nodded. "Right."

"You have followers, don't you?"

She winced. "Kinda. My mom follows me. And my hygienist." She bit her lip. "I'm not big on QuickFame."

He groaned. "What about the *Cloventia Gazette*? The circulation is huge, isn't it?"

"Sure is. And … I have an editor. And copyeditor. And advertisers. And advertising agencies. And sensitivity readers. And fact-checkers. And content uploaders. And three managers. Oh, and a legal team that has to approve everything. And—"

"Simone, what are you talking about?"

She sighed. "I can't just upload content to the *Cloventia Gazette*. It has to pass through an army of middlemen. We'll fight back. I know you don't own that skull. We'll clear your name. But it will take time. Maybe a few weeks."

"Within a few weeks, the Rangers' reputation will be destroyed. This isn't just about me. We must reach the cave. Fast. And confront her on camera. We don't have big QuickFame accounts of our own. But we can get on hers."

Simone looked around her. The supersaurus herd grazed nearby. Dozer had joined them, eating almost as much. The sauropods did not mind; there was plenty of food for anyone.

Vinnie was digging a cynodont out from the ground. Aside from humans, the only mammals on Mintari were these little fluffballs, an important food source for velociraptors. The grasslands spread toward distant hills, marshes, and a gorge lined with cycads.

"Joe." She looked back at him. "We're what, fifty kilometers from the Last Home Hollow? Twice that far? Even if Dozer walks nonstop, it'll take us two or three days to get back. By then Amissa will be long gone."

"There's a way," Joe said softly.

She nodded. "Right. Of course. We'll call the Rangers, order a tricopter service, and within an hour, we can—"

"No tricopters."

Simone heaved a sigh. "Joe, I admire your principles. But to reach her quickly, we need a tricopter."

"This isn't just about my principle," Joe said. "Tricopters are loud. Amissa would hear one approaching. She'd step outside the cave, gun in hand. She'd shoot a tricopter down. We must approach stealthily."

Simone looked at Dozer. The big dinosaur was stomping through the grass, grunting, groaning, belching, and passing gas. "Well, that rules Dozer out."

"There's another way," Joe said. "A skill my mother taught me long ago. It's dangerous. I'll go alone."

"Like hell!" Simone placed her hands on her hips. "I'm in this game, Joe. She murdered my sister. This is personal for me. I'm going with you."

"All right. Dozer! Dozer, look at me!"

The triceratops looked up, his mouth full of ferns.

"Dozer, I need a lift to the gorge past the cycads. And fast. Simone! Hop on. And hold on tight."

She frowned. "I thought we're not taking Dozer."

"We're not. Not the whole way, at least. Hop on."

Within a moment, Joe and Simone were riding the triceratops. Grunting and snorting, Dozer ran across the grass, leaving deep footprints. He weighed as much as two elephants, but when duty called, he could sprint at impressive speeds. Place a triceratops on an Olympic racetrack, and he'd outrun any human champion. And leave potholes so large a man could curl up inside.

As he hopped on Dozer's back, Joe glanced at his communicator. Amissa was still in his cave. She was sitting inside the upholstered T-rex skull, eating sausages, telling her fans how Joe was a hypocrite. Good. Let her rant for a long while. It gave him time.

A thought struck him.

Maybe she's waiting for me. Luring me into a trap.

Well, if she was, she was planning to trap a Ranger tricopter. Maybe an angry triceratops. Not this. Nobody would expect what Joe was planning.

You'd have to be crazy. And thankfully Joe Triplehorn was.

Within an hour, Dozer reached the gorge. The triceratops halted, breathing heavily. Joe dismounted and stroked Dozer's beak.

"Sorry for running you hard today, friend. I know you still hurt. You've taken us far enough. Rest now. Eat. Recover. When you're ready, make your way home."

Dozer snorted, tilted his massive head, and looked into Joe's eyes.

"Yes, friend, I'm leaving you for now. This is a journey you can't take with me."

Vinnie cackled. Joe knelt by the velociraptor and ruffled his feathers. "You too, buddy. Keep Dozer safe, huh?"

Vinnie cooed and began picking at his feathers.

Simone dismounted too. She gently laid her hand on Dozer's beak. She looked into Joe's eyes. "You're talking like you might never see them again."

"I'm flying to face a woman who just murdered two Rangers," Joe said. "It's dangerous. You can still stay behind."

Simone's eyes flashed. "And let you face Amissa alone? Not a chance. Just show me the way. Listen to me, Joe, and listen carefully. I promise you this. No matter what happens, *I will not stay behind.*"

Joe held her hand, walked with her toward the edge of the gorge, and they peered into the depths.

Pterosaurs nested across the gorge walls. Thousands of them. Every once in a while, one dipped toward a river below, grabbed a fish, and flew back to its nest. They ranged from small pterodactyls to the plane-sized quetzalcoatlus.

Joe gestured at the pterosaurs. "We're flying."

"I'm staying behind," Simone said.

She turned to leave.

"Wait. Simone! You said you wouldn't leave me behind. You said it's personal between you and Amissa."

She spun back toward him, eyes flashing. "It is! But I'll walk. A pterosaur already carried me off once. Not an experience I ever plan to replicate."

"Last time, a pterosaur grabbed you with its talons." He looked into her eyes. "This time you will ride one."

Her face softened, and she smiled. "Aww, I'll ride one, will I?" Her face hardened and she began stomping away. "When pigs fly, I can ride one of those. Goodbye, Jurassic Joe."

"Wait." He hurried after her. "Simone, you're right. I can't face my sister alone. I ... need you."

She stopped walking. Her shoulders slumped. She looked at him, eyes damp. "You need me?"

And he realized just how much he did.

I need you, Simone. When you came into my life, I was a wreck. Hungover. Barely leaving my cave. You came into that cave like a hurricane, messed up my home, messed up my life. And that's what I needed. I needed you. I still need you.

But he could bring none of that to his lips. He still felt too vulnerable. The walls around him were cracking but had not yet fallen.

"Well, I ... might need you to um ... distract Amissa. Or something."

Simone raised an eyebrow and placed her hands on her hips. "Or something."

"Just come with me. You'll be safe." Joe smiled. "Simone LaRue, you're tougher than you think. You rode a triceratops. You held a supersaurus in your arms. One more challenge. And you'll be queen of Mintari."

She groaned and approached the gorge. "A week ago, I was terrified of puppies. I hope you appreciate this, Joe Triplehorn."

They stood on the edge of the gorge, gazing down at the nesting grounds.

The pterosaurs bustled about their business—catching fish, roosting on eggs, snapping at one another. Pterosaurs were vulnerable on land. To protect themselves from predation, they nested on cliffs, in gorges, on mountaintops—places their foes struggled to reach. But no place on Mintari was entirely safe.

Sometimes brazen raptors scaled the cliffs. With their short wings, they could not fly, but with their claws, raptors were excellent climbers. Sometimes they reached pterosaur nests, snatched eggs, even grabbed adult pterosaurs to eat. That was life on Mintari. A life of constant danger. In this dino-eat-dino world, every day was a battle, every season a war, every scar a medal of triumph.

"Can you really fly these things?" Simone whispered. She was pale, and her eyes were damp.

"I did many years ago," Joe said softly. "The last time was the night my wife died. The shamans teach the skill. Skyriding, they call it. My mother taught me when I was a boy."

Nobody knew how many shamans lived on Mintari. Some said over a hundred. Some believed that fewer than ten still survived. The shamans made Joe look like an extrovert. They lived in the wilderness. Not even in caves but simple huts woven of branches and grass. They communed with dinosaurs, spoke to them, healed them, even worshipped them as gods. Joe had spent his youth in a grass hut, learning the ways of Mintari. How to ride a triceratops. How to tame a raptor. And how to fly.

He placed his fingers into his mouth and whistled. The sound echoed through the gorge.

Pterosaurs looked up, clacking their beaks.

Joe whistled again, adjusting the frequency, a long, loud sound like a siren. He blew three more short whistles.

The pterosaurs rustled their wings. A few ignored him. Others hissed.

Joe gave a third whistle, louder and longer than before. And a pterosaur soared.

The gargantuan beast rose from the gorge, dwarfing Joe and Simone. His wings spread as wide as a bus. His great beak opened, as long as a car. He let out a deafening cry—the same frequency as Joe's whistle. Here rose *Quetzalcoatlus northropi*, king of the sky. Q-pi for short. The largest flying animal that ever lived.

The giant flapped his wings. Blasts of air shook the cycads along the gorge's edge. Simone fell to the grass, gazing with huge eyes at the soaring titan. Joe had to grab his hat. The mighty quetzalcoatlus landed on the grass, a flying reptile the size of an airplane. He stood taller than a giraffe.

Simone gasped. "Darwin's beard, the size of it!"

Even Joe stood cowed before this legendary beast. Dozer only grunted. The trike was the size of a tank and not impressed.

"Climb on," Joe said.

Simone blinked. "Are you talking to me?"

"Well, I'm not talking to Dozer. Climb on!"

The Q-pi waited on the edge of the gorge. The enormous pterosaur clutched the earth with his talons. His wings were folded, the clawed tips placed on the ground for extra support. Q-pis were so big they could only move on all fours, using their folded wings like crutches. Even hunched over like this, the animal towered above the humans. He was the size of the mythical dragons of old. His fuzzy neck soared skyward. His beak clacked open and shut, as large as a canoe.

Simone gaped at the Q-pi, head tilted back.

"You've got to be kidding me. How do we climb this thing?"

Joe stroked the pterosaur's leg, whistling and cooing, using the sounds his mother had taught him. The titan crouched low, placing his beak against the grass. Joe patted the enormous head. Bright blue eyes stared at him, as large as bowling balls.

"Climb onto his back, Simone. Lie facedown, aligning yourself with his spine. Then wrap your arms around the base of his neck. These are huge animals, but they're deceptively lightweight. Be careful."

She blinked. "I should be careful? Well, gee, thanks for the tip, mister." She gulped and loosened her collar. "That beak is big enough to swallow me whole."

"Don't go near the beak. Climb onto its back. Hurry up. He won't wait forever."

Simone cringed. "You first. Like when we ride Dozer."

Joe smiled thinly. "We're going to fly on different pterosaurs."

She took a step back. "You want me to ride this thing *alone*?"

He nodded. "As I said, they're deceptively light. This quetzalcoatlus might seem larger than Dozer, but he weighs much, much less. These animals are the size of airplanes, but they don't weigh more than motorcycles. He'll struggle to carry even one person."

Simone cleared her throat. "Well, I might have put on a few pounds since the Slum Wars, I admit, but—"

The pterosaur snorted and clacked his beak.

"Hurry," Joe said. "He's getting restless. He's not used to lying down like this."

Simone took a deep breath, steeling herself. "Perfect. Just perfect. I'm going to fly a restless monster."

She started to climb, fell back onto the grass, and Joe had to boost her up. But finally, with a lot of cursing and some tears, Simone was lying facedown atop the Q-pi, holding the long, fluffy neck.

Joe gave a short, quick whistle and slapped the Q-pi on the side. The great pterosaur kicked off the ground, beat his wings mightily, and soared.

Simone screamed and clung on for dear life.

Despite his enormous size, the Q-pi struggled to rise. His wings pounded the air, flattening the grass. The animal was perhaps the size of a dragon, but his bones were light and hollow, his frame thin. A human was a heavy load.

Still, the brave Q-pi gave it his all. His wings beat again and again, shoving the air downward, until finally he rose high enough to catch an air current. From there, he glided.

"I hate you, Joe Triplehorn!" Simone could be heard screaming as the Q-pi flew into the distance.

Joe whistled again—a short, loud sound. Another quetzalcoatlus came rising from below. A big female this time.

Joe didn't even bother letting her land. He leaped off the gorge's edge, thumped onto the pterosaur's back, and gave quick, short whistles. The Q-pi soared from the canyon, following her companion in the sky.

They glided on the wind.

The two pterosaurs flew, struggling under their loads. Everything about them was slender, hollow, thin, optimized for gliding. Humans were tiny in comparison—smaller than their beaks. But humans were lumpy and compact. The Q-pis grunted, beat their wings, and flew onward, carrying their passengers. Perhaps they knew this was important. Perhaps they knew that Mintari was in danger, and they wanted to help. Joe was perhaps anthropomorphizing them. But he had never considered dinosaurs and pterosaurs to be merely dumb, slogging brutes, an evolutionary dead end. He had met dinosaurs whose intelligence rivaled chimps and dolphins. Dinosaurs who showed true emotions—loneliness, fear, respect, even love. They were dynamic, intelligent animals, and in this great war for Mintari, they would fight back.

Onward they flew, tumbling under clouds, rising higher, skimming along air currents, then dipping lower, rising again, sometimes tilting on the wind, sometimes leaping over air pockets, sometimes smoothly sliding on blue sky. Words of an old poem returned to Joe. An Earthling poet named Magee had written them long ago, and a thousand years later, Joe whispered those words into the sky of Mintari.

Sunward I've climbed, and joined the tumbling mirth
Of sun-split clouds, — and done a hundred things
You have not dreamed of — wheeled and soared and swung
High in the sunlit silence. Hov'ring there,
I've chased the shouting wind

Joe looked to his side. Simone was flying nearby, her red hair fluttering like a banner. Her eyes were screwed shut, but perhaps sensing his gaze, she opened them and looked at him. Her tears flew in the wind, and he knew those were not tears of pain or grief. They were tears of awe.

"Look down to see a herd of ceratopsians!" Joe cried to her.

"I am never looking down again in my life!"

"Don't look straight down. Just look enough to see the view. It's beautiful."

She screwed her eyes shut again. Well, Joe enjoyed the view at least. Here was Mintari as he rarely saw it. Ceratopsians herded across the grasslands, while parasaurs flocked along the rivers, blowing air through their hollow crests. Stegosaurs and ankylosaurs roamed in the forests, while the great sauropods loomed through the mist. Snowcapped mountains rose in the distance, their crests gilded with sunlight. On the distant horizon, Joe could just make out the sea, home to the plesiosaurs and mosasaurs. This planet teemed with life. With beauty nearly untouched by man.

Humans had populated this planet, using time-casting to revive dinosaurs, to give them a new home. The founders of Mintari had made mistakes. They mixed dinosaurs from different geological periods, letting Triassic, Jurassic, and Cretaceous dinosaurs compete in one biosphere. Sometimes the scientists got the cloning wrong, using their imagination to fill in gaps in the

DNA, and the resultant dinosaurs were not exactly like their ancestors. Certainly Ivan was a mutant. Some of the plants were wrong too; Mesozoic Earth probably never had this much grass. But Mintari was still a miracle. This wasn't a perfect recreation of Earth during the reign of the dinosaurs. But it was as close as anyone could get. Here on Mintari, humans had given dinosaurs another chance. To Joe, this was a noble endeavor. And this planet was precious.

It was a planet full of danger. A planet where predators lurked everywhere. But it was also a planet of majesty and beauty. To Joe, this was heaven. If Amissa had her way, she would turn this world into hell. Joe would give his life to protect Mintari and the wonderful dinosaurs who lived here.

Soon they saw it ahead.

Mudge Mountain. Joe's home.

It would take Dozer a day or two to catch up. The Q-pis had flown the distance within half an hour. By now, the enormous pterosaurs were exhausted.

Joe let out low, long whistles.

Descend, friends.

The pterosaurs began circling downward, wings spread wide to catch as much air as possible. They glided as silently as a stalking predator and as gracefully as swans. Joe spotted his cave below. He checked his communicator. Amissa was still streaming a video from inside. She was still sitting on the T-rex chair, talking about how Joe was the most bloodthirsty poacher in the galaxy—who else would own such a chair?

Suddenly Amissa froze.

She reached for her SmartSphere, stared at the screen, and her eyes widened.

"Gotta go, Tripletots! See you soon!"

She ended her stream.

"What the hell?" Joe muttered.

The two pterosaurs spotted a place to land—an outcrop of stone that jutted out from the mountainside. A waterfall cascaded nearby, filling a lake rich with fish. This would make a good nesting ground. The pterosaurs were naturally drawn there. It was only a short walk from the outcrop to the Last Home Hollow.

The pterosaurs were moments away from landing when Amissa emerged from the cave.

How the hell did she know we're here? Joe thought. The Q-pis flew silently. Had she set up a camera outside?

Amissa was carrying a rifle. A big one. The one she had killed the nodosaur with. The Dinoslayer.

She aimed and opened fire.

CHAPTER SIXTEEN
Big Brutes and Little Bugs

The quetzalcoatlus cawed in agony. The enormous pterosaur swayed in the sky. Joe clung to her back.

A second later, the sound wave reached him. A deafening boom. The gunshot rang across the sky.

The Q-pi wailed. Blood sprayed in a mist. Wind whistled through a hole in her wing, a cruel imitation of a skyrider's call. Amissa had scored a hit. The Q-pi was still alive, but she could barely move her wounded wing.

Again—a gunshot rang out.

Beside Joe, the other quetzalcoatlus wailed. Another shot to the wing! The big male screeched. Simone, riding on his back, cried out in terror.

Joe reached for his sleep-or-die, struggling to load the weapon while riding the Q-pi. But the great pterosaur was slewing, struggling to stay airborne. Joe slid across her back. He could not aim his gun. He fired as best he could. A bullet hit the mountainside. Not even close to Amissa. Joe could barely see. He—

More gunshots rang out.

The pterosaurs wailed. Blood splashed.

And the legendary flying reptiles plunged from the sky.

Simone screamed and clung on to her mount.

Even as they fell, Joe aimed his sleep-or-die. He saw the cave in the distance. He aimed. Fired.

A bullet slammed into the mountainside, missing his sister.

Dear God, I just tried to kill my sister, he thought.

Then he only thought of falling. The Q-pis were plunging fast. Both pterosaurs were still alive, but wind whistled through holes in their wings. They could not fly, not even glide. They flapped as best they could, trying to reach the lake, to land in the water. The waterfall roared nearby, and spray washed over Joe, and the lake was rushing up toward him, and—

A crash.

Cold. Terrible cold.

Water rushing over him.

Joe kicked underwater, struggling to free himself from the lashing wings and flailing neck of the pterosaur. He felt like a mouse trying to swim away from a drowning cat.

Another crash. The second pterosaur slammed into the lake. Still underwater, Joe saw red hair and kicking legs.

Simone!

He swam toward her, lungs aching for air. Her pterosaur was still alive, floundering underwater. A wing buffeted Simone, and she tumbled through the lake, bubbles rising from her mouth.

Joe swam faster. He caught her, kicked off the struggling pterosaur, and they both rose through the murky depths.

Their heads breached the surface.

They gulped down air.

"Are you all right?" Joe said.

"No, I'm not all right, Joe Triplehorn!" she shouted. "You made me fly a dinosaur, and an insane woman is shooting at us!"

"Pterosaur. It's a pterosaur, not a dinosaur." He winced when she punched him. "Never mind."

Miraculously, both Q-pis had survived the fall. They limped onto the shore, holes in their wings. Joe had seen such injuries before. In time, new membranes would grow over the holes. This was a good place for the pterosaurs to rest, find fish, and heal.

Of course, for that to happen, Joe must stop Amissa. Or she would shoot every creature within eyesight. Floating in the lake, he stared up the mountainside. He could just make out his cave from here.

An engine roared.

An astrolite took flight from the mountainside.

Amissa!

Joe aimed his sleep-or-die. He pulled the trigger, trying to hit her astrolite. But the weapon was waterlogged.

He swam toward the shore. Simone followed. They climbed onto the lakeside, coughing, covered in algae.

"Why is she flying away?" Simone asked. "Why isn't she still firing at us?"

"Because she's a predator," Joe said. "The greatest predators are always cautious. Even the mighty T-rex, the strongest dinosaur on land, carefully stalks his prey. He prefers to hunt the weak, the frail, or the young. Unless he's mad with hunger, he'll avoid attacking strong, healthy herbivores like Dozer. Headstrong predators die. Cautious ones live. Amissa couldn't know my gun would jam. She's cautious."

"But she'll keep stalking us," Simone said.

"You can count on it. Wait. Don't move."

He plucked a water snake out of Simone's hair. He tossed the little serpent aside.

Simone paled. She covered her mouth. "I—I—I hate it here. I want to go home."

Joe brushed back her wet tresses. "I can't take you to your home on Cloventia. But I can take you to my home. Let's see how badly Amissa trashed the place."

They climbed the mountainside. By the time they reached the cave, their clothes were dry and Nyx was setting. The portcullis, which normally secured the cave, was open. Amissa must have picked the lock. Winded after their climb, Joe and Simone entered the Last Home Hollow.

Yellow eyes shone in the shadows.

A creature darted forth, hissing.

Simone screamed.

Joe raised his sleep-or-die, heart pounding.

He recognized the dinosaur. A deinonychus. A fierce female, hungry and mean.

Its name meant terrible claw in Greek. And indeed, deinonychus bore a terrible sickle claw on each foot. That claw never touched the ground. It was purely a weapon. A type of raptor, she was smaller than achillobators, utahraptors, and others in her clade. She was about the size of a mountain lion. Tiny for a dinosaur. But like a mountain lion, she was fierce and—even worse—intelligent. Millions of years of evolution had honed deinonychus into a perfect predator. She opened her jaws, baring sharp fangs. The brown and white feathers across her back bristled, making her seem even larger.

With the gate open, the raptor must have sneaked inside while Joe and Simone had been climbing the mountainside. Or maybe Amissa had lured the predator into the cave—a little parting gift.

The deinonychus leaped at Joe.

He fired his gun.

And it jammed. Again. Still waterlogged.

The deinonychus slammed into him, jaws snapping. The dinosaur was heavier than him. All that mass shoved Joe back against the wall. He raised his sleep-or-die like a staff, fending off the terrible jaws. The raptor chomped down on the double barrel, losing a tooth. No big deal. Dinosaurs constantly grew and replaced teeth.

The hungry carnivore pinned Joe to the wall. She raised one leg. The sickle claw gleamed.

"Simone, the rug!" Joe shouted.

"What?"

"Pull the rug!"

The sickle claw lashed. Joe swung his rifle, parrying. The claw sparked against the barrel. The dinosaur leaned closer, jaws widening, and—

Simone pulled the rug from under the raptor.

The deinonychus, who still had one foot raised, crashed down.

Before the dinosaur could recover, Joe grabbed a tranquilizer dart from his belt. Normally he fired these darts from his sleep-or-die. Now he shoved the dart down with his hand. The syringe sank into the deinonychus, flooding the animal with relaxants.

The raptor rose to her feet. She blinked at Joe. Her eyes narrowed, and her legs wobbled.

All it took was a few gentle pokes from the rifle. Joe was able to herd the woozy dinosaur out the cave, then pull the portcullis shut. The deinonychus looked through the bars, yawned, then flopped down and fell asleep.

"Sleep it off, girl." He leaned down to stroke the jaws that had nearly savaged him. "You'll feel better in the morning."

He did not blame the predator for attacking. He blamed Amissa for placing the dinosaur here. A cruel trap to spring on him.

This whole thing was a trap, Joe thought. *The video. Mocking me. Just a way to lure me here. To kill me.*

And he knew that Amissa would not stop trying.

With the dinosaur safely removed, Joe looked around his cave.

Amissa had trashed the place. She had shattered his clay plates and mugs, overturned his bed, pulled his books off the shelves, and scattered food everywhere. The only thing she hadn't destroyed was the T-rex skull armchair. A hunting trophy was sacred to her. All else was contemptuous. Mina's picture lay on the floor. The glass frame was shattered. He knelt, lifted the photo, and shook off the shards.

Simone padded toward him, broken glass crunching under her boots. "I'm sorry, Joe." She looked around her and shook her head sadly. "What a petty, vindictive woman. I'll help you tidy up."

He looked at her, silent. Thinking.

She tilted her head. "Joe? Are you okay?"

He nodded. "Yeah. Yeah, I'm fine. Go rest. You've earned it. I'll clean up a bit."

"No way. I'm helping! You got a broom anywhere around here?" She looked around, then laughed. "Who am I asking? Of course not. This is a bachelor pad. Hang on, I can grab a frond from a cycad outside, and—"

"Simone, it's all right. We'll tidy up another day. It's late. We're exhausted. Let's get some sleep and reassess tomorrow."

She yawned. "I *am* exhausted. I carried a baby sauropod today. And flew on a pterosaur. I was shot at. Almost drowned. And finally pulled a rug out from under a dinosaur. This was definitely the strangest day of my life. Since yesterday, that is. Is Mintari always so … eventful?"

"It was a helluva lot more peaceful before you and Amissa showed up, I can tell you that much." He righted the bed, dusted off the blanket, and fluffed the pillow. "Get some sleep. I'll take the floor."

She climbed into bed, yawned again, and patted the mattress. "There's room for two. Don't worry, I won't ravage you in the night. I'm two seconds away from passing … out …"

And she was asleep.

Joe looked at her. Her hair spread across the pillow, the color of fire. Her face was a field of freckles like stars. She was so beautiful. Of course—she had to be.

Because I stepped into another trap, Joe thought.

Somehow Amissa had known. She had seen him flying over. Joe had found no evidence of hidden cameras on the mountainside. Yet once the pterosaurs approached, Amissa ended her video stream, grabbed her gun, ran outside the cave, and opened fire. Only one other person had known they were flying on those pterosaurs.

Could it really be you, Simone?

She looked like an angel, lying there asleep, a Titian masterpiece brought to life, a work of art made of porcelain and light. They had sent a goddess to trap one they thought a devil. No monster could have slain Samson. All it took was Delilah's touch.

He waited to be sure she was in deep sleep. Then he knelt, lifted her pack, and looked inside. Multiple bottles of sunscreen. Some trail mix and water. And her SmartSphere. A computer with a camera and microphone.

He lifted the SmartSphere. It unfolded in his hand, ballooning from a circle into a sphere the size of a peach. A light flashed on the side. Joe shut the camera off, but the light still flashed. He took a screwdriver, pried it open, and—

There.

His heart crashed.

His hands began to shake.

There inside—a bug. A parasite. A foreign piece of electronics, crudely welded inside. Eyes that forever saw, ears that forever heard. The little tracking device bore an unmistakable logo. A triceratops head.

Joe dropped the camera onto the floor. He crushed it under his boot. Hard. The components shattered. Including the bug.

"Show's over, Amissa," he said.

Simone stirred and opened her eyes. "Huh? Did I fall asleep?"

"Get out," Joe said.

She sat up in bed, rubbed her eyes. "What?" Her eyes widened. "Was that my SmartSphere? What—?"

"Get out!" Joe said.

She rose from bed. Her cheeks flushed. "Joe, what is going on?"

He barked a bitter laugh. "I found out. I'm onto you. You're a Triplehorn spy. Reporting straight to Amissa, aren't you?"

Simone laughed too—a shocked, mirthless laugh. "What? Joe! Are you pulling my leg?" She frowned. "Are you drunk?"

"I'm dead sober. I know exactly who you are. Ha! I fell for it. Like a perfect rube. You really are a good actress, do you know?"

"What are you talking about!" she said.

"Stop acting, tar it! The show's over. All those stories. About how Amissa killed your sister. How you're scared of animals and need the big, strong Ranger to protect you. Oh, what a performance!"

Her face flushed. "How dare you, Joe Triplehorn! I opened up to you. I shared my personal stories." Tears flooded her eyes. "And now you mock me, accuse me of lying?"

He rolled his eyes. "More acting! Give it up. I saw the bug!"

"What bug?" she cried. "I don't know what you're talking about!"

Joe knelt and lifted the crushed component. He waved it at her. "See this? You thought I'd never find it. This is a tracking device. It kept your camera constantly filming. And streaming the data right to Amissa!" He snorted. "I was such a fool. You strutted in here, a beautiful temptress, and I fell for it. Now get out of my cave."

Tears flowed down her cheeks. "Joe, I had no idea … I didn't know that bug was in there."

"Stop acting!" His body shook. His own eyes burned with tears. "I knew I should never have trusted humans. All humans do is betray one another. All they do is lie and cheat and kill. Get out! Get out, tar it! Go print your tarry story. Go laugh with my sister about what a gullible fool I am." He gripped his bed and hurled it across the room. The driftwood frame shattered, and he raised his voice to a deafening shout. *"Get out!"*

Weeping, she fled. She tried to open the portcullis, but her hands shook.

Joe lifted a chair and hurled it at the wall. It shattered. *"Get out!"*

She managed to unlock the gate, then fled into the darkness. Nyx was gone from the sky. Simone vanished into shadows.

Joe fell to his knees, shaking, tears on his cheeks.

Betrayed. Betrayed ...

"Why did I allow myself to be hurt?" he whispered. "Why did I let another person in? I knew humans were cruel. I knew it. I thought you were different, Simone. I thought you were real."

He lowered his head, and a sob wracked his body.

Even his dinosaurs were not here. Dozer and Vinnie were miles away. Joe had not felt so alone and broken since Mina had died.

Mina.

The only human he had ever trusted. Ever loved. An angel in a sea of demons.

He lifted her photo. He brushed off broken glass, cutting his fingers, and smeared blood on her cheek.

"I miss you, Mina," he whispered.

Her photo stared at him. Mina spoke in his mind. *Why did you send Simone away?*

"She was spying on me."

Maybe she didn't know.

"She knew."

Maybe she was as shocked as you.

"She knew! She's a human!"

So am I. So are you. Not all humans are bad.

"I don't know how to trust again. How do I trust anyone in a world where my sister exists?"

With time. Time turned single-celled organisms into dinosaurs. Time can change a fuzzy hatchling into a nine-ton T-rex. Time can topple mountains and grow forests over craters of fire. And time can heal a man.

Joe wiped his eyes. He rose to his feet. And he noticed an item on the floor. It must have fallen from Simone's pack while he was rummaging for the bug.

A plastic figurine. An action figure of Jurassic Joe.

Simone ran down the mountainside, tears in her eyes. She could barely see two steps ahead, but she would not slow down. She had to escape him. He was worse than any predator on Mintari.

He was a brute. A monster. How could Simone have ever trusted him?

A sob fled her lips. Seeing Joe like that ... it was like a demon possessed him. When he had smashed furniture, she worried he was going to kill her. She didn't care if he was drunk. Didn't care what his excuse was. The man was toxic, violent, dangerous.

She stumbled over a pebble, fell onto the mountainside, and slid down for a few terrifying seconds. She caught a tree root, halted her descent, and rose to her feet. Her knees and elbows were skinned. She kept running downhill toward the shadowy valley. Only the moonlight lit her way.

She knew it was stupid. Hopeless. She was a three-day walk from Dinovia City, assuming she found her way, which was doubtful. She had no map. No weapons. No supplies. She would never make it. She wouldn't last an hour out here! But she could not go back to that cave! She could not face that brute again! She would rather take her chances in the wilderness.

I was a fool to come here, she thought. *I was a fool to trust him.*

It all hit her at once now. Cody was dead. She would never see home again. She was going to die out here.

She reached the foothills. Tears flowed as she ran among the trees. All Triplehorns were cruel! First Amissa had murdered her sister. Now this …

She did not know who had bugged her camera. Maybe one of the Triplehorns back on Cloventia. After all, Tobias Triplehorn owned eleven percent of the *Cloventia Gazette* now. He could have gained access to the company equipment. Bugged Simone's camera to spy on Joe. It wasn't her fault. She had been duped too!

But Joe had not listened. He only wanted to shout. To smash things. To hate her. What did Joe care about the truth? To him, her word was meaningless. She was nothing but a *femme fatale,* apparently. Worse—a traitor! The things he had said … bringing up her sister like that …

She could not forgive him. Could never return to him. She had enough material for her story now. Oh, she certainly had enough. A caustic smile twisted her lips. She would smear him in the media! Show all her readers what a brute he was!

But no. Even through the storm of her fury, Simone knew she would not do that. She would drop the entire story. She would forget all about Mintari. Coming here had been the worst mistake of her life.

Her side was aching from running so much. She slowed down, breathing heavily, her body weak, her emotions a raging ocean. Where was she? She looked around her. She had reached the edge of Hell Valley. The trees were still dense here, but nearby she would find the sprawling grasslands. She must make her way there, walk west, and eventually she would reach the city. On the way, she might come across a tourist jippi and hitch a ride. Once she reached Dinovia, she was in the clear. The city had a spaceport. A few days from now, she would be home on Cloventia, and if she never saw a dinosaur again, she would die a happy woman.

Part of her knew she was being irrational. Overemotional. She should return to the cave, try to smooth things over with Joe. At least long enough to call for help. After all, she was a journalist. Talking to people, even angry or irrational people, was part of her job. But her fear drove her onward. She could not forget the rage in Joe's eyes. It had shaken her to her core.

And it was more than that. Not just the rage. His loss of trust. His accusations. Those cut as deeply as dinosaur claws.

A branch snapped. Somewhere in the shadows ahead.

Simone froze, heart galloping.

She stared but saw nothing in the darkness. The moonlight struggled to pierce the leafy ginkgo boughs.

A growl sounded.

Her heart raced faster.

A shadow moved. A huge shadow. A shadow the size of a building. Enormous feet cracked logs and boulders. And the beast emerged from among the trees in all his terrible glory.

Simone recognized this dinosaur. She remembered it from her field guide. The terrifying illustration had seared itself on her mind. Now she saw that old nightmare taken flesh and bone.

A giganotosaurus.

A predator as large as T-rex.

It was said that Tyrannosaurus rex was king of Mintari, but giganotosaurus was the tsar. The beast was truly gargantuan.

Crimson scales covered his bulky body, and bright red spikes rose across his back and head. A male, judging by the colors. He walked on two enormous legs, and claws like swords tipped his feet. Like a T-rex, his rival apex predator, the giga had short arms. But his jaws more than compensated. Those jaws were large enough to devour Simone whole. Rows of serrated teeth gleamed in the moonlight.

A giga had a smaller brain than a T-rex. Only about the size and shape of a banana. Which was also the size of his teeth. Unlike a T-rex or raptors, who were intelligent predators, the giga was a little slow. What he lacked in brains, he made up for with brawn. He was a big, dumb brute, all sheer power with no cunning. Every inch of him sprouted something that could cut, bite, or slash you.

This particular giganotosaurus was alone, rummaging for a midnight snack. And he had just stumbled across a delicious bite-sized ginger.

His eyes stared right at her. Oddly, in the darkness, Simone imagined the beast as a giant pit bull. Like the one that had killed Elize. And this spiky, dragon-sized pit bull was going to kill Simone. The dinosaur's mouth opened wide, and a deafening rumble washed over Simone.

She stumbled back, fear flooding her. She trembled. She could barely breathe.

"I—hate—this—planet!" she managed to blurt out.

Then she spun around and ran.

The giganotosaurus ran after her. And the dinosaur had some seriously long legs. Simone stood shorter than his knees. There was no way she was outrunning this thing. Her only chance was to find another cave, a burrow, a tree she could climb—something!

A massive clawed foot slammed down at her left side. Another foot to her right. They were like the talons of eagles. If eagles were the size of airplanes.

Simone leaped over a fallen log, hit the ground, and rolled.

The giga swooped down to bite. His jaws closed around the log, shattering it. Splinters and moss flew. The beast raised his head, for a moment confused. Where was his meal?

Simone was already running again. It took a moment for the giga to realize he had chomped down on wood. Then he ran again, his massive talons tearing through roots, cracking fallen logs, and shattering boulders.

Somehow I must outsmart him, Simone thought. *It's my only chance.* She laughed bitterly. *Some chance! Maybe I can challenge him to a game of checkers instead?*

After his slight delay, the giga caught up with her again. The dinosaur was tarry fast. Once more, the enormous mouth came swooping down, ready to scoop up Simone. Saliva sprayed across the forest.

She leaped again and rolled through the mud. The spiny snout slammed into the ground. God, the size of his head! That head was bigger than her entire body. The mouth was the size of a paddle boat. The eyes were like blazing red bowling balls.

The eyes.

His weak spot.

Simone grabbed a fallen branch. With a wordless cry, she thrust the branch at the giga's eyeball.

Right on target. The branch slammed into the eyeball ... and did nothing.

The stick shattered.

The giganotosaurus blinked his nictitating membrane—a hard, transparent casing that protected his eyeball like a contact lens of bulletproof glass. He turned his head toward her, and his pupils shrank to pinpoints.

"Darwin's beard!" Simone whispered.

She spun and ran again.

A ginkgo grew ahead, thick with wide branches like the rungs in a ladder. Should she climb? No, she'd never get too far up. She had only seconds before—

The giga's snout thrust toward her.

She whipped around the tree. The dinosaur closed his jaws around the trunk, shattering it. The great tree came crashing down. Simone ran, barely dodging the falling ginkgo.

And then she saw it.

There ahead! A burrow under the outstretched roots of another tree. A cave. Not a big cave like the Last Home Hollow. A small cave she could crawl into.

She leaped toward the little grotto, flattened herself on her belly, and prepared to crawl in.

A raptor's feathery head burst out, screeching.

Simone screamed right back at it.

The raptor hissed and snapped its teeth, nearly ripping her face off.

Simone scurried away from the cave. She slipped in the mud, landing on her back. The giganotosaurus loomed above her. A foot slammed down, narrowly missing her. The gargantuan predator salivated. Globs of drool splattered her. The raptor— who was no larger than Simone—squeaked in terror and fled into its lair. More squeals came from inside; an entire colony of raptors must live in there. Simone might as well seek shelter in a meat grinder.

I'm trapped, she knew. *It's over. This is the end. I'll be with you soon, Elize.*

Light flared in the distance, golden and beautiful.

I must be dying already, she thought. *This is the light of afterlife.*

She saw no tunnel though. And the giga hadn't even bitten her yet. Which was odd.

The light flashed brighter, then hurled across the sky, showering sparks. Simone gasped. A flare! Somebody had fired a flare!

A cry echoed across the forest.

"Hey there! Hey you! Yes, you! Here!"

Simone stared toward the east, and there he stood. There on the hilltop. A man in the darkness, limned in moonlight. A ceratop hat topped his head, and he held a double-barreled rifle.

"Jurassic Joe," she whispered.

The giga raised his enormous head, staring at the distant man. He opened his jaws with a furious bellow that rippled across the land, fluttering leaves. His teeth shone in the moonlight.

Joe's sleep-or-die boomed.

A tranquilizer dart slammed into the giga's neck.

Another dart flew. And a third. And a fourth. They all hit.

The giganotosaurus grunted, still awake, still furious, even with four tranquilizer darts in his body. The theropod probably outweighed three well-fed hippos, and he wasn't going down so fast.

Even with his puny, banana-sized brain, the brute realized that Joe was his top concern now. He turned away from Simone and charged toward the man on the hill.

Joe fired a fifth tranquilizer dart. It hit the giga. The giant theropod kept charging, crashing through trees. Simone remembered what Joe had taught her. Tranquilizers took a few moments to kick in.

Within a few moments, Joe would be inside the belly of the beast.

"Run, Simone!" he cried. "I'll hold him off. Run!"

Simone ran.

But not away from the dinosaur this time. She ran *toward* it.

On her way there, she scooped up the flare. It had fallen onto the forest floor but still shone. It crackled in her hand like a medieval torch.

"Hey you!" she shouted at the charging giga. "I'm over here! Here!"

The dinosaur spun his head toward her. She hurled the flare with all her strength. The light reflected in the giga's eyes. His pupils shrank, and he looked away, blinded.

"Over here!" Joe shouted from behind.

"Here!" cried Simone. "After me!"

The giganotosaurus spun his scaly head from side to side, bamboozled and overwhelmed. These puny little mammals *wanted* him to attack, which was terribly perplexing. Light was blinding him. Strange, unfamiliar sounds came from ahead and behind. Weird darts stuck out from him, tipped with feathers. And a strange warmth was oozing through him.

This was a bizarre night.

The giga took another step. Another. He was slowing down. Maybe he wasn't so hungry after all. With a grunt, he flopped down into the mud, snapping branches and shattering rocks. He laid his head on a pile of moss. Let the mammals run off. What he needed right about now was a good nap. Soon the dinosaur was breathing heavily, flitting in and out of sleep. He was down for the count.

Joe walked around the sleeping giant and faced Simone.

She stood in the dark forest, looking at him. She could only make out his silhouette. The night cloaked his face.

"Did you tell me the truth?" Joe said.

"Yes," she said. "Joe, I didn't know. About the bug. I didn't ..."

She could say no more. The shock of the night—of these past few days—was setting in. She trembled.

Joe was at her side at once. He pulled her into his arms.

"Oh, Simone, I'm sorry," he whispered. "I'm sorry. I'm so sorry."

She held him, her head against his chest, slowly calming down. She still feared him a little. She still remembered how angry he had been. But as he held her, as she felt his beating heart, she knew that he would never hurt her. He was like a beast who had been beaten too many times, still lashing out, still hurting. But he would never hurt her. He would always keep her safe.

"Can you forgive me, Simone? For acting like I did? For my anger, my cruelty?"

"Cruelty?" she said. "No, Joe, you're not cruel. You're broken. Maybe I am too." She laughed as she cried. "Maybe Mintari has to break you down before it can rebuild you."

He brushed back her hair and caressed her cheek. "The real monsters on Mintari are not dinosaurs. They're humans. I thought you were a monster too. I was so wrong. I trust you, Simone. I trust you."

He closed his eyes, and they held each other in the darkness. Beside them, the giganotosaurus slept on.

"Can we start over?" Simone said.

Joe frowned. "What do you mean?"

"The *Cloventia Gazette* bugged my camera. As of this moment, I quit. Joe Triplehorn? My name is Simone LaRue. I'm an innocent tourist here and definitely *not* a journalist. It's very nice to meet you."

He smiled. And for the first time, there seemed to be true joy in his smile. "It's good to meet you, Ms. LaRue. I have a cave nearby. It's not much, but I have a fireplace and food. There is a great big fool who lives there. And he promises to never hurt you again."

She took his hand. "I would love to see this cave."

Soon enough, they were inside the Last Home Hollow, sitting by the crackling fireplace, nursing mugs of tea. Surprisingly, the terrible Jurassic Joe made a decent cuppa.

"So, Ms. LaRue," he said. The firelight painted his face orange and gold. "Now that you're merely a tourist, any plans for the rest of your stay here on beautiful Mintari?"

She cradled her mug, gazing into the fire. "Yes. I plan to fight Amissa Triplehorn. Together, we'll stop her. And we'll save this world."

CHAPTER SEVENTEEN
Healing

Figaro spent the day with her grandmother, learning many things. Lifa was wise, even wiser than Long Tooth, the oldest achillobator in the pack. Maybe even wiser than White Tail, the pack matriarch who had died two winters ago, buried under an avalanche. All day, Lifa taught Fig her wisdom. How to mix herbs into potent medicine. How to build a campfire. How to season and cook meat so that it tasted better, offered more nutrition, and would not upset the stomach. She even gave Fig a special device made of something called "metal." When Fig pressed part of it, a spark came out, and she could light kindling. So much magic!

The old woman also groomed Fig in a special human way. She placed Fig into a wooden thing called a "barrel" and scrubbed her skin raw with something called a "sponge," removing years of grime, dried blood, and scabs. A strange substance called "soap" covered her body with suds. Next, the shaman used something called a "comb" to remove the lice and knots from her hair. After the hair was clean, Lifa placed a bowl atop Fig's head, then cut around the edges with metal claws called "scissors." It was certainly neater than the haircuts Fig would give herself in the wild.

She even gave Figaro a remarkable thing called a "dress." It was woven of fabric—same as the rug and bed. Fig hated it. It kept rubbing against her skin, all itchy and annoying. The "shoes" were even worse. Fig steadfastly refused to wear those and tossed them into the bushes. She kept pulling the dress off too, hissing, growling, and snapping her teeth when Lifa tried to force it back on. Finally Lifa came up with a brilliant idea. She pinned Fig's collection of red bator feathers onto the dress. Until now, Fig had simply tied the feathers to vines, then slung them loosely across her body. She had to admit: pinning them to a fabric dress was more practical. Fig wore it. She still refused the shoes, however.

While all this was going on, Red Scar kept himself busy running through the forest, hunting alone. At one point, he loped back toward the camp, holding a turtle in his mouth. His jaws were muscular, full of sharp teeth, and large enough to bite a man's arm off, but still Red Scar could not crack open the shell. He flopped the turtle down at Fig's feet, then mewled.

Open? Open it for me?

But before Fig could even try, the turtle raced into the stream and swam away. Fig had never known turtles could move so fast. But apparently, when the need arose, they could sprint.

Red Scar snorted in disgust, then ran back into the forest in search of an easier meal. The achillobator ignored Lifa, not growling or hissing at the woman. Humans were friends, he had learned. Not food.

After all her grooming, Fig stepped into her grandmother's hut, where she examined herself in the mirror. She barely recognized herself.

Her skin was clean. Her bowl-shaped hair was combed and neat, no longer a wild tangle full of leaves and lice. She wore actual clothes, not just feathers. A bone bracelet encircled her wrist, while a leather thong hung around her neck, engraved with coiling ivy. Her sickle claw hung from the necklace like a pendant.

I look like a human, Fig thought. Oh, there were still red feathers strewn through her dress, and that sickle claw was pure achillobator, but ... yes, a human. All doubts vanished from her mind now.

I'm human. Mina was my mother. Joe is my father. I am ...

She tried saying the word again. "Fi-ga-ro." She turned toward her grandmother. "La-ffff."

"Lifa," the old woman said.

"La-ffff!"

The old woman smiled. Wrinkles appeared across her face when she smiled, making her very beautiful. "Try saying it slowly, syllable by syllable. Li ..."

"Li!" Fig blurted out.

"Fa."

"Ffff! Li-ffffthh!" She ended up spraying saliva, then groaned and flopped onto the floor. "Arrrrroooo!" *I can't do it! My mouth is broken.*

Lifa laughed and stroked her hair. "Your tongue isn't used to making human sounds. It'll come with time. Keep practicing. Okay?"

"Oaey!" Fig grinned. That came out not half-bad.

"I have something for you," Lifa said. "A birthright."

She handed Figaro a ring with a large gleaming stone. The crystal was red with a golden streak like a reptilian pupil.

"This is a unique crystal that is found only on Mintari," Lifa said. "It doesn't have a name. But I call it the dinosaur's eye. It does look like a dinosaur's eye, doesn't it?"

Fig nodded—a gesture she had learned from Lifa. "Yi."

Lifa slipped the ring onto Fig's finger. "A perfect fit. Keep it. It belonged to your mother. Her spirit will always be with you."

Fig's eyes widened. She tapped the stone. "Mi-na?"

Lifa nodded. "She wore it often. She would want you to have it."

Fig admired the stone. It gleamed and seemed to watch her like a real eye. She treasured it. Achillobators had no concept of jewelry. They lived for practicality—eating, mating, surviving. But here in Lifa's hut, Fig had discovered the concept of beauty. Lifa had hung dream catchers throughout her home. Crystals covered her shelves. She wore jewelry of bone and tooth and stone. Fig didn't understand why humans collected shiny, pretty things, but she found them beautiful. Another sign of her humanity. She hugged her grandmother and purred, her way of saying thank you.

"Your mother would have been so proud of you," Lifa said. "You look so much like her."

Suddenly that horrible truth hit Fig harder than ever before.

My mother is dead.

Tears fled her eyes. Fig had never spent much time thinking about her mother. There had been the shaman long ago, a caretaker and nurturer. There were the achillobators. There was her grandmother. All these souls had touched her life. Mina was a stranger to her, but now Fig mourned her loss, craved the love of a mother, a love she had never felt.

Why am I here? she wanted to ask. *How did my mother die? Who was the shaman who tended to me, and where are the other shamans?*

She didn't know how to speak those words. But one question, perhaps, she could ask.

"Fa-de?"

Lifa wiped away Fig's tears. "What is that, sweetness?"

"Fa-de?" Fig bounded toward the photo album, flipped it open, and pointed at the photo of Joe. "Fa-de?" She looked around her as if seeking him. "Fa-de?"

Where is my father?

"I'll show you where he is."

Lifa unfolded a large parchment map. She placed it on the floor, holding down the corners with a geode, pine cone, theropod tooth, and ammonite shell. Fig leaned over and her eyes widened. She had never seen a map before, but intuitively, she grokked it at once. What a wonder! She needed to learn to draw maps herself in dirt. It would certainly help planning a hunt. She could not read the captions, but she recognized the landscape. There was the gorge where pterosaurs reigned, and there flowed the river where hadrosaurs came to drink. She spotted the grasslands where allosaurs prowled and the forests where stegosaurs roamed.

She tapped a place on the map, then gestured around her. Then at the map again. Then around her.

Lifa nodded. "Yes, that's where we are. Excellent! You're a natural."

Fig beamed. She had always had a good sense of direction. The pack trusted her. Often she led them to watering holes and hunting grounds, never losing her way.

The old shaman tapped a mountain on the map. "This is Mudge Mountain. It's not far from here. Just across the forest and meadow. Your father lives in a cave on the western slope."

"Fa-de!" Fig leaped to her feet. "Fa-de, fa-de!" She grabbed Lifa's arm and tried pulling her toward the door. "Yip yip, awooo!" *Let's go!*

Lifa smiled thinly. "Figaro, I'd love to go with you. But I'm an old lady. I walk with a cane, and I'm weary after my recent trek to the henge. Here in my neck of the woods, I know how to mark my home and trails with herbs that hide me from predators. But in the open … no, a limping old woman like me wouldn't last long."

Fig mimicked riding an achillobator, then pointed out the window. *Ride Red Scar!*

Lifa laughed. "He's learned to tolerate me to a degree. But I'm still a stranger. He would not let me ride him. Joe comes to visit me when he can. If you wait here with me, you'll meet him on his next visit."

Fig whined. *I want to see him now!*

"Wait!" Lifa laughed harder. "The impatience of youth. Joe will be here sooner or later. Maybe tomorrow. Maybe in a week or two. But he will visit again."

A week or two! Fig could not wait that long. And it wasn't just her impatience.

It was the pack.

With Red Scar away, Crooked Wing must be planning a coup. The big, barren female had been gunning for leadership for a while now. She was always testing Red Scar, nipping at his feathers, pecking at his food, testing her limits, probing for weakness. With Red Scar away, she would make a grab for power. The pack would not wait forever for Red Scar to return and assert his dominance. A few days more, and they might not welcome him home. Crooked Wing would slash and bite him, send him fleeing, and the pack would truly be hers.

Red Scar must return to protect his throne. Now. But the old male would not leave Fig, she knew. So long as she was away, he would stay with her. The tarry bator was loyal to a fault. And it might cost him everything.

Fig looked out the window. The scarred old predator was sticking his snout into the stream, drinking and searching for fish. This was no life for a bator. He needed to be with his pack, hunting big game. Fig had tried sending him away, going so far as to toss stones near his feet. But he remained steadfastly by her side.

Maybe after Fig met her father, after she learned more about her heritage, she would return to the pack. She would choose to live again among the achillobators. And Red Scar would come with her, a king in exile returning to reclaim his throne. Or maybe Fig would choose to remain with the humans, and Red Scar would understand and agree to leave her, though it would break both their hearts. In either case, Fig could not linger like this, teetering between two worlds. It was not fair for her friend.

I'll go to the mountain, she decided. *I'll ride Red Scar. I must leave Lifa today.*

She looked into her grandmother's eyes, not knowing how to communicate all this. But Lifa seemed to understand. She held Fig's hand.

"Are you sure, child? Are you sure you're ready to leave this place so soon?"

Fig nodded. "Fi-ga-ro … ca … bik."

I'll come back.

Lifa sniffed. "I know. I'll prepare you a basket. Hang tight."

The shaman filled a basket with fresh fruit, dry fish, jars of herbs, bags of nuts, a bottle of water, and a few flowers—just for their beauty. Finally she gave Fig one more thing. A long hug.

"I love you, wild child," she whispered. "You'll never be alone again."

I was never alone, Fig thought. *I had the pack. I still do.*

Outside, she called Red Scar to her. He ran up on his two powerful legs, crouched, and she climbed onto his back. They left Lifa's hut behind. But Fig knew that this place would be an anchor for her, that Lifa would forever be in her heart. She would return.

She rode Red Scar through the forest and across the grassy plains. The mountains soared in the distance, and the air kissed her cheeks. Already Fig felt a little better. She had felt warm and loved in Lifa's hut. But also cramped. Trapped. Here in the wilderness it was like a weight was lifted. The grass rustled, the sun gilded the snowy mountaintops, and clouds of dactyls glided above. Mintari was so beautiful. Fig could never live in a hut, hidden away from such majesty.

Nature was full of hunger, cold snow, punishing sunlight, dangerous insects, venomous snakes, and vicious predators. Nature was constantly trying to kill you. Nature made you fight every day, every moment to survive. Nature had left Figaro a scrawny thing with scabs on her arms, hunger in her belly, and lice in her hair. So why did riding here, leaving the hut behind, feel so right?

As she rode Red Scar across the grasslands, she buried her hands in his feathers, and more than ever, she felt herself trapped between two worlds. Between two species. Between two families.

Lifa stood outside her hut for a long time. Long after Figaro disappeared among the trees, Lifa stood there, watching as if she could still see her granddaughter in the distance. Grief and joy mixed inside her. She had not felt such joy since Joe had been born. She had not felt such grief since Mina had died.

"This will break you at first, Joe," she whispered. "But then it will heal you. It will heal our family."

She had kept her emotional storm hidden from Figaro, but now it flowed over her, and tears rolled down her wizened cheeks.

Twice Lifa's life had shattered. Thirty-two years ago, the first storm struck with unforgiving fury.

She had lived on Cloventia then. An expatriate. A Mintarian, wild at heart, trapped in the electric jungle of floating skyscrapers where billions of humans scuttled like bees in a hive. She had wilted there. But she had loved her husband then. Loved his strength. Loved his unstoppable force of will. He coated himself with steel armor, but she saw the broken shards of soul that rattled inside.

She had even left her homeworld for him, trapping herself in a world of steel and glass, a caged beast who yearned for the sky. Yes, she had left her beloved Mintari for Tobias Triplehorn. What a silly, lovestruck girl she had been! Naive. Broken. Manipulated. She had given Tobias everything. Her life. Two children from her womb. Her soul. She languished but she stayed for him, trapped inside her neon cage.

Until he built his wretched empire. Until leaving Mintari was not enough for Tobias Triplehorn. Until he decided to build weapons and unleash hunters on her world. All because of his trauma, his twisted need for revenge. Dinosaurs had killed his parents, but leaving Mintari was not enough for him. No. He had left Mintari behind, but Mintari's dinosaurs forever haunted his mind. And they would not stop tormenting him until they were all dead.

The storm raged over her. And Lifa left him. She returned to Mintari, taking her son with her. Joe had been only a boy, and Amissa had been only a baby.

And that innocent baby remained behind.

Lifa had tried everything, every lawyer, every judge, she had gotten on her knees, kissed Tobias's feet, begged him … but one child he kept. So Lifa had fled with her son and with her guilt.

The guilt crushed her. She had abandoned her daughter, and back on Mintari, instead of finding her home, she found only self-loathing. She lived in Dinovia City then, her childhood hometown, but she felt trapped, felt the eyes staring, heard the whispers.

She married a killer.

She abandoned her daughter.

She was a monster.

And they were right. All those whispers were true.

So Lifa had fled the city, and in the wilderness of Mintari, she met the wild women who danced on the mountains and in the rain. They welcomed her. Taught her how to heal, how to read the stars, how to worship the gods of Mintari. She danced with them in the moonlight between the stones. And she raised her son in the wild.

Those were hard years. The life of a shaman was often a short one. There weren't many old shamans on Mintari. They worshipped dinosaurs as gods, but some gods were cruel. Some gods devoured them. Sometimes the shamans starved during a drought, and sometimes they froze in winter. Sometimes venomous snakes and spiders felled them. Sometimes ticks bit them, and they wasted away, rotting inside until they died as skin and bones, riddled with parasites. Mintari was such a beautiful killer.

So many were gone. A shaman must have found the infant Figaro, then died like so many others, leaving the girl alone in the wilderness. The shamans who had taken Lifa in, who had taught the secrets of mud and stone and stars—they were no more. They were a dying breed, but Lifa remained, living in her little hut, hiding from her ghosts. Sometimes she felt like a mere husk of a woman, full of rattling demons.

Yet as the years went by, she slowly found peace. She learned to feel joy again. The first white strands invaded her hair, and the first wrinkles tugged at the corners of her eyes when she smiled. The guilt never left her, but she learned to live with that guilt. And in those years, after so long in the dark, she smiled often.

And then a second storm hit.

Then Mina died.

Joe had always been strong like granite. And like granite, when struck just right, he shattered.

He too left the city, moved into the wilderness. But not to seek peace as a shaman. He chose a different path. A path of war. He fought the poachers in the wild. He killed. At night he nursed his pain in a dark cave, a wounded predator. At dawn he fought again, defending his territory. And his territory was Mintari.

Tobias and Joe. Father and son. Both lost loved ones in the wilderness of Mintari. The father chose to exterminate the dinosaurs. The son chose to protect them.

My son survived that terrible night fifteen years ago, Lifa thought. *But Ivan took so much from him. Not just Mina but also his joy, his peace, maybe his soul.*

But now came one who could heal him.

One who could bring back joy to their family.

A scrawny child of the wild. *L'enfant sauvage.* Fi-ga-ro. They had all thought her dead, lost with her mother in the belly of the beast. But the gods had brought her back, and Lifa knew the girl was a miracle.

Tobias is lost forever down the path of shadows, Lifa thought. *Maybe Amissa is too. But maybe ... maybe this can restore Joe to the man that he was.*

"Ride well, my granddaughter," she whispered into the wind. "You are a blessing from the gods."

CHAPTER EIGHTEEN
We Are at War

Amissa stood on the mountaintop, her arm in a sling. Her astrolite idled nearby in the snow. From up here, she could see for many miles across the wilderness of Mintari. All the way across Skull Swamp, Mudge Mountain, Hell Valley, and Marshwood Forest. Beyond those misty woods it awaited. Dinovia. The only city on this planet. Headquarters of the Mintari Rangers.

The Rangers had declared war on her. And war was war.

It was time to muster her troops.

Amissa had come to this world by herself. But she was not alone. Her soldiers were already here.

She fished her SmartSphere out of her pocket. The device bloomed in her hand, expanding from flat circle to gleaming sphere. The round computer boasted many functions. Amissa's favorite app was QuickFame, the NyxNet's most popular social media platform. But her SmartSphere could do much more. It was a compass, an encyclopedia, a flashlight, a wallet, a communicator, a map, and ten thousand other things. Right now Amissa activated the scanner app. The sphere hovered above her and spun around its axis, scanning the landscape.

Triplehorn Incorporated sold many products to hunters. Rifles and shotguns and knives—of course. But also belt buckles, hiking boots, camouflage jackets, thermal tents, trail mix, sleeping bags, and a hundred other products hunters needed. Each product emitted a distinct signal, allowing Triplehorn HQ to track their hunters in the wilderness. Well, not the trail mix. But the engineers were working on that one too.

As heiress to the clan, Amissa could access this feature. Her SmartSphere now scanned for any Triplehorn product within range. And there they were. A dozen lights on the map. A dozen hunters loyal to her clan. Here within her reach.

Amissa grabbed the SmartSphere, turned off the scanner, and switched to camera mode. She tossed the sphere a few meters ahead. It hovered before her, filming her standing atop the snowy mountaintop, the wind in her hair.

This time she did not stream a video for her millions of fans. This time she broadcast her words on a private channel. She contacted only the dozen.

"Hunters! This is your girl, Amissa Triplehorn. Ladies and gentlemen, we are at war. Meet me at Dead Eye Crater tonight at sundown. And I will lead you to victory."

She hung up.

She got in her astrolite and flew.

The landscape sprawled below, rich with life. Forests spread into the horizons. Sauropods and ceratopsians herded across the plains, eating everything in their path. Flocks of pterosaurs filled the sky. This planet was a cornucopia of things to kill. But first Amissa must rid Mintari of the Rangers.

North of Skull Swamp, past the volcano range and the basalt sea, she saw it. Dead Eye Crater. A charred, lifeless depression in the land. No trees or grass grew there. No dinosaurs roamed within that shadowy bowl. Even the very dust was dead, and no worms or insects burrowed through it. Some tour guides said the crater was radioactive. They would bring no tourists near. Some Rangers said the crater was haunted. They feared to tread that barren land.

Dead Eye Crater. A good place for hunters to meet.

They call us poachers, Amissa thought. *They say we're monsters. But we are predators. And they are prey. We will bring them down.*

Most hunters could not afford astrolites. Not even tricopters, simple flying machines that couldn't even reach space. So Amissa arrived at the crater first. She landed her astrolite in the center, stepped out, and looked around.

It's like landing on an alien world, Amissa thought.

The crater was only about the size of a football stadium, but standing inside, one felt isolated. The crater's rim hid the forests, meadows, and grasslands of Mintari. One could see no life from here. No growing things. No animals. Not even pterosaurs dared fly over Dead Eye Crater. A towering volcano, located a few miles away, was tall enough to see from down here. Its vent was leaking lava and belching smoke, cloaking the sky.

It feels like standing on a lifeless gray planet, Amissa thought.

She could not see the sun behind the smoke. But Nyx seemed to be setting, and darkness spread across the crater like tar. Before long, the only light came from the volcano vent.

Then—new lights. High on the crater's stony lip.

Headlights. A jippi. A big one too. Its wheels were the height of a man, and its cargo hold could carry an elephant. Its cowcatcher could knock down a brontosaurus. The juggernaut came trundling down into the crater, blasting smoke, and stopped beside Amissa.

The door opened, and a rawboned man emerged. He wore a black coat and a wide-brimmed hat that shadowed his face. He walked with his head lowered like a man used to hiding his face. Bandoleers crisscrossed his chest, and two rifles hung across his back. Spurs jangled on his dino-skin boots. When he reached Amissa, he finally looked up, revealing a leathery face with sharp cheekbones, a jutting chin, and a wide mouth full of big yellow teeth. He gave her a sickly grin.

"Amissa Triplehorn." His voice was like gravel crunching underfoot. "My, my. The queen is here."

She nodded. "Hello, Rattlesnake. Catch any dinos lately?"

His grin widened, but no light filled his eyes. He had the eyes of a shabu addict. Eyes that were pure black, no white to them at all. The drug painted your insides black too, they said. Rattlesnake licked his yellow teeth. "A few. Look into the back of the jippi."

Amissa pointed her flashlight into the jippi's cargo hold. Her eyes widened in delight. "My goodness, it's huge! What is that, a triceratops?"

Rattlesnake nodded. "A big male bull. His head is eight feet long from beak to frill. Barely fit in the cargo hold. Wish I could have taken the body, but I'd need a bigger jippi." He barked a laugh. "The head will do nicely. I plan to place it in my living room."

Amissa whistled appreciatively. "If you can find a starship willing to smuggle it back to Cloventia."

"I have my contacts."

Yes, Amissa knew about the smugglers. A network of criminal organizations trafficked hunting trophies from the nature worlds to Cloventia. The Triplehorns knew all the bosses by name. Had them on speed dial. If anyone asked, of course, they were outlaw scum who had nothing to do with a reputable company like Triplehorn Inc. The silk emperors did not tolerate crime. And their silken robes hid many poison blades.

More lights shone above, interrupting Amissa's thoughts. Another vehicle came rumbling down into the crater. Another jippi. But this one was unusually small. Barely larger than an antique sedan.

The diminutive jippi rumbled to a halt beside them. One of the shortest women Amissa had ever seen hopped out. The top of her head didn't even reach Amissa's shoulders. She sported two blond braids, a tiny armored vest, and an enormous shotgun. The rifle was longer than her. The little huntress held it like a medieval pike. Her name was Avril Laurent, but everyone called her *La Petite Princesse*.

"*Bonjour, mon chéri*," Amissa said.

La Petite Princesse grinned. "Amissa, my darling!" She hugged her. "Good to see ya, queen. Loved the nodosaur video! Shame about the supersaurus fail. You needed me there. I would have taken the giant down." She winked.

If any other hunter had ribbed her this way, Amissa would have put a bullet through them. But she liked *La Petite Princesse*. She didn't take it personally.

"I'm sure you would have, little one."

"Hey!" *Princesse* glowered. "I'm not so petite with this gun."

Typical Napoleon complex, Amissa figured. What better way to compensate for her height? She was no taller than a child. So she hunted the biggest animals that ever lived.

Engines roared.

Two enormous motorcycles thundered down into the crater. Each bike was the size of a horse, and their tires were like those of a jippi's.

"Ah, the Guldner brothers are here!" said *La Petite Princesse*.

The men riding the motorcycles were shockingly obese. Each man wore a leather jacket, ripped jeans, and a bandanna. Their long beards fluttered in the wind. The skulls of saber-toothed tigers adorned their motorcycles.

"Weak men," hissed Rattlesnake. "Big bikes. Big guts. Few kills."

"They kill enough to stay well fed, old friend," Amissa said.

The Guldners did collect some trophies. But they primarily hunted for food. They had no appetite for the synthetic meats you found in Cloventian grocery stores. They craved the meat of legendary beasts, devouring tigers, mammoths, and dinosaurs.

More hunters arrived.

There was Madame Maria, a towering woman, close to seven feet tall. She wore a black velvet gown, a ruby choker, and opera gloves. Her midnight hair billowed in the breeze, and her arched eyebrows rose as she regarded the "little ones" with amusement. Next to Madame Maria, they were all small like *La Petite Princesse.*

The Scarred Man was here. That was what they all called him. He could not speak, and they did not know his name. Long ago, some ruthless predator had clawed and deformed his face. Now the Scarred Man could not speak, could not eat anything thicker than paste. Most of his face was gone. But his eyes were unharmed. Pale, pitiless eyes, almost colorless, completely emotionless.

The triplets were here too. They were willowy, pale women with long platinum hair. Their blue eyes were sunken, their cheeks gaunt. If Amissa hadn't known them better, she would mistake them for corpses. Maybe ghosts. They appeared weightless as they fluttered ahead. Their bare feet didn't seem to touch the ground. The triplets said little, ate little, slept little, and killed a lot. Despite their frail appearance, they were among the deadliest hunters in the galaxy. Their home on planet Dagon brimmed with skeletons of their hunts—a museum dedicated to killing the most wonderful creatures in the galaxy.

Tomahawk had come. He was an enormously muscular man, almost as broad as he was tall, and covered in tattoos. He looked like he could flip over a triceratops. A crest of red hair topped his otherwise bald head, four rifles hung across his back, and a dozen knives were strapped to his legs. Grenades dangled from his belt. Tomahawk had been a soldier once. He had fought on the battlefields of Earth, hunting down warlords. On Mintari he found more exciting prey.

Last to arrive were Buster and the Bean. Whenever those ones showed up, Amissa could not suppress a shudder. Buster was a handsome young man, athletic, tanned, with coiffed blond hair and a smile full of white teeth. The Bean was his twin. His parasitic twin. He grew out of Buster's chest, small and lumpy and cackling. His little arms were like the arms of a T-rex, and they held handguns. Among the two, Bean was far deadlier. Buster didn't even like hunting. He simply carried his sadistic little brother around.

They were all here.

The cabal of hunters gathered in the crater. Together, they numbered thirteen. Small for an army. Barely a squadron. But they were the deadliest killers this planet had ever known.

Amissa cleared her throat.

"Ladies, gentlemen, freaks, and friends!" she cried out. "Thank you for gathering here."

"What do you want?" grumbled one of the Guldner brothers. His mouth was hidden inside his great bushy beard. He slapped his ample belly, jangling his bandoleer. "We're hungry. We want to get back to hunting."

Bean cackled. It was a high-pitched, deranged sound. "Stop thinking of your gut, Guldner! Looks like you've eaten a brontosaurus already." The little parasitic twin cackled louder.

"At least my belly doesn't have a psychopath growing from it!" Guldner snapped.

"Boys, boys, please!" Amissa said, raising her hands overhead. "We're all on the same side here. We're all hunters. We're proud to be hunters. We came to Mintari because this is the greatest hunting ground in the galaxy. We face a common foe. The Mintari Rangers."

"Boo, hiss!" *La Petite Princesse* said, coning her diminutive hands around her mouth.

"They are naughty troublemakers," said Madame Maria. At seven feet tall, she towered over the others. She smiled crookedly. "I would love to teach them some manners."

The Bean cackled, twitching in delight on his brother's torso. "Slice the Rangers up! Slice and dice them! Give them to the dinosaurs to eat! Or to the fat biker twins, yes!" His high-pitched cackle echoed through the crater.

"The Rangers tried to kill me," Amissa said. "They've tried to kill all of us. We all know people who fell in this war. And make no mistake. We are at war."

Rattlesnake's thin lip curled in a snarl. "The Rangers must fall."

"They will fall," Amissa said. "I have a plan. Listen carefully, my fellow hunters. This is how we take them down ..."

It must all happen at once. A synchronized attack.

The thirteen of them together—they would get it done.

It took a lot of planning. Some bickering. Some returns to the drawing board. But as night fell, they were ready. They would do what no hunters had ever done before.

Attack the Rangers on their own turf.

Amissa crouched in the grass. The night was dark. Clouds hid the twin moons. But from where she hid, Amissa could see the towering wall that surrounded Dinovia City. Rangers manned the battlements like ancient soldiers. Spotlights scanned the valley where Amissa hid, but they would not find a small human hiding in the tall grass. The Rangers were there to protect their city from carnivorous dinosaurs. They had no idea of the true predators who lurked in the shadows.

Several lines of defenses surrounded Dinovia City. First there was an electric fence. It could deliver a shock powerful enough to stun a T-rex. Two generators inside the city kept the juice flowing. Next was a moat. Rumor had it that predatory beasts lurked in the dark waters. A drawbridge, currently pulled up, was the only way across. Next came the towering brick wall. Rangers stood there, armed with sleep-or-dies. They were trained to fire on any predator who approached the city. Sometimes pterosaurs flew near, but just the sound of a gunshot sent them fleeing. Fence. Moat. Wall. Rangers. Amissa must take them all down.

She planned an invasion of Dinovia City. An invasion from the ground, delivering ruthless punishment and devastation. She would bring this city to its knees.

She crouched lower in the grass. Crickets chirped and a cold breeze stung her cheeks. Amissa unfolded her SmartSphere, held it in her palm, and broadcast a message to her fellow hunters.

"They will never hurt us again," she said. "For years, they came to our territory. They attacked us in the forests and fields. They murdered our brothers and sisters. Now we bring the war to them. Are you ready, hunters?"

They reported in one by one over a secure channel.

They were ready.

"Let's roll," Amissa said.

The clock struck midnight, and Ronald yawned. Why had he agreed to take the night shift? Oh right, better pay. He wasn't thinking straight. How could he at this hour? He was exhausted.

Struggling to keep awake, he popped the lid on his thermos and took a long, luxurious sip of coffee. Lots of sugar. Lots of cream. It would keep him awake until the next sip. He stretched, and the buttons on his shirt nearly popped. Tarry shirt shrunk in the laundry again. He took another sip of creamy, sugary goodness.

Being a Mintari Ranger wasn't all glamour and adventure. Sure, some guys like Jurassic Joe were practically folk heroes. That dude wrestled dinosaurs and rescued damsels all day long. But other Rangers, like Ronald here—they did the grunt work. They couldn't all be legends. But if you asked Ronald, they were all heroes.

An electric fence surrounded Dinovia City, keeping dinosaurs out. It was the city's first line of defense against the predators who prowled the wilderness. A generator pumped power to the electric fence day and night. Somebody had to guard that generator. Ronald was that somebody. Like all Rangers, he wore a tan uniform and ceratop hat. Just like the action figures. Ronald almost felt like a hero.

He tucked his thumbs into his belt, feeling proud of his duty. Clearly his kids didn't appreciate his heroism. If you asked his teenage daughter, he was "totally lame." But tar it, Ronald sipped his coffee, and he stayed awake, and he manned his post.

It was a little past midnight when the girl appeared.

Ronald had just wandered back from brewing a second pot of coffee. He had only left his post for a moment. He had to. It was get coffee or fall asleep. Coffee won. When he returned to the generator, his thermos refilled, the girl was there.

"Wha— Who are you?"

The girl was facing the generator, her back turned toward him. She wore a pink dress, and ribbons adorned her pigtails. In one hand, she held a lollipop the size of a saucer. In the other hand, she held huge clippers. Ignoring Ronald, the girl was busy cutting cables in the generator. Snip snip. Cable after cable. As she worked, she sang a tune. "Ring-a-ring-a-rosies. A pocket full of posies. A tissue, a tissue. We all fall d—"

"Hey, what are you doing!" Ronald said.

The girl froze, her clippers poised over another cable. "Just disabling the electric fence, sir."

"Stop that!" Ronald grabbed her by the shoulder.

She spun toward him, and he stumbled back, eyes wide. It wasn't a little girl after all. She was a grown woman but very short. The height of a child.

"Oh, sir, but I just love to cut things." She snapped her clippers. "Arts and crafts, you see."

Ronald blinked, confused for a moment. Where was all the blood gushing from?

That's when he realized his fingers were no longer gripping her shoulder. They were on the floor. He opened his mouth to scream. But the clippers closed around his neck. And the scream came out as a gurgle.

La Petite Princesse smiled, covered in blood. She lifted the fallen thermos of coffee and sipped. Ah, nice and sweet!

She pulled out her SmartSphere and called her boss. "My queen! Your little saboteur reports. The generator is down."

On the holographic screen, Amissa Triplehorn smiled. "Good work, *mon chéri*."

La Petite Princesse licked her lollipop.

Crouching in the fields, Amissa tossed a pebble at the electric fence. It buzzed. Still working. Even after *La Petite Princesse*'s bloody sabotage.

The Rangers were stupid, yes, but they had taken some precautions. They had a backup generator.

Not a problem. She had a man on the job. A man-and-a-half even. Amissa watched through her SmartSphere.

On the other side of town, another guard manned his post. He was an elderly man. Eighty-two years young. He walked with a cane, and his hearing wasn't what it used to be. But he was still a Ranger, and he would not retire until they nailed his coffin shut. He wore the uniform and hat with pride.

When he was younger, he used to go out on dangerous missions. To fight poachers. To save dinosaurs caught in traps. He had shot and killed three hunters throughout his career, and he had put the fear of God in a thousand others. Years ago, when somebody broke into his house, he shot him too. He was a tough old bastard, and his knuckles were still scarred from his days as a boxer.

In recent years, he didn't sleep much. One curse of being old was lack of sleep. So he volunteered to take a few night shifts. To guard the city. They stuck him here in some back alley. Left him to guard a generator. Ha! Well, it wasn't as glamorous as manning the wall, but he took the job. At least he wasn't in bed, staring at the ceiling, the empty half of the bed so cold beside him. Since his wife had died, the bed always felt so tarry empty.

He was remembering the old days, reliving a boxing match he had won, when a shadowy figure approached.

The old man narrowed his eyes.

"Who goes there?"

The figure stepped closer. A young man in a trench coat. A lad with blond hair and an easy smile.

"Hello there, Gramps!"

"What do you want?" the old Ranger growled. "This area is restricted. Get the hell outta here, kid."

The young man raised his eyebrows, never losing his smile. "Calm down, old fella! I'm looking for the backup generator. That it behind ya?"

The old man grunted. "I'll tell you what you're looking for, punk. Trouble. And you found it." He drew his sidearm. "Now get lost before I put a hole in your gut."

The young man finally lost his smile. "You mean … this gut?"

He pulled open his trench coat.

The old man gasped.

A deformed creature grew from the young man's abdomen. It looked like some sort of conjoined twin. The face was bloated, the eyes yellow, the arms short and stunted. That's all there was. Just a face and two tiny arms.

"What the hell is that?" the old man cried.

The parasitic twin held a gun in each hand. He fired.

The old man fell. He never even got a shot off.

"Justice," said Bean. The little hunter fired again. This time at the backup generator. It buzzed and went dark.

Bean called Amissa and cackled. "We got it down."

When Amissa tossed another pebble, it clanged against the fence without a spark. The electricity was gone.

"Excellent work, hunters!" she said, transmitting the message via SmartSphere.

"No problem, big sis," said *La Petite Princesse*.

"My pleasure, toots," said Bean.

The Rangers on the wall probably didn't notice the power going down. But the Rangers inside the control room, several blocks away from the wall, most certainly did. They were all tired and bored, sipping coffee to get them through the night shift. The radio was playing old Mintarian folk songs—music for the soul. An array of monitors displayed views from security cameras atop the fence.

The Rangers had been sitting in this control room for hours. They did every night, sipping their coffee and watching their monitors. It was usually boring. Sometimes a curious iguanodon approached the electric fence, got a shock, and fled. The tyrannosaurs and raptors had quickly learned to avoid the fence; they were clever creatures. The pterosaurs had learned to fly around the city rather than over it. Only the iguanodons never seemed to learn. Dumb creatures. It was said that stegosaurus was the dumbest dinosaur, but at least they didn't repeatedly shock themselves.

So far, the night shift was quiet in the control room. The Rangers were still hoping for some excitement tonight. Maybe a bigger, meaner dinosaur would try the fence. Everyone kept dreaming of a giganotosaurus testing the fence—that would really be something—but the big brutes were rare, and none had wandered near Dinovia in decades.

Then the monitors all shut down.

The Rangers blinked, confused.

"What the hell?" somebody said.

"The power is down!" said another.

"Get the backup generator going!"

"Why isn't Hank answering?"

"Ronald, you there?"

"What's going on?"

They didn't know about *La Petite Princesse* and the Bean. The way they didn't know that two big, hairy bikers were heading their way.

Seconds after the power went down, the windows to the control room shattered. Two enormous motorcycles crashed into the room, destroying all in their path—chairs, desks, monitors, and Rangers.

Two obese men rode the motorcycles. They wore leather jackets, bandannas, and sunglasses. Their long beards flowed in the wind. Before their motorcycles even touched the ground, each man drew a handgun that was almost the size of a rifle. They opened fire, filling the room with bullets.

Every Ranger knew them. They were infamous poachers with an appetite for dinosaur meat. The Guldner twins.

A few Rangers managed to raise their guns, to open fire. They hit one of the brothers, but beneath his leather jacket, he wore a bulletproof vest. He didn't even fall off his motorcycle. Within moments, it was all over.

The Guldner brothers walked across the floor, killing the wounded. Blood mixed with steaming-hot coffee. They called Amissa. "The control room is ours."

A mile away, Rangers manned the walls and guard towers, protecting Dinovia City. They heard the gunshots. But when they tried to call the other Rangers, their communicators failed. Without the control room, they were cut off. The night was dark. The spotlights were dead. They could barely see anything in the fields beyond the walls. They were blind.

A handful of Rangers crowded atop the wall to discuss. Their flashlights painted their faces an eerie white. They knew something was up. The power going out. The gunshots. The jammed communicators.

"Somebody is messing with us," muttered a young Ranger.

"We're under attack!" said another.

"Hold your horses," said Don, the highest-ranking guard on duty. "This isn't a war zone. Nobody has ever attacked Dinovia City. Unless you mean a few dinosaurs clawing at the fence during power outages."

"Dinosaurs don't fire guns."

"Could just be a popping sound from the generators dying," offered Gary, a Ranger with a bushy gray beard.

"All right, boys." Don grabbed his sleep-or-die. "I'm going to the control room to take a look. Stay on the wall. I'll holler if I—"

He blinked and stared.

"What the hell?" whispered Gary, standing at his side. "You seeing this too, Don?"

Don saw it. Three young women, standing on the wall. Identical. Triplets. They wore pale white dresses that did not move in the wind. Their skin was colorless, their eyes sunken. They couldn't have been older than Don's daughters, but their hair was white as snow.

"Ghosts," whispered Don.

The triplets all tilted their heads as one, a perfectly synchronized movement. They spoke in unison.

"We are the living. You will be the dead."

They raised their hands. They held long, cruel blades. For the first time, their dead expressions cracked.

They smiled.

The Rangers didn't even have time to aim their guns. The triplets flowed over them, around them, through them. Blades lashed necks. Guns clattered to the courtyard below, unfired.

A few seconds later, the bodies of Rangers thumped down beside the fallen guns. Their necks were slit open.

Standing atop the walls, the triplets raised three lanterns with ghostly lights within. The signal to their leader.

In the darkness beyond the wall, Amissa saw and smiled.

Not far away from where the dead Rangers fell, living Rangers manned the city gate.

They heard the clatters and thumps from the shadows. When they turned to investigate, the Rangers found themselves facing the tallest woman they had ever seen.

The group of Rangers, all of them tall men, gaped in wonder. They didn't even reach this woman's shoulders. She wore a black gown, and her long raven hair spilled out from under a wide-brimmed hat. A red jewel shone on her choker, and sweet perfume wafted from her pale skin.

"Hello, boys," she purred, swaying closer. She wore opera gloves from whose tips sprouted steel blades.

"Stay right where you are, ma'am," said a Ranger.

But she sauntered closer. Her perfume intoxicated the senses. Her low-cut dress helped too.

"It's her," whispered another Ranger. "The famous poacher. Madame Maria."

The towering woman pouted. Her lips were the color of Pinot Noir. "Poacher?" She stroked the Ranger's cheek. Her steel claws scraped along his skin. "I prefer the term huntress. I hunt animals. And I hunt men."

She smiled, licked her lips, and slashed her claws.

Blood splattered Madame Maria's black dress. She licked her claws, savoring the coppery taste.

The other Rangers raised their sleep-or-dies. But Madame Maria moved with remarkable speed for her size. Before they could pull the triggers, she was spraying her crystal perfume bottle. Puff. Puff. Puff. Golden powder filled the night, scented of honey and lilac.

The Rangers' fingers slipped off their triggers. They smiled sleepily and wobbled on their feet.

"Go to bed, boys," Madame Maria said. "You've had a long day."

They thumped onto the ground, snoring. The madame decided to let these ones live. They had not insulted her, and she was not a monster. Maybe later she would play with them. But not yet. The night was still young, and Madame Maria had a lot of chaos to wreak.

She walked around the snoring boys, stepping on one's hand with a *crunch*, and approached the gateway. Wooden doors towered before her, even taller than her. They were thick, banded with iron, and locked for the night. She would deal with that later.

First, an easier task. Lowering the drawbridge over the moat.

She stood inside the city behind the defensive wall. The drawbridge was outside—just behind the heavy locked doors. A motor normally lowered the drawbridge, but with the power dead, the motor was dead too.

No worries. Two huge chains, accessible from here, kept the drawbridge raised. Maria flexed her fingers.

The chains were forged from solid steel. Maria grabbed them. Her hands were enormous. Her muscles bulged. She had the strength of three grown men. She strained, twisting one link in the chain until it bent and popped open.

The drawbridge swayed.

She approached the second chain, grabbed a link, and grimaced. Veins popped on her neck. She let out a growl ... and she twisted this link too.

Both chains tore free.

From this side of the wall, she could not see the drawbridge crash down. But she heard it. It made a spectacular sound.

Madame Maria climbed onto the wall and stared downward. The drawbridge spanned the moat. Perfect.

Now there was just the issue of opening the heavy doors. Normally, another set of motors opened these towering doors. But with the power out, the controls were dead. The doors were designed to stop a charging dinosaur. They were too heavy even for Madame Maria to force open.

She would need some help.

She pulled out her SmartSphere. "Tomahawk? It's your turn."

Tomahawk stood a foot shorter than Madame Maria, but he was even stronger, which was saying something. Instead of milk, the man poured protein shakes over his cereal. Instead of munching on popcorn, he snacked on steroids. He was almost as wide as he was tall. Often, Tomahawk hunted with his bare hands. Once, he had strangled a tiger to death. He used to be a wrestler, but no human foe could defeat him. So he turned to battling animals. Even dinosaurs.

Tonight he would battle heavy wooden doors.

The big hunter stood inside the city. The doors were closed for the night. A few hours ago, Tomahawk had sneaked into the city, hitching a ride in a tourist jippi. A few of his fellow hunters had slithered into Dinovia with him. Entering the city was surprisingly easy, even for a big, beefy poacher.

But there was a surprise outside, waiting in the fields. Something even bigger than Tomahawk. Too big to smuggle in. The doors must come falling down.

Tomahawk took a few steps back, lowered his head, then ran.

He barreled into the doors … then stumbled back, groaning.

The double doors hadn't even budged. Not so much as a crack marred the wood.

Tomahawk snorted and shook his head wildly. He stepped back farther this time. He leaned forward, pursed his lips, and charged.

He slammed into the doors with all the might in his massive, muscular body.

Not even a crack.

Tomahawk found himself sitting on the ground, stunned. Stars danced before his eyes.

"What the heck?" he muttered. He had knocked down doors before with ease. He had crashed through a brick wall once. He had yanked doors off cars, wrestled crocodiles to submission, and once—admittedly after a few drinks—killed a gorilla with his bare hands. He was renowned for his great strength, but this door still stood.

Impossible. He would not let a mere door defeat him!

He moved all the way down the block this time, then sprinted and slammed himself into the door.

He fell.

His eyes rolled back.

As he lay unconscious on the ground, Madame Maria sighed. The doors had won this battle.

Her SmartSphere rang. It was the Scarred Man. He stared at her from the screen. A dinosaur had mauled his face long ago. He could not speak now. His lower jaw was still mangled, his mouth covered in scars. But the mute man managed to smile.

When the camera panned out, Madame Maria's eyes widened. She hurriedly stepped away from the doors.

These doors were going down.

The Scarred Man drove his jippi across the grasslands. He gripped the steering wheel with scarred fingers, their tips missing. The dinosaur attack had savaged more than his face. Dinosaurs had deformed him. Crippled him. He got his revenge on the beasts every day. Someday they would all die, and he would be fully avenged.

But for now, he needed the dinosaur that rode in the back of his jippi. This dinosaur would serve him well.

He adjusted his rearview mirror. He could see the dinosaur chained behind him in the jippi. A pachycephalosaurus.

They were small dinosaurs, no larger than horses, and herbivorous. They had no sharp claws, no deadly fangs. But they were among the most feared dinosaurs on Mintari. Their weapons were their heads.

Bony domes topped their skulls, ten inches thick. These enormous helmets sprouted spikes and knobs. The dinosaurs used their fearsome domes to attack predators, rival males, trees, boulders—anything that irked them. Which was most things. Pachycephalosaurus was essentially a living battering ram.

Thankfully, the one riding in the Scarred Man's jippi was chained. Like this, he was harmless. But once unleashed, the domehead would hit the city like a hurricane.

The Scarred Man parked his jippi outside the towering doors of Dinovia City. He got out, pulled a spray can from his pocket, and began spraying the wooden doors. In the can, he carried the musk of another pachycephalosaurus. A big, strong male, seeking a female to mate with.

During mating season, the domeheads fought constantly. Males headbutted each other, competing for the females. The fights were the classic example of an immovable object hitting an unstoppable force. They were a sight to behold.

The thickness of their skulls left little room for brains. The domeheads were dumb dinosaurs. They lived to eat, to breed, and mostly to ram into things. Such as a rival male during mating season. Or a door that smelled like a rival male.

The Scarred Man unchained his captive dinosaur.

And the pachycephalosaurus ran.

The dinosaur drove his bony dome into the doors of Dinovia City.

The doors jolted and cracked.

The domehead stepped back, shook his head wildly, then charged and rammed the doors again. Wooden splinters flew.

A third time the dinosaur rammed into the doors … and the doors shattered.

The domehead tumbled into the city with a shower of wood. He rose, looked around, and snorted in triumph. In his tiny brain, a simple thought arose.

That'll show him.

Now where was that female?

The electric fence was powerless. The drawbridge was down. The doors were shattered. The Rangers were in the dark.

Amissa rose from the tall grass. She stood straight, stared at the city, and smiled.

"You're mine now, Dinovia."

She thought of those who had come before her. Brave hunters. Nature lovers. Outdoorsmen. Adventurers. They had come here to Mintari only for the Rangers to shoot them dead.

This was not just about her. Not just about Triplehorn Inc. This was for her fallen brothers and sisters.

The city's defenses were down. It was time to strike.

Amissa lifted her SmartSphere. "Rattlesnake, are you ready?"

On the screen, she saw his gaunt face. He grinned a cadaverous grin. "Ready. Here they come."

Excitement tingled through Amissa. This was going to be good.

She hung up, then tossed the SmartSphere into the air. It hovered above the dark field, filming her, the grasslands, and the city walls.

"Hello, Tripletots! It's just past midnight here on Mintari. I'm standing outside Dinovia City, the headquarters of the Mintari Rangers. Not long ago, the Rangers attacked me. They fired on me. They almost killed me. I was lucky. I survived. But many proud hunters are gone. Tonight we hunters strike back. I want you to watch this, my fans and my haters. This is what happens when you declare war on Amissa Triplehorn."

For a moment, the camera filmed only darkness. The grass rustled in the breeze.

Then, in the distance, a few miles away from the city— headlights.

A low rumble rose. Not the rumble of a dinosaur. Not yet. The rumble of a motor.

The jippi gained speed. It rattled across the grasslands, heading toward the city.

Amissa tapped buttons on her watch, operating the floating SmartSphere. The camera zoomed in, revealing a pale, gaunt man in the driver's seat. His grin revealed his yellow teeth.

Rattlesnake increased speed, roaring in his jippi toward the city.

The camera rose higher, revealing what lay chained inside the jippi.

Eggs. A hundred eggs or more, secured with rope. Amissa recognized those eggs at once. She knew them by their size, their brown shell flecked with orange.

T-rex eggs.

Dinosaurs had roamed Earth for two hundred million years before their shocking extinction. Over that time, they had evolved a fanatical, all-consuming need to protect their offspring. It was their strongest instinct. It trumped everything else— hunger, pain, fear. A dinosaur must protect the next generation. Thus had they survived for so long, grown so strong. Their parental instinct was a force of nature.

A dinosaur would stop at nothing to reclaim stolen eggs.

Rattlesnake drove faster, charging straight toward the smashed doors. The scent of the eggs wafted behind his jippi. Amissa could not smell it. But to a dinosaur, it would be an intoxicating lure.

In the distance, the forest rustled.

Trunks cracked.

Conifers crashed down.

And there they came. They emerged from the forest, rumbling, racing after the jippi.

A pack of T-rexes.

Five of them at first. Then two more burst out from the forest. Then several more. They were slower than a jippi, but they ran faster than an Olympic sprinter. They charged across the grass, consumed with fury. All they thought about was getting their eggs … and killing anything in their path.

Amissa was not in their path. They ran right by her, ignoring her. She stood no taller than their knees. The T-rexes were truly enormous. Truly magnificent. They were the greatest predators that ever lived, and Amissa gazed in awe as the pack thundered by her.

Across the galaxy, her fans watched. The comment section was dead. Everyone was simply staring in wonder.

"These creatures will destroy the city," Amissa whispered. "These creatures can destroy a world."

For a second, regret filled her. Hundreds might die. Maybe thousands. But she hardened her heart. It wasn't her fault if innocent people died. The Rangers had started this war.

"The blood that spills tonight is on you, Joe Triplehorn," she whispered. "Behold the might of Mintari. Behold Tyrannosaurus rex."

The pack was almost at the gates now.

A deafening grumble rose from the trees.

Amissa turned around. One more T-rex emerged from the forest.

He was larger than the others. Much larger. His scales were not brownish green but as black as tar. His eyes blazed red like two torches. The beast ran, his enormous claws cleaving the earth, shattering boulders and fallen logs. His low-pitched grumble rolled across the land like thunder.

Amissa lost her breath.

"Beautiful," she whispered, tears in her eyes. "He's beautiful."

She recognized this T-rex from the stories. He had not been seen in years, but it had to be him. The legend. The King of Mintari.

The T-rex that had devoured Joe's wife. The T-rex that would bring down the Rangers once and for all.

Ivan ran ahead of the pack, thundered across the drawbridge, and stormed through the shattered doors into the city.

CHAPTER NINETEEN
Sneaking Around

Earlier that day, several hours before the tyrannosaurs broke into Dinovia City, a much smaller predator hid in a tree.

She was an odd predator. She had no claws and her teeth were very small. Her name was Figaro, and like many small predators, what she did best was hide, watch, and wait.

Like a strange dactyl, she perched within the fronds of a cycad. She parted the clawlike leaves and stared at the mountainside.

She had climbed the tree that morning. It was the last tree before the forest gave way to the stony mountainside. Fig had been perched here among the fronds for hours. Waiting. Learning. Scared. Her muscles were cramping, and the spiky cycad leaves kept jabbing her skin, but she stayed put.

There on the mountainside, just a quick dash away—the cave. The place Lifa had told her about.

My father's home.

She wished Lifa could be here with her. But Lifa was too old to walk long distances. To reach Henge Hill, she had tottered on a cane, and the journey left her exhausted. She had told Fig that she was sixty-eight years old. Sixty-eight! Fig had nearly fallen over. She had not known anyone could live that long. An achillobator grew up within six or seven years, found a mate, and began to lay eggs. Fig had thought herself ancient at fifteen, but if humans could live to be almost seventy …

I'm barely more than a hatchling, she realized.

Thankfully, Red Scar was with her. The big achillobator hulked below the cycad. Bators were bulkier than humans, and while they were excellent mountain climbers, they struggled to climb trees. The poor bator kept wheezing and coughing. The scrub that clung to the mountainside irritated his lungs. To distract himself, Red Scar tried digging through the soil, searching for fluffy little mammals to torment, but he found none. Mostly Red Scar simply stood watch, sniffing the air and scanning the horizon for enemies.

They were both nervous. They were strangers in a strange land. The dreaded allosaurs roamed the nearby grasslands. Here in the forested foothills, the gargantuan megaraptors prowled. The raptors had covered the hills with their spoor, marking their territory. Fig and Red Scar were behind enemy lines.

But Fig must be here. She must learn more. She must meet her father.

Must I? she thought. Doubts filled her. She already had a pack. She had Red Scar, Sharp Eyes, Long Tail, all the others. Why was she risking her life out here?

But she sensed, deep inside her, that the bonds of family meant something. That they were precious. Even to her, this wild child who had grown up feral. When Lifa had hugged her, Figaro had felt down to her bones that this was right. This was human. For a few moments of warmth and love, she had felt like a real human girl.

Once Lifa had told her where Joe Triplehorn lived, Fig had rushed over at once. But now that she was here, fear gripped her. What if her father rejected her? What if he laughed and said Fig wasn't his daughter at all? What if human males were truculent by nature, and he attacked her? So she remained hidden, spying.

She had been here all day. And so far—nothing. Nobody entered or left the cave. A few times, Fig had almost climbed the mountainside. She ached to peer into the cave and investigate. But whenever that itch filled her, she hesitated. She remained here in the tree, perched among the palm fruit.

Her worries kept pestering her like mosquitoes. What if Joe had found another mate, replacing Mina? What if he had new hatchlings now, wild little humans with sharp sticks? What if his new mate attacked Fig? She had seen such things happen among bators. Or what if Lifa had been completely wrong and Joe wasn't her father at all? He would see Fig as an intruder, a menace. He was big and strong and would tear Fig apart. Or what if he was simply indifferent? Oh, you're my daughter? Well, good for you. A pat on the head and off you go.

Fig had traveled all this way, but she dared not take the last step. So she remained in the tree, watching, waiting, weaving all these scenarios in her mind, each one worse than the last.

Her body was aching. Humans were good climbers, perhaps, but even humans were not meant to sit all day inside a tree. Her stomach growled. She was famished. Lifa had packed her a basket of fruit and fish, but it was below the tree. Red Scar was guarding it. She should go down, eat, maybe go back to Lifa's hut. Maybe go back to her pack. Maybe all this had been a mistake, and—

Movement.

Movement from the cave!

Fig tensed, all her anxieties imploding into a single blazing point of terror.

Hidden in the cycad, she parted the fronds and stared.

A man emerged from the cave.

Fig's heart leaped. Her limbs trembled. The fronds shook around her. It was him. The man from the photo. Joe Triplehorn.

Her father.

From this distance, Fig couldn't see him clearly. But she saw enough to recognize him. He looked different from her. Bigger. Bulkier. Stronger. Hair grew from his face, and he wore those strange fabrics Lifa had called "clothes." A large, strange stick hung across his back. It was shaped like a stick, at least, but it was black and smooth like basalt. Clearly it was one of the magical artifacts humans used, though Fig could not guess its purpose. She feared it.

I must not fear him, Fig told herself. *He's my father. I must go to him.*

She took a deep breath, steeling herself. She was about to jump from the tree when a voice came from the cave.

"Joe? Joe, you all right?"

Fig froze, still hiding among the branches. Below her, Red Scar tensed and crouched in the tall grass.

A woman stepped out from the cave. A young woman. Fig stared in silent wonder.

She's beautiful. Her jaw dropped. *She's the most beautiful thing I've ever seen.*

The woman looked nothing like Figaro, who was scrawny and covered in sap and burrs. She looked nothing like Lifa, who was wrinkled and bent. This woman was … Fig had never seen anything so perfect. The woman's face was smooth and white like fresh snow. Hair the color of fire cascaded down to her waist. Even from this distance, Fig could see the blue of her eyes. Her body was full and strong and healthy.

Fig felt ugly. Skinny. A little pest like a tick that crawled out from the mud.

"Well, well, Simone," Joe said. "Finally up from your nap?"

The woman—this *Simone*—placed her arms around Joe. "Yep! Why aren't you making me coffee?"

Fig hissed. Below the tree, Red Scar heard her. He tensed and hissed too.

My father took a new mate! Fig thought. *After my mother died, he found another female!*

She began to shake. She was in danger, she knew. Fig had seen this happen in her pack. Achillobators mated for life. But in the harsh wilderness of Mintari, life could be short. Sometimes a mate died, perhaps in battle, perhaps from a snakebite, a wasting tick disease, or starvation during a long winter. Sometimes bators became widowers, left alone to raise their chicks.

Those chicks were in great danger.

During mating season, a widower was up for grabs. Strong, hungry females would court him. Aggressively. Sometimes a particularly aggressive female, desperate to breed, would kill a widower's hatchlings. She would then mate with the grieving male and lay her own eggs. It was brutal. It was cruel. But it was the law of survival. On Mintari, they all had to play this Darwinian game. A dead female was a weak female, and so her weak hatchlings must die. And a strong female wasn't afraid to kill them.

Right now this redhead was the strong, hungry female, gunning for the widower. Her babies would be strong, beautiful, healthy. Everything Fig was not.

That meant it was open season on Fig.

If Simone learns I'm his hatchling, she'll kill me, Fig knew. *She's big and strong. I'm a runt. She'll want to replace me with her own offspring.*

Fig hunched down lower among the fronds.

"Joe, you all right?" Simone said. The air was still, and her voice carried clearly across the distance.

"I thought I sensed something," Joe said.

"Sensed something?" Simone cocked her head.

"Yes. Maybe I heard it. Or smelled it. Or maybe just imagined it. Something ... new. But very old." He shook his head. "Probably nothing."

Red Scar tensed in the tall grass, ready to race forward to battle. Hiding above him in the tree, Fig made soft cooing sounds, too soft for Joe and Simone to hear. The bator calmed down.

"Come back inside, Joe," Simone said. "Make me coffee. I demand it."

He turned away from the wilderness. "Geez, princess, were you so bossy back on Cloventia with your servants?"

She gasped and placed her hands on her hips. "I did not have servants on Cloventia!"

"And you don't have them here. *You* make us coffee."

Simone snorted. "Oh please! Last time I made coffee, you said it tasted like mud."

"Fine!" Joe said. "I'll show you how to make a proper brew. You'll learn from the master. You see, the trick is all in how you grind the beans ..."

He reentered the cave, and his voice faded.

Just then, Red Scar let out a snorting cough. The bator had been holding it in.

Simone, who was halfway into the cave, paused. She looked at the wilderness. Right at the tree and grass where Fig and her bator hid.

Fig froze, not even daring to breathe.

She'll kill me. Oh stars above, she'll kill me. She's bigger, healthier, stronger. I'm dead.

Simone remained standing for a while longer outside, frowning at the area where Fig hid.

"Simone, you coming?" came Joe's voice from the cave. "You're missing this!" A grinding rumble came from inside.

"Coming, oh coffee master." She rolled her eyes. Muttering something under her breath, the redhead reentered the cave.

Fig exhaled in relief. For now, she was safe. Clearly this "Simone" was a vicious predator. A part of Fig suspected she was being silly. Sure, Fig was small. But she had taken down parasaurs before. Could she really not handle Simone? But Fig was used to hunting parasaurs. This was something alien. Frightening. In this strange land, her courage faltered.

She climbed off the tree and knelt beside Red Scar in the tall grass.

The bator tilted his head. "Arroooo?" *Are we going into their cave?*

"Heeeuuurrrrr," Fig purred. *Not yet. Caution.*

Red Scar snorted and twitched his sickle claw. Achillobators were patient hunters, but they did not like waiting this long. Red Scar was getting restless. He wanted to do what bators do. Run, hunt, eat. Not skulk in the tall grass for hours on end.

Fig didn't like skulking either. But she found herself torn. Should she return to the pack, live the rest of her life as a bator? Or should she summon her courage, enter the cave, and challenge Simone?

She felt trapped between two worlds. She stood at a crossroads. One path led toward life in the wilderness, wild and free, running with the bators. Another path led to humanity. To language, tools, clothes, a life unlike any other on Mintari, as foreign to her as life underwater or above the clouds. She must choose.

Red Scar purred and nuzzled her. *Choose me.*

Fig embraced him. She loved the bator. He was her dearest friend. Her family. Her pack. So many nights, she had found warmth among his feathers, shedding her tears into his plumage. So many days, she found courage in his strength, in the sharpness of his teeth and the swiftness of his claws. She had ridden him on so many hunts, had shared meat and her innermost secrets with him. How could she abandon Red Scar and his pack?

She turned to leave, to abandon this silly quest for humanity, to return to the pack where she belonged.

But after a few steps, she paused. She hesitated.

For years, she had thought herself an achillobator. Smaller than the others, certainly. A weird, malformed runt, yes. But still a bator. Now that she knew the truth, how could she live with the pack again? Would not her curiosity torment her, the lingering question: *What if?*

No. She had walked too far down the path of humanity. She had met the girl on the hill. She had met Lifa, her grandmother. She had seen her father on the mountainside.

I know who I am now.

"Fi-ga-ro."

She could no longer turn back. Tears streamed down her cheeks, wetting Red Scar's feathers.

I'll wait until night, she thought. *I'll sneak in while Simone is asleep. I'll talk to my father.*

The day went by in nervous anticipation. This was megaraptor country, and the big predators hunted by scent. Normally, Fig would be dead by now. Without a pack, a bator rarely lasted long. Especially not a puny thing like Figaro Triplehorn. Thankfully, Lifa had gifted her a jar of aromatic herbs. The old shaman had taught Fig how to crush the leaves, then smear them across herself to mask her smell. Fig had perfumed herself and Red Scar with the pungent ointment, and no megaraptor approached. The herbs seemed to work. It was probably how Lifa had survived so long in the wild.

Red Scar remained ever at her side. Fig had cooed to him, urged him to return to the pack. Every day that passed, Fig knew, Crooked Wing would grow bolder, more dominant. If Red Scar tarried too long, he would return to find that Crooked Wing had usurped him. He would then be driven away to die alone, too old already to form a new pack. The achillobator must know this. Yet he chose to remain with Fig. To guard her for as long as she needed. He had several offspring in the pack, but they were grown and strong. To him, Fig was like an eternal hatchling, one he would die to protect.

Sunset draped the land in gold. The stars wheeled across the sky. In the spring and summer, a glowing little spiral appeared in the night sky. The shape reminded Fig of a seashell, and it was about the size of a seashell held at arm's length. It wasn't a moon or a star but something unique. Next time Fig met her grandmother, she would ask the shaman about the meaning of the glowing spiral. But one thing Fig already knew. When the spiral reached its zenith during early spring, it was midnight.

And it was time to meet her father.

Red Scar was sound asleep. Fig kissed him on the snout, then tiptoed among the trees. She scurried from cycad to cycad, bounding across the foothills, and reached the mountainside. The cave was high up, but Fig was small and quick and a good climber. She scurried up the mountainside like a little brown spider.

She inched toward the cave, prepared to sneak inside, gently wake her father, and speak to him while Simone slept.

But the way was blocked.

Enormous teeth filled the cave! They were long and gray. Fig reached out, gingerly touched a tooth, then pulled her hand back. Hard and cold! Not a tooth. It felt more like basalt. Some strange material humans could wield. More magic.

Fig examined these "teeth" more closely. The strange sticks were placed in a palisade. Perhaps Fig could squeeze between them? She stepped closer, pressed her face between two sticks, and—

A feathered creature leaped toward her—from inside the cave!

Fig stumbled back.

A snout thrust between the hard sticks, and the creature screeched.

Fig exhaled in relief. She had nearly wet herself. It was only a velociraptor, a creature so small she could kick it over the mountaintop.

A deep, weary voice rumbled inside the cave. "Vinnie? Vinnie, are you growling out the bars again?"

The raptor looked over his shoulder and whined.

"Shut up!" rose the sleepy voice. "Just pee in your pot. I'm trying to sleep."

The velociraptor glared at Fig between the metal sticks—bars, as Joe called them.

"Go ... pee ... yo' pa'!" Fig said.

The raptor growled, snapped his teeth at her, then loped back to his master.

Fig waited, then inched closer to the bars. She peered into the shadowy cave. She couldn't see Joe from here. It was too dark. But she could make out Simone's flaming-red hair. The woman was sound asleep. Vinnie sat by the slumbering redhead, scowling at Fig. Clearly the velociraptor considered himself something of a bodyguard.

Fig tested the bars again. They were made to keep dinosaurs out. Fig, who was smaller than all but the smallest dinosaurs, was able to squeeze between two bars. Vinnie groaned and huffed but dared not wake his master again.

Fig crept through the cave. She had expected something like a typical theropod cave, full of old bones, shed feathers, eggshells, and rancid meat. But she found a place as cozy as Lifa's hut. Rugs covered the floor. Paintings of dinosaurs spread across the stony walls. A fireplace glowed with embers.

Simone was still asleep, lying on a sort of elevated platform built of wood and topped with fabric. It must be similar to the beds of leaves, feathers, and supple twigs achillobators built in their nesting grounds. Joe, meanwhile, slept on the floor. A T-rex skull rested in the back of the cave, filled with fabric beddings—somebody had turned the skull into a sort of nest. But nobody slept there.

Fig paused in the darkness, considering. Mated bators often slept nuzzled together. Were humans the same? If Joe and Simone were sleeping separately, maybe they were not mates after all. Maybe Fig was safe. Maybe Simone would not murder her, then try to bear a child to replace her.

She stepped around the redhead, tiptoeing toward her father. He sniffed, grunted in his sleep, and rolled over. Fig probably still smelled of Lifa's herbs. She cringed. She had gotten used to the smell. Of course Joe and Simone would smell her!

Simone sniffed too, rolled over, but kept sleeping soundly.

Vinnie hissed at Fig, then let out a deafening shriek.

Fig froze, heart pounding.

Joe leaped up. "Tar it, Vinnie, what is it?"

The tall, bearded man rose from the rug, looking around.

Fig crouched behind the T-rex skull, peering from the shadows. Joe blinked, rubbed his eyes, but could not see her.

Fig wanted to leap out, to tell him, "I am your daughter!" But fear pounded through her. She could understand language, but she could barely speak it. What if Joe didn't understand? What if he thought her a thief? What if he beat her while she begged? Again, all the worst-case scenarios rattled through her mind. Fear paralyzed her.

Vinnie grabbed Joe's leg with his clawed little hand. He began pulling Joe toward the T-rex skull, whimpering.

"Vinnie, what is it?" Joe said. "If it's a mouse, just—"

A loud beeping filled the cave.

Hiding behind the skull, Fig cringed. The sound! It was so loud and jarring. Like the *yip yip yip* of a ferocious raptor. She covered her ears. At first she thought it was Vinnie. But the velociraptor stood silently, his mouth closed.

The beeping woke up Simone. She blinked and rubbed her eyes. "What is it?" she mumbled.

Joe lifted a strange box from an alcove. Another photo album? No, this was some other form of magic. When Joe tapped the box, it went silent. Light shone from the box, illuminating Joe's face.

Fig peeked from behind the skull. She got her first good, up-close look at her father. He was a tall man. If she stood beside him, she guessed, she would not reach his shoulders. And broad shoulders those were, and his arms were muscular. Fig had always thought humans were all like her. Weak, skinny little things. But Joe looked like a predator, lean and powerful. It scared her.

Yet when she looked more closely, she saw more to him. She saw herself.

Their faces were different. His was harder, older, and sprouted hair. But the similarities were there. It was the tension in his muscles, always ready to spring forward. It was the dark somberness in his eyes. It was the tightness in his jaw. It was his body language which called out: *I am a human. I have no claws or fangs. But I'm strong. I bite.*

There could be no doubt now. This man was her father.

Joe lowered the device. He looked at Simone. "It's a call from the Rangers. Red Alert. The highest alert possible. Dinovia City is under attack."

Daniel Arenson

CHAPTER TWENTY
Ruler of the Pack

Joe rushed out the cave into the night. His sleep-or-die was slung across his back. His ceratop hat topped his head. Fire blazed inside him.

Dinovia City. Under attack.

His belly knotted, his heart raced, and his upper lip twitched in a sneer. The news had just come in. An urgent call for all Rangers across Mintari.

The city gates had fallen. The enemy was within. Joe knew who was behind this.

My murderous sister.

The twin moons lit the night. Standing here on Mudge Mountain, Joe could see the cycads on the foothills, the grassy plains of Hell Valley, and the dim shadows of Marshwood Forest. The city lay beyond the horizon.

Simone emerged from the cave too, hopping on one foot, then another, as she struggled to pull on her boots. "How will we get to the city? I hope not flying on dactyls again."

Joe shook his head. "We don't need a plane for this battle. We need a tank."

He placed his fingers into his mouth and whistled. The sound pierced the morning, carrying across the forested foothills and grassy plains. Roused from their sleep, dinosaurs raised their heads from their blankets of shadows. Their eyes gleamed in the moonlight. Then they returned to slumber. The sound must have just been some crazy dactyl, they figured. They were tired after a long day of hunting and eating, and they returned to their slumber.

All but one dinosaur.

This dinosaur had spent the past few days trudging across the wilderness, vacuuming up plants. He was wounded, but with every bush, fern, and tree devoured, he grew stronger. His body bore the scars of many battles. Carnivore teeth were lodged into his bony crest. Scratches covered his horns. His scaly hide still showed the marks of claws.

He was a triceratops. A big male bull. Among the strongest dinosaurs on Mintari. He had fought many great battles and won them all. He had crushed the dreaded sinraptors and allosaurs. He had even defeated the terrible spinosaurus and giganotosaurus. He was the terror of every carnivore on Mintari. He was like a living tank, an unstoppable beast, and there was no foe his horns could not slay. When he heard that whistle, he knew its meaning. He trudged through the grass and trees, not even pausing to eat. His friend summoned him.

Standing on the hillside, Joe and Simone saw the colossal shadow move through the foothills, knocking down cycads.

Dozer emerged from among the trees, snorted, and stamped his pillar-like feet. He was not a great mountain climber, so he waited at the foothills. Joe and Simone climbed down the mountainside to him.

Dozer lowered his enormous one-ton head. Joe hugged him, kissed his beak, and rubbed the base of his horns. The trike licked him and made low, affectionate grunts.

"Get a room, you too," Simone said.

Joe ignored her. "How are you, friend?" he whispered to his dinosaur.

Dozer rumbled and grunted. *Good. Strong. Ready. Let's fight.*

"Dozer, a pack of T-rexes is attacking the city," Joe said. "And they say a big black T-rex is among them." A shudder ran through him. "Ivan."

The T-rex that killed my wife and unborn child.

Joe's eyes stung. His jaw tightened. Ivan. He was still alive. He was back.

Dozer grunted and nuzzled him. Joe sometimes swore that the trike could understand him. Many offworlders thought dinosaurs were dumb, lumbering beasts, evolutionary failures revived and displayed here as theme park attractions. But Joe knew they were vibrant, intelligent, sentient beasts. If Dozer could not understand his words, he understood the emotion behind them.

The trike placed the tip of his beak on the ground, turning his head into a ramp. Joe grabbed the animal by the horns, climbed up his head, and hopped onto his back. Simone followed, a little clumsier, but she managed to climb the dinosaur without help. This time she sat in front of Joe. Better that way. She could hold Dozer's frill instead of crushing Joe between her arms.

Joe had decided to leave Vinnie behind. A battle was no place for a little velociraptor. Too easy for a trike or T-rex to crush the pint-sized raptor underfoot. Joe looked back at the cave, which yawned open on the mountainside above. Vinnie stood just outside the barred opening, watching him, yellow eyes glowing in the moonlight. The diminutive dinosaur was slender enough to squeeze between the bars. If he got hungry, he could go inside and raid the pantry. The poor guy was probably feeling left out, but he stayed put, obeying his master.

"Goodbye, Vinnie!" Joe called up toward the cave. "I'll be home soon. Hold down the fort."

Vinnie cawed, chattered, and tossed his head. He was not happy about being left behind. But the little raptor understood.

"Now ride, Dozer!" Joe said, patting the big dinosaur he sat on. "We must ride faster than ever before."

The triceratops shook his head, a gesture he had learned from Joe. He snorted.

"Dozer, ride!" Joe said. "The city needs us."

Again the trike shook his head. He reared on his back legs, opened his beak wide, and bellowed. Joe had never heard him cry out so loudly. The sound aroused sleeping dinosaurs across the land. Dactyls took flight from their mountainside nests, screeching. Grunts and groans and hoots sounded across the grasslands. A second time Dozer howled, a sound that echoed across the land. Still he did not ride, only kicked his front feet in the air.

"What's wrong with him?" Simone cried. With Dozer rearing, most of her weight was pressed against Joe. He wrapped his arms around her, securing her in place.

"I don't know!" he said. "He's never done this before! Maybe he doesn't want to leave Vinnie?"

A third time Dozer cried out … then finally lowered himself onto all fours, snorted, and was still.

For a moment nothing happened.

Then the land shook.

Trees collapsed. Stones cascaded down the hillsides. Dactyls fled across the moonlit sky, and grunts and grumbles filled the night.

They came from the grasslands. At first Joe saw only shadowy lumps. They moved closer, stampeding, splashing across streams, tearing down cycads. Steam rose from their backs. Their horns pierced the mist.

More triceratops.

They stampeded uphill. A full eight of them. Each one was bigger than a mammoth. Combined, they were a hundred tons of herbivorous fury.

Simone gasped. "Dozer, it's your family!"

Dozer snorted with pride. The eight other trikes came to stand around him. They ranged from young, powerful females to gruff old males with lumpy gray skin. The youngest looked barely full-grown, a cocky bull who snorted and reared and kicked the air. The older ones were larger, bulkier, and bore battle scars like badges of honor. One old bull was missing his central horn. One cow sported a row of T-rex teeth embedded into her frill; the bone had healed around the teeth, locking them in place. But every one, even the oldest and most scarred, was a force to be reckoned with. Together they were an army.

Simone looked over her shoulder at Joe. Her eyes were wide. "Where did they come from? What does this mean?"

"It means war." Joe slapped Dozer's side. "Now ride!"

Dozer reared in the moonlight, and his cry pierced the night. The trikes began to run. They charged through the brush, crushing reeds, bushes, and trees. The land seemed to shake. Joe held on tightly, and a savage grin spread across his face.

You declared war on this world, Amissa. Mintari is ready to fight back.

Hiding among the ferns, Fig watched and heard it all happen. The triceratops herd gathering. Joe and Simone mounting one of the horned herbivores, a scarred bull named Dozer. Talk of war at a city across the horizon.

Fig wasn't sure what a "city" was, but it sounded important. Possibly it was the nesting grounds of a large human pack. And T-rexes were attacking it.

A shudder passed through Fig. Long after the trikes vanished into the distance, she remained hidden.

With trembling lips, she took a stab at pronouncing a human word. "T-wik."

Well, she tried. In her mind, she heard it clearly. T-rex. But while she could understand human language pretty well, she struggled to speak it. Her mouth was used to making achillobator sounds. Her tongue stumbled around human words.

While she could not speak it, the word *T-rex* haunted her, a ghost from early childhood. She knew what the word meant. The shaman had used that word to describe the huge, ravenous predators. Every dinosaur on Mintari knew them. Every dinosaur had a word for them, be it a grunt, snort, yowl, or pheromone that cried out: *flee!*

Achillobators referred to T-rexes with a high-pitched, raspy screech. It was the harshest, loudest sound they could make. The pack feared these colossal carnivores. All dinosaurs did. Even the mighty triceratops gave them a wide berth. Even the heavily armored ankylosaurus avoided them, and those brutes could shatter boulders with their clubbed tails. Fig had seen a T-rex only once and only from a distance—a towering monster prowling in the sunset, his scales black, his eyes red. It was years ago. To this day, she sometimes dreamed that the dreaded meat eater was chasing her, and she woke up drenched in cold sweat.

That was no ordinary T-rex she had seen, Fig knew. She remembered his name. A name her caretaker had whispered by the fire in darkest nights. The shamans worshipped him as a god.

"Ayyyyvum," Fig whispered.

Ivan. King of Mintari.

Oh gosh, she needed to practice speaking. Well, there would be time for that later. Right now her father was riding toward the human nesting grounds. To battle Ivan and his pack of tyrannosaurs. It was foolish. Even with an army of triceratops, he could not do this. Perhaps Joe did not know how terrible T-rexes were.

But Fig knew. And she knew that Ivan was not just the deadliest dinosaur on Mintari. She remembered what Lifa had told her.

Ivan killed my mother.

This was personal. This was Fig's fight too. She must go help her father.

She turned toward Red Scar. The bator was crouched in the tall grass. He had been patient so far, watching her from hiding, ready to pounce if she needed help. But he was getting restless. An achillobator did not like skulking around like a mammal. He was born to run, hunt, fight, mate, and eat. Not hide in bushes. His muscles were tense, and his feathers bristled. But despite his nearly overpowering instincts, he had remained at her side, spying on the humans. He met her eyes.

What now? his gaze asked.

Fig pointed westward. Bators pointed with their snouts, and Fig did the best she could with her small nose. She purred, the word for a nesting ground. Then she marched around, legs as straight as sticks, chattering and gesturing with her hands. *Humans.* She pointed her nose westward again. *There's a human nest that way.*

Red Scar snorted and shook his feathers. *So? I care not!*

Fig repeated her chattering and funny walk, emulating a human nest. Then she tossed her head back and added a grainy screech that left her throat raw.

T-rexes. T-rexes at the human nest.

Red Scar snarled. He took two steps back. *We are strong, but we cannot win such a fight.*

Fig shook her head. "Aroorororrorroo!" *No, we must fight!*

He hissed, tossed his head, and mewled. *We'll die.*

Fig snorted and took a few steps westward. *Then I'll go alone.*

Red Scar hurried toward her, his sickle claws raised. *I won't leave you.* His red feathers bristled, and he bared rows of sharp teeth. *If you go, I go too.*

She bared her own decidedly less-impressive teeth. *We will fight together.* Then she lost her snarl and hugged him, burying her face in his feathers. She cooed softly. *I love you.*

The big, scarred predator licked her. *I'm always here for you, little one. We are pack.*

He crouched, and Fig leaped onto his back, straddling him. She tugged his feathers. But they were not heading west. Not just yet.

They both knew they could not do this alone. They needed help. They must summon the pack.

Amissa strutted across the drawbridge, a rifle in her hands, a grin on her face. Like a victorious empress, she passed through the breached gateway, entering the city.

The huge oaken doors lay shattered at her feet. The pachycephalosaurus had made short work of them. Ranger corpses lay among the splinters—the work of her assassins. Amissa refused to feel any guilt. These Rangers had started this war. They knew what they were getting into. Their blood was on their own hands.

A groan sounded below.

"Please ... help ... please."

Amissa walked toward the sound. A Ranger lay in the rubble, gurgling. Bullets bled across his torso. His skin was gray, his eyes sunken. He looked at Amissa.

"Help ... please."

He reached out a shaky hand to her.

She raised her rifle.

His eyes widened. A tear fled down his cheek. "Wait. Wait, I have kids, I—"

She fired a bullet between his eyes. He slumped down dead.

It was funny. It had not been long since her first human kill. Back then, she had felt nauseated, had nearly fainted. By now, shooting a man was no different from shooting an animal. No, she decided. It was even less than that. When she killed an animal, she felt a sense of pride. Now Amissa felt nothing.

"You are nothing, Rangers. Nothing more than mud beneath my boots. I will crush you, then wipe you away."

She walked deeper into the city, her smoking rifle in her hands. These little Rangers were a distraction. Pawns, that was all. She hunted a specific Ranger.

"Where are you, brother?" she whispered. "Do you still hide in the wilderness like a coward while your city weeps?"

No. He would come. Joe was foolhardy that way. His sense of nobility would kick in. He would come save those who had rejected him. And he would meet Amissa's gun. What a noble fool!

A rumble sounded far ahead, rippling through the city and interrupting her navel-gazing. Screams followed.

A smile spread across Amissa's face. Her pets were at work.

She walked down the cobbled road, moving between chunks of wood, scattered bricks, and corpses. The dead lay everywhere. Not all were Rangers. Not all were in one piece. A severed arm lay on the road, still holding a basket of fruit. Dates and persimmons spilled across the bloodied cobblestones. A house wall was cracked. A balcony had collapsed, shattering dozens of clay pots. Chrysanthemums lay in crimson puddles.

Huge three-toed footprints had cracked the cobblestones. Amissa followed the trail of destruction. It looked like a hurricane had passed through Dinovia. The round, clay houses were cracked, some shattered. Most people hid in their homes. Others ran down the streets. A pigtailed girl was wailing, holding a pink pliosaurus toy, calling out miserably for her mother. Amissa kept walking through the pathetic throng of crying, fleeing cowards.

She stepped into a city square, and her smile widened.

Two of the T-rexes were there, wreaking havoc. One was male, the other female. Both were equally gargantuan. They must have weighed ten tons each, maybe more. Their powerful feet crushed cobblestones. Their scaly tails swung, shattering buildings. Their tiny-yet-powerful hands grabbed balconies, ripping them off buildings. Their enormous snouts shoved through windows, sniffing, cracking the walls around them. A few corpses lay on the ground, crushed.

They were not randomly destroying the city. T-rexes were not movie monsters, hell-bent on destruction. There was purpose to their mayhem. These two were a bonded pair, and they were looking for their eggs.

Rattlesnake and the other hunters had hidden these eggs. Now a pack of T-rexes were stampeding through the city on a frenetic Easter egg hunt. Deep rumbles shook the city. Human screams pierced the night. The T-rexes would stop at nothing to get their eggs back. A lot of humans filled this city. A lot of humans stood in their way. And so a lot of humans were dying.

The big female T-rex stomped toward a round clay house. She grabbed the walls with her ridiculously small hands, steadying herself, then thrust her gargantuan muzzle through a second-story window. Her snout didn't fit properly. Chunks of clay fell to the ground. The T-rex shoved her head deeper, seeking her eggs. Screams sounded from inside the home. A gunshot boomed. The female rex screeched and pulled her head out from the window. A bullet hole bled on her snout. With a deep growl, she swung her tail again and again, shattering the house. The clay walls collapsed. Screams rose from inside, then fell silent.

I guess there are no eggs in that house, Amissa thought. *Not anymore, at least.*

Meanwhile, the big male T-rex was digging, tossing aside cobblestones and the underlying soil. He must be seeking the eggs underground. Before long, the beast hit a gas pipe, and a steaming geyser blasted from underground. The male T-rex stumbled back, grunting in annoyance. As he retreated, his claws sparked against the cobblestones. The gas leak caught fire. Flames roared skyward, lighting the square. The rexes howled and stepped back. The huge predators feared nothing but fire.

Amissa stared in wonder, eyes wide. The firelight washed over her. It was beautiful. Such beautiful destruction!

An engine roared.

A jippi rumbled into the square. Rangers leaned out the windows, aiming rifles at the rampaging rexes. They fired.

They were firing live bullets.

They were panicking, Amissa knew. Tranquilizers took a while to work. The fabled Rangers, the so-called conservationists of Mintari, were now trying to kill dinosaurs. Hypocrites!

Bullets plowed into the T-rex pair. They howled, trapped between flames and rifles. The female recoiled, stumbling into an alleyway, but the male was having none of it. Overcoming his fear of fire, the big rex charged. He ran around the flaming geyser, heading toward the Ranger jippi. Bullets crashed into him. His green scales chipped. Blood splashed the cobblestones. But still the T-rex charged.

The Rangers put their jippi in reverse. Too slow. The T-rex leaned down and caught the vehicle in his gargantuan jaws. A Tyrannosaurus rex had the strongest bite force of any animal nature had ever produced. The legendary predator could bite down with 35,000 newtons of force. That was equivalent to the weight of a full-grown Asian elephant pressing down on each single tooth. The T-rex crushed the jippi like it was made of tinfoil. The Rangers inside tried to jump out. They didn't make it. The terrible jaws ripped them apart.

With a flick of his neck, the T-rex tossed the jippi aside. The vehicle flew through the air, crashed into a house, and shattered the walls.

Amissa walked across the square, stepping around piles of debris and bodies. The firelight lit her way. The two T-rexes spun toward her, snarling. They were mad with fear, pain, and worry for their eggs. They stomped toward her, their great jaws opening, baring teeth the size of bananas.

"You are magnificent!" Amissa said as they charged toward her.

She pulled a gun from her belt and fired.

But she was not firing a bullet. And not firing at the T-rexes. She fired a cannister full of pheromones, aiming at a nearby street. The cannister banged off a haberdashery wall, then skidded across the road, leaking aromatic gasses.

The rexes spun toward the smells, forgetting all about Amissa. The scientists at Triplehorn Tech had crafted these cannisters. Many dinosaurs communicated with pheromones, excreting them in their urine, droppings, saliva, or from glands in their skin. The chemicals formed a complex language, one nearly as elaborate as human languages. The cannister Amissa had fired leaked a pheromone tyrannosaurs used to challenge rivals during breeding season. The T-rexes inhaled the scent. Their minds translated it as a furious cry: "Hey, you! I'm going to breed with your mate! If you get in my way, I'll attack you!"

The T-rex couple forgot all about Amissa. They thundered after the cannister, seeking the invisible challengers. They were intelligent predators, but instincts burned hot in dinosaurs. They could not resist the infuriating lure of these pheromones. On their way, they crashed through buildings, overturned jippis, and tore through a water pipe. A torrent gushed skyward, washed over the fire, and an eruption of steam flowed over the city. A few people were fleeing their shattered homes. The female T-rex stomped on one running man, flattening him against the cobblestones. The male scooped up a woman, crushed her in his jaws, and gulped down the remains.

Amissa kept walking through the city. More tyrannosaurs rampaged everywhere. Three big males, their scales dark green and their backs spiky, were swinging their tails against buildings, cracking walls, then rummaging through the ruins for their eggs. Whenever they encountered a human, they snapped their mouths or lashed their tails, crushing these annoying mammals who got in their way. To them, humans were little more than gadflies.

A Ranger emerged onto a roof and fired his rifle, hitting one of the green males. With a deafening grumble, the T-rex spun around, charged, and barreled into the building. His teeth scraped the rooftop. The Ranger leaped off the roof in a desperate attempt to flee. He landed hard on the pavement, breaking both legs, and screamed. The rex scooped him up and gulped him down.

This was all fine and dandy, but it would take the T-rexes weeks to destroy the city house by house. Amissa needed them to destroy more quality targets. She loaded a fresh cannister, climbed onto a nearby house, and saw it there.

Pangaea Hall.

It rose three or four blocks away, its domed roof looming over smaller buildings like a rising stone sun. Inspired by the Pantheon of Rome, Pangaea Hall was the largest, finest building on Mintari, built over four hundred years ago. Of course, on Cloventia it would barely be an outhouse, but here on Mintari, this building was legendary. Amissa stared, her lips tight. From that grand rotunda, the tyrannical government of Mintari reigned.

They would soon learn who the true rulers of Mintari were.

Amissa fired her cannister. It flew over buildings, passed between two columns, and clattered down onto Pangaea Hall's portico.

The three green T-rexes spun around at once, sniffing.

So did other rexes across the city. Amissa could see their heads swiveling across the neighborhood, staring over rooftops toward Pangaea Hall. The cannister leaked blue mist. These pheromones smelled like T-rex eggs. Eggs in peril.

The intoxicated predators charged, crashing through homes, racing toward Pangaea Hall. They reached the rotunda but found no eggs. They began ripping the curtain walls off, shattering the columns, seeking eggs that were not there.

I control them, Amissa thought. *I harnessed this might. This is the greatest army on Mintari. And it's mine.*

But as she watched the tyrannosaurs destroy Pangaea Hall, she noticed something. The greatest T-rex among them was not here.

Where was the mutant? The giant with black scales? Where was King Ivan?

Then she heard the distant rumble. It sounded nothing like the sounds the other rexes made. This sound was like a trumpet heralding an army of demons. It was like a foghorn from the depths of the abyss. It was a storm from hell, rolling through heaven.

The shamans worshipped Ivan as a god. Amissa could almost understand them. This was the cry of a dark deity.

And there he came, stomping through the city, crushing jippis, shattering buildings with his tail.

God, he was enormous. He towered over the buildings around him. His scales were darker than the night. Spikes like the blades of Lucifer sprouted from his back. His teeth were forks of lightning. His eyes were red cauldrons where the souls of sinners burned. In his jaws, he carried three corpses. His arms were perhaps small for his body, but they were large enough to carry one corpse with each hand.

He was boasting of his kills. He was not like the others, who simply cared about their eggs. When the other rexes killed, it was merely because humans got in their way. Ivan was different. Ivan delighted in killing for its own sake. With every step, he swung his tail and lashed his claws, slaying bystanders, covering the city with blood. Bullets bounced off his scales. Tranquilizer darts shattered against him. With a deafening rumble, he swept his tail through a crowd of Rangers, snapping their bones. He lunged at fleeing citizens, crushed them in his jaws, and spat them out. He was the angel of death passing over the city.

As he stomped toward city hall, the other T-rexes paused from their frantic search, stepped back, and bowed their heads in submission. They were enormous beasts. True giants. The greatest predators nature had ever crafted. And they were small by Ivan. The mutant black T-rex dominated them all. He was the true king of Mintari.

The beast swung his tail, destroying what remained of Pangaea Hall. The dome collapsed, burying anyone unlucky enough to remain inside. Ivan climbed onto the hill of broken stone, beams, and columns. He towered above all the other T-rexes in his pack. Clouds gathered above as if summoned by his very presence. Lightning flashed, illuminating his scales and terrible teeth. He tossed back his head, and his rumbling cry masked the sound of thunder.

Amissa stood in the courtyard, staring. And something strange happened.

Terror gripped her.

Terror like icy claws inside her.

"What have I done?" she whispered.

Fig and Red Scar ran hard across the grasslands.

She did not ride the achillobator today. They had a long way to travel, and Red Scar would need to conserve his strength. Fig didn't weigh much, but she didn't want to add even an extra feather of weight onto Red Scar today.

They ran side by side through the night, panting and tired but pushing themselves onward. The land rose and fell around them. It was a hard run for both of them. Achillobators were sprinters, not marathon runners. Humans were good at long-distance running, but they were slow. Each pushed themselves to their limits tonight. They both knew the stakes.

They must summon the pack. And fast.

Fig understood maps, but Red Scar led the way tonight. The pack left scent markers across the land. While bators communicated to some degree with yowls, growls, and yelps, their language mostly used smells. The wind carried the pheromones across forests and glens, warning all that here was a pack of achillobators. *If you are one of us, come closer for mating. Any other predator—stay away!*

Red Scar wasn't interested in mating tonight. He was an old bator and had already sired many hatchlings. What he craved was power. The pack was his, and he would reign again. And Fig was determined to help.

Finally, winded and wheezing, they saw the pack.

They stood by a moonlight stream. The achillobators had just taken down a juvenile iguanodon. Adult iguanodons were too dangerous to hunt. They were powerful, multiton herbivores, and their thumb spikes could easily kill a bator. So the pack normally waited in hiding for a juvenile to wander off. Then they pounced. Tonight's catch was just a yearling, but the young iguanodon was already bigger than any bator. The meat would feed the entire pack.

As Fig drew closer, she noticed something that made her wince. The iguanodon was still alive. The bators were ripping into its belly, sticking their snouts in, and feeding on the delicious entrails. The iguanodon twitched and kicked as the pack ate him alive. The smell of meat, blood, and offal filled the air, masking all other scents. The bators didn't even notice Red Scar and Fig. They were busy feasting. It was a grand old time. A banquet.

In Fig's absence, some eggs must have hatched. A brood of bator hatchlings bustled around, nipping at bones, sniffing at meat. One hungry hatchling leaped into the carcass to feed on the soft innards. Half Tail, a big male with many scars, tried to pull the greedy youngster out. The hatchling's mother growled, snapped her teeth, and shoved Half Tail aside. A few other hatchlings chewed on the iguanodon's tail, but their teeth were too small to pierce the scaly skin, and they must keep ducking as the iguanodon kicked. Their mothers ripped off bits of meat and fed their youngsters. The big herbivore finally stopped moving. It sometimes took a few bites to finally kill big prey.

Red Scar stomped forward, salivating. He was hungry after his long race, and the smell of food tugged his nostrils. He shoved his way between the other bators, reaching for a meaty iguanodon flank. Some of the younger females moved aside, making room for the big old male.

Before Red Scar could take a bite, a screech pierced the air.

A huge achillobator rose from behind the carcass, her jaws covered in blood. Her muscles rippled, and her red feathers bristled. She placed one foot atop the carcass, and her sickle claw twitched. One of her arms was crooked, the feathers white—an old injury from a fall down a cliff. But even with her injury, she was the strongest female in the pack.

Crooked Wing climbed onto the carcass, leaned down toward Red Scar, opened her bloody jaws wide, and shrieked. You didn't need to understand achillobator language to understand this.

There was a new sheriff in town. Red Scar was no longer welcome.

The old male bator took a step back.

Big mistake. That made him look weak. That emboldened Crooked Wing. She leaned closer to him, claws digging into the iguanodon carcass. She gazed down at him from her fleshy throne. A third time, she let out a terrible screech.

"Ayyyeeeeeeeeeeeeee! Ka, ka!"

The pack is mine! Be gone!

Her muscles twitched. Blood stained her teeth and claws, and her eyes blazed. The rest of the pack closed rank around her, gazing at Red Scar silently. They would not fight him. But they were showing their allegiance.

Your time is over, old one, they were saying. *Crooked Wing leads us now.*

Red Scar growled low in his throat. He was old. He was weary after his run. He had eaten nothing but fish and frogs these past few days. Now he faced a furious usurper, a big female who was younger and stronger. He growled threateningly, but he took another step back.

Crooked Wing raised her snout and yipped. She swung her head from side to side, looking at the others. *See? I told you. He's a weakling.*

Emboldened, Crooked Wing leaped off the carcass, landed on the grass ahead of Red Scar, and snapped her teeth. *Go, go!*

Red Scar growled. His feathers bristled. But he took another two steps back.

Crooked Wing cackled—an almost human display of laughter. She looked back at her pack. *See the weakling run!*

That was when Fig seized her chance.

She leaped toward Crooked Wing, her sickle claw flashing. The big bator was looking away. She never expected a runt to attack. Crooked Wing was several times Fig's size. But Fig lunged at her nonetheless, swung her sickle claw, and slashed through Crooked Wing's shoulder.

Feathers flew.

The bator screamed and kicked.

Fig leaped back, narrowly dodging her foe's claws. Crooked Wing had nearly disemboweled her.

The big bator stared at her, hissing, disbelieving. *How dare this runt attack me!* Blood trickled from her wound, beading over her feathers. But Fig had not cut deep. The thick layer of feathers had softened the blow.

Fig crouched, snarled, and raised her bloodied sickle claw. She snapped her teeth and slashed the air.

Crooked Wing quickly got over her shock. This impudent little runt had cut her! For too long, Crooked Wing had tolerated this mammal. No more. She did not belong in the pack. She belonged inside Crooked Wing's belly.

The bator lunged, reaching out her clawed wingtips. Bator wings were flightless but not useless. Mean claws gleamed on their tips. They were smaller than the claws on a bator's feet, but they were sharp enough to rip Fig to shreds. For a second, Fig could only stare in terror at the vision of oncoming death.

With a howl, Red Scar leaped forward.

He slammed into Crooked Wing with a *thunk*.

The two dinosaurs went down, snapping their jaws, kicking, clawing. The other bators surrounded them, hooting. Even the hatchlings watched and yipped. The meal was forgotten.

Fig leaped to her feet and faced the battle, her teeth bared, sickle claw in hand. She felt so small by the two battling bators. She was an ant watching scorpions duking it out.

But this ant could sting.

The two dinosaurs walked backward, putting more distance between them. They circled each other, maintaining eye contact. Their leg muscles stiffened, and their feathery tails stuck out straight. Then they both crouched, placing their bellies close to the ground. Like jousting knights, they were prepared to charge.

Fig bolted forward. While Red Scar was crouching, she leaped onto his back and tightened her legs around him.

With a screech, Cooked Wing pounced.

A split second later, Red Scar leaped toward her.

Both dinosaurs unleashed furious screeches. They slammed together. At once, they were biting and clawing. Crooked Wing twisted her shoulder away, narrowly dodging Red Scar's snapping jaws. She chomped down hard, catching Red Scar on the shoulder. Blood flowed between her teeth. Red Scar howled.

Riding his back, Fig leaned forward and plunged her sickle claw down.

The blade ripped across Crooked Wing's snout.

The bator opened her mouth to screech, releasing Red Scar's shoulder. Blood gushed from both dinosaurs. At once, Red Scar was lashing his wingtips. The claws ripped through his foe, tearing off feathers and strips of skin.

Crooked Wing stumbled back, shrieking, fluttering her clawed wings. *Unfair, unfair! Two against one!*

Fig didn't care. Nothing was fair on Mintari. Only survival mattered. Red Scar pressed the attack. He lunged forward, raised one leg, and lashed his sickle claw. Crooked Wing fell back another step. She thumped into the iguanodon carcass. Red Scar pinned her against the scaly corpse, lashing his claws, snapping his jaws, ripping out feathers. The big female landed a few blows of her own. Her clawed wingtip tore a gash along Red Scar's muzzle. One of her sickle claws nicked his leg, drawing blood.

Still riding Red Scar, Fig leaned forward, slashing her sickle claw. But she could not reach Crooked Wing. Curse her short arms! Fig rose to stand on Red Scar's back. For a moment she wobbled, arms windmilling. Then she leaped forward and landed on the dead iguanodon. Her feet almost slipped on the bloody hide.

The two bators battled below the corpse. Fig jumped again. This time she landed on Crooked Wing's back.

The female bator yowled. She bucked madly but could not shake Fig off. In a clever attempt, Crooked Wing leaped backward into the iguanodon, slamming Fig into the carcass with tremendous force. Normally, that would shatter Fig's bones. But the iguanodon's hard, scaly skin had been peeled away. Fig merely splashed into soft meat. Clinging onto Crooked Wing, she brought her sickle claw down hard.

Crooked Wing screeched.

Meanwhile, Red Scar kept attacking from the front. He clubbed Crooked Wing's jaw, knocking it aside. A tooth flew out.

Fig clung onto her foe. She climbed along Crooked Wing's back, nearing the bator's feathery neck. Reaching around, Fig placed her sickle claw against Crooked Wing's throat.

"HAEEEEeeee!" Fig cried. *Stop!* "Haeeee!" *Stop now!*

At once, Red Scar retreated and lowered his head.

Crooked Wing froze. She didn't like obeying the little mammal on her back. But she feared the claw on her neck. With a single movement, Fig could end the big bator's life. And Crooked Wing knew it.

"Haeee!" Fig said, more brusquely this time. *Enough!*

Crooked Wing made a sound halfway between growl and mewl.

"Harrrooo!" Fig said, shoving the back of Crooked Wing's neck. *Get down!*

The dinosaur obeyed. She lay down on the bloodied grass, panting. Her adrenaline was wearing off. She was bleeding, hurting. When Fig climbed off, Crooked Wing rolled onto her back, exposing her underbelly. *I surrender.*

Fig took a deep breath. *It's over. We won.*

But she had to make sure Crooked Wing was not humiliated, that she would not hold a grudge. Not against Fig or against Red Scar. A leader who led with fear would forever be looking over his shoulder, just waiting for his enemies to pounce. A leader who earned true respect and loyalty would command his pack forever. So Figaro knelt, and she began to lick Crooked Wing's wounds. It was a way of saying: *I can hurt you, but I can also heal you. If you rise against me, I will strike you down. But if you bow before me, I will raise you up.*

Red Scar knelt beside her, and he too began to lick Crooked Wing's wounds. The big female bator made soft, subservient purring sounds. She bared her teeth in something resembling a smile. In human body language, that indicated joy or mirth. Among achillobators, a smile was a show of submission, the opposite of a snarl.

You rule over me, Crooked Wing was saying. *I'm sorry. I serve you.*

Everyone in the pack had witnessed Crooked Wing beaten. And everyone had seen the mercy given and the mercy taken. She would never rise up again. The other bators would not accept it. Perhaps someday, after Red Scar died of old age, Crooked Wing might reign, or perhaps someday she would strike out on her own, form her own pack in another territory. But one thing was certain. She would never so much as snarl at Red Scar or Fig again.

"Yirrr yooorrr," Fig purred to Crooked Wing. Then she snarled, eyes blazing. "Yeeeuuur, yae yaep!"

I need more than your groveling. Will you fight for me?

Crooked Wing rose to her feet. She was bleeding, panting, but her tail struck out straight, and her upper lip peeled back. *I will fight.*

Fig turned to Red Scar next. He too was bleeding and panting. But none of his wounds were serious. Crooked Wing had not tried to kill him, it seemed, only to humiliate him and drive him away. Still, Fig took some of the healing herbs Lifa had given her. She crushed the leaves and placed them into his wounds. Red Scar winced but let her keep working. Crooked Wing would never allow anyone to touch her wounds like this—silly runt behavior! But Red Scar understood. He accepted Fig's medicine. His wounds stopped bleeding, and the herbs would prevent infection.

Fig stroked his snout, gestured with her chin, tilted her head, and mewled. *Can you run?*

He gave a low snort and crouched in the grass. *Climb on.*

Fig climbed onto his back, and he rose to his feet. She pointed northwest. She used her finger to point—a human mannerism.

"Hai, hai!" she barked.

Red Scar began to run, and the pack followed in the darkness. They left their meal behind for the scavengers, showing ultimate loyalty to their leader. Yet as they ran across the grasslands, Fig wondered: *Do they follow Red Scar ... or me?*

CHAPTER TWENTY-ONE
Rex Rampage

All night long the tyrannosaurs rampaged, devastating Dinovia City. And the hunters helped.

The surviving Rangers tried to mount some pathetic defense. They hopped into their jippis, prepared to roll into battle, only to find their tires slashed. They raced toward the armory, seeking more tranquilizer darts, only to find the place burning, all their weapons gone. A squad of Rangers ran down an alleyway, heading toward the city square where the rexes raged. They didn't get far. Snipers on the roofs took them out.

Amissa was one of those snipers. She lay atop the roof of the Tar Pit, one of Dinovia's run-down hotels, and blew smoke from her muzzle. Rattlesnake crouched at her side, his own muzzle smoking. The other hunters lurked farther back, shadows in the night.

"Good work, boys and girls," Amissa whispered.

All night, while the T-rexes searched for their eggs, the hunters kept moving through the city like shadows, picking off the Rangers one by one. The Rangers fashioned themselves warriors. They were no such thing. They were just glorified zookeepers. But Amissa and her posse had been stalking big game for years. To them, hunting men was no different.

Sounds of destruction came from her left. Amissa turned her head. A T-rex stood in a nearby yard, tearing apart a domed house. The dinosaur had cracked open the roof. Clutching the house with his tiny hands, the T-rex stuck his snout through the roof, rummaging for eggs. Screams sounded from inside. Apparently the rex didn't find eggs, but he did enjoy some lovely snacks.

A shadow darted. A young Ranger ran up toward the T-rex. He looked barely twenty, new to his badge and ceratop hat. Probably fashioned himself a hero. He aimed his sleep-or-die at the T-rex and opened fire. He was using bullets. Ha! Bullets! Watching from a block away, Amissa laughed. The kid was like some medieval knight facing a dragon with nothing but a sword.

With a rippling rumble, the T-rex raised his head from the house. A severed arm was stuck between his teeth. The dinosaur spun toward the young Ranger. The kid held his ground. He fired again, and bullets chipped the T-rex's scales.

The dinosaur pounced. With an enormous three-toed talon, he kicked the kid down, crushing every rib in his body. Then, almost delicately, the T-rex used one claw to knock the sleep-or-die aside. With the indigestible metal stick removed, the T-rex gulped down the poor Ranger. Smart dino. Amissa wondered how many guns the T-rexes had swallowed before learning they were indigestible.

This was what the Rangers did not understand. They built walls around their city like a medieval fortress. They feared dinosaurs. They thought them monsters. But dinosaurs were merely animals. Big, powerful, and majestic, yes, but just animals nonetheless. The T-rexes were simply looking for their eggs and maybe a bite to eat. The true monsters were humans. Humans like the Rangers, who terrorized good hunters. Humans like Joe, who betrayed his clan. Humans like Simone, who spread lies with her pen. They acted like they were above nature. Amissa was part of nature. The savage part, yes. A predator. A huntress. But still part of nature. The Rangers were an abomination.

She rose on the rooftop and faced her fellow hunters. They rose too, standing on roofs across the city. They raised their glowing spheres, communicating across the darkness.

"Tonight we end the illegitimate reign of the Rangers," Amissa said. "When dawn rises, Mintari will be ours. The self-righteous Doctor Dolittles will be gone. And we, the hunters, will be masters of Mintari. Move through the city with me, friends. Find every last Ranger who still lives. And kill them. For the hunt!"

"For the hunt!" they all cried.

Amissa hopped off the roof and landed in a garden. She stomped over the petunias, made her way onto the street, and cocked her rifle. The other hunters joined her. They spread out, slinking from shadow to shadow, seeking their enemies.

There ahead—two Rangers were running toward a rampaging rex. One was a burly, bearded man, the other a young and slender woman. Both had auburn hair and broad faces. They looked like father and daughter. They must have been out of ammo, or maybe they realized bullets were no use here. Instead of firing guns, they were swinging a chain.

The T-rex wasn't paying the two Rangers any attention. The dinosaur was digging through the ruins of a school; Amissa had tossed a cannister of egg-scented gas in there an hour ago. Working together, the father-and-daughter duo managed to lasso the chain around the rex's neck.

"Dad, we got him!" the younger Ranger cried. She grinned.

Foolish. The titanic theropod merely swung his head. The younger Ranger flew through the air, slammed into a house, then crashed onto the ground. The slender woman moaned, her body broken. Amissa walked toward her. The Ranger lay on the cobblestones, groaning in pain. Her ceratop hat had fallen off, revealing her bloodied auburn hair. The skull was probably fractured. The Ranger looked at Amissa through squinting eyes, unable to speak.

Amissa put a bullet in her head. It was a mercy.

The older Ranger let out a strangled cry.

"Daughter!" he cried.

The T-rex stomped toward him, snarling. To his credit, the bearded Ranger did not back down. He swung his chain in wide arcs, then lashed it against the rex's snout. Scales shattered. The dinosaur grunted in pain.

Amissa's rifle boomed. The brave Ranger fell. Amissa had shot his leg. She could have hit his head, made it quick, but ... eh, she was out of mercy tonight. At once, the T-rex was on him, ripping him apart.

Amissa kept walking. Two more Rangers down. Not many left to go now. She would purify this city.

As she walked past the bodies, a chill gripped her. Her legs began to shake. Her head spun.

What am I doing? Oh God, I'm killing people. I'm murdering them.

Blackness spread across her peripheral vision. The domed houses swam around her. Sounds distorted, seeming distant, and Amissa swayed on her feet. Panic was creeping in. She took a deep breath, burning away the terror with her fury. Her vision cleared. Her mind steadied.

This is war. There can be no mercy in war. Tonight I am a soldier.

Two Rangers ran toward her, guns firing. Amissa leaped aside. The bullets hit a domed house. She crouched and returned fire, mowing them down. Both Rangers fell. Amissa examined her arm and winced. A bullet had grazed her skin. Another inch to the left, and the bullet would have shattered her bone, maybe even torn her arm off. Lucky.

Gunshots sounded across the city.

As the tyrannosaurs terrorized Dinovia, hunters and Rangers clashed. Bodies fell. Warriors died on both sides. The mighty Tomahawk crashed down, bullets in his barrel chest. Madame Maria stomped through a crowd of Rangers, lashing her steel claws, lacerating Rangers. Their bullets hit the seven-foot-tall woman. She howled and fell. Rangers were on her at once like sinraptors crawling over a fallen sauropod.

But for every hunter fallen, they took down ten Rangers, maybe more. And Amissa knew: *This city is ours.*

As she fought onward, shooting from the shadows, she noticed that the shadows were no longer so dark. The first hint of daylight gilded the rooftops. The night was ending. And her conquest was almost complete.

Then she heard it.

A rumbling.

A chorus of snorts, grunts, and thumping feet.

The T-rexes stopped their rampage. Across the city, their scaly heads rose over the rooftops. They stared east, sniffing, squinting in the rising sun.

The rumbling grew louder. Louder still. The cobbled alleyway shook below Amissa's boots.

She climbed onto a pile of rubble, hopped onto a balcony, and pulled herself onto a rooftop. She still couldn't see anything. The city was shaking now. Dust danced across the ruins. The T-rexes hissed and bared their teeth and whipped their tails.

Amissa hopped from roof to roof, moving to higher ground, until she could see the eastern wall of the city. The sun was rising. Light blinded her. The rumbles deafened her. She squinted, waiting for her eyes to adjust.

There.

She saw them.

They came charging from the dawn. A herd like a tank battalion. Triceratops.

The horned dinosaurs raced over the drawbridge. They stormed through the shattered gates. One T-rex was near the gateway, a young female with green scales. She snapped her teeth at the charging herd, then lost her courage, turned tail, and fled. A T-rex, the mightiest predator on Mintari—fleeing.

Amissa stared in silent horror.

Then she saw something else. A gasp fled her lips.

A man and a woman rode the lead triceratops. The man wore a ceratop hat and carried a sleep-or-die. The woman's flaming-red hair billowed in the wind.

Rage flared over Amissa's horror. Standing on the rooftop, she raised her binoculars. Ah yes. Just as she had suspected. A thin smile stretched across her lips.

"Welcome, Joe and Simone. Welcome to your graveyard."

The triceratops herd charged into the city, cracking cobblestones, sending a T-rex fleeing.

Joe rode at their lead, staring ahead with narrowed eyes.

"Dear God," he whispered.

Dinovia teetered on the edge of destruction. Much of the city lay in ruin. Hundreds of round, domed homes had cracked open like eggs. Chunks of clay spread across the desolation, and clouds of dust sparkled in the morning light. Bodies lay across the cobbled roads. Bodies of Rangers. Of civilians. Children too. Some of the bodies had tooth marks and claw marks on them. But others were riddled with bullets.

Amissa had stopped filming herself a while ago. But she had done this. Joe was sure of it. And he would put a stop to it.

A pack of T-rexes would not simply invade a human city, trapping themselves between walls and houses. They were not monsters hell-bent on destruction. Like all dinosaurs, they were simply interested in survival. A city was full of danger and only small, bony humans to eat. Amissa must have done something to lure them here. She would have no bond with them, not like Joe's bond with Dozer. No. She must have …

"Eggs," Joe said. "She must have stolen their eggs."

Simone sat before him on Dozer's lumpy back. She clenched her fist. "Amissa! Tar her. How do we fix this, Joe?"

He thought for a moment. Joe could try to herd the T-rexes out of the city with brute triceratops force. That might work. But the rexes would resist. It would not be pretty. Perhaps Joe could find and remove the eggs. Judging by all the shattered buildings, the T-rexes had already done a thorough search. How would Joe, without a tyrannosaur's keen sense of smell, find what they could not?

"If I'm right, Amissa hid T-rex eggs here. And she'll know where they are." He raised his voice. "Amissa! Tar you, Amissa, where are you?"

No reply.

His cowardly sister was hiding.

He bulldozed onward through the city. Dozer's enormous feet crushed cobblestones, leaving deep footprints. The trike weighed a dozen tons, enough to pulverize the city streets. Ahead, Joe saw more T-rexes moving through Dinovia, stomping between buildings, furious and confused. They seemed torn, desperately wanting their eggs but also seriously concerned about the charging triceratops army.

The two species were mortal enemies on Mintari. They were about the same size—both bloody massive. T-rex was taller.

Triceratops was broader. T-rex had the most powerful jaws known to nature. Triceratops had the most powerful horns. In the wild, they gave each other a wide berth, but sometimes they did come to blows. Their battles could go either way. Joe had seen rexes kill trikes before. But just as often, trikes killed rexes. They were the two greatest warriors on Mintari. Now they were trapped here in this gauntlet.

Dozer smelled the T-rexes ahead. But he did not cower, not even hesitate. He actually gained speed, raring for battle. The burly triceratops charged through the city, leaving potholes in his wake, overturning carts, knocking down trees. People fled before him. But Dozer would not harm a human. It was his old mortal enemies he smelled here. The T-rexes had slain many of his kind. He had lost brothers and sisters to the terrible tyrannosaurs. Now they threatened humans, whom Dozer considered allies. He was eager to thrust his horns into any tyrannosaur foolish enough to get in his way.

One T-rex was foolish enough. She was a big female, driven mad by the loss of her eggs. Scars ran across her scaly green body like red rivers, and her black eyes blazed with fury. The prodigious predator stomped into an alleyway and faced the charging herd. She was a Tyrannosaurus rex. An apex predator. The greatest predator that ever lived. She did not fear some herbivores! What could they possibly do? Nibble some grass around her? Facing the charge, she placed her feet at a wide stance, opened her jaws, and unleashed a deafening rumble.

Normally, facing such an opponent, even the mighty triceratops would flee. But Dozer was no normal triceratops. He kept charging, opened his beak, and unleashed his own furious cry. Emboldened by their leader, the other trikes charged with him, shaking the city.

Sitting ahead of Joe, Simone clung to Dozer's frill. "I want off, I want off, I want off!"

"It's too late to get off Dozer!" Joe said.

"I mean off this planet!" she screamed.

The trike kept charging. The green T-rex stood her ground, teeth bared. Joe winced. Simone ducked behind the frill. The two animals charged closer, closer, and—

The world shook.

Trike and rex slammed together.

The horns drove into the T-rex's chest, shattering scales, drawing blood. The theropod howled. But she did not die or flee. In blind animal fury, the tyrannosaur leaned forward. Her legendary jaws chomped down on Dozer's frill.

Screaming, Simone pulled her arms back. She nearly lost them to the terrible teeth.

The tyrannosaur jaws squeezed like clamps. Banana-sized teeth punched into Dozer's bony frill. A T-rex had the greatest bite force of any animal alive. It made a shark's bite seem like a gentle kiss. Bone snapped and cracked.

But the triceratops kept charging.

Dozer shoved his horns deeper into his enemy's flesh, carving through muscle and bone. His thick legs shoved against the ground. Those legs were so muscular they made elephant legs look like toothpicks. Even with those dreaded teeth chomping into his frill, the triceratops kept shoving, digging his horns deeper, brutalizing his foe.

And then the other trikes were with him, running, barreling forward, a great stampede.

For a moment longer, the T-rex clung onto Dozer's frill. She was like a dog refusing to release a favorite toy. It seemed she would rip Dozer's head right off his body.

Then the combined might of the triceratops herd overpowered even the great Tyrannosaurus rex. One second, the tyrant was gnawing on Dozer's head. The next second, she was beneath his stomping feet. Then the feet of the herd. The T-rex was an enormous dinosaur, weighing more than two mammoths. And the trikes steamrolled over her, crushing her bones.

The herd kept plowing through the city. One young T-rex, a powerful male with gray scales, found himself in their path. He glanced down at his dead sister, up at the herd, then turned tail and ran. There were few things in this universe that could make a T-rex flee. Right now a dozen of those things were stampeding through Dinovia City.

"Amissa!" Joe cried. "Where are you, Amissa? Did you hide eggs here? Oldest trick in the book! Where are you?"

Then he saw it. A figure on a distant rooftop.

Dinovia Library was the largest building still standing in the city. Its dome rose several stories high. The library would barely be a hut on Cloventia, but for Mintari, it was a colossus, taller than even the rampaging rexes. Joe had spent most of his life in the wilderness, but whenever he visited the city, he would take time to visit the library, to drown himself in books. To him, books were like nature. They took him to places of danger and wonder.

Now Amissa stood on the library dome. Her chestnut hair streamed in the wind. She seemed almost to glow in the sunrise.

"Good morning, big brother!" she said. "And good night."

She aimed her rifle at him and fired.

"Can I hold her, Mother?" the boy asked. "Can I hold my baby sister?"

Lifa lay in bed, recovering from a difficult birth. This baby was eight years in the making. After having her son, she had tried again. And again. Over and over. But her first birth had broken something inside her, and for years, doctors told her she would never have another child. Here, finally, in this hospital floating above the neon sea—a miracle. A baby girl.

"Mother, can I hold her?" asked the boy.

Lifa smiled thinly. Her son spoke with a Cloventian accent. She herself had been born and raised in the savage beauty of Mintari. But she had followed her husband to this synthetic world. She was raising her son in this so-called civilization, a place of metal and light where the only leaves were made of plastic. Lifa was wilting here in her exile, trapped inside the floating skyscrapers, and all the wealth of her husband could not set her free. He kept her in a neon cage.

Joe, this sweet and somber boy, was her light. Her life. She taught him the ways of Mintari, taught him about the great animals who roamed there, the mountains that soared, the air that was scented of pines, not chemical purifiers. And still he spoke with a Cloventian accent. But Lifa knew his heart was wild.

Now in her arms she held a new blessing. A miracle baby. A daughter.

"Amissa," she whispered. "I name you Amissa."

"Mother!" Joe said. "Can I hold her?"

She laughed weakly. "Of course."

The eight-year-old held his newborn sister, rocked her gently, and kissed her forehead. "Hi, Amissa. I'm Joe, your big brother. I love you. And I'll protect you forever."

Thirty-three years later, as the gunshot rang out in Dinovia City, that memory flashed through Joe. He had suppressed most of his memories of Cloventia. It had not been a happy childhood. But that day always remained with him. One last day of light before the long shadow years.

Now that gunshot snapped through his reverie. The bullet missed him. It slammed into Dozer's central horn, embedding itself into the bone. The trike reared and howled. He was already wounded from long days of battle. T-rex teeth were still stuck in his frill. But his fury flooded through him. It would take more than a bullet to stop him. He charged onward.

Riding the trike, Joe raised his sleep-or-die. He aimed at Amissa.

For a second, he almost fired from the right barrel. A live bullet. Then he quickly flipped the switch and fired a tranquilizer dart at his sister.

She vanished behind the library's domed roof. The dart flew overhead.

Joe's jaw clenched. "After her, Dozer!"

He didn't need to knee the trike in the right direction. Dozer knew his mission. It was no longer to trample over rexes, as much as he enjoyed the activity. It was to crush the little human. His master's sister. Like humans, trikes had strong family bonds, and Dozer knew that the human on the rooftop had broken that sacred bond. With a bullet in his horn and teeth in his frill, he rumbled toward the library.

Yet as they got closer, the streets narrowed. The library was located in the Old City. These streets were five hundred years old, dating back to the first colonists from Earth. Back then, the city had been only a town, and the colonists walked everywhere. The streets were too narrow for jippis. And certainly too narrow for dinosaurs. Dozer found himself stuck.

The triceratops was forced to stop on Horner Lane, a cobbled street that led to the library. The entire herd crowded behind him. Clay buildings rose alongside, grazing the trikes' lumpy flanks. These buildings were ancient. Some still had the original shops on their bottom floors, while the shopkeepers lived above.

Trapped in the narrow road like a potato in a man's throat, Dozer swiveled his enormous head around. He looked at Joe with one eye. He grunted something that sounded like a question. "Hau?" *What now?*

Joe knew that if he ordered it, Dozer would keep going, simply bulldozing over the buildings. But he had come to save this city, not cause further devastation. Especially not to historical buildings.

"I'll keep going on foot," Joe said.

"I'll go," Simone said. "Somebody needs to lead the trikes, and—"

Gunshots boomed.

Bullets pinged off triceratops horns and thudded into scaly flesh. The dinosaurs reared, trapped in the narrow road.

Tar it! Joe saw them. Snipers on the rooftops. All along Horner Lane. So Amissa had brought a posse.

Joe aimed his rifle and took a shot. A bullet hit a sniper. The man grunted and fell back. More bullets rained down. One grazed Joe's thigh, and he hissed in pain. Dozer bellowed.

"Back, get back!" Joe shouted. "Dozer, get out of here!"

The triceratops tried to retreat, but Horner Lane was cramped. A perfect place to trap a herd of bulky dinosaurs. In a panic, a few triceratops leaned into nearby buildings. Walls collapsed, revealing the insides of a millinery shop, a toy store selling wooden dinosaur skeletons, a gallery of paleoart, and a chocolatier offering dino-shaped treats. More bullets whizzed. The trikes were trying to spin around, toppling more buildings. A statue of Mary Anning tipped over. A perfumery crumbled, spraying the alleyway with a thousand aromas.

More bullets flew. Dozer reared. The dinosaur ran through the clouds of perfume. His scaly flank grazed a doll shop, peeling off the wall. A few little girls cowered inside, perhaps seeking shelter in a familiar place of comfort. They screamed. Dust and broken dolls filled the alleyway.

Then Joe heard it.

A low, rippling bass that raised his hackles. Pebbles danced on the ground. His chest ached.

The sound of grumbling tyrannosaurs.

One T-rex came from behind. Another from the front. They blocked both ends of Horner Lane. The gargantuan carnivores slammed into the herd, front and back, biting, kicking, shoving the trikes closer together. One triceratops fell with an earth-shaking *thud*, and his neighbors trampled him. And the bullets kept flying.

I led us right into an ambush, Joe realized.

"Joe, lead the herd out of here!" Simone shouted. "I'll go after Amissa!"

"Simone—wait!" he said.

But the tarry redhead was already leaping off Dozer. She landed on a pile of rubble, hopped down to the road, and ran, vanishing into a cloud of perfumed dust.

The T-rexes shoved harder against the herd. Clouds of dust hid their bodies, but their jaws emerged from the storm, biting at the trikes. Joe bared his teeth, aimed his gun, and fired a tranquilizer dart at one rex. The dart snapped against the scaly skin, only enraging the carnivore. More tyrannosaur howls came from behind.

And in the distance, miles away, rose an even deeper rumble.

A familiar rumble. A sound like thunder. Like an earthquake. A sound that ached in Joe's bones. It was a sound so low in frequency Joe could barely hear it. But he could *feel* it. The sound waves thumped against him.

It was a sound Joe had not heard in years. And a shiver ran down his spine.

"Dozer, pull back to the city square!" Joe said. "We'll lure the big green rex out. Go!"

The trike could not understand human language well, but he understood the tone, the situation, and the urgency. He managed to spin around, crumbling more walls. He lowered his head and charged, his horns shoving aside rubble.

The triceratops made his way off Horner Lane and onto Bakker Road, which was just as narrow. Barbershops, restaurants, and souvenir shops lined the cobbled road. A few other triceratops followed, fleeing the gauntlet on Horner Lane. As they charged, the dinosaurs shattered cobblestones, cracked the walls of shops, and knocked over a water fountain. Merchant stalls overturned. Locals fled. A few tourists snapped photos.

Joe held on tight. Dozer led the trikes down Bakker Road. The herd trampled everything in its path. Horns grazed balconies. They collapsed, and balustrade rails clattered down everywhere like pickup sticks. A teashop cracked open, spilling aromatic leaves across the cobblestones. Dust filled the air. Joe's eyes burned. He could barely see.

He glanced behind him, blinking the dust out. He could make out several rexes and trikes still battling along Horner Lane. Simone had vanished, seeking Amissa in the destruction.

A deep rumble sounded farther down Bakker Street.

Joe tried to see the source. Too much dust. When you built a city out of clay and stone, then raced a herd of triceratops through it, apparently that caused a lot of dust. Who'd have thought? The rumble sounded again, closer now. Joe leaned over Dozer's head, trying to see, then gasped. Dust filled his mouth.

"*Rex!*" he shouted, coughing.

Dozer understood that word. He crouched, snarled, and lowered his head, aiming his horns ahead.

A brown T-rex burst out the clouds of dust. The predator crashed through a balcony, shattering stones, and lunged at the triceratops.

Dozer charged at full speed, driving twelve tons of triceratops ferocity into the T-rex. His horns pierced the scaly skin with sickening *thunks*.

The T-rex leaned back, howling in rage. How dared this herbivore make him bleed! He took a few steps back, then lunged forward, prepared to finish this impudent vegetarian. Dozer was already charging and rammed into the rex again. A second trike, then a third added their bulk, plowing over the combative carnivore.

The tyrannosaur had enough. He was used to hunting docile hadrosaurs. At worst, he dealt with an iguanodon and their terrible thumbs. A herd of truculent trikes? No meal was worth this. He fled down a narrow road, which the trikes were too bulky to enter. His chest was bleeding, and his pride hurt even more, but the T-rex would live to terrorize smaller herbivores another day.

That deeper rumble sounded again in the distance. That old familiar bass.

Joe knew he should try to herd the rexes out of the city. He knew he should fight the poachers on the rooftops. The last thing he needed to do was chase that old deep bellow.

But that sound had been haunting him for fifteen years. It echoed through his dreams every night. Now it was here, pealing over the city.

The sound of King Ivan. The dinosaur that had devoured his pregnant wife.

Joe could not see the tyrant from here. But he would recognize the monster's rumble anywhere. Joe's upper lip rose in a sneer. Let Simone track Amissa down. He had another battle to fight.

He dug his heels into Dozer's sides.

"Go, Dozer! Follow that sound. He awaits us deeper in the city. Ivan is here, Dozer. Charge!"

The scarred old triceratops ran, stomping through the city toward the echo of a nightmare.

CHAPTER TWENTY-TWO
A Dinosaur in the Library

Simone ran down Horner Lane, coughing and waving aside the dust. The sounds of rumbling, stampeding, and battling dinosaurs rose all around. A chunk of building slammed down ahead of Simone, blocking her way. She skidded to a halt, wheeled away, and ran down another road.

"Where are you, Amissa?" she shouted. She had last seen the huntress hiding behind the library. But where was the library? Simone no longer knew left from right, up from down. She could barely see anything through the collapsing city.

She raced down the cobbled road, then leaped back. A salmon-colored triceratops, a big female with a cracked frill, raced down an intersecting road. The dinosaur was wounded and bugling in terror. A T-rex stomped after the horned herbivore, leaning down and snapping his jaws. He managed to catch the trike's tail, severing the tip. The two dinosaurs stumbled aside and slammed into a building. Balconies came crashing down. A bell tower collapsed. The bell clanged as it rolled down the road.

The dueling dinosaurs shoved off the crumbling building, then wobbled sideways, lumbering toward Simone. The rex's tail swung. Simone ducked. The scaly tail slammed into a pottery shop, shattering the wall. A thousand clay pots and mugs spilled onto the street. The triceratops charged, thrusting her horns at the T-rex. Simone screamed and leaped away, narrowly dodging the trike's foot. A music shop's wall collapsed. Guitars, cellos, and violins fell across the street with a discordant symphony. Simone felt as small as a mouse, trapped between a battling dog and cat.

The T-rex managed to get past the bony frill, to close his jaws around the herbivore's neck. But the salmon-colored triceratops kept fighting, shoving her bulk forward, goring her tormentor with her horns. Simone didn't stay to see who won. She ran onward, leaving the mortal enemies behind.

There! There past that fallen statue! The library.

The domed building still stood, an island rising from a sea of dust. Amissa was no longer on the roof. Had she gone inside, perhaps to regroup with other hunters? Or had she fled to another neighborhood?

Shadows darted across the road. Screeches rose above. Simone pressed her back against a wall, heart pounding. She glanced up. Pterosaurs! Pterosaurs above Dinovia City!

A flock of them flew above. Joe had told her that pterosaurs dared not fly over Dinovia. The Rangers on the walls shot them with stinging pellets. Now many Rangers were dead, the walls were abandoned, and the pterosaurs flocked.

Simone screamed and cowered as pterosaurs swarmed down toward the road. The beating of their wings blasted her hair back and raised swirling dust devils. They were only dactyls. Members of the *Pterodactylus* genus—relatively small members of the broader pterosaur clade. But each dactyl was still big enough to rip her apart. Memories of her time in the hatchlings' nest spun in her head.

Thankfully, the pterosaurs ignored her. They flew down the block, then landed on … Simone gasped. A triceratops corpse!

For a terrible moment, Simone thought it might be Dozer. But it was a different triceratops, a young bull with blue-gray skin. A big male T-rex stood above the fallen herbivore, one foot on the carcass. The theropod tried to swat the pterosaurs away, but with his tiny arms, he wasn't swatting anyone anytime soon. He must content himself with sharing his meal. The T-rex tugged back the frill, revealing the soft meat of the neck, and tucked in. The dactyls began to peck at the tougher torso.

Simone took a few deep breaths, then coughed out dust. She needed to find Amissa—and fast. If the poacher had indeed hidden eggs across Dinovia City, the only way to stop the rex rampage was to find those eggs. And only Amissa knew where they were.

Another T-rex ran down the road, sniffing, shattering everything in her path. Simone retreated into the Fossil Garden, a small restaurant. It served Mintarian fare—lots of meat, potatoes, and beer. Mintarian fare, yes, though it was all likely imported from the farming world of Dagon. Same place Cloventia got its food. In any case, the kitchen was now closed. People huddled inside the dining hall, hugging one another, their faces pale. One man had lost an arm; a tourniquet wrapped around the stump. Simone peeked out the window. Would the predator visit the restaurant for a meal? Yes, waiter, I'll have the redhead journalist with a glass of Merlot. Thankfully the T-rex ran by, searching for her eggs.

The people hiding in the restaurant began to pray. A few invited Simone to join. But she wasn't here to hide for long. She pulled out her SmartSphere. Joe had shattered it back in the cave, and bits of tape held it together. It looked clunky, but when she tapped a button, the device unfolded into a glowing digital sphere. Simone ran her hands over the sphere, selecting menu options, and found Amissa Triplehorn's QuickFame profile.

Bingo!

The poacher was broadcasting. Right now.

Simone ground her teeth. Why that vain, monstrous woman! She looked so pleased with herself. Simone wanted to reach through the SmartSphere and strangle her.

"Yes, my Tripletots, it's war!" Amissa was saying. She had taken time during the battle to fix her makeup and brush her hair. "The Rangers are attacking from all sides. They vow to kill me. And every other hunter. If they can, they will kill you too. Do you eat meat? The Rangers want you dead! Do you go fishing? They will shoot you! The Mintari Rangers are a fanatical, misanthropic hate group that places animals above humans. But don't worry, my fans. I'm here in Dinovia City to crush them once and for all. If you hear this broadcast, join me. Bring your weapons, bring your fury, and come fight with me for freedom!"

"Why you tarry little—" Simone began. But she was so angry words failed her.

Then she looked more closely. Amissa was speaking from a shadowy place. When Simone increased the sphere's brightness … there.

Bookshelves.

Amissa was in the library. The mystery section.

"Gotcha!" Simone said.

She didn't have a weapon. She walked toward a table in the restaurant and lifted a steak knife. The waiter stared at her, pale, and gulped.

"I'll bring it back," Simone said, tucked the knife into her belt, and ran outside.

She raced down the street, sending a few dactyls flying. She headed toward the library.

"Ma'am, ma'am! You have to stop, ma'am. Head back now!"

Simone was only a block away from the library. A big, beefy Ranger came walking toward her, holding out his hand in a "stop" gesture. His uniform was a size too small and covered with dust, and a gash bled on his cheek.

Simone skidded to a halt, panting. "Sir, I'm a journalist. I don't have my press badge, but—"

"Ma'am, step back now!" he said. "Get into one of the shops and—"

The sound of stomping feet silenced him.

The Ranger looked to his left. He cursed and raised his sleep-or-die.

A second later, a T-rex thundered toward him. He was a big male, his scales green, his eyes yellow. Bullet holes bled on his chest.

The Ranger didn't even have time to fire. The T-rex grabbed him and ripped him apart. Clearly the predators had learned to hate the Rangers and their horrible guns.

Simone stood, frozen like a deer in the headlights. She knew she should flee. But she just stood there, panting.

The T-rex nudged the dead Ranger with his snout, grumbled, and kicked the body aside. Then the beast raised his head and looked at Simone. He actually made eye contact. Simone could see intelligence in those yellow eyes. This was no mindless monster. He was sentient. Simone had heard that T-rexes were as smart as dolphins and chimps. Right now she believed it.

She wanted to run, but she stood her ground. Running would mark her as prey. She simply stared back.

The T-rex sniffed the air, then loped away. He was not hungry. He had only killed the Ranger in self-defense. Simone was not a threat, so he let her live. The dinosaur walked onward, sniffing, searching for the eggs Amissa had stolen.

Simone kept running. With every footstep, the T-rex had left potholes. Simone had to zigzag around them. Finally she reached the library.

Back on Cloventia, there were no libraries. Paper was a rarity, available only to the elite; no trees grew on Cloventia. The *Cloventia Gazette* did publish a paper edition, but barely anyone bought it. Most Cloventians read everything on their SmartSpheres. Some people—not Simone, but some—got neural implants that fed information directly into their brains. But Mintari was a world beyond time. A world where the past came to life. That didn't only mean dinosaurs. It was also how people lived. Their ancestors had colonized space, but here on Mintari, people looked back in time. They still built libraries and filled them with paper books.

Columns lined the library portico. The double doors were open. Simone raced inside.

For a moment, she almost forgot about the T-rexes rampaging through the city.

The library was beautiful. Breathtakingly so.

Simone had seen old movies and photographs featuring libraries. Well, she had also seen photos of dinosaurs. Seeing some things in person was a completely different experience.

A stained glass window glittered between the bookshelves, dappling the library with light in every color. Upholstered armchairs nestled in nooks, little havens for bookworms to sit and escape into a book. Antique globes stood in brass holders, depicting the five rocky planets of the Nyx system. Cloventia, the neon world, a planet for humans. Dagon, the grass giant, a farming world. Borealis, a cold planet for Ice Age animals. Thalia, a warm planet for victims of the Holocene extinction. And Mintari, a world of dinosaurs.

The globes were works of art, adorned with precious metals and gems, but the books were the star attraction. Shelves soared several stories tall, lined with spiraling metal staircases and wheeled ladders. Simone resisted the temptation to slide on a ladder, one arm stretched out. Millions of books covered the shelves, centuries old. Most were bound in leather. The smell of old paper filled the air, intoxicating. There was so much knowledge here! Millions of books that could take Simone to another world. Many were books written here on Mintari, but most were books from old Earth. From the days before the Slum Wars and the nuclear fallout. Back when dinosaurs still hid underground and the stars were but a dream.

Completing the tableau was a massive fresco. The painting spread across the domed ceiling, depicting dinosaurs. The fresco was arranged like a pie graph, divided into four geological eras. The Permian era featured dimetrodons with spiky sails on their backs, a hungry scutosaurus with lumpy plates of armor on his body, huge insects bustling in a marsh, and other animals that predated the dinosaurs. The Triassic section of the mural featured turtles, crocodiles, a tanystropheus with a ridiculously long neck, and the earliest dinosaurs, who were still humble and small. The Jurassic era featured the dinosaurs coming into their own. Stegosaurus roamed the forest, massive sauropods dominated the land, and dreaded theropods like allosaurus preyed upon them. Finally, the Cretaceous section of the mural depicted the golden age of dinosaurs. Here appeared the classic dinosaurs. Tyrannosaurus rex. Triceratops. Velociraptor. The largest of the sauropods. Here the dinosaurs were at the top of their game.

The Cretaceous ended with a bang—literally. The asteroid doomed the dinosaurs on one terrible day. Gaping at the mural, Simone wondered. What would have happened had the asteroid never wiped out the dinosaurs? What new eras might have followed? How would they have continued to evolve? Would the sauropods have grown even larger? Would T-rex have lost his vestigial arms? Would new, wondrous species take form? Nobody would ever know.

But then again—maybe they *would* know. What the asteroid had interrupted was continuing here on Mintari. Using time-casting, scientists had rescued dinosaurs from before the asteroid impact, regrew them from DNA here on Mintari, and let them loose. They were irresponsible, those old scientists. They mixed animals from all four eras on one planet. They opened it up to tourism. They played god instead of letting evolution take its slow, delicate course. But that was centuries ago. Those old visionaries were gone, and Mintari was in danger. Amissa and her poachers were hitting Mintari like the asteroid had hit Earth. Yes, the dinosaurs were big and strong, and they could kill a few humans. But they could not survive humanity for long. Not with poachers like Amissa running wild. Even the mighty T-rex would not fare much better than the lions, whales, and elephants of Earth. The dinosaurs too, confronted with humanity, could face extinction again.

And Simone realized what this war meant. What the stakes were. Not just to save a few dinosaurs. But to save them all. To let evolution continue its grand game. It was too late to stop the asteroid from hitting Earth, but they could stop humanity from polluting Mintari. This was a noble war. It was a war Joe had dedicated his life to. And Simone, who had come here as a journalist, realized that she was now a soldier.

"I could have shot you ten times by now, you dumb tart," came a voice from the shadows. "You're in a war, and you're gaping at a ceiling."

Simone started, drew her knife, and stared toward the shadowy bookshelves. "Amissa, I'm not here to fight!"

Amissa still remained hidden in shadows, but her laughter echoed through the library. "And you draw a knife. How cute! Hasn't anyone ever told you not to bring a knife to a gunfight?"

A shot rang out. The blade shattered in Simone's hand.

It took Simone a moment to realize what had happened. Amissa had shot the blade!

With a trembling hand, Simone tossed the hilt down. It clattered. "All right, I get it! You're a good shot. You have me in your scope. I'm at your mercy. Believe me or not, I didn't come here to kill you. I want to talk, Amissa. I want to know where the eggs are."

For a moment, silence filled the library.

Then Amissa stepped out from between the bookshelves.

Her SmartSphere floated beside her, a ball of light like a small moon, filming everything. Even here, even now, Amissa was putting on a show. She swayed as she walked—an exaggerated strut designed to accentuate her curves. She smiled crookedly and raised one perfectly groomed eyebrow. In the chaos of battle, she had found time to fix her makeup, and her cleavage was so deep Simone worried a pterodactyl would try to nest there. Dramatically, Amissa blew smoke off her muzzle. She was playing a role, the seductive huntress, the perfect social media queen. Her QuickFame followers were eating it up.

Simone had known such women all her life. She had gone to journalism school, reported from war zones, and written hard-hitting stories of serious journalism. And she had never gotten one percent the ratings of QuickFame Queens like Amissa Triplehorn. On their popular channels, they broadcast themselves across the galaxy. QuickFame Queens were always young, attractive, seductive. They posed aboard luxury starships, inside penthouses, or—in Amissa's case—with the corpses of slain dinosaurs.

Simone was pretty, or so she had been told. She knew that with her looks, she could abandon the *Cloventia Gazette*, open a QuickFame channel, flirt on camera, and make more money. *Much* more. She had always resisted that path. She went into journalism with a sense of purpose, while Amissa disgraced mass media.

"Did you hear that, Tripletots?" Amissa said. "She wants to talk! How cute. Is she going to beg for her life? How about we have a vote, my fans? Should I let her talk? Or should I put a bullet through her head?"

Simone raised her chin. "Boasting for your followers, huh? Go ahead. Shoot me on live stream. Let everyone see you're a murderer. Murder me like you murdered my sister. Maybe finally you'll face justice. Or you can end this charade! Tell me where you hid the eggs, and we can end this senseless destruction!"

Amissa tossed back her head and laughed. This time her laughter was higher in pitch, almost deranged. It echoed through the library. "Do you hear her, Tripletots? Making those baseless accusations again. She lost at court! The judge was clear. I'm innocent of killing her silly, stupid twin. Yet still she slanders me! And she came at me with a knife. You all saw it." Amissa aimed her rifle. Her face hardened. "You declared war on me, Simone LaRue. You fought me in the courts. Now you fight me on Mintari. You've lost. This is your end. You'll finally be famous, Simone LaRue. Your death will get a hundred times more views than anything you've done in life."

That's all this is to her, Simone realized. *Drama. She's putting on the biggest show of her life. I can use that.*

"Please, Amissa … I beg you," Simone said.

Amissa's eyebrows rose. She smiled. "Ah, you want to grovel, do you? Do you want to see her beg, Tripletots?"

Comments and likes came flooding in, hovering as little holograms around Amissa's SmartSphere.

The QuickFame Queen stared at Simone, eyes hard. "They want to see it. Get on your knees and beg."

Simone stepped closer.

Careful. I must be careful.

"Amissa, I shouldn't beg you. I should beg your fans. *They* should decide if I live or die."

Comments burst around the sphere. The fans were loving this. Millions were watching. Amissa dedicated herself to her fans. She could not reject Simone's suggestion.

"Very well," Amissa said, unable to hide the note of annoyance from her voice. "Look at the camera, LaRue. And beg them."

Simone turned toward the camera. She took a deep breath. It was the largest audience she had ever spoken to. But she was no stranger to cameras.

It's showtime, she thought.

She tossed her luxurious red hair. She pouted, making puppy dog eyes at the camera. "I beg you, Tripletots. Please let me live."

"Get down on your knees," Amissa said. "Let's see some proper groveling."

Simone obeyed. She stared up at the floating camera. "Please, oh please let me live." She shuffled forward on her knees. "I beg you. I would do anything."

"Beg harder!" Amissa said. "Put your back into it!" She was loving this.

Simone sniffed. She inched even closer to the floating sphere. The camera tilted down toward her. "Please. I'm nothing compared to Amissa Triplehorn. I'm only a lowly, useless girl, while she is rich, beautiful, and ..."

While Amissa was basking, Simone reached out and grabbed the SmartSphere. The round computer was logged into Amissa's QuickFame account. Simone held the sphere in both hands, staring right at the camera.

"...famous," Simone said.

She tapped a few buttons, deleting Amissa's QuickFame account.

With a quick confirmation tap, it was gone forever. Along with her hundreds of millions of followers.

Simone turned toward Amissa. "You lose."

Amissa stared in silence for long seconds. It wasn't sinking in. The huntress just blinked, face blank.

Then it clicked. And Amissa screamed.

It was a scream of pure heartbreak. Of unstoppable fury. A scream of a mother who lost her children, of an empress who lost her throne. Amissa Triplehorn had lost her fame, and to her, that was a tragedy worse than a thousand deaths. Her tortured scream echoed through the library. Outside the windows, the grumbles, snorts, and huffs of rampaging dinosaurs ceased. They must have heard that terrible sound.

"I'm sorry, Amissa," Simone said softly. "I know it hurts. But your addiction to fame drove you mad. It drove you to kill. You can still redeem yourself. There is a path back to forgiveness. Where are the eggs?"

Amissa's scream died on her lips. She gazed at Simone, but her eyes were blank like doll eyes. Her face was pale, expressionless. Something had broken inside her, devouring whatever last shreds of humanity she had possessed. There was no more soul there, Simone realized. Only a hollow space for demons to haunt.

Amissa spoke softly as if trapped in a dream, her eyes still unfocused. "Death by bullets is too good for you. I can't believe I almost showed you such mercy. That's off the table now. Your death … will be far more agonizing. I killed your sister with a dog. And I will kill you with an animal much, much bigger."

She lowered her rifle and pulled a spray can from her vest.

"Amissa, the show is over," Simone said. "Nobody is watching us now. Let's talk. Just two women. Tell me where the eggs are, and we'll—"

Amissa sprayed her from the can. Simone coughed. The miasma covered her clothes, her hair, her face.

"What are you doing?" Simone cried.

Amissa tilted her head. "You wanted to know where the eggs were, didn't you? Well, truth is, I don't know. My people hid them across the city. Maybe the dinosaurs found them already. But oh, don't worry. I brought backup. Spray that smells just like T-rex eggs." She pouted. "Oh, I am afraid that right now … the eggs are *you*."

A grin spread across Amissa's face.

For a moment silence filled the library.

Then a rumble like thunder rolled outside. Footsteps thudded. *Thump. Thump. Thump.* The books danced on the shelves.

"What did you do?" Simone whispered.

Amissa pouted and waved. "Bye-bye, Simone. Say hi to your sis from me."

The huntress spun on her heel and strutted away, vanishing between the bookshelves.

The grumble rolled again. It was coming from right outside the library's western wall. Simone turned, facing the huge stained glass window. A thousand hues of light dappled her. The window was shaking. A shadow loomed beyond. The parti-colored light dimmed, leaving Simone in darkness.

Then a Tyrannosaurus rex burst through the stained glass window, crashing into the library with a furious bellow and a hailstorm of colored glass.

The gargantuan predator landed in the center of the library. It was the big green male. The one Simone had watched slaughter a Ranger. The beast whipped his scaly tail. Bookshelves shattered. Books fell to the floor, scattering pages. The T-rex shook wildly, tossing off shards of glass, then raised his head and howled. It was a cry every bit as horrible and heartbroken as Amissa's scream. She had lost her fame. This dinosaur had lost his unhatched children.

Then the beast saw Simone.

He lowered his head and sniffed. His pupils dilated. *Eggs! My eggs!*

Simone ran.

She raced between two bookshelves, arms pumping. The T-rex followed. The colossal predator barreled down the aisle, shattering shelves. Books rained, thumping onto Simone. She ran through the storm. The dinosaur huffed and grunted behind her, jaws thrusting out to bite her. She could imagine his thoughts.

You stole my eggs! I smell them on you, thief! Die!

The terrible mouth snapped shut. Simone leaped away just in time, rolling between bookshelves. The T-rex found himself biting a bunch of history books. He spat them out, then crashed through the shelves, following the little egg thief.

Simone rolled through piles of books, leaped up, and ran onward. Shelf after shelf collapsed behind her. Genre after genre tumbled. Mysteries, science fiction, romance—they all crashed down. Simone ran with her arms over her head. Books thumped onto her, bruising her pale skin. Other books ended up crushed inside the maw of the T-rex.

Simone whipped around a corner, then shoved a bookshelf with all her strength. The shelf collapsed onto the T-rex, showering the dinosaur with books. She might as well have tossed confetti onto him. The dinosaur burst through the shelf with flying pages and chips of wood.

Simone ran. The T-rex lashed his tail. A shelf came crashing down, blocking her escape. She turned, leaped over fallen cooking books, and slid into the classic literature section. The predator followed, crushing the books under his enormous feet. Arms pumping, Simone made her way toward a metal staircase. The stairs spiraled up toward a mezzanine—the early Cloventian literature section. She wasn't going to make it. The beast's breath washed over her. The terrible jaws opened wide, and—

The T-rex slipped.

He slipped on books!

Literature—saving the day again!

It took the T-rex only a few seconds to leap back up. By then, Simone reached the staircase and ran up, spiraling higher and higher.

The tyrannosaur lunged forward. His mouth closed around the corkscrew staircase. Simone leaped several stairs upward, dodging the terrible teeth. The metal stairs and railing shattered below her feet. She scrambled higher. The jaws snapped again, tearing through more metal stairs.

She leaped onto a long mezzanine and ran. Bookshelves stretched to one side. At her other side, a railing protected her from a fall to the library floor. The dinosaur ran on the ground floor, crushing the fallen books, knocking over globes, shattering the study tables. The mezzanine was probably three stories tall, even taller than the T-rex. For a brief moment, Simone thought she was safe.

Then the rex jumped. His head slammed into the mezzanine from below. Simone jolted and fell.

She pushed herself up, ran onward.

The dinosaur jumped again.

The mezzanine cracked in two. Simone wobbled. She found herself sliding down the tilting mezzanine. The dinosaur's mouth widened below, waiting to devour her.

She grabbed a piece of mangled railing, halting her fall. Her legs kicked in midair. The rex leaped up to bite. Still clinging to the railing, Simone curled her legs upward. The jaws snapped shut just inches below.

"I don't have your eggs!" she cried. For all the good it did. Her terror and rage exploded from her with tears and a passionate cry. "I hate! This! Planet!"

She pulled herself back onto what remained of the mezzanine. The T-rex leaped up, his head shattering the support beams. The entire mezzanine ripped off the wall, along with an ungodly amount of books.

As the mezzanine collapsed below her, Simone leaped into the air.

She sailed for a terrifying second that lasted an eternity.

She grabbed a chandelier and swung. Crystals tore off, pattering into the T-rex.

Simone let go, flew for another eternal second, and landed on another balcony.

"Holy shit!" she blurted out. She almost regretted turning off Amissa's video stream. That was one for the record books. Maybe she should turn on her own SmartSphere and try again.

Wait a minute ...

That gave her an idea.

The T-rex blinked, covered with sharp crystals. He shook them loose, looked round, and saw Simone on the other mezzanine. He stomped closer. Bits of mangled metal hung between his teeth. This balcony was lower than the last one. She was eye level with the dinosaur.

Simone chewed her lip. All right. She had a plan. Of sorts.

"All right, all right! I do have an egg!" she said. "Easy, boy. Easy ... I'll give you what you want."

Standing on the mezzanine, she reached into her pack.

The T-rex tensed, ready to pounce but waiting, watching. In a sudden moment of terror and hilarity, the dinosaur reminded Simone of a dog waiting for its master to toss a stick.

Inside her pack, she felt her SmartSphere. It was switched off and flat like a pancake. She didn't pull it out yet. Glancing into her pack, she tapped a button, and the computer ballooned from a circle into a sphere. She tapped another few buttons. The sphere turned white.

The T-rex took a step closer, sniffing. She stood on a balcony, he stood on the ground floor, but they were still eye level. Bits of stained glass and broken chandelier crystals clung to his green scales. Shredded books dangled from his claws. He let out a terrible cry. His rancid breath blew Simone's hair back. *Where are my eggs!*

Simone pulled out the round, white computer. She cradled it in her hands.

"Here you go! An egg. The only egg I have."

She placed the SmartSphere on the edge of the mezzanine.

The dinosaur bolted forward. Simone scurried backward until her back hit a bookshelf. The T-rex thrust his enormous snout closer, nostrils flaring, sniffing the SmartSphere. The size of that head! The skull in Joe's cave had seemed large. But covered with muscle, fat, and lumpy skin, a T-rex head was even larger. Easily large enough to devour a redhead with a single bite. Yet for now, the dinosaur ignored her. He was still sniffing the sphere.

He's not going to fall for it, Simone thought. *He's too intelligent. He'll know I duped him. Who am I kidding?*

The dinosaur's eyes narrowed. Those eyes appeared tiny on the massive head of the carnivore. But standing so close, Simone realized the eyeballs were the size of grapefruit. He must have impeccable eyesight. Now he focused those eyes on the strange, round object. Simone could imagine his thoughts. *This is strange. It doesn't look quite like an egg. Too small. Too round.* He sniffed. *But it smells like an egg!*

Finally, with surprising gentleness, the dinosaur lifted the SmartSphere in his mouth. He had teeth the size of bread knives, yet he managed to hold the sphere without shattering it.

Ah well, he was probably thinking. *I'm just a male. What do I know of how eggs look? I'll bring this one back to my mate. She'll know more. The redhead can live for now.*

The T-rex turned away. He stomped out of the ruined library, gently carrying the "egg" in his mouth.

Simone slumped to the floor, shaking, head spinning. She let out a weak laugh, and tears flowed down her cheeks.

I'm alive. I faced a T-rex. An actual T-rex, the worst dinosaur of them all! And I'm still alive.

She stood up, trembling, and descended a staircase to the ground floor. Yes, she was alive. But she had failed. Failed to talk sense into Amissa, to find out where the eggs were. Even if the triceratops drove the T-rexes out of Dinovia, it would be temporary. The tyrannosaurs would simply bide their time, then come back. They would not stop until they found their eggs. One SmartSphere would not satisfy them. Especially when they realized it wasn't a real egg.

Something shiny caught her eye. Simone looked down at a pile of books.

A SmartSphere lay there. At first Simone thought it was her own computer. Had the T-rex dropped it, realizing he'd been duped? But no. It wasn't hers.

This was Amissa's SmartSphere.

A trap? No, Simone realized. Without her QuickFame account, the sphere was useless to Amissa. She had discarded it like a piece of garbage. It lay among torn books, a crack along its round screen.

Simone lifted the computer. She tapped a few buttons, scrolling through screens. A few photos, that was about it.

Then …

Simone gasped.

"Bingo," she whispered.

A map of Dinovia City. And on the map—red dots marking the locations of the hidden eggs.

"So you *do* know where they are!" Simone said.

A bunch of dots glowed in different locations. Eggs. Scattered across the city. And the dinosaurs were after them too.

Simone's heart sank. She had hoped all the eggs would be in one location. Simone had barely survived an encounter with one T-rex. How would she survive an Easter egg hunt across so many locations, competing with the frenetic dinosaurs?

"How the hell do I collect all these eggs, take them out of the city, and avoid being eaten?" she whispered.

No wonder Amissa had let her find the map. The knowledge was useless. It was impossible.

CHAPTER TWENTY-THREE
Egg Hunt

As the noon sun beat down, Figaro Triplehorn rode into the city, leading her pack of achillobators.

She had never seen anything like this place. None of them had.

Houses rose everywhere. Fig had thought that Lifa had lived in a proper house. That was nothing, she realized. Houses here weren't made of branches and grass. They seemed built of hardened soil like termite mounds, but they were as big as brontosaurs. And the people! There must have been *hundreds* of them! Figaro had never imagined so many humans could exist, let alone live in one place. There were as many humans here as ants in a colony. Indeed, the entire city reminded her of a huge hive.

Many of those strange, stinky, metallic machines rumbled about, belching out smoke. Humans rode inside. Lifa had told her about those. What were they called again? Right. Jippis. Terrible things! Lifa did not use one, nor did Joe. Smelling the exhaust and hearing the rumbles, Fig understood why. She realized that Joe and Lifa, while so strange to her, were still beings of the wilderness, more like Fig than these urbanites with their terrible machines.

It truly sank in now. How different humans were from dinosaurs. How different Fig was. Humans were unlike any other animal on Mintari. They were not like dinosaurs. Not truly like insects either, despite their bustling hives. Not like fish or frogs, certainly. They were something entirely alien to her. Fig suddenly felt very afraid. Of this city. Of herself. Of who she was.

I'm not a real bator. But neither am I truly human.

She wanted to turn around and flee. To escape into the wilderness. To hide among the bators and live as one of them. Even if she would always be the runt. She had been happy with the pack. Why had she ever gone into this world of humans?

Red Scar was nervous too. He snorted and sneered and his eyes kept darting between the buildings. Like her, he felt trapped. The other achillobators snapped and snarled at everything. Crooked Wing lunged toward a human child, her toothy jaws open wide. The boy fled down an alleyway. Fast Foot, who had the quickest legs but slowest mind in the pack, began chasing a jippi, biting at its bumper. The pack was scared. Becoming too wild. Too aggressive. This was not their natural habitat. They had followed Fig here dutifully, but now they acted like animals in cages.

Riding Red Scar, Fig tossed back her head. She let out a loud howl. "Arooooo!"

Red Scar tossed back his head too. "Aroooo!"

The other bators returned the calls. Their howls echoed through the city.

"Ahhh-woooo!" Fig cried. *Gather here! Unite! Be together! Be strong!*

The pack formed rank behind her. They were on a mission. Fig had been spying on her father. She didn't understand everything that was going on. But she understood enough. The city was in danger. And her father was here. She must help him.

"Arooo!" the pack members cried. Battle cries.

And from the distance came a deeper, louder sound.

A bass rumble.

The sound of a T-rex.

So what Fig had heard was true. The rexes were attacking the city.

The bators sniffed the air, then sneered and moved closer together. Their sickle claws twitched. Fig couldn't smell it, but her hackles rose. Her heart burst into a gallop. The greatest enemy of the achillobators was here. In this city. The creatures they feared most on Mintari.

The rumble rolled again.

Footsteps thudded in the distance.

A huge shadow fell upon the road.

Fig's lip twitched. Her hands trembled. She wanted more than anything to flee. But she forced her fear down. Still riding Red Scar, she straightened her back, raised her chin, and lifted her sickle claw high. She let out the loudest cry her lungs could manage.

"Ahh-ooooooooeeee!"

To battle!

Just then, the T-rex burst from behind a building.

Fig almost fainted. Her heart skipped a beat. Tears sprang into her eyes.

She had never seen a Tyrannosaurus rex up close before. Now she stared at a towering female, a true goddess of hunger. By the stars, they were massive animals. Even larger than she had imagined. This dinosaur dwarfed the achillobators. Every one of her teeth put a sickle claw to shame. Not that a T-rex would even need teeth against Fig. This dinosaur could gulp her down whole, no chewing required. True to their name, they were tyrants. Tyrannosaurus rex ruled Mintari.

And this one wasn't even fully grown, judging by the fuzz across her back. Rexes sported fluffy feathers as hatchlings, then gradually shed them as they grew, unveiling their hard, scaly skin. This T-rex looked just old enough to begin laying eggs. She might be here searching for her first brood. At this young age, she had only lost the feathers across her flanks and snout, revealing snaking patterns of brown and yellow scales. She stomped closer, shattering the cobblestones with every step. Her jaws opened wide, ready to destroy this pack of puny predators. This was her territory now.

Fig liked giving dinosaurs names in her mind. She named this towering foe Featherback. A silly name, perhaps. But there was nothing silly about that hungry hellmouth.

"Ahh—ooooo!" Red Scar cried and charged.

"Aooo aooo!" the pack replied.

They all ran to battle.

Featherback stopped in her tracks. The young T-rex blinked. She must have been thinking: *Who are these little feathery creatures attacking me? They must be crazy! I'll teach them a thing or two.*

The enormous predator thrust down her primary weapon—the most powerful jaws nature had ever created. She reached for one achillobator. The one the puny human cub was riding.

Fig stared upward, eyes wide. Featherback's mouth widened above, prepared to close around her. Fig raised her sickle claw. It felt so pointless. She might as well be wielding a twig.

But Red Scar was fast enough. The bator bolted under the T-rex's snout, carrying Fig to safety. Featherback's jaws snapped shut behind Fig, missing her but catching the tip of Red Scar's tail. The young T-rex spat out red feathers. Red Scar let out a deafening "awoo!" Thankfully, he only seemed to have lost some feathers, not any flesh.

Tail trimmed, the bator raced alongside the T-rex. Figaro didn't waste a second. She leaned sideways and lashed her sickle claw against Featherback's leg.

Nothing.

Nothing!

This sickle claw could disembowel a hadrosaur. It barely even scratched Featherback's scaly skin.

The other achillobators attacked together. They leaped at Featherback's legs. One brave bator bit the giant on the tail. The T-rex howled and kicked and lashed her tail, shaking them off. Annoyed now, the prodigious predator tried using her main weapon again.

Success! This time she grabbed an achillobator!

Fig stared in horror. It was Slender Snout! A female and new mother. Her hatchlings were only a few days old, waiting back at the nesting grounds with an iguanodon leg to sustain them.

Featherback chomped down with relish. Ah, this was better! Not just feathers but actual meat!

Slender Snout screamed. The sound was so horrible that Fig would never forget it. Bones crunched. Blood spurted. Featherback hurled the mangled body aside, then seemed almost to grin, showing off her bloody teeth.

Fig shouted in rage.

She tugged on Red Scar's feathers and pointed at a nearby house. "Yi, yiii!"

Red Scar understood. He ran, scaled up the house walls with his sharp claws, landed on the roof, then jumped toward Featherback.

The achillobator landed on the tyrannosaur's feathery back. Fig swayed, but she managed to keep riding Red Scar, clenching her thighs tightly around him. Beneath them, the young T-rex bucked and howled and danced around, but Red Scar held on. His claws dug through Featherback's coating of fluff and found her skin. Fig leaned over, lashing her own sickle claw. She sliced through the juvenile T-rex's feathers and nicked the scales beneath.

Featherback was not happy. She was only a youngster, not used to battles. There was a nasty little stabby thing on her back. And more stabby things were attacking her legs. A few were scurrying up walls, then launching themselves at her flanks. Terrible little predators! They stung and it hurt. A few of their claws made it through her scales. Blood seeped. Featherback bucked and wriggled, shaking them off.

Red Scar tumbled off the T-rex, thumped down hard onto the road, and growled. Fig spilled onto the cobblestones, skinning her elbows, but leaped back onto Red Scar at once. She bared her teeth and raised her claw.

"Ahoo, ahoooo!" Fig cried. *Keep attacking!*

The achillobators were intelligent hunters. They learned from Red Scar. Instead of attacking Featherback from below, they climbed onto buildings, then swooped from above. Their wings spread, helping them glide through the air. They could not fly like pterosaurs. They were too heavy. But their wings made them decent gliders, and they mobbed the T-rex, attacking from everywhere.

Featherback snapped her jaws, catching Curly Tail, a young bator with resplendent plumage. Featherback crunched him between her jaws, then spat out red feathers. Meanwhile, her tail walloped Long Tooth, a brave and experienced hunter. The old achillobator flew through the air and slammed against a house. The wall cracked. Long Tooth's leg bent with a sickening *snap*. Clouds of feathers filled the road. But the survivors did not flee. They kept clawing and biting, and more and more blood seeped down Featherback's flanks.

Finally the big carnivore had enough. Fig could imagine her thought process. This was pointless, the rex must have decided. She was searching for her eggs—her very first brood. Why was she risking her young life fighting these little assassins?

Not worth it! Very dangerous creatures, these snapping, biting things with red feathers. She would avoid them in the future.

The T-rex ran, heading toward the city gates. The pack of achillobators chased her, snapping at her heels and tail, until the mythical beast was out of Dinovia City.

Fig gasped in shock and relief, her body shaking. For the first time, the pack had defeated a T-rex! They won the battle!

But then tears flooded her eyes. The victory was not without sacrifice.

With their enemy scared away, the survivors of the pack approached their fallen.

Figaro let out a hoarse cry of grief.

Three bators lay on the road. Slender Snout and Curly Tail were dead. Featherback's teeth had crushed them. T-rex teeth were dull. They were designed not to cut flesh but to crush bone. The bator bodies were broken, but their heads were still whole, gazing skyward with blank eyes. Long Tooth lay on a pile of rubble, groaning. His leg was broken. Maybe several ribs too. To an achillobator, that was a death sentence.

Figaro fell to her knees, and tears flowed down her cheeks.

I led us here. This is my war. Now three of my pack members are gone.

The surviving bators nudged the dead with their snouts, then cried in mourning.

Tears in her eyes, Figaro pointed at the shattered gates. She made a series of groans, yips, and mewls.

Go, pack. Return to the wild. I'll continue alone. This is my war.

Achillobator language was not complex enough for so many words, but she conveyed their meaning with her tone and body language. They understood.

Growling, Red Scar came to stand at her side. *I'm with you.*

Crooked Wing joined them, head raised. She snorted. *I'm with the little runt.*

The others joined too, surrounding Fig. They were pack. They would fight for her. They would never leave her.

Their loyalty touched Fig. But how could she continue? If she stayed to fight, more bators might die. Should she leave Dinovia, leading the pack back into the wild?

But the pack moved down the road, heading deeper into the city.

They want to continue, Fig realized, tears running down her cheeks. *For me.*

Sniffing, she joined them.

They left behind Long Tooth, the old hunter with the broken leg. As they walked, they heard his pitiful wails. He was calling out to them. *Don't leave me! Don't leave!*

But they left him. With a broken leg, he could no longer hunt. Nor could he lay eggs, being a male. He was useless to the pack now. So they left him to die. His death would be slow and torturous. It would take him days, maybe weeks to starve to death. But that was the way of Mintari. Of survival. The lone bator died but the pack survived.

I wonder if humans would leave one of their own, Fig thought. *I wonder if they would think us savage. Maybe humans are nobler than us. But we are pack. We are survivors.*

And strangely, here in this city full of humans, Fig felt more like a bator than ever.

Gunshots rattled in the distance.

A dinosaur howled, then a thump shook the earth.

Fig jumped. The bators snarled. The pack looked toward the source of the sound.

Down the block, a T-rex had fallen. A big male with brown scales. Only his head was visible, lying across the road. Several holes gaped open on his skull.

Over the past few days, Fig had learned a little about these terrible weapons humans wielded. These things called "guns." They struck with the force of many claws. During her time outside Joe's cave, eavesdropping on her father, she had learned about poachers hunting with these guns. Killing dinosaurs for sport.

And Fig realized something. This mission here in Dinovia City—this wasn't just *her* war. This wasn't just about finding her father.

It was a war for Mintari. A war between those who wanted to protect Mintari and those who sought to destroy it. That was why Joe had come here. To fight for Mintari. And that was why the pack must fight too. Maybe the bators had understood this before Fig. Maybe they had been trying to tell her.

Motors hummed. Smoke wafted from down the block, obscuring the dead T-rex head. Voices sounded from around the corner.

"Good shot, brother! Tarry good shot."

"Got a T-rex! Even Amissa hasn't killed one of these bastards."

"We're the first ones, brother! The first hunters to ever kill a Tyrannosaurus rex!"

"And the first ones to eat a Tyrannosaurus rex. Tuck in, brother!"

Fig could not see who was speaking. But those words shot trembles of rage through her. Those were cruel voices. She knew enough about humans to recognize that.

She gestured to the pack with her eyes. They understood. Fig climbed onto Red Scar, and they slunk down the road, silent, approaching the dead T-rex. They could only see the head. The dinosaur's body was still hidden behind the corner.

Fig heard the sound of eating. Not, not just eating but guzzling. It was a wet, gurgling sound. Years ago, Fig had stepped on a beached jellyfish, squelching it under her foot. It had made a similar sound. Riding on Red Scar, she turned the corner and saw them.

Two enormous humans sat atop the dead T-rex. Fig's eyes widened. They were the largest humans she had ever seen. They had round bodies like a brontosaurus but without the graceful necks. Without *any* necks for that matter. They both had messy hair and big bushy beards. They looked exactly the same—twins, she surmised. While eavesdropping outside the cave, Fig had heard Simone talk of having a twin.

The hirsute brothers did not notice her. They were busy devouring the dead dinosaur. With big blades, they were peeling back the skin, sawing off chunks of meat, and stuffing their cheeks. Saliva and blood matted their beards. They paused only to belch, then kept guzzling meat down. This was not eating to survive. It was sloth, conquest, a show of dominance. It disgusted Fig. She growled low in her throat. So did the others in her pack.

One of the obese twins looked up. He wiped blood off his mouth and grinned.

"Look, Gus!" He elbowed his twin, who was still guzzling down raw meat.

"Not now, Grant. Eating."

"You'll like this. Look!"

Gus wiped his lips and looked up. Both brothers stared at the pack. Both grinned.

"My, my, what are those?" Gus said. "They look like big red chickens."

Grant licked his lips. "And there's a little slip of a girl on one. What's your name, sweetheart?"

"Maybe we should eat her too." Gus laughed, belly jiggling. "What do you say, brother? I've never tasted human flesh."

"All right, let's kill them and taste them." Grant aimed his rifle.

Fig tugged Red Scar's right flank feathers. The bator leaped to the right. The gun roared. A hailstorm of bullets hit the cobblestones, narrowly missing Red Scar. This was not like the guns the Rangers used, which only fired one bullet at a time. This terrible weapon was spitting out bullets faster than a velociraptor pecking at bugs.

"Aahhhrrrra!" Fig cried. *Attack!*

The pack swarmed.

Gus raised his rifle too. Both twins opened fire.

One bator fell, riddled with bullets. Then another.

Zigzagging to avoid the bullets, Red Scar raced toward the dead T-rex. The twins sat atop the carcass, dealing death from on high. A bullet hit Red Scar's wingtip, ripping off a claw. He yowled and wobbled. Fig tightened her thighs around his flanks, barely clinging on. A bullet grazed her arm. She hissed, bared her teeth, and raised her sickle claw.

They managed to reach the dead T-rex. Growling, Red Scar scurried up the carcass, then leaped toward the twins. Riding the bator, Fig let out a battle cry. "Arooo!"

One of the twins—Gus—raised his rifle. The muzzle faced them.

Fig grimaced, seeing death ahead.

Gus's finger twitched over the trigger.

With a screech, Crooked Wing leaped from the side, slamming into the poacher.

His gun boomed. Bullets hit a nearby balcony, just missing Fig and Red Scar.

With furious screeches, Crooked Wing lashed her claws, carving open Gus's neck. Blood spurted. An instant later, Crooked Wing was chomping down on his head, crushing the skull.

The second twin, Grant, screamed and tried to flee. But Long Tail snarled at him, blocking his escape. The obese man turned the other way, only to meet Narrow Eye's snarling jaws.

But it was Red Scar who leaped onto the man, knocking him down. And it was his claw that sliced the man's throat.

The bators dragged the two dead poachers onto the roadside. Fig stood on the bloodied cobblestones, watching, feeling hollow. Two humans dead. She had not killed them herself, but she led this pack. Those deaths were on her.

I killed two of my fellow humans.

She didn't know how to feel.

Crooked Wing looked up at her, panting. Long Tail tilted his head and licked his chops. The entire pack was watching her. *Can we eat?*

Fig snapped her teeth and grunted. *Eat.*

The bators leaped onto the corpses and tucked in. They had not eaten yet today. They were famished and they feasted. T-rex meat was tough, but fat humans were delectable.

Fig turned away, eyes burning. Disgust filled her belly. *Maybe I'm not so human after all. Maybe I'm just a predator. Maybe I'm a monster.*

She stumbled into an alleyway, wrapped her arms around her belly, and vomited.

The survivors of the pack continued through the city. The achillobators were well fed and riled up. They were already raring for another fight, but Fig's stomach was a knot. Chaos filled Dinovia. T-rexes rumbled through the city, looking for their eggs, destroying buildings in their frenzied search. Trikes raced after them, trying to herd them out of the city, but only infuriating the predators. Rangers raced everywhere on their jippis, trying to tranquilize the dinosaurs. One rex was slumbering, her scaly body bristly with tranquilizer darts. But most of the T-rexes brushed off the darts and savaged the Rangers who fired them. The city folk were fleeing their crumbling homes, racing everywhere, shouting, praying.

Fig walked through this nightmare, seeking her father.

"Yaooo!" she cried.

Red Scar looked at her and tilted his head. The other bators seemed just as confused. Yaooo? What command was this?

Fig tried again. "Yaooo!"

She was trying to say "Joe!" but her tongue was clumsy. If Joe heard her, he probably just mistook her for a dinosaur. This talking thing would definitely take some practice.

"Fa-de!" she tried calling. "Fa-de!" *Father! Father!*

Ah, that was a bit easier to pronounce. But of course that was pointless. Even if Joe *could* hear her, and even if he *could* understand her, he wouldn't realize she was calling him. As far as he knew, his daughter had died fifteen years ago. Devoured by King Ivan before ever being born.

Then Fig realized how she could find him.

Because Ivan was in this city. And Joe would go straight to the tyrant, seeking his vengeance.

Well, how hard could it be to find a mutant dinosaur with black scales, eyes like fire, and teeth that made a normal T-rex seem like a herbivore? It couldn't be too hard. Fig just needed to follow the screams.

She moved onward through the city. Indeed, screams filled Dinovia. Human screams. But they were coming from everywhere. People were running every which way. Rexes were still trudging down the streets, cracking open buildings, sniffing for eggs, and sometimes pausing for a human snack.

Fig couldn't see very far. The buildings rose everywhere, crammed closer than trees in a forest. Tar it, how did anyone *see* anything in this city? Every street was like a canyon. Fig couldn't imagine living in a place like this.

She climbed onto a rooftop and looked around her. Even on the domed roof, she wasn't high enough to see very far. Only a block or so in every direction. Better than nothing. Dinosaurs were still roaming through the city, heads rising above the buildings. From here, Fig could see two rumbling triceratops, a few dactyls picking at a corpse, and several green and brown T-rexes. None with black scales. Ivan must be beyond her field of vision. A few neighborhoods rose behind hills, and Fig couldn't see those streets from here. The city was larger than she had imagined.

A flash of red caught her eyes.

Not the red feathers of an achillobator either. Red hair.

Standing on the roof, Fig gasped. Simone! Simone was just a block away!

Fig had spent long hours outside the cave, spying on her father and his redheaded friend. The two were clearly close. But where was Joe? She couldn't see him. Surely Simone would know where he was!

Fig climbed back onto the road and ran. The pack ran behind her. A triceratops came rumbling down the road, his gargantuan feet leaving potholes. The achillobators hopped backward, narrowly avoiding being trampled. Then they raced onward. People fled from the pack in terror. It hurt Fig to see them run.

Don't fear my pack! she wanted to cry. *We're here to help!*

But then again, her bators had just eaten two humans. Maybe the city folk were right to run.

The pack raced around a corner, sending a family fleeing, and Fig saw that flash of red hair again.

"S'ma!" Fig cried. "S'ma!"

Closest she could manage to "Simone." Hopefully close enough. Tar it, why couldn't her mouth shape these human words? Simone didn't acknowledge her. She was far down the block, unreachable behind a throng of people.

Fig herded her pack into a shadowy alleyway. No need to cause a panic.

"Rrrrr," she purred at Red Scar and the others. *Stay here.*

Leaving the achillobators in the shadows, Fig raced down the crowded road, elbowing her way between humans.

"S'ma!"

Now that she was afoot, Fig noticed something. She was very small for a human. Smaller than anyone but children. She had to hop to peek over people's shoulders. Was this because she was still a hatchling? Would she grow taller? Or was she a runt even by human standards? Well, she had plenty of time to worry about that later.

Simone was closer now. Her red hair stood out in the crowd like a flame in a field of deadwood.

"S'ma!" Fig called out again.

It worked! Simone turned toward her. Her blue eyes narrowed, scanning the crowd. She didn't see Fig. Tar it! She was too short. She needed to clear this crowd.

Fig whistled, and the pack burst out from the alleyway. People screamed and ran.

The bators scrambled forward, causing a panic. People fled, screaming. A few bators leaped onto the nearby buildings and hopped between balconies, sending flowerpots cascading down. Crooked Wing snapped her jaws at a few men, ripping the seat of one's pants. They ran for their lives. The crowd was clearing the street.

Simone perhaps could not see Fig. But she definitely saw the pack of red-feathered theropods. Her eyes widened, and she turned to flee.

Fig groaned in frustration. Her plan was backfiring.

"S'ma!" she cried out. No response.

Red Scar ran up to her. Fig leaped onto him, and she pointed at the fleeing redhead.

"Waoo, waoo!" she cried. *Follow her!*

The pack ran, whipping around and above fleeing people. Simone ran down the road, arms pumping. Clearly she was terrified. Who could blame her?

"S'ma! Um na har a!" *Simone, I'm not going to hurt you!*

Oh, this talking thing was pointless. How did humans do it? The redhead kept fleeing. Fig pursed her lips. She tugged on Red Scar's feathers, directing him. The bator leaped sideways, clutched a building with his sharp claws, and raced along the wall like a big feathered spider. He scrambled higher, vaulted off a domed roof, and landed in a cobbled square. Just ahead of Simone.

The redhead screamed and spun around. But Crooked Wing was behind her, teeth bared and eyes wild. Simone tried to run in another direction, but Blue Eyes blocked her way, his feathers bristling. The pack surrounded her. The young woman drew a knife, ready to go down fighting.

All around, other humans were fleeing, leaving Simone in the circle of bators. So much for humans being the nobler species. They too, it seemed, were quick to leave one of their own behind.

"Stand back!" Simone said, weapon raised but voice trembling. "Or I'll cut you!"

"S'ma! Um na har a!"

Fig hopped off Red Scar and stepped closer.

Simone looked from side to side at the bators. The feathery carnivores were snarling, keeping her trapped in a tight noose. A few were salivating. They were predators by nature, and they saw Simone as prey. Already they were hungry again. Crooked Wing licked her chops.

Fig glared at them. "Hai, hai!" *Back off!*

They sneered. She had led them on a hunt! Now she would deprive them of meat? Blue Eyes growled and bared his teeth. But Fig snarled right back at him. She stared the bators down one by one. They lowered their muzzles and stepped back.

Simone was watching her curiously.

"Who are you?" she said softly.

Fig tapped her chest. "Fi-ga-ro." She pointed at Simone. "S'ma?" She tried again. "S'maannn?"

Simone's eyebrows rose. "Yes, I'm Simone. Do I know you?"

Suddenly tears flowed down Fig's eyes, and she didn't even know why. She tapped her chest again. "Fi-ga-ro ... Yao's ... da-ta."

I'm Joe's daughter.

Simone stepped closer, eyes narrowed, scrutinizing her. Then she gasped. "I see it. You look just like her. Like the woman in the photo. Like Mina ..."

And now Fig was trembling, and tears rolled down her cheeks. Simone pulled her into her arms, engulfing her in a warm hug. Figaro barely reached Simone's shoulders. She felt so small, so afraid, but also so warm and protected.

She tried talking again. "Waaaooo Fi-ga-ro fa … da?" *Where's my father?* She was almost getting the hang of this talking thing. Almost.

Simone placed her hands on Fig's cheeks and stared into her eyes. "Listen to me, Figaro. I don't know how you're still alive. I don't know by what miracle you came back. And I believe you are a miracle. And I believe there's a reason you came back now, today, at our hour of need. I'll take you to see your father soon. But first I need your help." She looked around at the pack of bators. "All your help. We need to dig out the T-rex eggs."

The achillobators raced through the city like wildfire, zipping down the streets, leaping from balconies and archways, bounding across rooftops. They swerved around, slipped under, or hopped over the rumbling triceratops. If a T-rex snapped at them, the smaller and quicker bators fled. They ran onward.

They knew the way. Fig was leading them. And she had a map.

Back in the wilderness, Lifa had explained to Fig what maps were. She had shown her a map of Mintari, displaying the locations of mountains, forests, and glens. But this map was entirely different. Simone had given it to her, and it was truly magical. The map was located within a floating sphere. Fig didn't even need to hold it. No matter how fast she rode through the city, the sphere hovered beside her.

Inside the sphere, Fig could see the labyrinthine streets of Dinovia marked with white lines. Red dots showed the location of T-rex eggs. A blue dot indicated Fig's own position. As she kept riding, the blue dot kept moving through the labyrinth.

It was funny. Only days ago, Fig had thought human clothes were totally bizarre. A simple mirror had boggled her mind. Now a spherical computer was floating beside her, displaying her location on a map, and Fig simply went along with it. Strange how fast one could get used to human miracles.

Fig couldn't help it. As she rode through the city, and as the sphere floated beside her, she laughed. Running beside her, Crooked Wing cocked her head and glanced at her sideways. That only made Fig laugh louder.

This is wonderful, she thought. *This is the most wonderful day in my life.*

A T-rex came stomping toward them. Fig tugged Red Scar's feathers. The pack swerved onto a side road. The map kept updating their location. The pack rushed down the cobbled alleyway but hit a roadblock. A triceratops! The burly dinosaur came stomping their way, horns lowered, ready to plow into the pack. Fig yelped and tugged the feathers again. The pack schooled onto another road, dodging the charging juggernaut.

An entire herd of triceratops awaited them ahead. The huge herbivores had no love for any theropods, be they towering T-rexes or bantam bators. They lowered their horns and charged.

Fig tugged feathers with both hands, leaning backward, and let out a cry. "Ayyeee!"

The pack ran, hopped over merchant stalls, and scrambled onto rooftops. They raced onward, leaping over the triceratops horns, then jumping from roof to roof. Ah yes, much easier to navigate the city this way.

As the pack hopped along the rooftops, a jippi roared down the road, doing its best to keep up. Simone sat behind the wheel. They had found the jippi a few streets back. A Mintari Ranger jippi with big wheels, a loud engine, and dinosaur scales painted onto the sides. Hopefully, the Rangers wouldn't mind Simone borrowing it. The redhead was driving fast, yanking the wheel from side to side, swerving at breakneck speed down the streets. Every once in a while, she knocked over carts, flowerpots, and road signs. The woman wasn't very good at driving but she *was* tarry fast.

Fig's job was to lead the bators to the T-rex eggs and dig them out. Simone would carry them in her jippi.

When Fig looked up from the jippi, her eyes widened.

A T-rex was stomping a few streets away, shaking the nearby buildings, moving toward the road Simone was driving down. A big gray male, his eyes narrowed and nostrils flared. Fig, who always gave dinosaurs names, decided to name this one Lumpy, due to the warts across his body.

She was still riding Red Scar, hopping from roof to roof. From up here, she had a good view ahead. She looked back down at the jippi. Simone was still driving straight ahead, oblivious. The redhead could not see Lumpy from down there.

"S'ma!" Fig shouted. "S'ma, laa aooo!" *Look out!* "S'ma, a da-ra!" *A T-rex!*

Simone looked up from her jippi. She gave Fig the thumbs-up. "All good down here!"

Fig groaned in frustration. "S'ma, laa aoo—"

Just then Lumpy burst around a four-story hotel. Simone finally saw the dinosaur. She yelped and tugged the wheel hard. The jippi swerved around the T-rex, rose on its side wheels, slammed down hard, and kept racing down the road. The dinosaur grunted and gave chase. Angry at the loss of his eggs, Lumpy was ready to take out his rage on this malodorous machine. His muzzle thrust down, reaching toward the back bumper.

With a battle cry, Fig tugged Red Scar's feathers. The bator leaped off the roof, landed on Lumpy, and slashed his warty back. The T-rex rumbled and bucked, trying to shake off this small, impudent dinosaur. Red Scar hopped off Lumpy, landed on a barbershop's roof, and yipped, taunting the much-larger predator.

Lumpy forgot all about Simone in her jippi. The T-rex made a lunge at Red Scar, but he only managed to shatter the barbershop. Clay bricks clattered down. Clouds of dust filled the air. A striped barber's pole rolled down the road. Red Scar leaped from the crumbling roof onto another house.

The other bators evidently thought this was some delightful game. They too began jumping onto Lumpy, slashing his back, then hopping away. The poor tyrannosaur could not swat them off. Not with his puny arms. Out in the countryside, he could chase bators down and crush them between his jaws. But here inside Dinovia, Lumpy was trapped in a canyon, and the infernal feathered menaces kept dive-bombing him.

Finally poor old Lumpy had enough. He would find some other jippi to terrorize. One that wasn't guarded by feathered little devils. Grunting and bleeding, the T-rex stomped away in disgust.

They were nearing the first egg now. According to the map, it was right ahead inside a bakery. Fig wasn't sure what a bakery was. Simone had told her it had something to do with food. Very well then. Toward the bakery they jumped.

Dinosaurs had an excellent sense of smell. They could smell eggs from a mile away. But to confound them, the poachers had sprayed egg-scent across the city. Right now the entire city smelled like eggs. The T-rexes couldn't pinpoint the real eggs. With her map, Fig could.

They reached the bakery. Fig rode through the front door on Red Scar's back. A few more achillobators burst through the windows. The bakers inside screamed and fled through the back door. At once, the pack began rummaging around, sniffing, seeking the egg. They ripped through sacks, and powder flew everywhere, painting them white. Fig coughed. A few bators sneezed. What was this powder? Probably more human nonsense. Fig would ask Simone about it later. Right now—the egg.

Fig helped the bators look. A shelf held strange, aromatic lumps. Fig sniffed. Food? It smelled good. But it was not meat, not berries, not fruit. What could it be? She lifted one of the warm loaves, sniffed more closely, and took a bite. Her eyes rolled back. Yum! Good food. Whatever this was—good!

Then she saw it. There behind a few loaves.

A T-rex egg.

She grabbed it and left the bakery. Simone was waiting outside in her jippi.

"Ga eh!" Fig cried. *Got it!*

She tossed the egg to Simone. The redhead caught it, fumbled, and nearly dropped it. But she managed to steady her grip, then place the egg into the jippi. Were all humans this clumsy?

"Good job, Figaro. Now let's keep going. We've got lots more to find!"

They kept racing through the city, chasing the second egg. They found this one inside a saloon called the Fossil and Firkin. The egg was hidden among bottles above the bar. A third egg they found in an old man's garden. It was nestled among his rock collection. More eggs hid among the laundry at the Tar Pit, a cheap hotel popular with price-conscious tourists. Other eggs hid inside a kindergarten among the dolls.

As they kept retrieving eggs, anger grew in Fig. This poacher, this Amissa, had hidden eggs among human cubs! The cubs could have died! And Fig realized how truly different humans were from dinosaurs. All dinosaurs, from the smallest raptors to the biggest sauropods, simply struggled to survive. If they killed, it was to eat or defend themselves. If they left a member behind, it was so the pack could survive. They were not evil. Nor were they good. They were simply interested in living another day.

But humans were different, Fig realized. Some were noble like Simone, endangering themselves to save others. Some humans were wicked like Amissa. If Fig integrated in human society, she wondered what kind of human she would become.

Well, first she must save the city. She could contemplate good and evil to her heart's content once the rexes were out. They kept hunting, following the map, finding the eggs one by one. It was Red Scar who found the last egg. It was in a flower shop, hidden inside a clay jug. Fig placed it into Simone's jippi. The search was complete.

By now, the sun was setting, the wind was blowing, and the artificial egg-scented spray was dispersing. Meanwhile, Simone's jippi was exuding a strong, concentrated smell. Eggs! T-rex eggs! A whole pile of them, wafting their aroma for all to smell. They nested in the jippi's cargo hold, secured with bungee cords.

Snorts and sniffs sounded across the city. Then footfalls and grunts.

The T-rexes were no longer confused. With the eggs in one place, they knew where to go. They came charging down the streets. Heading right toward the jippi.

"We need to get out of here—now!" Simone said.

Fig reached into the jippi and grabbed her. "S'ma! Cam, cam!" *Get away from that jippi!*

Simone shook her head. "No, I can't just leave the eggs here. We need to lure the dinosaurs out of the city. Hop into the jippi!"

Fig heard the T-rexes stomping closer. She could see a few of their scaly heads above the rooftops.

Jippi? No, thanks. Fig hopped onto Red Scar. She'd ride the bator instead.

Simone floored the gas pedal, and the jippi roared down the road. The clutch of eggs rattled in the cargo hold. The bungee cords kept them in place.

One T-rex began to chase her. Then another. And a third. Soon an entire pack of the huge predators was stomping down the road, chasing the jippi with the precious eggs inside. Their feet shattered cobblestones. Their tails whipped buildings down. Clouds of dust rose behind them.

Simone drove faster. The rexes stampeded in pursuit, crashing through houses, knocking over parked jippis, destroying merchant stalls. Barely any humans remained on the streets now; they must have fled the city. As Simone drove, Fig and her pack hopped from roof to roof, following the procession.

Finally they saw it ahead. The towering wall that divided city from wilderness. Simone roared in her jippi toward the archway where the great wooden doors had stood. Those doors still lay shattered across the road. Simone just had to drive out, and the rexes would follow.

But Simone didn't see what Fig did.

She was riding Red Scar, vaulting from roof to roof. From up here, she saw it.

There was no way out.

Somebody had destroyed the drawbridge. Most likely, it was Amissa or another poacher, trying to keep the dinosaurs inside the city. The bridge had been torn apart. Chunks of wood floated in the moat.

If Simone kept driving out the gateway, she would plunge into the moat and perish.

"S'ma!" Fig shouted from the rooftops.

But Simone couldn't hear her. The jippi's engine was roaring. Hot in pursuit, the T-rexes were rumbling just as loudly.

"S'ma, S'ma!"

The woman couldn't hear. And in the shadows of sunset, she couldn't see the destruction ahead. Simone was driving faster, faster, almost out the gates now.

Fig tightened her lip.

"Yip yip!" she cried, tugging Red Scar's feathers.

The bator obeyed. He leaped from the rooftops and landed on the jippi. Fig jumped off Red Scar, swung into the passenger seat, and grabbed Simone.

"Stap stap! Bri din!" *Bridge down!*

Simone's eyes widened. She understood. Seconds before racing out the gateway, she tugged the steering wheel. The jippi swerved down a side road, burned rubber, hit a wall, and jolted to a stop. The engine coughed and died.

For a moment, Simone and Fig sat in the dead jippi together, taking deep breaths. Amazingly, not a single egg had cracked. The entire clutch still sat in the cargo hold.

In the rearview mirror, Fig saw the T-rexes approach. Stars above, they were enormous. There were seven, maybe eight or nine. They barely squeezed onto the road. Their flanks grazed the nearby buildings, cracking walls. The entire pack stomped toward the jippi, raising dust with every footfall.

Simone and Fig leaped from the jippi and ran.

The dinosaurs did not follow. They didn't care about two measly little morsels of meat. Only the eggs mattered now. One rex ripped the tailgate off, revealing the precious cargo.

The T-rexes lost all their anger. They no longer bared their teeth. They did not grumble, snort, or bellow. They made soft cooing sounds. One rex stuck her snout into the jippi and nuzzled the eggs. The other dinosaurs whimpered, and it sounded almost like they were crying with joy.

Simone and Fig stood in the shadows, holding hands, watching. The pack of bators gathered behind them, silent and watchful.

One by one, the rexes gathered eggs into their mouths. They had the most powerful teeth in nature. They had ripped the tailgate off the jippi like it was made of straw. They could bite through brick walls. Yet they lifted the eggs so gently that not a single one cracked.

Simone sniffed, and when Fig looked up, the redhead had tears in her eyes.

"They're not monsters," she whispered. "They're beautiful."

The dinosaurs couldn't leave the city with their eggs. Not with the drawbridge at the bottom of the moat. But T-rexes were intelligent animals. Several T-rexes, all bulky males, began shoving the thick wall that surrounded Dinovia. With their huge mass, they cracked the wall, then toppled a chunk of it. Bricks rained into the moat, and dust rose in a cloud. And the dinosaurs had their way out.

Carrying their eggs, they stepped over the pile of rubble, crossed the moat, and vanished into the wilderness.

Fig was surprised to find tears in her own eyes. She knuckled them away.

Then she realized something, and a chill ran through her.

She had not seen a spiky black T-rex leave the city with the pack.

And then she heard it. A terrible rumble like thunder. It came from deep inside the city. A sound like an erupting volcano. Like a crashing wave. A sound that reverberated through Fig's very bones.

He was still in the city. The king.

"Ivan," she whispered.

CHAPTER TWENTY-FOUR
The Battle of Buckland Hill

All day, Joe had been hunting him.

All day, as the battle raged across Dinovia City, Joe focused on his quarry. Throughout a day of crumbling buildings, of dying Rangers, of rampaging rexes and trampling trikes, Joe had stalked the beast.

Now Nyx had set. Now the twin moons shone their eerie light—just like on that night long ago. And now Joe saw his nemesis.

There ahead he rose, towering over rooftops, a shadow in the night.

King Ivan.

Joe's upper lip twitched. His fists clenched. There he was! There was the bastard! There was the beast! There was the tyrant who had murdered his wife. The monster who had swallowed his unborn child. There he was, this freak of nature, this thing that should not be, this creature that stained the world.

Staring from a distance, Joe was suddenly back there. Fifteen years ago. A rookie Ranger in the wilderness, afraid, hurt, watching the great black T-rex devour the love of his life. He was shaking. His eyes burned.

Sitting atop Dozer, Joe leaned forward and gripped the trike's frill.

"Are you ready, Dozer?" he said through stiff lips. His voice shook with anger and fear. "Are you ready to face him?"

Dozer grunted, stamped his feet, and tossed his head. *Let's roll.*

Behind Dozer, several more trikes grunted and reared and swiveled their heads from side to side, brandishing their horns. Several trikes had died in the battle so far. Several more were elsewhere in the city, searching for any remaining tyrannosaurs. But Joe had seven of the hardy herbivores here with him. Seven tanks. Seven of the most powerful weapons nature had ever created, rivaling any carnivore. And tonight he would lead them to victory.

"Charge!" Joe cried, raising his sleep-or-die overhead like a banner.

Dozer burst into a gallop, and the others followed. The triceratops army rumbled along the street, pulverizing the cobblestones beneath their feet.

"There he is!" Joe cried, pointing the way. "There on the hilltop! *Charge!*"

The triceratops rumbled up the coiling road, heading to the top of Buckland Hill, the highest place in Dinovia City.

Five hundred years ago, the first pilgrims from Earth landed on this hill. The first humans to set foot on Mintari. Here on this good world, they decided, they would create a safe haven for dinosaurs. A place to restore these majestic animals from Earth's past and let them roam free. Their starship, *Darwin's Ark*, still stood on the hilltop all these centuries later. The ship was rusty and bent now. But she was still a grand monument to Mintari's history and purpose.

The small research camp the pilgrims had built around their starship had grown into a city. To this day, the founders' vision lived on. To ensure Mintari belonged to dinosaurs. To remember that humans were only here as caretakers, not masters. Some Mintarians forgot this purpose. They raced dinosaurs for sport in the derby. They drove tourists around in rattling jippis, disturbing dinosaurs in their natural habitats. But Joe remembered. He still honored the vision of the first pilgrims. It was a vision Joe dedicated his life to.

Now Ivan was slowly, methodically dismantling the starship on the hilltop. With jaws the size of a car, he kept crunching through the rusty hull, ripping off chunks of metal, and scattering them across the hilltop. It was as if Ivan knew what this old monument represented—and he was destroying it.

Like he destroyed my life, Joe thought.

Because Ivan was not natural to this world. He was a mutant. A freak. A monster. And Joe would end him now.

The triceratops battalion charged uphill toward the beast. Ivan spun away from the mangled starship, placed his foot atop a chunk of rusty metal, opened his jaws wide, and let out a deafening rumble. Strings of saliva quivered between his teeth. His tongue vibrated. His cry echoed across the city and the wilderness beyond, rattling pebbles and dust with waves of bass.

The trikes hesitated. Even Dozer slowed down. They had slain T-rexes before. But this was different.

"Charge!" Joe cried. "Charge at him, Dozer!"

The trike gained heart and galloped with a new burst of speed, his horns pointing the way. The other triceratops hesitated only a moment longer, then kept running uphill, following their leader. Dozer was the largest among them, a scarred old bull, the victor of many battles. The others herded behind him, ready to fight with their master.

They were very close to the hilltop now. Ivan awaited there like an ancient god upon Olympus. The triceratops battalion rumbled higher and higher up the hill. The road coiled between tall, narrow houses like a snaking canyon. It was, Joe realized as the trikes herded along, the perfect place for—

Gunshots rang.

Smoke filled the night.

Bullets pounded the herd.

An ambush.

Triceratops yowled with pain—horrible sounds, sounds that broke Joe's heart. The headstrong herbivores reared. All their armor was on their heads. In nature, they always turned those heads toward an enemy. Evolution had denied them armor on their bodies, but it had given them incredibly agile necks. They could swivel their skull on ball joints, using their frills as a shield. The strongest predators struggled to penetrate a triceratops frill. But now hidden snipers were firing on their unprotected bodies. Their skin was thick and scaly but no match for guns. Bullets plowed into their flesh. The trikes cried out in agony.

Two bullets hit Dozer—one on the tail, one on his bony frill. He let out a raspy cry.

Joe opened fire. In the night, he couldn't see who he was firing on. He shot toward the rooftops, simply laying down suppressive fire, trying to scatter the attackers. Somewhere in the night, he heard a familiar laugh. Feminine. Deranged. Amissa was here. Probably with a bunch of her fellow poachers.

"Dozer, keep going!" Joe cried.

He must reach the hilltop. There, in the open moonlight, the poachers would have no place to hide.

Dozer understood. He kept charging. One trike fell behind him. But the others trudged onward through a storm of bullets.

A motor roared.

A heavy armored jippi burst out from an alleyway. It was twice the size of a normal jippi, so big it dominated both lanes. A spiky metal cowcatcher thrust out from the front. A cadaverous man was driving. He wore a black coat, a wide-brimmed hat, and crisscrossing bandoleers. His cheeks were gaunt, his mouth like a slit in leather. His sunken eyes were pure black, no white to them

at all. The eyes of a shabu addict. A drug that made you strong
but drove you to madness.

Joe recognized that weathered face. He had seen it on
wanted ads before. Rattlesnake. One of the most notorious
poachers in the galaxy.

Clutching the steering wheel, Rattlesnake grinned,
showing brown teeth. He raced his jippi toward a big female
triceratops with bluish scales. The cow saw him coming, but the
road was too narrow for her to turn around. The jippi was roaring
up from behind her.

Rattlesnake plowed his cowcatcher into the dinosaur.

The triceratops bellowed. She was a huge beast. As large
as this gargantuan jippi. But Rattlesnake had hit her with
tremendous force, possibly even breaking her legs. And those legs
were as thick as tree trunks. The blue dinosaur stumbled aside,
wobbled, and fell down hard, shaking the hill.

Rattlesnake leaned out the jippi window, aimed a machine
gun, and opened fire.

Another jippi burst out from an alleyway, peeling off the
walls of nearby shops. And a third one. And a fourth. A poacher
rode in each vehicle, firing out the window. Another triceratops
fell, riddled with bullets.

The herd crumbled.

A few triceratops were dead. A few others tried to flee,
trampling the others. Some brave trike charged at the jippis. One
big cow slipped her horns under one jippi, then hurled it through
the air. The vehicle spun several times before crashing into a
house. More poachers on the roof opened fire, riddling the cow
with bullets. One jippi tried to flee only for a triceratops to charge
in pursuit, ramming the back bumper. The jippi skidded and
crashed into a café. The windows shattered. Strudels and coffee
spilled across the road.

As the herd fell apart behind him, Dozer kept charging uphill. He knew his mission. He would not be distracted. Even if he must leave some dinosaurs behind. With Joe on his back, Dozer raced up the last length of road and burst onto the hilltop.

He awaited there.

Ivan. The King of Mintari.

Dozer was an unusually big triceratops, heavier than most other trikes, even heavier than most T-rexes. He could easily flip over jippis. Were he on the ice planet Borealis, Dozer would make mammoths look puny. And even Dozer, this colossal beast, seemed small before the black Tyrannosaurus rex on the hilltop. Looming over the city, Ivan was like a dark god overseeing his shadowy domain. The bones of his enemies lay around his feet, and the fury of hellfire burned in his eyes.

Yet still Dozer charged.

Riding his back, Joe aimed his sleep-or-die and fired from both barrels at once.

A bullet and a tranquilizer dart slammed into Ivan. Both shattered against his scales. Hundreds of dents and scars already covered the towering tyrannosaur. A few bullets were embedded into his chest. The Rangers who had fired them lay dead at Ivan's feet, bodies crushed, some half-devoured. It would take more than a few guns to kill a god.

It would take the most powerful weapon on Mintari. A triceratops.

Grunting in fury, eyes narrowed and blazing, Dozer charged uphill and lunged toward the tyrannosaurus.

Dozer's horns were weapons of legend. They were a foot wide at the base. They grew outward like stalagmites, narrowing to sharp points. When Dozer thrust those horns, he put all his twelve tons of weight behind them. Even a titan like Ivan could not hope to survive such a blow.

And Ivan knew it. He stepped aside with surprising speed for a dinosaur so large. Dozer's horns just missed him.

But a triceratops was more than just his horns. A triceratops was also a bony frill larger and thicker than Rattlesnake's cowcatcher. A triceratops was a bulky body of muscle, fat, and scales that would not shame any tank.

And while the horns narrowly missed the T-rex, the rest of Dozer did not. The bony frill and Dozer's right shoulder plowed into Ivan with a terrible *crack*.

It was a sound like thunder. Like a booming cannon. Like the ground ripping open in an earthquake. Like an asteroid plowing into the earth. Across the city, they could hear it. Outside in the wilderness, dinosaurs would look up, startled, and all would know that atop Buckland Hill, titans were clashing. Here on this hilltop, where the first pilgrims had landed, the fate of Mintari would be sealed.

Ivan tossed back his head and bellowed in fury and agony.

Riding the trike, Joe held on tight, teeth bared. Next to Ivan, Joe was no larger than a mouse by a cat. But he would not abandon his triceratops. Nor would he abandon the memory of Mina. This was a battle for Mintari. But it was also Joe's personal battle. He would defeat his nemesis or die in his jaws like his wife.

Ivan's colossal head loomed above. Joe could see the old scar along the snout. Over the years, the injury had faded to a crimson gorge among the black scales. Joe had given the titan that scar. Fifteen years ago, he had lifted Ivan's fallen tooth, then thrust it like a sword, slashing the dinosaur's snout.

Joe still had that fallen tooth. It hung from his belt. An old memento. A sword.

Ivan's red eyes stared at the tooth. Then the T-rex made eye contact with Joe.

The dinosaur remembered. He recognized Joe.

Joe stared, eyes narrowed. He gripped the tooth, hand shaking, but did not draw it yet. More than anything, Joe desired to thrust this blade into the heart of his foe. To finish what he had started fifteen years ago. But he was still out of range.

With a furious rumble, Dozer charged again. The trike headbutted the tyrannosaur. Once more, Ivan had to step sideways to dodge the horns.

Then Ivan struck back.

He had the most powerful jaws on Mintari. Most likely the most powerful jaws in history. He tried to reach Dozer's back, to crunch through his scaly hide, muscles, and bones. But like all triceratops, Dozer had a unique design to his head. His entire one-ton skull was mounted onto a ball joint, able to swivel in any direction at incredible speed. No other animal could move its head like a trike. And as the gargantuan jaws of the tyrant came thrusting down toward his flank, Dozer wheeled his head around, bringing his horns to bear on Ivan.

The T-rex nearly impaled himself on those horns, but he had fought triceratops before. He knew how deadly they were. He had seen lesser tyrannosaurs fall to their horns. He quickly adjusted his attack. The horns thrust past his neck, slicing only air. Ivan was unable to reach Dozer's scaly body, his most vulnerable part. But he managed to close his jaws round Dozer's bony frill.

A trike's frill was the most perfect armor nature had ever crafted. It was formed of solid bone as thick as a wall. Hornlets lined its fringe. A triceratops frill was bulletproof, fireproof, and could withstand almost any predator's bite.

Almost any. Ivan was not just any predator. When he chomped down, he exerted staggering force, equivalent to the weight of a jippi shoving down on each tooth. He had jaws that could shatter tree trunks, crush boulders, bite through solid walls. Against Dozer's frill, two of his mighty teeth shattered. But three teeth crunched into the frill, sinking into the bone.

Dozer's beak opened in a terrible howl.

Ivan tugged on the frill, his neck muscles bulging. Joe had seen rexes decapitate trikes this way, yanking their heads off the ball joints to reach the soft neck meat. Dozer cried in agony, shaking his head, unable to free himself. Ivan kept tugging the frill as if trying to open a tin can.

Joe stood up on Dozer's back, holding on to one horn for support. He aimed his sleep-or-die right at Ivan's eye.

He fired.

He fired a live bullet.

Ivan turned his head away. The bullet pounded his muzzle, chipping a scale. The T-rex grunted, a sound more annoyed than pained.

Dozer seized the opportunity to shake his head free. Holes punctured his frill. That frill was wider than Joe's arm, and Ivan had bitten holes clean through it. The trike must be in agony, but Dozer still bellowed and charged back to battle.

The two great dinosaurs slammed together again.

Ivan—the greatest predator on Mintari.

Dozer—the mightiest of herbivores.

Two titans. Two kings. Two ancient enemies who had once fought for dominance of Earth. The asteroid that ended the Cretaceous period had left their war unresolved. Now, millions of years later and a thousand light-years away, T-rex and triceratops would settle the final score.

Dozer's horns grazed Ivan's side, peeling off scales.

Ivan's claws slashed Dozer's flank, ripping lumpy gray skin.

The two dinosaurs pulled apart, bleeding and enraged. With battle cries, they lunged at each other again. The *crack* of their slamming bodies rippled across the city.

Claws lashed.

Horns thrust.

Teeth crunched through bone.

The combatants pulled apart, attacked again. All Joe could do was ride the triceratops and fire his rifle. He felt useless in this battle between gods.

Again the two dinosaurs pulled back. Dozer bled from several gashes. He was panting, slowing down. Three long scars bled on Ivan's side. A hole pierced his thigh. But the predator rumbled in rage, and his swordlike teeth gleamed in the night. Again the T-rex lunged to battle. He closed his great jaws around Dozer's left horn, trying to rip it off, only for the triceratops to plow into him, to shove him against the *Darwin's Ark*. Chunks of the rusty old starship shattered. The dueling dinosaurs pulled apart, then charged again. Their bellows filled the night.

Buckland Hill was the highest point in Dinovia. The city planners had wanted everyone to see the starship on the hilltop, to remember their history. Now all in Dinovia watched this epic battle.

Horns hit scales.

Claws crushed bone.

Teeth tore flesh.

The hill shook. The city rumbled. The night sky trembled. The stars themselves seemed to quiver and shake as rex and trike slammed together again and again, biting, clawing, goring, bloodying each other upon the hill.

Again and again they charged.

Dozer plowed his horns into Ivan's leg.

The T-rex grabbed Dozer by the frill, shoved the enormous horned head down, and clawed the trike's shoulder.

The triceratops shoved his back legs against the hilltop, bulldozing forward, slamming his foe to the ground.

He was down! King Ivan was down! And the world shook. And the sky cracked in two. All of Mintari trembled.

The fallen tyrant kicked. A great clawed foot slammed into Dozer, knocking his armored head back. Dozer stumbled. Ivan pushed himself back up, then lunged. His huge muzzle thrust forward.

Joe fired his rifle again. Again and again. Ivan recoiled from the bullets, but they didn't cause any real damage. Nothing could stop those jaws.

Joe fired his last bullet. It did little more than chip a few scales.

Out of ammo, Joe stood up on Dozer's back and raised his T-rex tooth. The same tooth he had been carrying all these years. With a hoarse cry, Joe thrust the tooth like a sword.

He aimed at the old scar. Ivan had never regrown his scales there. If Joe could just hit him in the same spot ...

But Ivan knew his Achilles' heel. He leaned back, protecting the scar.

Instead of hitting flesh, Joe hit one of Ivan's front teeth.

It was as if Ivan were actually parrying. The two teeth— one in Joe's hand, one growing from Ivan's gums—clanged together.

For a second, they remained deadlocked like two medieval fencers crossing swords.

Then Ivan thrust his hungry maw toward Joe.

Joe had to leap off Dozer.

One of Ivan's teeth grazed his leg.

Joe hit the ground. Pain exploded through him. His leg was slashed open. He tried to rise but could only roll away. His blood spilled, and Joe grimaced. He tried to stand up, but his leg buckled. He fell again.

He had failed. He was out of the fight. It was up to Dozer.

The two titans kept battling. All Joe could do was lie and watch.

T-rex vs. triceratops. A battle as old as time. Here on Buckland Hill, this ancient rivalry flared.

The enormous teeth of the T-rex snapped shut like a bear trap. At the last second, Dozer managed to raise his frill, to protect his neck. Ivan's jaws clamped down on the frill with tremendous force. Cracks ran through the bone. Ivan dug deeper, punched holes into the frill, then yanked off a chunk the size of a knight's shield.

The sound was horrible.

The sound of cracking bone.

The sound of Dozer's cry of agony.

The sound that came from Joe's own lips—a cry of pure terror.

Ivan spat out the chunk of bone. It thumped onto the dirt beside Joe. A piece of bone so large Joe would struggle to lift it.

Joe stared at Dozer, terrified that the trike would collapse. Dozer wobbled on his feet. His frill was missing a chunk shaped like T-rex jaws. For a terrible second, Joe imagined a giant cookie somebody had taken a bite out of. It was a horrific wound. But it was not life-threatening.

Dozer growled deep in his throat and charged back to battle.

Ivan seemed almost taken aback. Clearly he had not expected Dozer to still fight. Ivan must have slain thousands of dinosaurs in his long life. He probably never saw one who would still fight after such an injury.

Yes, King Ivan hesitated for a second. And a second was all Dozer needed.

The enormous triceratops drove his horns into Ivan's thigh, ripping scaly skin, muscle, fat, maybe even bone.

Ivan tossed back his head and gave a terrible bellow of pure agony.

Even as the horns were embedded into his thigh, Ivan thrust down his jaws and closed them around Dozer's back.

His back. His unprotected back. A place with thick, scaly skin—but no armor.

The T-rex's teeth punched through that thick skin like it was paper.

Dozer bellowed.

Ivan pulled his head back, ripping out skin. Blood ran down Dozer's flanks.

"Dozer!" Joe cried, wanting to help, knowing he could not.

The tyrannosaur swung his great tail. It was thick, powerful, rippling with muscles, covered with hard scales. The tail slammed into Dozer like a whip of pure agony. A terrible *crunch* hinted at cracked ribs.

Dozer howled. He stumbled aside, legs wobbling.

Ivan lashed his tail again. And again. And again. The blows hit Dozer. With each blow—that terrible *crack*.

The triceratops moaned. His legs shook. He sidestepped, swaying.

Ivan plowed his head into him, and Dozer fell.

The triceratops slammed down with enough power to shatter stones, shake the hill, and break Joe's heart.

Ivan placed an enormous foot on Dozer's battered flank, pinning him down. The three terrible claws dug fresh wounds. The triceratops was still alive—but barely. He was moaning, his tongue hanging loose. He was taking deep, ragged breaths, struggling for each one. His eyes narrowed in pain. His blood flowed.

One foot upon his fallen foe, Ivan tossed back his head, thrust out his little arms, and howled in victory.

Then he lowered his jaws, prepared to snap Dozer's neck and seal the deal.

Joe could only stare in horror, out of bullets, out of hope.

Yips and howls sounded in the night.

Shapes leaped through the shadows. Red feathers fluttered.

Joe looked up, gasping.

Ivan raised his head, staring around in confusion, giving Dozer a brief stay of execution.

Teeth and claws flashing in the moonlight, a pack of achillobators leaped through the darkness toward the T-rex.

Riding Red Scar, Fig let out a battle cry.

The pack leaped from all sides, hurling themselves at the gargantuan tyrannosaur.

Achillobators were not small predators. They were not puny like velociraptors or eoraptors, the lightweights of the food chain. They were heavier and bulkier than the dreaded deinonychus. Lifa had told her about a carnivore on Earth called a lion—at one point an apex predator. Bators, the old woman had explained, were larger than lions. Yet lunging toward King Ivan, the bators seemed barely more than insects.

"*Ayiiiii!*" Fig cried.

Red Scar vaulted through the night, his wings spread wide, his red feathers ruffling. It almost seemed like he could fly. The bator landed on Ivan's back and chomped down on the tyrant's black scales.

Several of Red Scar's teeth shattered. It was like biting a boulder. The old bator yowled, slipped off the T-rex, and thudded onto the ground. Fig fell off his back and rolled through the dirt. Ivan's foot slammed down, and Fig scurried aside, just barely dodging the terrible talons.

With war cries, the other bators landed on Ivan too. Crooked Wing began biting and clawing the king's tail. More bators attacked his legs. A few gripped his flanks, digging their sickle claws between his scales, and climbing higher.

The T-rex moaned, whipped his tail around, and flailed his tiny arms, shaking off several bators. Ivan swung his massive head from side to side, clubbing the bators that clung to his flanks.

One bator thumped down, bones cracked.

Ivan managed to grab another in his huge jaws. He chomped down, pulverizing the poor dinosaur. Red feathers flew through the air. Blood splashed the hilltop.

But that did not deter the pack. It only infuriated the survivors.

"Ayiiiiii!" Fig cried.

She hopped onto Red Scar, and they vaulted back into the fray. The surviving bators rose to their feet, shook off the pain, and rejoined the assault. They attacked relentlessly. Mercilessly. They scaled the tyrant. They climbed his neck. They bit his head. They learned fast to avoid the lashing tail, the swinging head, the mean little arms.

Ivan craned his neck around and managed to grab Fierce Mother, a bator who had raised many hatchlings. He crunched the poor theropod between his teeth, then spat out the mangled body. But the others kept striking. Long Tail managed to peel off a black scale. Crooked Wing was still savaging Ivan's swinging tail, her eyes burning with bloodlust. The big, barren female seemed rabid, her claws flashing so quickly they blurred. With startling audacity (or perhaps foolhardiness), Blue Eyes attacked Ivan's snout head-on. The brave bator managed to hook his sickle claw into Ivan's nostril, yank back hard, and rip the flesh. Bellowing in pain, Ivan crushed the impudent little dinosaur between his jaws.

As the pack kept fighting, Red Scar clung to Ivan's back. He was clawing and biting, but the black scales were thick here. Even worse, spikes rose across Ivan's back, stabbing Red Scar, slicing feathers, drawing blood. The bator could not break through.

"Haooo haoo!" Fig cried, tugging Red Scar's feathers.
Move up! Higher up! Toward Ivan's head!

Red Scar understood. He scampered along Ivan's back, heading toward the muscular neck. Ivan shook and bucked, but he couldn't shake off the bator. Changing tactics, Ivan craned his neck around, thrust his snout over his right shoulder, and snapped his teeth. Red Scar scurried onto the left shoulder, fleeing the bone-crushing teeth.

But the old bator was too slow. Ivan managed to bite off half his tail.

Blood spurted and feathers flew. The bator yowled. He had already lost the tip of his tail earlier in the day. But back then, Red Scar had only lost a few feathers. This injury was far more severe. Maybe life-threatening. Ivan had crunched through bone and flesh.

Red Scar's claws loosened. He slipped off Ivan's back.

But Fig did not fall.

As Red Scar tumbled to the ground, leaving half his tail behind, Fig hopped off the mutilated achillobator.

She landed on Ivan's back. Alone.

She ran.

Her bare feet padded across Ivan's scales.

With a wordless cry, she leaped and landed on the king's head.

She stood there for a moment, shocked at herself.

I'm standing on the head of Mintari's largest T-rex.

This was *not* how Fig had imagined her night going.

From up here, she could see the entire battle. Below, her bators were attacking Ivan's feet. Red Scar curled up. Joe lay on his back, clutching his wounded leg and gazing up in shock. Farther down the hill, trikes were overturning jippis full of poachers. Below the hill, buildings lay toppled across the city.

Fig took this all in within a second. Then she bared her teeth, raised her sickle claw, and plunged it down with all the strength in her skinny arms.

She drove the claw into one of Ivan's eyes.

It was a massive eye. The eyeball appeared small from a distance. And it *was* small compared to the size of Ivan's head. But up here, Fig realized the eyeball was the size of a coconut.

The eye was not soft. A thick nictitating membrane protected it. Achillobators had such membranes too—transparent layers to protect the eyeball. But Fig held the sickle claw of an achillobator, a weapon crafted and honed over a hundred million years of evolution. It was one of the sharpest, deadliest weapons on Mintari. And with her rage, she shattered that membrane and clawed the mushy eyeball.

That claw was long. Fig drove the whole thing in, then sank her entire hand into the goo.

Ivan let out a cry.

But it was not the deep rumble a T-rex was famous for. This was a different sound. High-pitched. Almost a whine. The sound a bator hatchling made if you stepped on its tail.

Ivan's head shook madly, and Fig flew through the air. She landed on a patch of grass and fallen red feathers. The fall knocked the air out of her, but she was unhurt. Sitting down, legs splayed out, she stared up at the beast.

Ivan took a few steps, whimpering, tossing his head around. His little arms flailed. The sickle claw was still embedded into his eyeball. He yowled. A torn sound. A sound like ripping skin.

The pack knew this was their best chance.

The achillobators lunged, savage and wild, attacking with berserker fury. For many years, the tyrannosaurs had bullied the smaller bators. This was their revenge. They lunged at the wounded titan, clawing, biting. Crooked Wing lashed her claws, hamstringing the prodigious predator. Even with one eye gone, bleeding from many cuts, Ivan still tried to fight, whipping his tail, snapping his teeth.

And then something amazing happened. Something Fig was not expecting.

Dozer rose to his feet.

Fig had thought the trike was dead. A chunk of his frill was missing, and gashes bled across him, but the triceratops let out a horse cry and charged.

His horns drove into Ivan's leg, ripping muscle, cracking a bone.

And the king fell.

He hit the ground with a *thud* they could hear across the city.

Fig stared with wide eyes. Joe gasped. Dozer and the bators stepped back, barely believing what they had done. Ivan lay on the ground, breathing raggedly, a claw in his eye, his leg mangled. He was still alive. But he was staying down.

The king was defeated.

CHAPTER TWENTY-FIVE
Leave-taking

Joe struggled to his feet. His injured leg blazed with pain, but if he favored it, he could walk a few steps. His head spun. He had lost a lot of blood. But this wasn't over yet. He limped closer to the fallen Tyrannosaurus rex.

His nemesis lay there on the bloody grass, breathing raggedly. Joe had seen injured dinosaurs before. He knew that Ivan was not getting up anytime soon. His leg was broken. His eyeball was cut and blind. He was down for the count.

Dozer stood above his vanquished foe. The triceratops was injured just as badly. He struggled with every breath, wounds gaped on his sides, and a chunk of his frill was gone. But the big herbivore remained standing, victorious. With a grunt, he placed one foot on Ivan's neck. All Dozer had to do was lean forward, press his weight down on his foot, and rid Mintari of Ivan. Forever.

The triceratops swiveled his head around on its ball joint, looking at Joe. He gave a low moan, rising in pitch at the end. *Can I kill him?*

Every cell in Joe's body screamed: *Yes! Yes, end him! End this now!*

Joe thought of Mina's face, innocent and beautiful. He remembered her disappearing into the jaws of this beast. He thought of the life he had been denied. A life with Mina. With their child. A life of joy. He thought of fifteen years of grief and despair.

Yes! he wanted to cry. *Yes, crush his neck! Kill him!*

And then Joe thought of his father.

Tobias Triplehorn had been born on Mintari. He grew up here. He lost his parents here to a dinosaur attack. And he chose a path of vengeance. Chose to sell weapons to poachers, to mastermind the mass killing of dinosaurs. To Tobias, dinosaurs were monsters.

But they were not monsters. They were magnificent animals. They were majestic creations of evolution. They were wonders brought back to life, rising again, proud and free.

Even Ivan.

Joe had sworn to protect dinosaurs. Because he knew that despite their size, their sharp teeth, and their long claws, they were vulnerable. Humans could drive them to extinction as easily as any other animal. Little humans, with their weak, soft bodies, had driven the great cats, the elephants, even the whales to extinction. Against the devastating industry of mankind, dinosaurs would fare no better.

But at least one man still stood for them.

Joe still wore the hat of a Ranger. He still wore the badge on his chest. And in his heart, he still loved dinosaurs.

"Let him live," he said in a low voice. "Show him mercy, Dozer. Let him live."

Dozer grunted. He seemed disappointed. But he removed his foot from Ivan's neck.

Joe stepped closer to the fallen king, opened his pack, and pulled out medical supplies. He began treating Ivan's wounds.

As he worked, bandaging the injured T-rex, Joe was aware of the strange girl watching him. The girl who had ridden here atop an achillobator. She stood with the feathered theropods, daring not approach but clearly curious.

Joe too was curious. Riding dinosaurs was nothing new on Mintari. After all, just outside this city, jockeys rode in the Dino Derby every weekend. But Joe had never seen a girl so connected to a pack of predators. She seemed almost like one of the pack, making sounds in their language, fighting with them, wielding one of their claws. And there was something else about her. Something haunting and familiar.

After Joe had stopped Ivan's bleeding, he turned away from the wounded rex. Ivan lay on the hilltop, breathing deeply, sliding into an uneasy sleep. It would probably be days before he walked again. There were only three paleonarians in the city, and tonight the dino docs had their hands full. They would treat Ivan when they could. For now, Joe had done all he could.

He looked at the slumbering dinosaur.

Yes, you killed my pregnant wife, he thought. *And no, I will not take revenge. I am not my father. Sleep well, King of Mintari. And when you can, leave this city and never return.*

He felt that Mina was watching. He hoped she understood. Maybe she would not approve, not agree. But he hoped she understood.

He turned away from the sleeping T-rex and looked at the strange girl.

She stood in the shadows among her pack of bators, watching him. In the chaos of battle, he had only caught glimpses of her face. Now Joe got his first good look at her. He blinked. A shock bolted through him.

Mina! It was Mina!

For a second, Joe thought he was looking at a ghost. But no. This girl was younger. Only a teenager. She had tanned skin, almond-shaped eyes, and bowl-shaped black hair. She wore a dress adorned with red feathers.

"Thank you," Joe said to her. "For helping. You saved my life."

The girl took a step closer, hesitated, took another few steps. Her pack remained behind, muscles tense, ever watchful. Each achillobator was the size of a polar bear and twice as ruthless. Any one of them would tear Joe apart. They knew it. He knew it. But the feathered dinosaurs stayed put, simply watching.

Joe took a step closer. The bators bristled. Their scaly lips peeled back, baring their teeth. Joe froze.

The girl glanced at the bators, made cooing sounds, and they calmed. She then walked closer to Joe, stepping into the moonlight.

Darwin's beard! Joe thought. She really did look like Mina. In the moonlight, she seemed like his wife reborn.

"Who are you?" he whispered.

The girl tapped her chest. "Fi-ga-ro." A tear fled her eye and rolled down her cheek, gleaming in the moonlight. "I ... em ... Fi-ga-ro. I ... em ... yow ... da-te."

Joe blinked. The girl was struggling with every syllable.

"Did you just say you're my daughter?"

More tears flowed down her cheeks. She nodded. "Yes. I ... Mi-na ... da-te. An . . yow ... da-te."

Rage exploded through Joe. What was this? Some kind of sick joke? Amissa must be behind this! She must have found a girl who looked like Mina, put her here, and ...

Then Joe noticed it.

A figure was limping up the hill, leaning on a cane.

It was Lifa. His mother.

The shaman stopped a few steps away. The moonlight lit her necklaces of beads and bones. It had been years since Lifa had left the wilderness. Shamans chose a life of solitude. If Lifa was here in the city, this was truly a momentous night. Her tears shone in the moonlight. She looked at Joe and gave a slight bow. She did not need to speak. Her eyes said it all.

It's true, Joe. She's your daughter.

"How?" Joe whispered to the girl. "How is this possible?" His own tears were falling now. "I saw you die. I saw Ivan, I saw ..."

And he remembered.

Mina going into labor.

Mina crumbling in the dark grass, crying out.

She gave birth that night, Joe thought. *While I was battling the beast. And I never knew it. I never knew ...*

A great sob fled his lips, and he pulled Figaro into his arms.

"I'm sorry," he whispered. "I'm sorry, my daughter, I'm sorry, I'm sorry. This is a miracle. A miracle ..."

He could say no more. The years of grief flowed from him, wetting Figaro's dress of feathers with a thousand tears.

For a long time, Fig stood in her father's embrace. He was crying, and she felt how broken he was. How sorry he was. He was like a great wounded animal, old and battle worn, only now beginning to heal.

Vaguely, Fig was aware of Simone parking her jippi on the hilltop, stepping out, and gazing at the scene with soft eyes. But the redhead gave them space. Simone joined Lifa in the shadows. Both women knew this moment belonged to father and daughter.

"Figaro," Joe said, looking into her eyes. "That's a beautiful name."

She smiled shakily. "Fi-ga-ro."

"I have so much I want to ask you," Joe said. "So much I don't yet understand. I don't know where you were all these years. I don't know how you survived. I'm sure you have many questions too. But one thing I want you to know right now. I didn't abandon you. I thought about you every day. I thought you were gone. And I'm so glad you're here. I've only just met you, Figaro, but I love you. I'm your father. And I'm here for you."

Her smile grew, and she trembled and shed tears. She laid her head against his chest. She had spent so many years thinking she was an achillobator, some orphaned chick the pack had adopted. That had never felt right to her. Not throughout all those years in the wild. *This* was true. Joe was true. This felt right.

This is who I am, she thought. *Fi-ga-ro. A human. A daughter.*

A soft nickering came from behind her.

Still held in Joe's arms, Fig looked over her shoulder. Red Scar had taken a few steps forward, leaving the pack behind. Lifa had bandaged the stump of his tail, and despite the brutal injury, dear old Red Scar was already on his feet. Even the bite of a T-rex couldn't keep him down. The bator nickered again, then purred and bobbed his head.

Little one? Come back. Rejoin the pack.

Now fresh tears fell. Gently Fig disentangled herself from Joe's embrace. She stepped hesitantly toward Red Scar. The bator lowered his snout and nuzzled her palm. He purred, a sound of soft pleading tinged with grief.

You're not coming back, are you?

Fig sobbed and pulled his snout into a hug. His head was larger than her entire torso, his jaws full of terrible teeth, but to Fig, there was nobody kinder, softer, or braver in the world. She hugged that huge scarred beast, and her tears wet his feathers. She cooed into his ear, shaking, holding him so tightly.

I love you, Red Scar. I love you. I'll miss you so much.

He was an old bator. He had taken her in years ago, a young orphan girl in the wild. He had raised her. Seen her as one of his pack. For all those long years in the wilderness, he had been there for her. Mentor. Protector. Friend.

How could she go on without him? How could she find a life away from her companion?

But she knew that she must. She had grown up. By the reckoning of human years, she was no longer a hatchling. In the wilderness of Mintari, few hatchlings reached adulthood. Starvation, disease, or predation took out most of them. Red Scar had seen her through the dangers of childhood. He had scared off predators, brought her meat, groomed her for ticks, raised her to be quick and strong. But now she must leave the nest. Now she must forge her own path. Now she must return to her people.

In her soft cooing, she explained all this to him without words. Just with her hug and tears and loving noises. And when he looked into her eyes, Fig knew that he understood. Perhaps he had always understood. Perhaps he had always known this day would come—long before Fig herself had known.

She held his snout in both hands, and she looked into his eyes. For the first time, she tried to speak to him like a human. "Re-Sar ... Fi-ga-ro ... ruv you."

He licked her face, and she giggled. She would stay with the humans. But she would visit him, and part of her would always run wild with the pack.

Suddenly Red Scar stiffened.

His nostrils flared, and his lips peeled back with snarl.

In his eyes, Fig saw a reflection. A figure in the night, aiming a rifle.

She spun around to see Amissa. The poacher came slinking through the night. She must have been hiding behind the ruins of *Darwin's Ark*.

She aimed her rifle right at Fig.

Red Scar howled, knocked Fig to the ground, and lunged toward Amissa.

The poacher's gun boomed.

Red Scar made a terrible, high-pitched squeal. Blood flew from his neck. He took three more steps, then crumpled.

Fig screamed.

At once, Joe was running at Amissa, limping and bleeding but still propelling himself forward. He was out of bullets, but he raised his T-rex tooth sword. Simone ran toward her jippi, perhaps looking for a weapon. The other bators raced to battle. Lifa was shouting, "Amissa! Amissa, my daughter!" But the old shaman was barely audible over the shrieking bators.

Amissa fired again.

Joe cried out.

A bullet hit his leg. The same leg Ivan had already savaged.

Joe fell. He was not getting up anytime soon.

The bators pounced toward Amissa. She leaped back. The poacher raced behind the mangled remains of *Darwin's Ark*.

"Amissa!" Joe howled. He tried to rise, fell again, bleeding. "Get back here, coward!"

The bators whipped around *Darwin's Ark*, chasing Amissa. But then engines roared. An astrolite soared skyward on a pillar of fire. Fig watched, eyes wide. She had never seen a flying machine before. The astrolite rose higher and higher, then vanished into the night, leaving nothing but a streak of light.

Amissa was gone.

Lifa hurried toward Joe, moving as fast as she could with her cane. She knelt and began treating his wounds.

Fig, meanwhile, raced toward Red Scar.

The old bator lay on the ground, his blood wetting the grass. The bullet had pierced his neck. He gurgled, struggling for breath. A lot of blood was flowing from him.

Fig's hands shook. She wanted to cry out for help, but Lifa was busy tending to her son. The other bators crowded around, watching, cooing, and Fig trembled. She knelt and nuzzled Red Scar, cooing too, but her voice shook. She placed her hands on his wound. Such small hands. They could not stanch the blood.

Don't die, Red Scar. Don't die. Don't die. Please …

Her tears splashed him.

Red Scar looked into her eyes. There was intelligence in his gaze. Awareness. Love. He purred, laid his huge head on her lap, and closed his eyes. She held him as he took his last breath.

Fig lowered her head, overwhelmed with grief. Her best friend was gone.

CHAPTER TWENTY-SIX
Homecoming

They never found Amissa.

Many Rangers had died in the terrible battle of Dinovia City. Those who survived searched for Amissa throughout the night. And the next day. And the day after that.

They flew tricopters over the wilderness. They gazed toward the stars with their telescopes. They looked in every cave, under every rock. They questioned the poachers they captured.

Nothing.

Amissa Triplehorn was gone. Perhaps she had left the planet. Perhaps she was hiding in some hole in the wilderness. Perhaps someday she would strike again.

For now she was gone. And Mintari had to heal.

They wanted Joe to stay in the city. They wanted to give him some medal. They wanted a big ceremony with a crowd, cameras, the whole shebang.

Joe had refused. He was no hero. He had failed in this battle. Failed to stop his sister. Failed to save the hundreds who died. He wanted to go back to his cave, to nurse his wounded leg, to remain in isolation. He had almost lost that leg. Ivan's tooth and Amissa's gun had both savaged it. The doctors said he would keep the limb. In time, with proper care, he wouldn't even limp, they said. But the road to recovery was long, and Joe wanted to recover at home.

Lifa had already left the city, returning to her burrow. The shaman did not like crowds. Joe could sympathize. He had definitely inherited his introversion from his mother.

It was Simone who convinced him to stay in Dinovia a while longer.

"You and Dozer are no shape to take the journey to Mudge Mountain," she told him. "We're staying in the city until you boys can walk. There are rooms in the Fossil and Firkin. I already rented one."

Joe sat beside her in the jippi, his leg wrapped in bandages. She was driving through the narrow streets of Dinovia City. Figaro sat in the back seat.

Poor Dozer was limping behind them. There was no jippi on Mintari large enough to carry him. The trike took careful steps, favoring one leg. Bandages covered his body. Metal bolts held his frill together. The paleonarians had reattached the chunk Ivan had bitten off.

"Look, he can walk!" Joe said. "So can I. Let's head back to the cave."

Simone groaned. She was driving in first gear, slow enough for Dozer to follow. She pointed at his bandaged leg.

"*You* cannot walk, mister. Amissa almost shot your leg off."

"Almost!" he said. "That means I can still walk home." Riding Dozer was out of the question until the big dinosaur healed.

"If you behave, I'll let you walk from your room to the bar," Simone said.

Joe thought for a moment. Then he grunted and nodded. "Your terms are acceptable."

They finally reached the Fossil and Firkin. One of the walls had been knocked down during the rex rampage, revealing the common room. Dust and rubble lay everywhere. But the regulars were undaunted. They still sat inside, nursing their mugs of ale. It took a lot to rattle a Mintarian. Widespread dino destruction was no reason to stop drinking.

Simone parked the jippi outside the saloon. Dozer grunted and wheezed, winded after the long walk. The triceratops could have stayed on Buckland Hill. The paleonarians had been treating him there—along with Ivan and a handful of other triceratops. The historic hill had become a field hospital for wounded dinosaurs. But Dozer insisted on trudging along, and besides, Joe would never leave him behind. The weary trike plopped himself down outside the Fossil and Firkin, taking up three parking spots and cracking the asphalt. He laid his head in the garden, which he began to devour plant by plant. He especially loved petunias.

Joe patted the dinosaur, then limped toward the saloon's batwing doors. When he swung them open, one door clattered to the ground. Joe winced. Oops.

The patrons looked up at the sound. Barnum, the rotund barkeep, paused from cleaning a mug. Everyone stared at Joe in stunned silence.

"Jurassic Joe himself!" whispered a man with a huge handlebar mustache covered with beer foam.

"Back from the dead!" whispered another barfly, a woman with two blond braids, freckled cheeks, and a big ceratop hat.

Joe froze. He used to be a regular here. Back before Mina had died. He would visit daily for Barnum's famous shepherd's pie. For the cold ale. For the warm company. Now, standing here with everyone watching, Joe's cheeks flushed beneath his beard.

He should not have come back. He should have ignored Simone and taken Dozer to the cave. It was not too late.

He took one step back when Barnum hurried around the bar. The portly man rushed toward him, his belly swinging from side to side.

"Joe, my boy!" he cried. "It's good to have you back." He gripped Joe's hand, shook it, then changed his mind and hugged Joe instead. "Come on, come inside! I have fresh shepherd's pie cooling on the counter. And the beer is cold, or there's coffee if you prefer. Come, my friend, sit down. Ah! Look at that!"

Simone entered the saloon next. She waved shyly. "Hi, Barnum."

The old barkeep's eyes twinkled. "Why, if it isn't the lovely Ms. LaRue. I see you found Jurassic Joe."

She smiled. "We've met, yes. It's been ... interesting."

Barnum burst out laughing and slapped his ample belly. "I can imagine. Come inside, come inside. I'll fix you a plate. And—oh." The old man peered at the doorway. "And who might you be, young lady?"

Figaro tiptoed into the room. She sniffed, noticed everyone staring, then bared her teeth and growled.

"It's all right, Figaro," Simone said. "We're among friends."

Barnum took a step closer. "We're all friends here, we—"

Fig growled, lunged forward, and snapped her teeth. Barnum stumbled back.

Simone looked at Joe, concern in her eyes. "I don't know what's wrong," she whispered.

But Joe understood. He turned toward his daughter and stared into her fierce, almond-shaped eyes. "Figaro. Look at me. You're a predator. I know. You feel cornered in strange territory. I understand." He smiled thinly. "I feel the same way. Come, let's sit by that broken wall. Easy escape. If we need to run, we can hop out the hole in the wall. Is that all right?"

Fig stopped snarling. She looked around the room. Lots of people. Lots of places to be trapped. But one wall had crumbled, and Dozer could be seen lounging outside, munching on petunias. He would keep them safe.

Fig nodded. "Ow wite."

They sat down at a wooden table. All the tables, the chairs, even the bar were carved from live-edge wood. The legs were made from branches stripped of bark, still coiling and full of knots and knobs. It wasn't quite like being in the wilderness, but it put Joe at ease. Fig seemed to calm down too. She began grooming Joe's hair, searching for bugs. He knew it was a show of affection.

Joe kept expecting odd looks, mutters, somebody to point at his Triplehorn pin and grumble. He expected people to toss bottles. To insult him. To curse his clan.

But instead, one lady approached and shook his hand. "Thank you, Joe," she said, voice choked with emotion.

An octogenarian with a walrus mustache stepped over and saluted, tears in his eyes. "I was a Ranger for sixty years. You, sir, are the finest Ranger I've met. I would love to buy you a drink."

Others approached too. They patted Joe on the back, shook his hand, bought him more drinks than he could manage. Simone not-so-furtively sneaked a few drinks back to the bar. Fig delivered a beer to Dozer, spilling it into his beak. Joe would have to talk to her about that.

As Joe sat there in the crowded saloon, he felt trapped. He wanted the ground to swallow him. He had not been among so many people for fifteen years now. But he found that tears of gratitude filled his eyes.

He looked at his lapel. At the small silver triceratops pin he wore there, so tarnished it had turned black. His clan crest. Not long ago, people would have ripped it off, would have cursed his name. There were still cruel Triplehorns out there. And many poachers still carried guns with the same symbol on the barrel.

But Joe had done something here. He had shown this city another type of Triplehorn. Maybe someday his daughter would not be ashamed of her family name.

"I wish Mina could have been here," Joe said softly. He looked at Fig and smiled through the tears. "But you're here, Figaro. And I know your mother is proud of you."

Barnum approached, carrying a tray with three servings of shepherd's pie. Joe, Simone, and Fig all tucked in. The meal was delicious. Fig inhaled her serving, then quickly ordered seconds. And thirds. Joe laughed. The girl was scrawny, but soon enough, she'd put some meat on her bones. She would improve her speech. She would integrate in human society. Maybe even better than he did.

We both have a long way home, he thought. *But we'll get there.*

He put his arm around his daughter. She leaned against him, closed her eyes, and smiled softly.

Joe looked at Simone. She looked back, eyes solemn.

He wanted to ask Simone so many things. Would she return to Cloventia? Would she stay here on Mintari? Would she live in the city, or would she live with Joe in his cave? The *Cloventia Gazette* had betrayed her. She would no longer be a journalist. But would she still be in his life? A friend? Something more?

So many questions, but when Joe looked into her eyes, he realized that Simone herself did not know. They would need time. To recover. To heal. To see what happened next. Him. Simone. Figaro. Yes, it would be a long road, but they would walk it together.

"Joe." Simone lowered her eyes, suddenly blushing. "I … wanted to ask you something."

His heart lurched. He tried to hide his nervousness. "Go ahead."

She looked up at him from under her lashes. "Barnum told me that … you used to play the piano here. Will you play for us?"

"Absolutely not!" Joe said.

"Oh please!" Simone held his hand. "I want to hear."

"No!"

Fig, who had been dozing off, opened her eyes. She tilted her head. "Wae pano?"

Simone pointed. "There. That thing. It's a musical instrument."

Fig tilted her head the other way. "Mu … huh?"

Simone grinned. "Show her, Joe. Come on. Play us a song."

He rose to his feet. "I'm going home. To my cave. Alone. You're not invited."

Laughing, Simone grabbed his arm and pulled him toward the piano. Fig scampered after them, curious. Joe noticed that she walked funny. Not like a regular girl. She hopped forward like a bator. Maybe in time, her walking would become more humanlike. Maybe it wouldn't. He would accept her either way.

Simone practically forced him onto the piano bench. "Play, mister. That's an order."

He glowered. "It's been fifteen years. I forgot how."

"Just try!"

He played a C chord. "There, happy?"

She grinned. "No. I want more. Here, I'll remind you how to play." She sat beside him on the bench. "Scooch over." She stretched her fingers. "Seven years of lessons at Clover Heights, here we go."

She played a tune. She played well. Joe played a few more chords. It was slowly coming back to him. He felt as clumsy with the piano as Fig did with speaking. But soon they were playing a simple song together. She played the melody on treble, he played the bass chords. "Dinosaur Road." A classic Mintarian folk song. And everyone in the saloon sang.

When they returned to their table, Joe glowered at Simone. "Are you always like this? Thriving on attention?"

She nodded. "Yep. I'm a journalist, after all. Well … was. But maybe you need somebody like me, Joe Triplehorn. Somebody very different from you."

"Well, maybe you should stick around!" he grumbled.

She placed her hands on her hips. "Maybe I will, Mr. Triplehorn."

"Well, good then!"

"Good!"

Figaro looked at them. "Hoo-mans weir-da."

Simone laughed. And Joe couldn't help it. He laughed too. Uproariously. He had not laughed like this in years.

When their laughter faded, Joe spoke softly.

"We spent too long in the darkness. All three of us. We suffered loss and pain. We wandered the shadows alone. But now the three of us are here. Together. Now we can heal."

Simone hugged him. Figaro cooed and groomed his hair.

Joe closed his eyes, and he thought of Mina.

I will never forget you, Mina. I will always love you. You were here for me during all those years of shadow. Our daughter is back. And I promise she will know you.

He felt something then. Something odd, alien. Something he had not felt in fifteen years.

He was happy.

Amissa knew they were searching for her. And she knew that nobody would find her. Not here.

This was the safest place on Mintari. All she had to do was lie low.

Standing outside, one could barely see the shaman's hut. It looked like a mound of earth covered in grass and leaves. Ferns, flowering bushes, ivy, and a hundred herbs grew around the burrow, an explosion of flora. Jars of scented leaves kept dinosaurs at bay. Concealed wind chimes, cleverly attached to vines strung along the ground, would warn of anyone approaching. A stream provided fresh water and fish. Fruit trees offered plenty of sweet nourishment. For thirty years now, Lifa had lived here, hidden away from the world, surviving on the most dangerous planet in the galaxy.

As the Rangers searched for Amissa, she could think of no better hideout.

And Lifa would never turn her in. What kind of mother would turn in her only daughter?

Amissa walked through the herb garden, careful to avoid the tripwires. She pulled back a curtain of vines and entered the hut.

On the inside, the hut was far more than a mere mound of soil and leaves. It was a home. A cozy hideaway full of rugs, dream catchers, and glistening crystals. Lifa moved about the hut, tending to a pot of tea, dusting the crystals, and watering the plants. When she noticed Amissa, she paused and turned toward her.

"Daughter." Her smile was kind. "I thought you might come. I've made mint-and-jasmine tea. I want us to talk."

The shaman sat down on a tasseled cushion. Amissa remained standing.

"Won't you sit?" Lifa said.

Amissa stared down at the old woman. She looked nothing like a Cloventian. She looked … old. Back on Cloventia, women of a certain age got face-lifts. They dyed their hair. They surgically altered their bodies. But Lifa—wonder of wonders—looked her age. Her hair was long and white, her skin was wrinkled, her body sagged. She did not even remove the warts on her chin. To Amissa, she looked like a witch. She was just missing the hunchback.

Did this wrinkly old creature truly give birth to me? Amissa thought. Disgust filled her. *If I ever look like that, I'll kill myself.*

Lifa seemed to read her mind. Her smile softened. "I know you're not used to this life. I know I don't look like a fine Cloventian lady. I know my home is nothing like the fancy penthouses that float over the neon sea. But I hope you can understand why I chose this life."

Amissa clenched her fists at her sides. "I understand that you abandoned me. I was only a baby. And you left." Tears burned her eyes.

Lifa stood up. Her eyes dampened. "I tried to keep you. I fought for you. I begged the courts to keep you. But they divided you and Joe. Divided two siblings between two parents. So—"

"So you left!" Amissa shouted. "You left Cloventia! You left me!" Tears ran down her cheeks. "You could have stayed. Even if you divorced my father, you could have stayed on Cloventia. You could have visited me."

The tears ran down Lifa's wrinkles like rivers through canyons. "I was wilting on Cloventia. I was dying."

"So you ran into the wilderness!" Amissa cried. "Like a coward. You fled! You escaped me!" She fell to her knees, and suddenly she was sobbing. "I grew up without a mother. Because you abandoned me."

Lifa lowered her head. "You're right. No more excuses. I'm sorry, Amissa. I love you, and I'm so sorry."

The shaman stepped forward, reaching out to hug Amissa.

But Amissa took a step back. "Your sorries are useless, old woman. Why did I even bother coming here? You mean nothing to me." She spat on the rug. "Nothing. While you were cowering here, worshipping your crystals, my father raised me. He raised me to be strong! A huntress!"

Lifa met her gaze. "And now you, the proud huntress, hide in the den of a shaman. There is no strength in a gun, Amissa, only loud noise and violence. There is strength in stone and leaf and starlight. It's not too late for you. I abandoned you. And your father broke you. Let me heal you."

Amissa slapped her.

She slapped the old woman so hard Lifa reeled back.

The shaman clutched her cheek. She stared at Amissa, and fear filled her eyes.

"What are you?" Lifa whispered. "What did Tobias do to you?"

"Raised me to be strong. I'm glad you left us."

"Get out," Lifa whispered. "Get out of my home."

Amissa barked a laugh. "Home? This is nothing but a rat's nest." She stepped toward the fireplace, grabbed a poker, and fished out a smoldering log. "I should burn it to the ground!"

She flung the burning log onto a hanging tapestry.

The fabric caught fire at once. With remarkable speed, the flames spread to the rug, then raced toward the thatched roof.

Chin raised, Amissa walked out of the hut. The fire was spreading behind her. The *Huntress* was hiding under a pile of leaves, branches, and vines. As the hut burned behind her, Amissa pulled the greenery off the astrolite. She popped the hatch, entered the cockpit, and fired up the engines.

As the *Huntress* rose through the sky, Amissa looked down. The hut was ablaze. Lifa stood outside the inferno on a scrimshawed boulder, gazing up at the astrolite. Then smoke rolled over the old woman, and Amissa looked away.

I've lain low long enough, Amissa thought. It was time to emerge from hiding. To be the huntress Tobias Triplehorn had raised. She had lost a battle. But she vowed to win the war.

She flew higher, scattering a flock of pterosaurs, and kept rising. When she looked down again, only a few minutes later, the fire was spreading across the forest. Dinosaurs were fleeing the inferno, racing toward the open plains. Too slow. The fire washed over a herd of iguanodons. A family of sauropods stampeded toward a river, but the flames grabbed them and pulled the mighty titans down.

Amissa took no pleasure in killing with fire. A huntress should kill with her arrow, knife, or gun, then mount her trophies. There was no honor in flame. She had acted impetuously, perhaps. This fire was like her rage, exploding and expanding, consuming all in its path. This was no longer a hunt. This was war, and there could be no honor in war. She would keep this rage burning until this entire planet was nothing but ashes.

She flew higher until she breached the atmosphere. The Rangers mostly operated jippis, boats, and tricopters, navigating land, sea, and air. But they did own a few ships capable of reaching space. Nothing that could fly to another planet, of course. Interplanetary starships were expensive. The Rangers owned none of those. Even Amissa's astrolite could not cross the vast distances of space. But the Rangers could still reach Mintari's orbit. They could still hunt her here.

She was careful. Amissa had cleverly disguised her vehicle as a simple tourist astrolite. Even if the Rangers did penetrate her stealth cloak, they would see a bumbling tourist enjoying the view, maybe a discreet businessman who wanted to keep his visit quiet. No more. And if any Ranger did fly in for a closer look, well ... her astrolite boasted the best guns money could buy.

Amissa picked up her transmitter and sent a message to Cloventia. From here, the neon planet was a bluish dot, nearly lost among the stars. But in half an hour, traveling at the speed of light, her message would reach her father.

"Dad? It's me. I'm going to need some backup."

It was a month before Dozer was well enough to travel. Finally the big old triceratops lumbered out of the city. Scars ran down his flank, and bolts still held his frill together, but he was healing nicely, and he still had many years of munching leaves and battling carnivores in him.

Joe, Simone, and Fig rode the trike out of the city. All three of them easily fit on his back. Dozer grunted as he lumbered into the wilderness.

"Are you sure he can carry us?" Simone asked.

Joe nodded. "He's a big boy. He barely even feels our weight."

Joe himself was healing. His leg still hurt, and he still limped, but his doctors expected him to make a full recovery. Even now, it was hard to accept that Amissa—his own sister—had shot him. That she had murdered so many people. If the stories were true, it was Amissa who was behind the wildfires in the east. She was still out there. Here on Mintari or near the planet. Joe knew he must face her again someday.

But not today.

Today was a day for family. For homecoming.

They rode through Marshwood Forest where the stegosaurs roamed, feeding on ferns, and the ceratosaurs prowled, feeding on stegosaurs. Under a blue sky, they crossed the sprawling Hell Valley, a flowering land they all found heavenly. Iguanodons and parasaurs swept across the grasslands, sauropods vacuumed up industrial amounts of greenery, and the year's first young allosaurus hatchlings were learning to hunt. Gould River flowed by, lined with cycads, coiling toward the swamps where the spinosaurs guzzled down fish—and any dinosaur who ventured too close.

Finally, three days after checking out from the Fossil and Firkin, they saw it ahead. Mudge Mountain. Joe's home.

With his thick, stumpy legs and bulky frame, Dozer could not climb the mountainside even at full health. But the triceratops was happy to remain on the foothills, where he could munch on cycads, rebuild his herd, and perhaps even make some baby trikes. The megaraptors who prowled the foothills would not dare approach a trike who showed the scars of T-rex teeth. Anyone who had faced a T-rex and lived was not to be trifled with.

Joe climbed the mountainside, leaning on a walking stick. His leg hurt. But it was getting stronger every day. He wore his Ranger uniform, and his sleep-or-die hung across his back. He was ready for anything.

Simone walked at his side, wearing a safari uniform. Her braided hair spilled out from under her ceratop hat. She no longer looked like a Cloventian tourist lost in the wild. She looked like a Mintarian. Figaro bounded up the slope with them, her dress of feathers fluttering. Sometimes she lowered her nose to the ground and sniffed. Sometimes she paused, cocked her head, and listened to distant birds. Sometimes she growled and chased lizards and mice, vanishing into the brush. But whenever Joe got too far ahead, Fig was sure to hop after him.

A familiar face greeted them outside the cave.

Vinnie loped toward them, yipping with excitement, his feathers fluttering. The little velociraptor leaped into Joe's arms and nuzzled him. Joe laughed and mussed his old friend's feathers.

"Vinnie! I missed you, boy. I bet you thought I was never coming back, huh?" He kissed the feathery theropod. "You held down the fort for me, did you?"

Then Vinnie did something completely unexpected. He began to cry. But it was from joy and relief. He refused to walk, and Joe had to keep carrying him.

They reached the cave. His home awaited. The Last Home Hollow. A comfortable burrow with fresh water, a warm hearth, stores of food ... and years of pain. For a long time, Joe had hidden away there, withdrawing from the world. It had been a hiding place. But now, with the people he loved, he could make it a true home.

Simone gazed at him softly, caressed his cheek, and smiled. With her fiery hair, blue eyes, and dazzling freckles, she was a beautiful woman, and Joe knew that her beauty was more than skin-deep. She was an intelligent woman. A brave woman. Most importantly—a kind woman. And Joe realized that there was room in his heart for more than one woman. That he could love Mina but still feel new love.

Fig hopped toward them and nuzzled Joe. He mussed her dark hair, and she grinned up at him. Joe would always regret missing Fig's childhood, but he knew that her return was a miracle. Over the past month, his love for her had grown and grown. It filled his heart to the brim.

My cup runneth over, he thought. *I am blessed.*

Before entering his cave, he turned and gazed down from the mountain. Hadrosaurs herded across the misty valley while sauropods trudged through the shallow lake. Pterodactyls flocked above, and their shadows raced over the flowering meadows. There it was. Mintari, a world of dinosaurs. A world beyond time.

A world Joe loved. He vowed to forever defend this world, to forever fight for the majestic animals that lived here. This was their world. He was only a guest. A caretaker. It was the greatest honor of his life.

He put his arms around Simone and Figaro, and he sighed contentedly. He was home.

The End

NOVELS BY DANIEL ARENSON

Mintari:
A World of Dinosaurs
Where Dinosauars Roam
March of the Dinosaurs

Starship Freedom:
Starship Freedom
The Cost of Freedom
We Fight for Freedom
For Death or Freedom
Let Freedom Ring
In Pursuit of Freedom
The Guns of Freedom
A Time for Freedom

Alien Hunters:
Alien Hunters
Alien Sky
Alien Shadows

Earthrise:
Earth Alone
Earth Lost
Earth Rising
Earth Fire
Earth Shadows
Earth Valor
Earth Reborn
Earth Honor
Earth Eternal
Earth Machines
Earth Aflame
Earth Unleashed
Earth Remembers
Earth in Darkness
Earth, Our Home

Soldiers of Earthrise:
The Earthling
Earthlings
Earthling's War
I, Earthling
The Earthling's Daughter
We Are Earthlings

Children of Earthrise:
The Heirs of Earth
A Memory of Earth
An Echo of Earth
The War for Earth
The Song of Earth
The Legacy of Earth

Kingdoms of Sand:
Kings of Ruin
Crowns of Rust
Thrones of Ash
Temples of Dust
Halls of Shadow
Echoes of Light

The Moth Saga:
Moth
Empires of Moth
Secrets of Moth
Daughter of Moth
Shadows of Moth
Legacy of Moth

Dawn of Dragons:
Requiem's Song
Requiem's Hope
Requiem's Prayer

Song of Dragons:
Blood of Requiem
Tears of Requiem
Light of Requiem

Dragonlore:

A Dawn of Dragonfire
A Day of Dragon Blood
A Night of Dragon Wings

The Dragon War:

A Legacy of Light
A Birthright of Blood
A Memory of Fire

Requiem for Dragons:

Dragons Lost
Dragons Reborn
Dragons Rising

Flame of Requiem:

Forged in Dragonfire
Crown of Dragonfire
Pillars of Dragonfire

Dragonfire Rain:

Blood of Dragons
Rage of Dragons
Flight of Dragons

Misfit Heroes:

Eye of the Wizard
Wand of the Witch

Standalones:

Firefly Island
The Gods of Dream
Flaming Dove
Utopia 58
Star Stuff

KEEP IN TOUCH

www.DanielArenson.com
Daniel@DanielArenson.com
Facebook.com/DanielArenson
Twitter.com/DanielArenson

www.ingramcontent.com/pod-product-compliance
Lightning Source LLC
Chambersburg PA
CBHW022232020726

47496CB00004B/870